THE SONS OF GYGES

PREVIOUSLY BY PHILIP J. GOULD

Fiction

The Girl in the Mirror

Non Fiction

The Book of Alternative Records (Metro Publishing Ltd)

And Coming soon...

Fiction

The Whisper of Persia
(Book three in *The Girl in the Mirror* series)

PHILIP J GOULD

THE SONS OF GYGES

A GIRL IN THE MIRROR NOVEL

THE SONS OF GYGES

First Published in Great Britain in 2016
Wildboar Publishing, 3 Ashton Close, Ipswich, IP2 9XY

A CIP catalogue record of this book is available from the British Library

ISBN 978 0 9934167 1 2

Cover Illustrations and Interior Formatting by Streetlight Graphics
Author portrait © Hayley Waller

Dedicated to my parents, Gwen and Terry Gould, the two people I'm lucky to have known the longest through chance, good fortune and circumstance. Raising me probably wasn't easy, but I thank you for all that you did, and continue to do. I hope this goes a little way towards making you proud…

THE SONS OF GYGES

Gyges (pronounced *jahy-jees*) was a humble shepherd in the service of the king of Lydia. According to legend, after an earthquake whilst tending to his flock, Gyges discovered a cave in a mountainside. Curiosity getting the better of him, he entered the cave and discovered a tomb within which contained the corpse of an extraordinarily large man. He wore a golden ring which Gyges pulled free and pocketed for himself. He later discovered, upon wearing the ring, he had the power to become invisible. Masquerading as a messenger, he visited the king, and using his newly acquired power of invisibility he seduced the queen. With her help, he murdered the king and took the kingdom of Lydia for himself.

Glaucon, the brother of the Greek philosopher Plato, asked Plato whether it was possible for a man to remain so virtuous as to resist the temptation of carrying out any act, if it was possible to avoid being discovered. The legend was debated at length. It was suggested that morality was only a social construction, the source of which being the desire to maintain one's reputation of virtue and justice. If the chance of discovery was removed, it was proposed that one's moral character would evaporate and the temptation to use it for ill gains would thereafter be too great. They concluded, nothing good could ever come from possessing an item that gave the bearer a means to turn invisible.

A translation of *Book 2* from Plato's *Republic* (380BC)

PROLOGUE
NASCENT

DEEP BELOW THE SCORCHED ground within a large, desolate stretch of desert eighty-three miles north-northwest of Las Vegas, in an area of America listed as Area 51, a large laboratory the size of two Wembley football stadiums was spread out with various machines, scientific apparatus and what appeared to be hundreds of large translucent polyethylene bags filled with liquid. Suspended in racks of five and hanging hammock-like atop of one and other, there was just a couple of inches gap between each. Tubes and wires were connected to each bag, an electronic console flashing and flickering data was situated alongside every bag, affixed to the rack. There were ten rows in all.

Many personnel milled around the facility, dressed in sealed biochemical hazmat suits, some holding clipboards, others wheeling trolleys containing equipment or chemicals.

The one entrance into the laboratory was heavily fortified with three sets of security doors, each manned by two armed guards, all identically attired. Despite being indoors with the absence of sunlight or bright light they wore matching aviator sunglasses.

At the first security door, having travelled for two minutes within the elevator (at a speed of two mph) down to the laboratory, George swiped his security card and placed his right eye level with the scanner, a small ten-inch monitor to the left of the steel door. A moment later a green line of light coasted across the screen, taking a retinal scan and cross-examining with images stored within the security database. Facial recognition images flashed upon the screen flickering at fifty per second, finally resting upon a picture of George Jennings, with the word: 'MATCH' in bright neon green. The door glided open to allow George admittance.

The second and third security doors required vocal recognition and finger and breath analysis, together with further swipes of George's security pass. No chances were being taken.

At each security door the guards stood on either side of George as he underwent clearance, poised to seize at the slightest sign of rejection, hands gently wrapped around the butts of their holstered weapons, at the ready.

When the final door closed behind him, George audibly sighed his relief and made his way to the conference room, an office nestled between a store cupboard and the toilets along a short corridor that ultimately led to the large underground laboratory.

Inside, five men and one woman were sitting behind the large rectangular desk that took up the whole of the centre of the room. All wore military uniforms of varying rank. At the furthest end, to the left, a fifty-inch screen sat at the head of the table. Milo Calland was sitting in his office more than 2,000 miles away – the same office George had found himself in a little less than three weeks earlier.

"George, glad you could make it," a note of sarcasm in Milo's voice.

"Yeah, well… I didn't want to keep you waiting," George replied smugly, taking his seat.

"President Harrison is keen to know how things are progressing. I take it the facilities are as you required."

"Yes… better than expected."

"And the product?"

George looked a little apprehensively at the man on the screen, brushed a hand through his hair and then composed himself. He felt nervous and noted a tinge of fear in his voice when he spoke:

"They are nascent," he said. "I've been successful expediting the programme to phase two – all embryos are growing normally within the pods, all at their expected growth cycles, and all on schedule."

"And the modifications we talked about, George?"

"I've incorporated the emotion inhibitor as you instructed."

"Good."

"What does that mean, exactly?" The woman in the room, Warrant Officer Mary Taylor-Marsh, a tall woman in her mid-fifties, shoulder-length black hair and a face that, for many, would explain her meteoric rise up the Army's ranks, regardless to her ability or work ethic. She spoke with a southern accent.

"Well, simply, it means that we have stripped out the bits that get in the way," Milo stepped in, saving George the task of explaining a modification that he'd been dead set against. Milo continued, "Fear... anxiety... love... hate... All – and *any* – feelings that hinder one's ability to function efficiently... all gone."

"So, I guess no women, then?" One of the men in the room, his name not known by George, spoke up, chortling at his own joke. George paid little attention to him.

Also ignoring him, Milo readdressed George. "When can we expect the first delivery from your so-called Project *GYGES*?"

"In two months... your first 250 soldiers will be ready to begin their training."

One of the other men in the room, the eldest and most senior officer, General Bill Eastman, raised his hand to speak.

"Yes, General," Milo was straightening his tie on the big screen at the end of the table.

"You say 'first 250', how many more are there to be?"

"Well, General," Milo replied with a smile, "just ask the question:

how many soldiers, including Army, Navy, Air Force, Marines, Coast Guard and Reserves, does the US have now? Your conservative guess?"

"Conservative guess, " he shrugged, "two-and-a-half million."

Milo crossed his arms and looked each person around the table in the eyes, ending on George Jennings. He then smiled and nodded, almost as though he had answered the question verbally.

George turned away, suddenly engulfed in shame and guilt. He looked down at the desk, focused on a smudge of black ink worked into the mahogany surface and closed his eyes, wondering whether the nightmare for him was over… or whether it had only just begun.

What have I done? he pondered.

Beyond the corridor behind the office, through a fourth set of security doors, the laboratory the size of two football pitches; ten rows of racks laden with large polyethylene pods filled with liquid and… and something moving inside each of them.

A small foetal hand, barely formed, pressed against the inside wall of one of the pods, causing the plastic to bulge outwards. A moment later the hand was quickly pulled back, as though stung by a nettle or burnt by a naked flame… only to be replaced by an indistinct face, its small, dainty nose distending the pod's translucent wall much like the hand seconds earlier. Though obscured by the pod's hazy barrier, one could see that the face was human.

The foetus' eyes popped open and took its first glimpse of the world.

CHAPTER ONE
SOPHIE

IT HAD BEEN NEARLY three months since she'd last seen her father; barricaded behind the door within the dimly lit corridor of the warehouse where the CIA had been holding her mother captive. The image of him as he had been, still appeared when she closed her eyes, the desperation never fading from his imploring features:

"Go get your mother," the words had been muffled but Sophie had heard them clearly; they still haunted her. It was almost as though he were still standing within easy reach. *"I will try and find another way in, but if not… meet me by the hole in the fence!"*

The way he looked to her now had altered slightly. Ryan and Thomas' opinions had cast an ugly shadow over her father, tarnishing the image of the man who had created her. Created her yes, but not before manipulating her DNA makeup in such a way that it left her reliant on an ochre-coloured serum that controlled her invisibility, something she considered a majorly debilitating side-effect.

To the uninitiated, being invisible is a major attraction. It has its advantages – and Sophie appreciated that. Who hadn't wanted to disappear at some point in their lives? It has its much championed benefits; the ability to go to the bank for an involuntary cash advance; being able to visit the theatre despite the cashier at the box office insisting that the show was all 'sold out'. Not to mention being able to just become *absent* whenever one pleased.

But for all its advantages – and there were many – it came with a whole trunk-load of issues, not least the increasingly painful administering of the serum that her father had developed to counter the invisibility side-effect. As she'd grown and developed towards maturity, her body had needed a greater dosage of the stuff, and with each increased dose her body reacted more and more negatively, each and every cell screaming out in agony to the invading antigen that attacked its fundamental right to existence, resisting the antibodies with increasingly greater success.

And of course, the serum wasn't in endless supply. With her father stolen away, the source of her medication was gone too.

As was any imminent cure to her perceived disability.

She'd taken every vial of serum from the refrigerator in the apartment in Chelsea after the attack, filling a sport's holdall with a couple of hundred bottles of the stuff, and for a time the supply looked vast, far outweighing demand – but that was changing every day. Keeping visible had its costs.

When George had created the serum, the effects of one dose lasted more than a day. This was no longer the case, the effects had decreased exponentially since then. So much so that Sophie now required three vials of serum, which, reluctantly, she needed to administer three times over the day.

Three months had passed since she'd said goodbye to what was left of her family. In the car park of the *Little Chef* restaurant a woman with glasses had turned up to collect Meredith, Stanley and Charlie, to whisk them off to their grandfathers', an errand on the say-so of Ryan Barber. She wasn't wholly sure how Ryan fitted into the situation, but he had assisted her father in his attempt at rescuing her mother, and helped her directly in the hours thereafter.

That plan had only been marginally successful, seeing as her mother was now dead; besides the man had had his own agenda. The truth was, Ryan blamed Sophie's father for the death of his daughter, Clara, who had died at the laboratory where she worked. The long and short of it was he had plans of his own for meting out justice.

That all seemed like such a long time ago now, standing there by the road, thousands of miles away from home on a different continent, hitching for a lift. Of course, she didn't need to stick a thumb in the air if she didn't want. Much easier would it be to just climb into a car, van or lorry invisible, and steal a ride. But she had her some morals; she didn't enjoy the thought of taking something that didn't belong to her, whether it was physical like a... *diamond*, or not, like a lift. For her conscience, she preferred to receive things given... not taken. Not to say that she *wouldn't* resort to 'appropriation' if it was necessary.

Sophie couldn't deny the thrill she'd experienced back in July when, under duress, she'd entered the exhibition building in London with the leanest of plans and undertaken a daring robbery that saw her come into possession of the *Whisper of Persia*. The adrenaline had given her a buzz never before experienced. She'd felt giddy with excitement and enjoyed the danger and the white-knuckle fear that fired every neuron in her brain. It was for those moments that she had been created, her genetic makeup designed for combat and daring missions. She allowed the memory to glide away on a stiff breeze. Although elated at the time, she'd sworn never to undertake such things again.

It was a false promise.

Such a beautiful diamond, though, she reflected.

A couple of days after she'd found her mother dead, she'd packaged up the diamond and sent it back to London with a slip of paper with just one word scrawled across it:

Sorry.

A car sped past, pulling her mind back to the present. The driver was ignorant or oblivious to Sophie's thumbed plea for a ride. Although legal in most states, hitchhiking was not as easy as it would appear in the movies.

Sophie watched the sporty car disappear into the distance. It had been the first car to drive by in more than an hour, and the fourth car to give her little or no thought since she'd walked onto the highway.

The young woman sighed, quickly glancing at herself for reassurance that she'd not disappeared without realising it. It was something that happened from time-to-time – but mostly at night.

"No, I'm still here," she said to herself, half-disappointed. Had she been invisible, she'd at least be able to explain why no one had stopped to give her a ride. A young, attractive woman, all alone on a quiet highway; a damsel in distress, normally ripe for a passing weirdo – or at least someone for a Samaritan to bestow a caring deed upon.

After half an hour she accepted she was going to have to think of something else with regards to her travel plans. There was no way she was going to be able to walk across two states, so stealing a ride was beginning to look very appealing.

A horn blared, startling Sophie into dropping her sports holdall to the ground. The backpack slung over her shoulder barely moved. She peered behind her as the red *Chevy Equinox* drove past, coming to a grinding halt ten or so yards ahead of her. It had a 2013 number plate.

Sophie scooped up her sports holdall and jogged after the stationary car. Where it had parked off-road, a cloud of dust had been kicked up.

"Where you headin' littl' doll?" The guy in the driver's seat smiled a toothless grin, his voice gravelly with a South Texan drawl. It was unexpected, seeing as she was in the heart of North Carolina, one hundred miles slightly north-east of Charlotte.

Taking the first flight from Heathrow Airport had seemed like a good idea at the time, and using her invisibility made it easy to avoid security. In her haste she hadn't considered the distance from which Charlotte was to Washington, thinking she might be able to use public transport or something. With little money, the idea of a taxi journey or use of any other means of paid transport soon evaporated, and it soon dawned on her that she would need to make the journey by any means necessary.

Though dangerous, hitchhiking seemed like a good idea. Plus she enjoyed the company.

"Well?" The guy in the car was growing impatient, the top of his head hidden beneath a dark blue baseball cap with a 'T' emblazoned in white with a red shadow behind it. Sophie didn't know what the 'T' signified, but it was in support of the *Texas Rangers* baseball team. A sticker in the rear windscreen attested to the fact.

"Washington DC," Sophie replied meekly.

"I can getcha as far as Richmond," he said. "Hop on in."

"Thanks." Sophie tossed her holdall and the backpack into the rear seats of the car, climbing in after. The car set in motion before Sophie could secure the seatbelt.

"That's quite an accent you hav' ther', doll, you Australian or somethin'?" excitement in his voice.

"English."

"That sure is a pity," he sighed. "I knew a gal once, said she was from Bromley or some such place, I don' know. Not good with maps, especially from overseas. She stole me heart... and me money!" he went forlorn. "Never trusted a Brit ever since. Still, can't help where your roots lie..."

"I guess," was all Sophie said. She closed her eyes and tried to forget where she was for a moment, allowing her thoughts to wander through a passage of memories from before things went seriously screwy.

Images of Meredith, Stanley and Charlie flitted into her mind.

She focused on the rare meals she'd shared with them, and her father. Her thoughts settled on *The Pig and Whistle*. Food was making her hungry. The memory evaporated and Ryan's face appeared, so vivid – it was though he was in front of her.

"You can go to sleep if you like," said the driver interrupting Sophie's reverie. "I'll put something on radio, maybe to your liking." He pressed a button at the centre of the car next to an LCD display and watched it flicker through a number of digits before settling on one. *Coldplay* filled the car, *Paradise*. "Of cours', don' like this music me-self. Reminds me of Jacqui... I'm more a country man, but you can listen for sure."

Sophie nodded in the direction of the driver but said nothing. She had little interest and limited experience of music. People who didn't know her would think her to be in her late teens or early twenties, based on her appearance. Her passport, provided by Ryan, gave her a birth date that made her twenty-one – which matched her physical appearance; her actual birth date was more recent than that – but who would have believed this young woman was just three-and-a-half-years-old?

It was just *one* of the genetic *mal*adjustments... courtesy of her father.

Of course, her body had developed to that of a twenty-one-year-old woman – which was obvious from the shape and form of her features – her ageing, having been so rapid, had decreased dramatically now to less than a tenth of a normal, *unmodified* person. She would have the body (and the facial appearance) of a young person in their early twenties for the equivalent of a human lifetime. She couldn't contemplate how she was going to explain that in future years; though by then it might not be a problem – if she ran out of serum no one would be able to see her anyway.

With her eyes closed, Sophie listened to the radio and allowed further memories to surface of the people she missed.

Queen came on, filling the void between her and the driver, *I Want It All* which was then replaced by *U2*'s *Hold Me, Thrill Me, Kiss Me, Kill Me*, which was the last song she heard before sleep blanketed over her.

The distance between Charlotte and Richmond was just short of three hundred miles and, on a good day, would take four hours, eighteen minutes to drive using Interstate 85. Excepting the first twenty minutes, Sophie slept the whole distance, not stirring once – not even when the driver pulled into a service station for fuel – and not waking still, when the car came to a complete halt in an empty parking lot outside a dilapidated single storey motel; the neon sign in the reception window declaring 'vacancies' in bright pink – though the second letter in the word was faulty, as was the second from last; flickering on and off intermittently.

It was dark, the clock on the dash indicated it was 9:12 p.m. Around the parking lot were a couple of roadside lamps dimly lighting the area, but for all their refulgence very little light filtered through to the car's gloomy interior.

The small light in the ceiling of the *Chevy* afforded very little light, creating more shadows than obliterating them. The man with the *Texas Rangers* cap was accustomed to the gloom and had been kneeling in the back of the car for nigh on ten minutes when he made his move.

Something cold touching her neck shocked Sophie awake.

The something cold touching her neck was a five-and-a-half-inch bolster knife, its wooden handle clenched within his grubby fisted hand. With the blade pressed against her skin, Sophie could sense the keenness of its edge.

With the slightest of glances, she found the driver was kneeling on the seat in the back of the *Chevy* to the left of her.

"Don' m-," *ove*. Before he was able to finish his warning, Sophie had reacted with barely a thought. In less than an eye-blink, Sophie's left hand had shot upwards and slammed the driver's knife-holding hand into the ceiling of the car, grappling about his wrist and smashing it repeatedly until he loosened his grip. The knife slipped from his grasp, his hand still pressed against the ceiling of the *Chevy*, the blade falling, point downwards, which Sophie snatched mid-air with her right hand. In a single, fluid motion she continued the blade's descent into her assailant's inner thigh, slamming it down hard.

"Agghhhhhh!" screamed the driver. Sophie released the driver's hand from the ceiling, which immediately fell upon the protruding knife, wrapping back round it, his instinct making to remove it.

"I wouldn't do that if I were you," Sophie said as she opened the door, grabbing her holdall and backpack and making ready to go. "I have just nicked your femoral artery. If you try pulling that out..." Sophie looked quickly around the desolate parking lot. "...around here, I figure you'll probably bleed out before anyone notices you..."

"Please... Please... I'm sorry. I'm sorry..." he was sobbing, the Texas drawl less prominent.

She went to walk away, changed tack and turned back, hunching down to peer into the car through the open door. "Mister, I figure I've done you a favour. How would you have lived with yourself after what you might have done to a poor, defenceless girl?" She slammed the car door behind her with the flat of a hand.

"I know, I know. I beg ya. I'm sick... I need help! Help me..." barely audible through the door.

Unable to hear the driver's stifled pleas, Sophie walked towards the motel's reception.

Crying freely now with tears trickling down his pain-stricken face, the *Chevy* driver watched the young woman walk a little distance, fear and loathing filling his head, expletives exploding from his lips, until something strange occurred.

The young Brit seemingly began to vanish before his eyes, fading like a picture on one of those heat sensitive magic mugs when the liquid within cools down.

"I'll be damned..." For a moment the pain from the knife protruding from his leg, and the sight of blood leaking from the wound, was forgotten.

Nobody saw Sophie enter the reception area of the motel, and despite setting the bell attached to the door a jangling as she entered, she was unseen.

She walked past the service desk, through the gap between the desk and the wall (that allowed staff access behind it) and crossed to a small key cupboard screwed into a false wall a little further back that partitioned the reception and a private area. Sophie could hear from out back, the motel's owner lumbering about and slowly making his way through to respond to the bell and his expected visitor. Reaching in, she took the first key her hand fell upon. It instantly disappeared within her grasp.

The man wore a dirty grey T-shirt and a faded black, buttonless cardigan opened at the front. He appeared behind the service desk as the bell jangled once again as the door was opened and reclosed.

"Come again!" called out the owner in disdain, feeling depressed that a customer had seemingly changed their mind about spending a night at his motel. It had been two days since he'd last had a paying customer book a room for the night. Convinced that the recession was solely the reason for the lack of business, as opposed to the deteriorating state of the building (and the fact a Holiday Inn had opened less than a mile away), the motel owner returned sluggishly to the back room.

Sophie checked the number cheaply scrawled in red felt pen on the yellow plastic key ring fob:

11.

The single level motel was built in the shape of a reversed 'L' with the reception office at its top and rooms numbered from one through to twelve running in order to its right. The key Sophie had stumbled upon by chance was furthest but one from the office. She hoped the space would allow her presence to go unnoticed, despite knowing that she herself would not be seen without a heavy dose of serum, or the aid of a thermal-imaging ocular device. Although she wanted to be seen, wanted to be normal like any other young woman, it was times like these, without money or any means of paying for overnight accommodation, being invisible was a definite blessing.

Sophie stopped outside number eleven. Despite the gloom (the nearest roadside lamp was across the parking lot) she glanced around to check no one was watching, before inserting the key and opening the door. Still parked where she'd left it, the red *Chevy* and its occupant remained unchanged. For a fleeting second she wondered what the man inside was going to do, had almost started to worry, before remembering the knife touching her throat.

She dismissed the thought totally and went into the darkness within, closing the motel door behind her.

CHAPTER TWO

EMILY

SINCE TOM KAPLAN'S DEATH, the intelligence section of the business had all but severed its interest in pursuing George Jennings and his family (a decision made the easier with George's abduction). Under Jennifer Ratcliff's leadership, all agents, assets and employees within that division were reassigned or rewarded for their failure with a large box to help with emptying their desks.

No one was beyond reproach, including its Director, Samuel Jackson who was far from safe, despite being romantically linked to the company's CEO. Neither was his short-lived second in command, Assistant Intelligence Officer Emily Porter. After just two weeks in the role she inherited from Ryan's widely reported disappearance, she found herself in a queue outside the local Job Centre.

The whereabouts of Kaplan Ratcliff's former quarry (and employee) George Jennings was no longer a topic on the agenda, neither was the product of George's imagination, *Sophie Jennings*. Both were still at large, though analysts and agents (who were no longer looking for them) had grown to the conclusion that George – now understood to be a traitor and CIA agent – had disappeared to America; his daughter's whereabouts though, were unknown…

Well, unknown to most.

Despite joining 2.5 million other people out of work, Emily Porter had valuable information that many would pay a fine price to know.

"Emily Porter?" A tall, skinny woman with a face like a bag of golf balls came to the front of the office. Her name badge indicated that her name was Edwina. "This way."

Emily followed the woman into the main part of the Job Centre and took the seat in front of the desk, behind which the woman had now sat.

Edwina located a small booklet upon which Emily's details were recorded and started to punch in a few letters and numbers on the keyboard in front of her. She glanced up at Emily and smiled warmly.

"So, what have you done in the past two weeks to find yourself a new job?"

And so Emily proceeded to outline a number of activities she'd undertaken to procure employment: speculative letters sent out; networking; applying for part-time jobs. She explained the obstacles she was facing – her qualifications and the fact that she was trained to be a spy.

"You see, no one wants to hire someone who has the ability to tell whether you are lying, just by the expression on their face."

"Not even McDonalds?" Edwina asked genuinely.

Emily could not find any words to answer. She could not believe that after all the years at university, the extensive training programme at Kaplan Ratcliff and her experience, she was going to be reduced to taking a job at a fast food franchise.

"McDonalds are hiring at the moment," continued Edwina in an insistent tone. "Ronald McDonald is happy to take anyone on these days. Delivering his happy meals! Shall I book you in for an interview?"

"I, um, err..." Emily was aghast at the suggestion.

"Of course, if you refuse to take my offer of an interview it may affect ongoing payments of your job seeker's allowance..."

Emily faked a smile and reluctantly agreed with a nod of the head. *I can't believe I'm being reduced to this.* She felt like screaming.

Edwina smiled smugly. "Sign here," she said, passing the form which confirmed her fortnightly attendance, allowing her employment benefit to continue. "I will arrange for your interview and be in touch."

Emily took her signing-on book and left the Job Centre quickly before Edwina could make her sink to new depths of depravity, perhaps by offering her a job cleaning out public toilets…

Outside the Job Centre the familiar figure of Ryan Barber stood waiting, his hands deep in his black quilted bomber jacket pockets, despite the October temperature being above normal.

"How did it go?" he asked, starting to walk alongside the woman down the high street.

"How d'you think? I'm on the scrap heap and I'm not even thirty. They want me to get a job in *McDonalds* for *Christs'ake*."

"Did you ask if they wanted fries with that?"

"It's not funny Ryan. What am I going to do? I have a mortgage. I have a cat with expensive tastes in food."

Ryan shrugged, going silent for a moment. Emily could see from a side glance that he was deep in thought, mulling over something. When he next spoke he stopped walking. Emily walked a few feet further before realising that she was all alone. She backtracked and stood in front of her former boss.

"What?" she demanded. "And why were you waiting for me?"

Ryan contemplated not telling her, but thought better of it upon seeing the need and expectation in her eyes. "I may have a job for you. Something you're suitably skilled for."

"Go on," she implored, almost desperate.

"I've had contacts with the Secret Intelligence Service for years and have done a little moonlighting for them in the past – nothing too dirty, just a little field work, off-the-grid sort of stuff. Occasionally our paths would cross, so I'd chip in with a few morsels of info. Nothing too innocuous..."

"You've been a double agent?" Emily exclaimed indignantly.

"Well, no... nothing so melodramatic – not entirely," he continued. "My associate within the service has given me a paid position, company car, expenses account and a good benefits package; he wants me to head a small, specialist team," he paused to allow for his information to filter in. "It has caveats, but... I'd like for you to join me."

Emily went quiet for a moment, almost contemplative. The Secret Intelligence Service were more commonly known as MI6. Like Ryan, she'd had dealings with them in the past.

"What's the purpose of this 'team'?" Emily asked, almost flabbergasted. "I mean, what would we be doing?"

"I can't tell you Emily. It's classified. Only those on the inside are privy to the finer details. If you really want to know just say 'yes' and join my team; I can promise, you won't be disappointed. And that's without the pay and benefits. Would you like to think about it, say, over a coffee or some lunch? I'm starving. There's a *McDonalds* round the corner, they do a nice mocha. You could hand in your C.V whilst you're there." Ryan started to snigger.

Emily wrinkled her nose at the man but couldn't help smiling. "Okay."

"Okay?"

"Ryan, I'm in. I'll do it, whatever it is. I trust you." The pair of them were walking once again. "So, what is the work we'll be undertaking with SIS?"

"Before I tell you there's some forms you need to sign and a little thing regarding your employment status to sort. Her Majesty's Government insist that we follow strict protocol. Once the 'I's are dotted and the 'T's are crossed we can get to work. Also, I wasn't kidding about lunch. I'm afraid I could eat the backside off a dirty old homeless guy – *that's* how hungry I am."

"Ergh…" Emily screwed her face up in disgust.

CHAPTER THREE
DOMINIC – TWO MONTHS AGO

THE DEAL HAD GONE horribly wrong for Dominic Schilling. In the warehouse the night George Jennings had been abducted and flown to Langley, Dominic had lain unconscious in the dark - albeit for a fading glow stick - slumped across the floor of the holding cell where Harriet Jennings had been locked up for more than twenty-four hours. An injection of *Profonol*, enough to knock an elephant out (or two *Michael Jacksons*) had been administered, courtesy of Sophie, who'd claimed it for herself during a bungled attempt at apprehending her. For three hours Dominic had gone unnoticed, forgotten by his recently acquired allies, having defected from Kaplan Ratcliff to the CIA with the promise of a handsome reward – that in part being the *Whisper of Persia*.

It wasn't until a team of 'cleaners' drafted in by the CIA carried out their work that they came across his paralysed body. To most, a 'cleaner' was someone who slipped into *Marigolds* and pushed a *Dyson* or a little *Henry* vacuum cleaner, dusting and sanitising. The CIA's 'cleaners' did all that, but on a much grander scale – they also were skilled at making things disappear, leaving buildings and scenes of interest with barely a trace. When the CIA's 'cleaners' were finished, the warehouse would be as if they'd never been there in the first place.

Brayden Scott had been clear with his instructions. Strip the warehouse and get rid of all the evidence.

Dominic Schilling, lying on the floor of the holding cell, was thirteen stone of fleshy evidence. The 'cleaner' – one of a team of eight scouring the premises (a man in an all-in-one white coverall, who wouldn't look out of place at a murder scene, face mask concealing his appearance, and surgical gloves completing the look) – had crouched down at the body and checked for a pulse. Finding the rhythm of the man's heart thumping strongly, the 'cleaner' sighed. He didn't deal with the living. Cadavers, no problem – though messy, he was very skilled. To take someone out was outside of his pay grade. Reaching into the pocket of his all-in-one he retrieved a mobile phone and punched in a number.

The dialling tone sounded for about seven rings then the call was answered by Brayden, his voice distant, interspersed with interference and the thrum of a deep engine.

"I've found someone." The 'cleaner' explained the scene, described the man lying unconscious on the floor and asked for further instructions. He'd been praying that he wasn't about to be ordered to kill the man.

"Take off his clothes, relieve him of his possessions and dump him. Somewhere... remote," he said, before cutting off – either deliberately or through the terrible cellular reception.

During the 'clean-up' Dominic remained deep in sleep, comatose to his displacement, unaware as he was dragged naked from the room, through the corridors, out into the balmy night, and tossed unmercifully into the back of the *Black Hawk UH-60* that had returned to the site after completing escorting duties to Mildenhall airbase.

The 'cleaner' gave the pilot some instructions and climbed into the back of the helicopter, quickly harnessing his seatbelt. Another passenger closed the door and moments later the war machine – a veteran of various US combat missions since first entering active duty in 1983 during the invasion of Grenada – lifted off noisily from the ground, its twin engines deafening to any without protective earphones.

Fourteen hours later Dominic Schilling was roused from his chemically induced slumber, his head pounding and his skin – from scalp to his toes – was dappled with moisture. The sound of waves crashing from the sea, perilously close by. He lifted his head up from the sand and looked around, a baffled expression spreading across his face.

I'm outside. His second thought was: *I'm dreaming.* A swift tug on some hairs to the back of his left wrist convinced him that he wasn't.

Awareness permeated through to his neuron-senses; he was on a beach, and fear and alarm was heightened even more when he realised he was bereft of clothing – even his underwear!

"What the...? What's going on?" He jumped up and whirled around to take in the spectacular scenery, feeling the wind whipping around him and a cold draught caressing the delicate regions not ordinarily exposed. A thick whiff of salt assailed his nostrils, clinging to every molecule of air.

"Where am I?" he whispered. Behind him there were a number of cobble houses in the distance, many derelict; the remnants of a village street from long ago. Dominic turned a full 360°, taking in the entire panoramic surroundings.

"Where are all my clothes?" he muttered to himself, deciding on the direction to take. He took a step towards the village street, just a little way beyond a set of hills, on what was all that remained of the settlement on Great Britain's remotest set of islands, St. Kilda, the westernmost islands in the Outer Hebrides.

The archipelago comprised of Hirta (upon which Dominic, unknowingly, found himself) and three smaller islands (Dùn, Soay and Boreray). Behind him was a rough and inhospitable sea – much like any, Dominic would later muse, that surrounded Mother England.

Hiding his modesty with his hands, the fingers interlaced and overlapping above his groin, acting as a shield. Dominic made his way to one of the cobble houses that had stood for what could have been a millennia.

Despite the month being August, the sea winds and the time of day barely past sunrise made it feel very chilly. Dominic wore goose bumps instead of clothing, and shivered on his approach to the first of the cobbled houses.

Initially he had believed the old village was derelict and abandoned, but on closer inspection he could see signs of restoration and recent habitation. One such building provided little protest in accessing. A shoulder shove against a loosely-locked door gave way with barely a whisper, just a whine as rusty hinges grated, metal-upon-metal. On entering the single level building, he was immediately warmed by the shelter, relieved to be out of the biting wind.

He sat down to gather his thoughts.

What had happened?

How did I get here?

Where am I?

Questions collided in his head, all vying for answers but all falling short of one. Were they to have been spoken aloud it would have made little difference in view of the lack of an audience.

Dominic hadn't a clue where he was; how he'd arrived on the island (though he didn't know that it was an island), or what events had transpired that had resulted on his arrival there. The last memory he had was…

The image of Harriet Jennings and the girl, invisible to the naked eye but observable through the thermal goggles, flitted into his mind. He remembered all the events up to the moment he blacked out.

Why was that? Why did I lose consciousness?

Dominic touched the nape of his neck and felt a slight swelling from where the needle had penetrated his skin. Rubbing the area, it felt tender beneath his probing fingers.

Now he understood. He'd been drugged.

"Clever girl," he whispered.

Looking around the almost empty room, he found half a dozen hessian sacks lying discarded in a corner, and rope fragments scattered here and there. With a little patience and creativity he fashioned some clothing with two sacks tied about his waist and a couple of others he draped over his shoulders. Though rough and scratchy, and looking worse than a tramp, or like a badly dressed caveman, the hessian provided a little warmth and restored his virtue. He wrapped the remaining hessian sacks and rope fragments, double-thickness, around his feet for makeshift shoes.

❖

After moping about for half a day, Dominic had taken a walk along the ruins of the street that faced St. Kilda Bay, checking for signs of life, for a telephone, for food, and essentially, for water. He was ravenous and his throat felt dry, swollen, and more scratchy than the makeshift hessian clothing felt upon his skin; so much so, that he was beginning to think that if he didn't quench his thirst soon his oesophagus would shrivel and close up.

With the onset of night he'd searched most of the houses, a futile exercise, doing nothing but use up vital energy that he knew was unlikely to be replenished, not in this Godforsaken place, at any rate.

Perhaps this is hell, he surmised.

He would be the first to admit that he was hardly innocent of ever committing a sin. Harriet wasn't the first unarmed person he'd shot point-blank. Maybe this was his punishment.

He sat down on a pile of rocks overlooking the bay – the village street behind him – and watched as darkness slowly stretched across the sky from the east; a blanket peppered with the most brilliant arrangement of stars he'd ever seen, each constellation somewhat closer and brighter than he could ever remember. With each passing minute the temperature dipped lower, the Atlantic surf kicking up a cold wind that bit through his meagre clothing, beginning to chill him to the bone.

Dominic shivered and wondered what would become of him.

I'm going to die, he mostly thought, calmly. Most people go through five stages when faced with a life threatening event, and usually in the standard order of:

Denial. Anger. Bargaining. Depression and finally, Acceptance.

Dominic skipped four of them and settled on acceptance. With his knees drawn to beneath his chin, his arms folded together above them, he rocked back and forth wishing sleep to come and take him.

Soon, it was completely dark and the moon had crept silently up the sky behind him, illuminating the island brighter than he thought possible. He closed his eyes to the milky white luminance.

On reopening his eyes he saw an orange ball of light flickering in the distance from the peripheral of his vision. Turning slightly to the right, he looked towards the orange glow, placing a hand over his eyes to shield them from the moon's brilliance, as though it would visually aid him.

It didn't, but the orange ball of light was unmistakeable.

It was a fire.

Almost feeling its warmth, Dominic stood up and started towards what couldn't be anything other than a campfire. Hope ignited within his belly, and with it a fresh wave of energy suffused his body. Without realising, he was running headlong towards the cosy heat that was on offer, not stopping for anything – not even the hidden ravine that took him totally unawares, and which took his feet out from under him. For a moment he felt like he was suspended in midair, like *Wile*

E. Coyote in those *Road Runner* cartoons, before gravity realised its purpose.

"Ya-uuuuuugghhhhh!!" Though falling through the gap in the landscape, Dominic's flailing hand had managed to find purchase on a craggy, damp rock on the other side of the narrow ravine – a natural fissure in the land, thirty feet below which a runnel ebbed inky-black water back to the sea.

"Help!" Dominic cried desperately, certain that his voice would carry to those responsible for the campfire burning not too far in the distance.

"Help me!" he caterwauled. "Heeelppp Meeeeee!" He continued to cry out for what felt like an eternity.

Just before his voice gave out he felt all his renewed reserves of energy dissipate, his grasp on the craggy rock begin to lessen and the dark, yawning chasm of the ravine below hungrily beckon him to drop into its icy maw.

With his final guttural cry, Dominic felt his fingers slowly slip from the rock, too numb and fatigue too total, to retain a grip. Once again he accepted that it was time fate dealt its final blow.

As unconsciousness engulfed him and his fingers finally loosened from the rock's flint-like surface, two pairs of hands snaked out from above and took a hold of his limp wrists, just managing to pull him to safety before the ravine took him to the fish for supper.

⁕

When he awoke it was as though the day on the desolate, harsh landscape of what was Hirta was just a terrible dream. Momentarily, thoughts of the days leading up to that moment were forgotten.

Lying in a single bed, an eiderdown duvet drawn close to his chin, a jug of crystal water, ice-cubes clinking subtly within, and a half-full glass on the bedside cabinet placed beside him; he could easily have been fooled into believing that all was well, and that he was snuggled up in bed holidaying in some distant sunspot.

With his eyes shut he could hear the crashing of the waves adding further credence to his imagined vacation, images of palm trees and beach babes, of sunbeds and pina coladas with straws and little umbrellas, conjured delightful thoughts to mind.

"Mornin' sunshine..." His eyes were still closed, not wishing for the fantasy to end. The voice spoken was female, and strongly accented with a Scottish brogue, *Glaswegian* – Dominic thought – but she spoke clearly – unlike some from the region who he'd often struggled to understand, thinking their utterances nothing more than incoherent babblings. "You wer' nearly a gonna. Lucky us finds ya like we did."

Dominic opened his eyes and sighed. He had still half-hoped that the women speaking was just room service. Giving her a quick cursory glance, he sized the woman up and quietly appraised her. Immediately, he could tell from her appearance that she wasn't room service. Clinging to the dream, it was possible, he thought, she might be a cleaner woman. Shabbily dressed and not unattractive, she had the appearance of a homeless-shelter worker, dowdy grey sweatpants (the knees wearing thin), black V-neck jumper (made by granny) over a grubby looking white collared blouse and steel-toed boots that climbed above her ankles. Her hair was dark-ginger and untidily tied into a tail. Matching her hair, the woman's face was slightly red from windburn and characterised by freckles (especially the cheeks).

With the sound of the waves still crashing outside, Dominic desperately held onto the thought that he was still on holiday, although memories of the previous day were breaking through like streaks of sun splitting banks of cloud.

Sighing, he spoke with a rasp, his mouth and throat parched dry. "Where am I?"

"Aye, we guessed you weren't here by choice." She smiled.

"We?"

"Aye. Clarence and Dougal… my colleagues. I'm Elspeth – or Ellie. Ya donnay how lucky you really are. We're here, part of a conservation team on the island. We're due to sail back to mainland in a couple-a dee-s."

"Island?"

"Aye. St. Kilda. It's uninhabited. No one else here currently, so had we not found ya, you'd've been stuck on the island on your own for don't know how long; save for the odd sheep and the large population of *Leach Petrels*…"

"Scotland?"

"Aye, *Caledonia*. Where else? Any hoo, you'll be famished I'm sure. Dougal is about your size; he's loaning you some clothes – begrudgingly, mind! You'll find what you need in the room next door. Nothing too grand – though better than those rags we found ya in! When you're dressed, come down to the 'but and ben'. There's sausage and bacon on the skillet, and some scrambled egg in the pan."

CHAPTER FOUR
SOPHIE

THE MOTEL HAD ALLOWED the young woman a good deal of rest. What was intended to be one night's sanctuary, unwittingly ended up being her place of residence for three whole days. Within that time business at the motel went from 'sluggish' to 'all but extinct', which basically meant Sophie's room remained vacant for her continued undiscovered use, as did ninety percent of the other rooms; no cleaner or motel staff came within a whisker of disturbing her up to that point.

The *Chevy* and its scumbag occupant were long gone. The car was in the parking lot when Sophie had closed the door to room 'eleven' that first night. She'd gone to bed and fallen immediately asleep upon hitting the pillow. When she'd awoken (around lunch time) and peered out through the curtain – the *Chevy* was no longer there. The 'when' and the 'how' were outside of her knowledge; in truth, she didn't care a single iota. The actuality was a police cruiser had happened by early that morning, followed soon after by medical assistance. The 'who' and the 'why' in relation to his predicament was omitted by the impaired driver in his statement, not wishing to admit that he'd been incapacitated by a mere girl. He instead concocted a story about a failed carjacking, his description of the perp vague and pinpointing somewhat towards America's stereotypical black gangland culture.

Sophie had half-hoped the *Chevy* was still there; morbidly, she'd expected to find the driver – her attacker – having ignored her advice regarding the knife and having pulled it out of his leg, (wishful thinking) bleeding to death. It wouldn't have been pleasant, but it would have given her an easy transport option (stowing his body in the boot of the car would not have caused her any bother), and she wouldn't have shed a tear or held a moment's remorse.

Food options had been limited. Even if she were a paying guest there were no restaurant facilities at the motel. With little money (and no desire to rob a bank), and not excited at the prospect of being discovered, she maintained invisibility, using it to liberate fruit (apples, a banana and a melon), packaged goods (*Lays* crisps, *Oreos*, *Hersheys* chocolate bars and *M&Ms*) and soft drinks (mainly bottled water plus a bottle of diet *Pepsi*) from a convenience store half a mile away. Stealing went against her conscience and she made a mental promise: she would return to the store one day and pay for what she'd taken.

Feasting in the motel room on crisps and *Oreos*, it reminded her of the day three months earlier when she'd revealed herself to Meredith and Stanley in Meredith's bedroom at Willoughby Rising. Stanley had brought her a plate of food and a big bag of *Doritos*. This was before the sky had all but caved in and the world had simply ended; Meredith and Stanley's innocence had been lost forever.

Sophie had been just as hungry back then. The memory summoned a pang of guilt. Although ravenous, she slowed her eating, almost abandoning it.

Meredith, Stanley and Charlie.

With her father missing and her mother dead, they were her closest family. And she'd left them behind with their grandfather, Theo.

"I miss you guys," she whispered to herself. She took a swig from the *Pepsi*, pulling a face as the gas threatened to volcano from her mouth.

On a small table big enough for just one chair, a mobile phone began to vibrate. Sophie had switched off the ringtone, not wishing to announce her presence, no matter how deserted the motel appeared.

Pushing aside the packets of calorific snacks and wiping a greasy hand on the front of her jeans, she picked up the phone and accepted the call.

"Sophie?" The caller ID on the phone had given no clue as to the caller's identity, meaning he was either calling from outside the country or, an unscrupulous salesman.

It was the former. The voice belonged to Ryan Barber, a man she had mixed feelings for. On the one hand, he had acted as a friend, ally, and, as it turned out, her grandfather, giving her sanctuary when she needed it and providing assistance with her personal mission. On the other, he made no pretence of hiding his hatred for her father, blaming him for the death of his daughter Clara, who, to complicate things, turned out to be her biological mother. Though they both wanted to find George, Ryan's motives were maligned, as opposed to hers.

"Who else?" she spoke petulantly.

"How are you? How's America?"

"I'm broke, Ryan; America sucks, and I feel like Marlin in the frigging *Finding Nemo* film. I'm living on snacks, and so far the people of good ol' U. S. of A are turning out to be more Norman Bates than Dr Doolittle." Sophie surprised Ryan with the movie references. One of the perks of being left on her own by her father for days at a time meant she could watch whatever she wanted. She gave Ryan an update on her most recent ride, and the good Samaritan who turned out to be 'not' so good.

Ryan had listened to his granddaughter quietly. Most grandfathers would have been horrified to learn of Sophie's assault, but Sophie wasn't your normal granddaughter. "Where are you now? You still on course?"

"I'm in a dump near Richmond, a motel straight out of the Psychopath's Handbook, about a hundred miles from Langley. But, yeah… to answer your question, making reasonable progress."

"When you make Washington, I'll hook you up with our contact in the agency. Working for MI6 has its advantages."

"Are you sure this guy is on the level… I mean, you're expecting him to dish dirt on the people he works for; the last thing I want is to walk into a trap and end up like *Bonnie Parker*." She also did a lot of reading, her enhanced abilities enabling her to sponge information much like an upsalite absorbs water. Bonnie Parker being one half of the infamous outlaws *Bonnie & Clyde*, who were ambushed on a rural road in Bienville Parish, Louisiana on May 23, 1934. Lawmen opened fire on their approaching vehicle allowing them absolutely no opportunity to escape or reciprocate.

"Sophie, relax. We can trust him. Besides, nothing comes free, you'll do well to remember that." *And I'll remind you of it when the time comes…* Ryan thought. As part of the agreement to utilise SIS resources, and the deal sweetener in securing a position for Emily Porter within the Secret Intelligence Service, Ryan had shared knowledge germane to George Jennings' research, not withholding details of Sophie's unique abilities and skill set. Kept from Sophie, this fine print detail would eventually come back to bite them in the ass – but for now, it benefited the situation. Besides, Ryan often appeased his conscience, Sophie *had* stated to him prior to stepping through the entrance doors to Heathrow's international airport, she would do *anything* to see her father again. More to the point, *he* was willing to do *anything* to get her father back also.

A knock at the door startled Sophie. For a moment she ceased all movement, including breathing. Her ears pricked up as she strained to hear any clues as to the identity of the visitor.

Despite him being her grandfather, they remained on first name terms. "Ryan. I'll call you back."

"Sophie..." She disconnected the call and stood up. She was facing the door as she heard the jangle of keys and the sound as one was selected and then slipped into the lock. Slowly and carefully, the key was turned.

Although invisible, Sophie still harboured a fear of being discovered. She glanced around the room. Without a doubt, anyone stepping in would see that it was inhabited, least of all because of the half-eaten snacks spread across the table. She just hoped that whoever was now about to enter vacated swiftly, allowing her time to collect her personal effects to enable a speedy departure.

The key fully engaged the lock and a moment later the door began to open.

"Howdy, I know you're in there!" The man looked dirty from head to toe and was wearing the same T-shirt and black cardigan that Sophie had seen him in three days earlier when she'd helped herself to the room key. "I don't know how you thought to get away with this, but your game is up sonny... Come on out and you can settle up for the room, I'll give you a good rate; no questions asked. Hell, I'll throw in a discount if you come quietly. We don't need no trouble. I won't even call the fuzz... not too keen on them sniffing about. Not good for business... if you know what I mean."

As the man came deeper into the motel room, bright afternoon sunshine washed in from behind him through the open doorway. It gave him an ethereal appearance.

Sophie's first real look at the man came almost as a shock. To accompany the well-worn appearance of his clothing, his face – quite long – had a sallow complexion; his eyes were sunken in and his cheekbones prominent, the skin pulled taut across them. Two days' worth of stubble had grown in patches, making him look decidedly strange. His head was bald and marked all over with *lentigo senilis*, commonly known as 'liver spots'. He didn't look a well man, and as he walked closer to Sophie, she wrinkled her nose. He didn't smell well either!

Intermingled with the overpowering odour of weeks' old sweat, a musty, nauseating stench of mouldy clothing, wet dog, garlic and rotten meat threatened to cause Sophie to retch, bringing tears to surface.

It surprised her not at all that business was slow if this specimen of a man was all the motel had to offer for front of house welcoming.

"There's no point hiding..." he continued, his eyes scouring the room, noting the telltale signs of habitation. "I can smell you..."

Sophie was surprised he could smell anything over his own awful stink.

The newcomer pulled out a gun from inside his trousers' pocket having caused a bulge in a place Sophie had not wished to contemplate. A small *Cobra CA380* handgun was held in a tight fist, finger at the ready. Knowing her guns, Sophie immediately identified the weapon as a budget pistol. Retailing at $129 (just under eighty British pounds in current exchange rates), it was the cheapest method of home defence available on the market. It was also one of the shoddiest, least reliable handguns available, reportedly jamming frequently, and firing slightly off-target. Magazines carried no more than five rounds – adequate against a single intruder at point blank range, but no use against a group, or against anyone from a distance. It would never win a shooting contest.

Sophie's weapon of choice was a *Glock 19* pistol, selected by many in the military and law enforcement. What Sophie liked most about the *Glock* was its durability, reliability and capable magazine size.

Each standard cartridge held fifteen 9mm rounds, the gun having the ability to seat seventeen or thirty-three round magazines – useful if, and when, heavy firepower was desired.

It was with regret that Sophie had come to the States unarmed, leaving an assortment of handguns, knives, explosives and myriad gadgets behind, her luggage consisting of little more than essential clothing, three months' worth of serum (all that remained) and her father's *Nexus* tablet computer, his GPS tracker coordinates still being tracked, but thus far falling short on locating him.

The motel's grubby proprietor was walking around the room, eyes roaming over Sophie's backpack. He peered inside (seeing nothing of interest – the glass vials of ochre liquid hidden beneath a sweatshirt and undergarments), his interest lingering on the unkempt bed, its duvet covers flung aside with no attempt at tidy or remaking.

Sophie watched the man disappear from the room into the bathroom. Not wishing to alert him to her presence or wanting to engage physically with him she stayed sitting invisibly at the table, barely breathing.

"I could have sworn I heard a voice…" grubby man muttered to himself, returning the *Cobra CA380* to his pocket, satisfied he was on his own. "Still, someone was here, someone who hasn't paid…" He crossed over to the bed and reached out for Sophie's backpack, picking it up swiftly, ruffling through it, hearing the tinkling of small glass bottles. Digging deep, he retrieved one. "He-llo?" The small glass vial had no identifying labelling. He rolled it around the palm of his left hand, considering its worth.

Sophie silently sneaked up and waited for him to be totally immersed in his foraging. As he continued to examine the contents, she thrust a hand out with force, grabbing the man's throat and pressing a thumb into one of his carotid arteries, and her fingers into the other.

Unable to see Sophie, grubby man did not know what was happening; he dropped the backpack, his hands flying to the sudden pain that burned at his neck.

Two seconds passed and grubby man was clawing at the invisible force squeezing his throat; feeling light headed, the strength in his hands started to weaken. At six seconds grubby man passed out. Sophie released the pressure around his throat, allowing his body to fall backwards onto the unmade bed.

Sophie checked grubby man's pulse, knowing that had she torn either one of his carotid arteries, her actions could prove fatal. She had no wish to be responsible for this poor excuse of a man's death, no matter how repugnant he was. She was content to find his heartbeat pounding strong.

Relieved, Sophie went about the room collecting her sparse belongings, hastily packing her backpack and sports holdall, sweeping up the uneaten snacks and bottles of water which she would finish off later.

Two minutes later, she'd injected three vials of serum. Once again she could be 'seen' by the world and was now walking along the side of the road heading in the direction the signposts indicated was Richmond City Centre.

With a thumb hooked out above her left shoulder, she aimed to hitch a ride beyond Richmond, cadge a lift up Interstate 95. If at all lucky, she'd end the day in Washington DC.

At the very least, the nauseating smell of grubby man was no longer threatening to bother her.

CHAPTER FIVE
DOMINIC

THE STORMFORCE 11 BELONGED to a private tour operator, hired to carry the small team of researchers off Hirta and back to the main land. The boat was tied to a mooring post at the end of a small narrow jetty that had seen better days; wooden boards were rotting in places and signs of past attempts at repairing it were patched everywhere. Eleven metres in length and bobbing up and down upon the choppy North Atlantic Ocean, the *Stormforce 11* looked out of place against the backdrop of the island that time appeared to have forgotten.

Dougal, Clarence and Elspeth were hurrying towards the jetty dragging large suitcases on casters and carrying bags and forty litre rucksacks on backs and shoulders; Dominic, trailing them, helped transport some of their belongings by carrying a couple of sports holdalls – each containing scientific equipment and weighing what he believed was a ton each.

Standing beside the boat was a young man smartly attired in what looked like an air pilot's fancy dress costume, but without the hat; the vessel's operator, Skip Williams. His birth name was Mark, but he fancied himself as a Captain. Knowing the title would not fit a mere tour boat driver he adopted the name 'Skip' early on, thinking it sounded nautical and authoritative. It was neither; most Scottish tourists thought it was a nickname meaning he liked to 'take time off" or shirk his duties.

Elspeth glanced over her shoulder in Dominic's direction. The involuntary visitor was struggling with the weight of the sports bags, his face bright red from the exertion.

"Ar' you oka-yee?" Elspeth was nearing the boat, Dougal close by. Clarence was already climbing aboard the vessel.

"I'm good..." Dominic grunted under the strain. "Thanks." *What on earth was in these bags?* It felt like he was shifting forty kilos in each.

"Com'on then, let's get going. We'd like to make home before the weather turns..." The truth of it was strong gales were forecast for that night, with reports of ninety to one-hundred mph winds expected to batter and bruise the coast; not desirable weather to be out within a small boat only big enough to carry fourteen passengers.

Dominic had heard the weather forecast on the radio over breakfast and seen the downcast looks on the faces of the three islanders sitting with him, around the kitchen table.

"It takes fourteen hours to get to Oban from here – in good weather!" It had been Dougal who had answered the unasked question, Dominic reflected. The man's subtle Scottish accent giving each word additional punctuation. The boat wasn't expected to turn up at the island until just before lunch time (12:00 p.m.) meaning they weren't expecting to dock until after two in the morning.

In actuality, the *Stormforce 11* didn't moor at the jetty until after one. Doing the calculations was simple. In good weather they couldn't expect to arrive on the mainland until three a.m. In bad weather the E.T.A was anyone's guess. It was common for trips to be cancelled halfway owing to the weather, meaning the boat would return to the start to wait out the storm – not good if you were five hours or more into the journey.

Skip Williams supported Dougal onto the boat, helping him balance as he took a big step off from the jetty, over the gap between boat and dock, and propelled himself forward. Next came Clarence followed by Elspeth who hung back a moment for Dominic to catch up, breathless.

"Did you find gold on this damn island of yours, and had me carry it for ya?" he lamented between gasps for air, his shoulders and back aching painfully.

"Chance would be a fine thing there, laddie," she said, launching herself onto the boat. "Nothing of value in these parts. The soil is barren of everything; why d'you think the island is uninhabited?" Not since 1930 had the island been inhabited after a gradual decline in self-sufficiency since the turn of the century; the land was unfit to grow produce, and with an increasing reliance on the outside world the small community decided to evacuate for the mainland.

Dominic grunted. He'd assumed no one lived there because of the inhospitable climate. He climbed on board the *Stormforce 11* and followed Elspeth into the cabin which was comfortably furnished. There were six pairs of seats, three either side), and two single seats set at the front (one for the driver).

Dougal and Clarence were seated already at the front of the boat, each taking a pair of seats. Dougal sat behind the driver, getting comfortable.

Leaving her suitcase at the rear of the boat within a shelved recess set aside for luggage (next to a small sink and opposite a toilet), Elspeth made herself at home on the middle set of seats on the left, sitting on the inside next to the window.

Dominic heaved the two sports holdalls into the cabin and shoved them close to the luggage recess, unable to lift them to one of the empty deep shelves (noting that Dougal and Clarence had taken the lowest ones with what appeared to be light backpacks). Not sitting with any of his travelling companions, Dominic took the pair of seats at the rear of the cabin to the right and closed his eyes.

Elspeth looked back over her shoulder towards the strange man who'd suddenly appeared in their lives in such a dramatic fashion just a week earlier. She knew nothing about him, not a single fact. She knew more of *Lord Lucan's* whereabouts than she did of Dominic Schilling sitting there a little ways behind her. From a carry-on bag she retrieved a paperback novel; a romance or some such pulp fiction.

Reopening his eyes, Dominic spied Elspeth pick up her book. He exhaled noisily. Fourteen hours of sheer boredom. No iPod; no magazine or reading material; no in-cabin entertainment of any variety. There wasn't even any alcohol to numb the senses (he'd seen the prohibition signs).

Skip Williams untied the rope mooring his touring vessel to the jetty and had entered the cabin, closing the cabin door behind him with a loud clatter. He strode to the front and took his place in the driver's seat. Pulling down a microphone attached to a coiled wire – a bit like a *CB Radio* mic, Dominic thought – Skip spoke into it, his voice amplified through speakers set into the ceiling above each set of seats.

"Good afternoon, and welcome to this Island-hopper tour boat. As you'll be aware there have been weather warnings issued for these parts for later. The latest is we may hit a squall or two in around nine hours time." Squall being a nice name for a sudden, violent gust of wind accompanied by rain. What had actually been predicted was more severe but Scottish people are a hardy folk. "For anyone who's new to travelling with us (aimed completely at Dominic), this is a non-smoking vessel and absolutely no alcohol to be consumed on board. As it can get a bit rough, sick bags can be found at the rear of the cabin next to the toilet. I hope you enjoy travelling with us to Oban today."

A little sooner than nine hours later the small boat lurched from one side to another, riding waves that Dominic didn't know existed in the seas that surrounded Great Britain. Half expecting a tsunami to swallow up the vessel at any given moment, Dominic stood from his seat and staggered to the small toilet situated just behind him. Closing the door behind him for privacy, he knew the flimsy door would do nothing to mask the sound of his vomiting as he stood, towering above the porcelain bowl designed for its function rather than cosmetic appearance. He felt a wave, stronger than that lashing the side of the boat, churn inside his stomach, followed a nanosecond later by a geyser of upchuck cascading into the toilet faster than one could say 'gastroenteritis' – which he wished he had; at least there were some medications available to settle that.

"Oh God…" he gurgled between bouts of vomiting.

Ten minutes later, his stomach empty and his throat raw from retching, he felt that it was safe to return to his seat.

Five more minutes he found himself back in the small toilet cubicle, wrestling to keep hold of his intestines as there seemed to be no end to what seemed to want to explode from his mouth.

"Are you alright in there, laddie?" Elspeth had knocked on the door announcing her presence.

"I'll be one minute…" mumbled Dominic hoarsely.

"Would you like a *Fisherman's Friend*? A glass of salt water, maybe?"

Dominic chose to ignore the woman.

———◆———

Twenty hours after first stepping onto the boat and with an empty stomach, Dominic stepped onto the shores of mainland Great Britain, relieved to be on dry land. Well, *wet* dry land. It was raining heavily (as it had done at sea for the better part of the journey) as Skip Williams tied up the *Island Hopper* touring boat and Dominic clambered weakly off. Fat rain drops fell in a sheet that obscured visibility to just a dozen feet.

Having exchanged phone numbers, they said their goodbyes on the boat, and Elspeth – *Ellie* – watched the man shuffle away from the quay in Oban's Marina, once home to RAF's flying boat squadrons during World War Two. She was slightly sad to see him go, though she barely knew a thing about him. During the few days he convalesced after being rescued, he'd spoken little about himself, instead choosing to learn about St. Kilda and the work Dougal, Clarence and herself undertook on the island. All she'd gleaned from Dominic was he worked in private security and that he 'wasn't a nice man'. To what extent, he'd not been willing to expand upon, but from his silence and the glare he'd momentarily given her, she guessed he carried with him a number of demons locked up inside.

"Godspeed, Dominic Schilling…" she whispered to herself as the man disappeared within the blur of heavy rain.

Having accepted a small donation of currency, Dominic used a shiny pound coin received from Dougal to make a phone call. The public phone box was situated just outside a small cafeteria. He deposited the coin, heard the dial tone and keyed in a mobile phone number. A half dozen rings later and a voice came on at the other end, female; it was a recorded message. The call had gone to voicemail, the recipient either too busy or unwilling to accept what was a 'withheld' number.

"Hi, this is Jennifer Ratcliff. I'm not available at the moment. You can leave a message or contact my secretary on…"

Dominic replaced the handset reluctantly, disconnecting the call. He couldn't leave a message, could he? She'd sworn him to never call her, never burden her with his problems, no matter what.

But to hear her voice again…

For a moment his hand remained on the handset, poised to make a further call. He tried to think of someone else who could be of assistance. He racked his tired, hungry brain.

Who else was there?

Everyone else thought he was dead, killed in a car accident on the Seabrook Road less than two weeks earlier, his body barbecued within the *Mercedes* emergency services had found wrapped around a tree. So convinced everyone was that he was the victim in the car, little was done to identify what remained of his charred, shrivelled body.

Dominic lifted the handset to his ear once again and punched in the mobile number. Like before the dial tone was replaced with ringing and then the voice he *oh so remembered*. How he longed for her.

"Hi, this is Jennifer Ratcliff. I'm not available at the moment. You can leave a message or contact my secretary on ..." He didn't bother listening to the rest of the message, pulling the handset away from his ear, composing himself, desperately thinking of something to say. He heard a beep that announced that it was time to leave a message.

Placing the phone to his face Dominic began to talk casually:

"Hi, Jen. Guess who? Just like *Lazarus* I'm back from the dead," he chuckled. "I know you said not to call you but... I'm kind-a in a fix. Those CIA mongrels dumped me in Scotland, bastards. Worse still, on a remote island. I'm back on mainland UK now, which was lucky but... Jen, I really need your help. I'm on a payphone. Please call me." He left the number and hung up.

Outside the phone box the rain continued to fall in thick, icy cold sheets. He could just make out the sodden forms of his three travel companions heavily laden and dragging with them their suitcases slowly through the squall. He wondered what would become of them, especially Elspeth. Despite her homely appearance there had been something quietly attractive about her. She was different to all the girls he'd ever been with or sometimes met.

He whiled away the time, waiting to see if Jennifer Ratcliff would return his call. Sheltered in the phone box, he thought pleasant thoughts and daydreamed about the dark-ginger haired woman with her freckled, ruddy face.

He resolved to give her a call sometime.

CHAPTER SIX
SPENCER

THE CALL HAD BEEN taken at home during the early hours of that October morning. He glanced quickly at the alarm clock to his left, its bright numerals coating the room in an unearthly lime-green lustre. Even without checking the time it was easy to grasp that it wasn't anywhere near time to get up.

The time: 3:16 a.m. Eastern Daylight Time. Washington DC.

Alexandria lying next to him, her face hidden beneath a thick coverlet of dark-brown hair, had stirred from the chime of his mobile but did not wake. That was the way of things. No matter what the noise Agent Spencer Roberts' wife did not wake for anything, which had been especially annoying after the twins were born. It invariably meant that he saw to his daughters' night time needs more often than not, regardless of his sleeping requirements and the type of work he undertook, which required absolute focus.

The phone ringing had been a major annoyance for two reasons:

One, he'd only been asleep forty minutes after feeding Brianna and Rachel their night-time bottles.

Two, he'd only had forty minutes' sleep that night in total and he was especially tired after putting in a twelve hour shift at the agency prior to retiring to bed.

"Y'ello...." he yawned the greeting, talking softly.

"Hi, Spencer... it's Ryan Barber, UK intelligence..."

Agent Roberts looked at the alarm clock having not registered the time. It was too Goddamn early in the morning for someone to sound so chipper.

"D'you know what time it is?" His voice was subdued. He tried waking himself up, suddenly craving coffee.

"Seriously, don't you guys have watches over there?" Ryan was being sarcastic and the American knew it. *"It's quarter past seven in London. Aren't you a few hours ahead of us?"*

"No. We're four hours behind you…"

"Oh, sorry. My bad. I didn't mean to wake you…"

"What d'you want?" Spencer was now fully awake and sitting up in bed. Alexandria had woken up beside him and had turned on the light. "What's goin' on?" she asked in annoyance.

Ryan continued to speak into Spencer's ear. *"Some information…"*

"That figures."

"Spencer… you see what time it is?!" Alexandria hissed at her husband. He fanned her question away with his free hand, the other holding his mobile handset up tight to his ear.

"I have someone in the States looking for her missing father."

Spencer sighed. "Ryan, this is not my area… There's approx nine hundred thousand missing persons in the US alone; you'd be better off contacting the FBI…"

"Spencer, the FBI won't be any help because your guys have him."

Agent Roberts went silent for a moment.

"Did I hear you straight? The CIA have him? Who is this guy, what makes him important to us?"

"He was a special scientist, unique within his profession, a real visionary. He was also one of you…"

"None of this makes any sense, Ryan…"

"Have you ever heard of Project CHAMELEON?"

With the sudden silence it would be easy to hear the beat of a moth's wing.

"Say again?"

"Project CHAMELEON..."

Agent Roberts had heard of a project from the UK, but details of the research were sketchy and almost far-fetched. Something about *invisible soldiers*. He couldn't stop himself from laughing.

"You called me in the middle of the night to talk about an urban myth or some-such nonsense?"

"No, Spencer. I've called you for help locating my granddaughter's father."

Ryan Barber had spent the best part of the next hour filling in his old contact at the agency with details of the events that had occurred three months earlier. Though wanting more sleep, Spencer had continued Ryan's call downstairs in the kitchen, pouring himself a decaf coffee he felt he so needed. It helped him to focus.

When the call was over, ideas of getting further sleep were long gone, compounded by the relentless screaming of both infants from the twins' bedroom. One needed a nappy change; the other just liked the sound of her voice and seemed to take pleasure in depriving her daddy of sleep.

Two hours later and he was commuting to work. Getting the Metrorail into the city, Spencer gave all of Ryan's story some serious thought, mapping out in his mind where to start digging around, thinking of who to contact for further information, and what to say when asked for reasons for his enquiry.

Initially, he decided, he would do some research from the comfort of his leather chair behind his cluttered desk at the DC office of the agency. Then he would speak to the most senior analyst within the local operation, his friend and mentor, Paul Lebrock, and see what he might've heard. But so covert were most of the agency's operations, and with only specific clearance on information relevant to his role, he half-expected to draw a big fat blank.

Spencer almost slipped from his chair when finding – almost without any effort – information about the missing person whom Ryan Barber had sought his help finding.

Using a simple algorithm, Spencer typed a command searching for information regarding George Jennings within the Central Intelligence Agency's records database. As Ryan had indicated, the man indeed belonged to the agency, so it stood to reason that it was possible a personnel record existed for him, though likely encrypted in view of the clandestine operation he was involved with.

Remarkably, a page appeared on the web browser almost immediately, displaying an account of George Jennings' service history, an old photograph (the same image of George that Ryan had found printed on *Kodak* paper in the man's locker shortly after his disappearance), and a brief outline of the man's area of expertise. The information corroborated the British Intelligence analyst's claim to a point. Unsurprisingly, the intelligence was years' out of date.

When Spencer searched again, keying in a command for information using a more specific and more recent date range, the web browser returned a warning screen with a password prompt, the words in angry red. Spencer glared at the screen:

Classified – Authorised Personnel Only
PASSWORD:_______________
By order of Deputy Director Milo Calland

Spencer had rarely been blocked from information. His pay grade and authority level surpassed the majority of analysts, so the mere suggestion that the information he requested was outside of his domain indicated that the man was being kept hidden for an important reason. The fact that Milo Calland had ordered it just added weight tenfold.

Knowing that any attempt to gain access to the information would likely flag his identity, Spencer closed the web browser and took the only other option available to him.

Paul Lebrock.

Lebrock was in his late fifties, though looked fifteen years younger on account of his clean-shaven look and the jet-black hair courtesy of an over-the-counter bottle dye. It didn't hurt that he had a two-hour fitness regime that included a run around the National Mall. He'd been with the company since leaving Stanford University, and had a reputation for having an encyclopaedia for a brain, which meant he knew a lot about a lot, absorbing information like a best brand kitchen towel. He answered the phone almost immediately upon Spencer's dialling.

"Lebrock," the voice on the other end of the phone was relaxed, almost distracted. Spencer imagined the senior man had the phone wedged between his shoulder and the side of his head, whilst his hands continued with some other task – possibly the *Washington Post* crossword puzzle. Or rolling a cigarette.

"Hi. It's Spencer Roberts." There were two Spencers within the agency so he always announced his name in full.

"Hi Spence… what do I owe the pleasure…?" Still distracted, very casual sounding.

"Does the name *George Jennings* mean anything to you?"

Spencer heard the clunk of the handset slipping from Lebrock's wedged position; it clattered to the desk noisily, bouncing a couple of times. The sound of rustling papers followed as the senior man scrabbled to retrieve the handset.

"Where've you heard that name?"

Ignoring the question Spencer probed further. "What can you tell me about his whereabouts?"

"*Agent Roberts, I can't help you...*"

Agent Roberts? He never called him that. Lebrock's tone was sharp and momentarily took him aback.

"Paul... it's important. You know I wouldn't ask if it wasn't. I need to locate him," he said, adding, "for someone."

Lebrock went quiet for a long moment. Spencer guessed his mentor was wrestling with his conscience. They'd been friends a long time, and colleagues a bit longer.

Also, there was the matter of 'owing him one' on account of the time when the younger man had saved Lebrock's life, but that was another story.

Just when Spencer thought the line had gone dead, Lebrock spoke up:

"*Okay, Spencer. But not here. I warn you though, you're sticking your head into a hornet's nest.*"

Eleven miles away within the CIA's headquarters at Langley, a computer alerted a bespectacled man operating an entire bank of highly sophisticated electronic surveillance equipment to a telephone conversation that was then taking place. Programmed to scan telecommunications across the nation, the 'spyware' had been installed under *George W. Bush's* presidency to help detect calls between terrorist cells – that was the pretence that gained senate approval. A number of keywords and phrases (more than a thousand) had been pre-programmed so that, when uttered within a single conversation, they would automatically activate the CIA's surveillance system to record and analyse the call. It would then go onto highlight what, and if, there was a potential threat. If a number of keywords or phrases were flagged, the computer would sound an alarm.

Piggybacking off the system, the CIA had also programmed in other keywords that would assist with investigations and help highlight unwanted attention on matters.

One such phrase was: *George Jennings*.

The sophisticated surveillance equipment started digitally recording the telephone conversation taking place in a CIA building in Washington. Pinging an electronic memo simultaneously with the phrase or keyword in its title, it would audibly 'ding' on arrival within a mailbox permanently opened on a laptop computer situated within a closeted room. Such emails flagged high alert topics for the bespectacled man to review. He'd cross reference the rubric against an up-to-date list detailing the threat, the level of importance, and the escalation process.

Hearing the 'ding' of an email, the man casually wandered back to the laptop and opened up the email. Headed *George Jennings*, it contained a link to the call's recording. Sitting down, bespectacled man picked up an A4 ring binder within which were a hundred pages listing all the keywords and phrases in operation. It took him less than ten seconds to locate the name on the sheet.

"Holy Christ!" Had he been drinking coffee as he'd read it (as he often did) he would've spat a geyser from his mouth. Luckily he'd left his coffee to cool on a different desk at the other end of the room.

George Jennings' name appeared on the first sheet (also known as the 'red list' or what bespectacled man considered the 'Hot One Hundred') sandwiched between names of wanted fugitives, terrorists and known codenames used by insurgents.

For *George Jennings* to appear on the first page indicated to the bespectacled man that he was someone of significance. For what reason, he could not guess. The accompanying information all but confirmed it:

Threat:	Classified
Importance:	High
Escalation Contact:	DD *Milo Calland*

The fact that the contact was the CIA's Deputy Director was intriguing and highlighted the importance of this *George Jennings* guy. He reached for the landline phone and dialled a number. A moment later a voice at the other end answered.

"Deputy Director Calland's office…"

The bespectacled man introduced himself, pausing for breath before speaking further. "I have an audio file flagged as code red. Someone has been discussing George Jennings…"

The name was familiar to the secretary who, without hesitation, said: *"The Deputy Director is with the President at the moment. Hold one moment; I'll just patch you through…"*

CHAPTER SEVEN
EMILY

THE VIRGIN ATLANTIC BOEING *747* landed just ten minutes late at Dulles International Airport after an eight-and-a-half-hour flight. Tired and travel weary, Emily Porter stepped off the aeroplane and traipsed the corridor with all the other passengers, like a horde of hamsters piling through a tube for the promise of some nuts. All heading with trepidation towards the arrival lounge via Passport Control. She joined a long queue for non-US citizens to pass through. Despite the purported legitimacy of her visit, she couldn't help feeling guilty of something.

It had to do with uniformed men, she mused. Authority figures, in general, dressed in such a way had frightened her for as long as she could remember. Just a mere glance from one had made her go wobbly at the knees. Of course, getting older had solved much of that problem, but there was always something about the officers at border control, the way they scrutinised your passport and stared deep into your soul. Such inspection turned her to jelly.

Before she could dwell any further her turn arrived and she stepped up to the border control kiosk, the officer seated behind the desk with just a short *Plexiglas* screen partitioning himself from her.

Emily handed the customs officer her passport. He accepted it and opened it up to the page with her photograph and personal information displayed. A moment later he held it against a biometric passport scanner and waited for her information to appear electronically on his computer screen.

Emily smiled softly, a nervous twitch starting to aggravate her left eye.

"Ma'am, what brings you to Washington today?" The customs officer spoke without an accent or any hint of humanity.

"It's for pleasure... visiting friends... sightseeing, that sort of thing," Emily replied serenely, her nervous twitch cancelling it out.

"Anywhere particular?"

"Oh, the usual," she tried nonplussed. "*The Smithsonian*, the *Lincoln Memorial*, all the other memorials and what not. I might take a gander at the International Spy Museum..." she shrugged non-committed, "perhaps take in a show at the John F. Kennedy Centre..." She'd bought a cheap tour guide from *Waterstones* a day earlier and had read up a little during the flight. It was plausible and wasn't altogether a lie as she hoped to make the most of her all-expenses paid 'holiday', but the main reason for her visit was to lend assistance in Sophie's search for her father.

"How long's your visit?" The expression on the custom officer's face was vacant. He'd heard the patter a million times before from a million different visitors.

"A couple of weeks, maybe three..."

The customs officer stamped Emily's passport and closed it, making to hand it back, gently smiling. The interrogation was over. "The memorials and other famous buildings look spectacular at night," he said, "be sure to visit them then. Less busy also."

Emily smiled appreciatively, accepting the passport. "Thank you."

"You're welcome, ma'am. Enjoy your visit..." She picked up her hand luggage and followed the signs for baggage reclaim. Sighing with relief as she moved steadily away, she felt like she'd just cheated an examiner in a practical test. Her mouth was sandpaper-dry, her throat just as rough. She couldn't wait to get out of the airport, away from perusing eyes and into a comfortable hotel room.

She travelled light, easily finding and retrieving a small purple suitcase that a five-year-old could carry from a heavily crowded conveyor belt. She brought clothing and sundry personal items for her visit; things a woman needed for comfort and peace of mind. Anything else Ryan had assured her would be provided in Washington by MI6 or his contacts.

Outside the airport Emily hailed a cab by stepping off the kerb and raising an arm. A black *Washington Flyer* pulled up. She climbed into the back. A moment later the vehicle pulled off, the driver not waiting for her to buckle up.

"Hyatt Regency, Capitol Hill please," she said. The driver, an Indian man with flecks of white in his black beard and a dusty-grey coloured turban nodded in acknowledgement. She guessed he spoke very little English. A local radio station aired advertisements endlessly for background, not breaking for unnecessary chit-chat or (heaven forbid) a song. Emily closed out the noise and focused on the busy sights of daytime Washington as they drove on by.

⎯⎯◼◆◼⎯⎯

She glanced around the room, silently appraising the accommodation and decor. Her hotel room was clean, modern and sparsely furnished. Working for MI6 was proving to have its perks.

It was mid-afternoon as she stepped in through the door to her tenth floor room. The bellhop had opened it with a key card, handing it to Emily as he escorted her in. The walls were beige and matched a small arm chair and plain curtains. The bedside cabinets standing sentinel beside the double bed (made up with a duvet dressed in a black covering) were black, as were the desk and the television unit opposite. A thirty-two-inch *LG* flat screen took up precedence upon it.

Atop the bedside cabinets were a pair of futuristic lamps wearing cream shades, with one keeping a digital alarm clock for company, doubling up as an *iPod* docking station. On the walls were framed prints, a sketch of the *Abraham Lincoln* memorial above the desk, the former president in his seated pose; another hanging above the armchair next to the bedside cabinet, a sketch of an external shot of the memorial building within which Lincoln sat.

Beside the bed closest to the room's entrance (behind which was the bathroom) was a floor-to-ceiling mirror.

"Nice," exclaimed Emily, carefully examining the room. The bellhop placed her small suitcase next to the bed and stepped out of the way. Emily walked past him and crossed to the window, peering out and taking in the panoramic Washington view. The Capitol Building, its magnificent dome atop which stood the statue of freedom, appeared ahead of her, a colossal landmark which sent goose bumps marching up her spine. "Amazing," she whispered, in awe.

"Ahem." The bellhop was loitering in the room making no attempt at leaving. Initially Emily was puzzled, before it dawned on her.

"Oh," Emily smiled apologetically. She reached for her hand luggage, unzipped a side pocket and removed a purse from which she pulled out a wad of notes she'd changed up at Heathrow airport. She removed a couple of one dollar bills.

"Here," she said, "thank you."

The bellhop accepted the tip with half a smile and left, closing the door behind him. When he'd been gone a couple of minutes she tested the bed by throwing herself down onto it, checking its 'bounce' before lying down fully, stretching out. Fatigued from almost a day's worth of travel, she deferred her shower in favour of an afternoon nap.

It seemed no sooner had her head hit the pillow her sleep was interrupted by ringing from somewhere in the room. It wasn't her mobile phone, that was still packed in her hand luggage, turned off.

Bedraggled, Emily pulled herself off the bed, allowing her ears to follow the sound and locate its source. Rubbing her eyes she could see on the desk the room's phone, a small red light flashing in tandem with the discordant ringing.

Emily sighed. *Can't I have a few minutes sleep?* she wondered to herself. She hadn't noticed how dull and dreary the room had become.

She reached for the handset of the landline phone and pressed it against her ear.

"'ell-o," she said, sounding tired.

"*Hi Miss Porter, I have a call for you from London, England. Are you happy to accept the call?*"

Ryan.

Emily sighed. She glanced at the clock behind her on the bedside cabinet. 8:32 p.m. She'd been asleep for more than five hours.

"*Miss Porter... are you there?*"

"Hi, yes. Yes... put him through. Thanks."

"*You're welcome, ma'am...*" A moment later and the recognisable voice of Ryan Barber filled her ear.

"*Your phone's turned off,*" he griped. "*I had no end of hassle finding the number for your hotel. It's a good job it wasn't a life or death situation...*"

"Ryan, it's been a long day, I need some rest. Can't we do this tomorrow?"

"*No, afraid not. You're not being paid to sleep, Emily. Besides, didn't you get enough rest on the plane?*"

"Ha-ha," she said sarcastically. Despite MI6 flying Emily in 'Economy Class', she had travelled in relative comfort, or would have were it not for the thirty stone man from Bristol sitting next to her, his immense backside encroaching on her personal space, pressed up against her outer thigh. "Go on, then."

"I've just had some alarming news from Stateside," he paused, gathering his thoughts. The hiatus went on too long.

"Ryan, I'm listening."

"I'm sorry…" he sounded upset. *"It's just…"* he couldn't finish the sentence.

"Ryan? What is it?"

"They killed her," he sounded distant and in shock. *"It's too dangerous. Our mission is over. I can't expect it to go on."*

CHAPTER EIGHT
MILO

T HE LEARJET 85 TOUCHED down on the baking hot tarmac of Homey Airport's newest runway. Before beginning its taxi to the designated area (as instructed by the control tower), a small convoy of military vehicles sped towards it.

The base was known by a few different names. Homey Airport. Groom Lake. But most notably, Area 51.

Until the early nineties the US government denied its very existence, no matter its name, never disclosing its uses. Even now everyone in the know was coy as to Area 51's functionality. Some claimed it to be a top secret test centre for military war craft and weaponry, whilst others swore it's where the Americans kept captured aliens for experimentation. Either way, it was a no-go area for non-authorised personnel, and contracted guards armed to the teeth were regularly seen driving around in jeeps, patrolling the perimeter religiously.

The passenger of the *Learjet 85* was an authorised visitor to the base within sun-scorched Nevada desert. Dressed in a dark-grey *Ralph Lauren* Gabardine suit and *Ray Ban* sunglasses, the man immediately regretted leaving the comfort of the air-conditioned cabin, a sheen of sweat instantly coating his face as he took the portable staircase to the waiting entourage. In his right hand he carried a black leather briefcase; the other hand he used for balance, sliding it down the handrail which guided those alighting the aircraft.

"Deputy Director, welcome to Area 51…" General Marcus offered his hand to Milo Calland, who shook it firmly. He was in his late-fifties and wore the markings of his rank upon his uniform. Either side of him were four soldiers nursing rifles and wearing blank expressions. "You know, we're not used to receiving *VIPs*…" he said the word with a sneer, "… to the base. Not even the President has been here," adding acerbically: "We're deeply honoured…"

"Spare me, General Marcus… I'm not a tourist. I've come to see how our *mad scientist* is getting on…"

General Marcus shrugged, nonplussed. "Whatever. This way." He led the Deputy Director of the CIA to a waiting armoured personnel carrier. They climbed in, Marcus closing the door. The four accompanying soldiers disappeared within two other vehicles, one leading the convoy, the other tailing. Another armoured vehicle, its occupants unseen, was placed between General Marcus's car and the lead soldiers.

The four vehicles sped off from the *Learjet 85* towards a number of buildings, passing a dozen hangars that housed God-knew-what, their closed doors protecting their contents from Milo Calland's prying eyes. Three minutes later they passed a hangar marked as number '17' and carried a little further east to a big building, its giant front doors opened wide enough to allow the small convoy to enter unhindered. Once inside, the vehicles parked up on the far side of the building, alongside each other in no orderly fashion. Only General Marcus and Deputy Director Calland climbed out.

The large hangar was big enough to house two Premier League football stadiums with ample space either side; excepting the four vehicles, it was completely empty.

"Is this some joke?" Milo removed his sunglasses, taking in his surroundings.

"Deputy Director… this way." General Marcus led the CIA man away from the parked vehicles towards the far wall and what appeared to be an outline of a hidden double-door set within the brickwork. Painted the same uniform colour of battleship-grey, it was barely noticeable. "Oh, you'll be needing this." The General tossed Milo a visitor's swipe card on a braided lanyard. Using his own, he inserted it into a discreet slot set into the wall next to the electronic doors and waited a moment.

From behind the wall gears and pulleys began to sound, followed by the thrum of internal mechanisms moving.

A moment later the double-doors slid open to reveal a sizeable elevator – the biggest ever built – with enough space to carry a whole platoon or three *Abrams* battle tanks.

"This way." General Marcus stepped into the elevator, taking eight or nine giant steps, before he stood dead centre of the lift.

Milo Calland couldn't hide the fact that he was visibly impressed. Flanked by the soldiers, two still to each side, he walked tentatively into the elevator, eyes flitting around the immense space. The ceiling of the lift was three times his own height. "Quite something, this…" Milo indicated the elevator with a wave of his hand.

"Isn't it just…" The General never entertained other's small talk, not even with his wife of twenty-eight years. He preferred to do the conversing rather than the listening.

The doors of the lift closed seemingly by themselves; a motor from above began to whirr for a moment, before Milo felt the floor beneath his feet shift slightly, indicating the lift was beginning its descent.

"How far down does this thing go?"

General Marcus harrumphed at the Deputy Director's attempt at further conversation. "I thought you said you weren't a tourist?"

Milo shrugged. "Just curious. I have *taphophobia*."

"*Taphophobia*? What's that? A fear of taffy candy?" The General began to laugh. The soldiers standing around him were all smirking. One laughed too heartily and drew disparaging looks.

"No. I'm afraid of being buried alive…"

General Marcus allowed his mirth to subside. "Don't worry CIA man, no one's getting buried here. Perfectly safe. But, to answer your question; this thing goes down half a mile, giving access to over fifty levels of operational room, each of which stretching out beneath the airbase for approximately a mile."

"Jeez… that's huge… what on earth is the need…?" Milo left his question hanging, guessing at the likely possibilities.

"Of course, it's not the deepest underground labs, that will be in the Black Hills of South Dakota at nearly a mile deep; but we have the record for the largest underground building – unofficially, of course!" The General took a moment for Milo to absorb the information before continuing. "Your guy, George Jennings' lab is situated somewhere close to the bottom."

"Great…" Milo felt nauseous at the thought. Barely moving, it seemed, after two minutes of descent the elevator came to a sudden stop. Comically, like the sound of a cheap microwave announcing the end of cooking time, a 'ding' sounded meekly from above the mammoth-sized doors. Milo looked quizzically at the General who could only shrug.

Within the conference room, Milo had made himself comfortable at the head of the table. Behind him, just above his shoulder the flat screen TV was hanging from the wall, set-up for conference calls, but easily adjusted to showcase the *Super Bowl* or the *NBA All Star Game*. It was within this room he usually viewed George Jennings through the TV-screen from Washington, receiving weekly updates regarding what he'd termed emotionlessly as the 'product'.

From a vending machine placed at the opposite end of the room (closest to the entrance door), he pressed for a can of *Minute Maid.* Pink Lemonade. The machine clunked, rattled and thumped as the can was dispensed, clattering to the collection tray. Sitting at the large table and using an index finger, he pulled the ring to open the can, pouring the ice-cold drink into a glass tumbler he'd found on a tray at the centre of the table.

The only thing Milo liked about visiting military bases was the free vending machines. Not only were drinks *gratis*, so too were the snack foods. The food machine was symmetrically placed on the other side of the door, containing bags of crisps (labelled *chips*), pretzels, chocolate bars and packaged-up pastries. Milo was considering helping himself to a couple of *Twinkies* and a doughnut when the double-rap of knuckles against woodwork gained his attention. He kicked into touch his musings, gently placing down the glass of pink lemonade and sliding it out of easy reach, beyond his briefcase (which was lying flat directly ahead of him) to rest alongside the landline telephone.

"Come." Said loud enough to be heard through the fireproof door and the toughened glass walls.

Outside the conference room, two of the soldiers who'd accompanied General Marcus had been assigned to the Deputy Director as his personal guard – or his babysitters, he reflected. One of the two soldiers opened the door into the conference room and guided a man in.

Still dressed in his white lab-coat, George Jennings walked

confidently into the room, stepping past the soldier who was half-heartedly barring his entrance.

"Milo… this is most unexpected…" a note of concern in his voice. "Why…?" The soldier who had escorted him in turned about and left, closing the door behind him.

Milo smiled reassuringly. "Why? Can't an old friend stop by and say 'hi'?"

"There's stopping by to say 'hi' if you lived around the block, it's another thing travelling two-and-a-half-thousand miles across country… so, excuse my reticence…"

Milo's smile disappeared. "You're quite right George, bang on the money. I thought it was time to have a little 'face-to-face' with you. See for myself how the 'product' is coming along. Get a feel for things on the ground." *Or under it*, he reflected, slightly unsettled.

"I gave an update just the other day. Little has changed."

"I know, I know, and the President is most pleased. All of Washington is. Excited too."

"So, why the visit? Is it news from England? Have you heard from my wife?"

Milo had turned his head slightly away and was avoiding eye contact.

"You said my family were safe. You gave me your word…"

"I know what I said George…" Milo looked down at his briefcase, his thoughts wandering to the file it contained.

"So, I want to see them. I've done everything you asked… as I promised. And more. It's been more than three months, you owe me that much…"

"George… it's… not that simple."

"Why? We had a deal. I agreed to do this on one condition, that when it was done I would be free from all…, from all the running…"

"And is it done George?" Milo interjected. "Do we have our super soldiers?"

"They are coming along, Milo. Growth enhancements have been made, but full maturity won't be reached for six months. Batch one are currently at infant age, physically and mentally advanced, all exhibiting the special abilities that my research promised." Sounding satisfied, George continued: "My job here is all but over, save for repeating the process for batches two through to twenty, but anyone can do that... Tutors and formalised programming are taking over with our infants' continued development."

"Good. Congratulations, George. It would appear that your job IS done." Milo unlatched his briefcase and dipped his hand within. A moment later he waved a light-brown foolscap folder in front of him. "Here. Within are the details regarding your family." Milo tossed the folder across the table where it slapped the surface and skidded to a stop just ahead of George. "As promised."

George straightened the folder in front of him and opened it up like it were a book with one hand. Inside was a single sheet of A4 paper.

"What is this?" George asked looking up, his face confused.

"Answers," Milo said. "A report put together by the agency regarding the whereabouts of your family."

George picked up the piece of paper and read the brief report, his face draining of colour. One line stood out above all others:

Harriet Jennings: DECEASED

As the details sunk in, he slumped back into his seat and allowed the piece of paper to slip from his grasp; it fell to the desk and glided across the lacquered surface to rest at the centre.

"I'm sorry George," Milo offered solemnly.

"When?"

Milo shook his head, like he didn't know. "I only received the report this morning," he lied. In truth he'd learnt of Harriet's death the day after George had been extracted, back in July. Her body had been discovered at the side of a road outside a US airbase in England by a group of USAF Airmen returning from an excursion into a nearby town.

"And my children?" ventured George absently, his mind trying to comprehend the news.

"As the report states. Missing. We assume they've gone to ground with the help of your… *pet project*."

George glared at the Deputy Director. "SHE HAS A NAME!" he bellowed, referring to his daughter.

Milo raised his hands in surrender. "I didn't mean anything by that comment," he said.

George closed his eyes, trying to picture Harriet from when he'd last seen her. It was the day before Charlie had fallen from the crab-apple tree, back at Willoughby Rising.

He shook his head slowly, regretfully. "I can't even remember what she looks like," he whispered weakly, beginning to cry.

Milo stood up from the table and walked round to where George was seated. He placed a hand gently upon the man's left shoulder. Offering comfort wasn't something he was good at, and it felt awkward and clumsy. He could feel the man's grief vibrating beneath his palm.

"I'm sorry, George. You will remember her; grief has just temporarily blocked her from your memory."

George swallowed, fighting hard to regain his composure. "You didn't keep your end of the deal," he said quietly, adding with a little more vigour, his tone resentful: "I guess my work here is done…"

For a moment Milo left his hand on George's shoulder. He sighed. "I was afraid you were going to say that." The Deputy Director removed his hand and reached down to the gold chain that hung about the scientist's neck. "I'll be taking this." Milo tugged it sharply, snapping a couple of links. The small spherical pendant which encased a tracking device dangled in his hands. "It's best I have this now."

Absently, George's hand clawed at the vacant spot around his neck.

"What? Did you think we didn't know about the tracking device?" Milo tutted, then laughed. "Shame on you. Of course, totally useless this far down in the ground." He walked the short distance to the room's exit, opened the door and indicated for the two guards to come in.

"Mr Jennings has resigned his post here," Milo directed the soldiers loaned to him. "His level clearance is revoked with immediate effect. Can you see that he is taken somewhere for debriefing."

"Right you are," Soldier One replied in a deep growl. He towered over George still sitting in his seat, quietly crying. "Sir, come with us. Please, this way..."

George slowly rose to his feet. "I don't have to leave just yet... I can give you some notice period."

Milo shook his head but said nothing. His decision was made.

It had been made back in Washington hours earlier, the President himself giving the authorisation.

"Sir..." Soldier Two had muscled in and had laid a hand ominously on George's arm. He had a lighter, almost boyish, voice. "We insist you come with us."

Reluctantly, George allowed himself to be escorted out of the conference room. Before exiting, he turned to Milo, catching the Deputy Director's eyes.

"Milo?" pleading in his voice. "We were friends..."

"Goodbye George."

Soldier Two manhandled George out through the door, which swiftly closed shut.

Through the wall Milo could hear George's shouts and curses. He reached for the glass of pink lemonade and drank deeply, leaving just some dregs at the bottom. Stifling a small burp, Milo pulled out his mobile phone, unsurprised to find he had no signal. Reaching for the landline phone just ahead of him and his still-open briefcase, he picked up the receiver and dialled a number General Marcus had earlier given him.

"*Deputy Director, I guess your visit is concluded.*" It was General Marcus who seemingly had been waiting at the other end of the line.

"Indeed."

"*Tell me,*" started the General, "*what are we to do with your mad scientist?*"

"There are people searching for him. He needs to disappear."

"*Permanently?*" the General enquired.

"No, no. Good God, not permanently. He used to be a friend." Milo paused as though giving it some thought. He held George's gold chain in a fist, the pendant dangling. "Tell me, General. Are we sending anyone to Guantanamo Bay these days?"

"*Officially? No. Unofficially?*" General Marcus guffawed. "*Hell, yea…*"

CHAPTER NINE
SOPHIE

SITTING ON THE STEPS leading up to the Abraham Lincoln memorial, Sophie looked out over the reflecting pool that stretched out for six-hundred-and-eighteen-metres ahead of her; the world's tallest stone structure, the obelisk of the Washington monument standing proud in the foreground, the largest expanse of sky she'd ever seen stretching out beyond it, making her feel so small, fragile and powerless.

It was evening and darkness was descending fast; spotlights situated strategically around the Lincoln memorial and the Washington monument made them glow majestically. Sophie couldn't help marvelling at how impressive they were.

Despite being on her own, the many tourists milling about and the locals walking or jogging around the national park, helped her relax and made her feel comfortable. She didn't feel alone.

Walking for the best part of an hour after vacating the motel room and leaving the grubby man behind, she had managed to hitch a lift from a group of *Alpha Omicron Pi* sorority girls, returning from a road trip on their way back to George Washington University – which, as it turned out, was a stroke of luck. University campus was close to DC's city centre.

Excitedly, the three young women, all appearing roughly Sophie's age (one blonde, one brunette and one auburn-haired), babbled animatedly about their travels. Sophie hardly heard a coherent word due to the speed in which they talked (together with their American accents); she just smiled politely.

For two hours the girls talked and talked, and in some way, became friends. As Sophie was from England the sorority girls were interested to hear of her life, not knowing that she'd barely lived one, growing into the young woman sitting in their presence in less than four years. They'd quizzed her on all manner of things, though mostly (Sophie felt) on the boys back home. She didn't let on, but she had no experience in that department. Instead, she faked a traumatic break up, insisting she didn't want to talk about it.

The lead *Alpha* girl (named Jody), who happened to be driving, agreed to take Sophie directly into the capital by way of some of the more noticeable landmarks (which wasn't difficult as the route into DC was via 14th St. SW, which would directly pass the White House).

A short time later Sophie thanked her newly gained friends, asking Jody to let her out anywhere along the stretch of Constitution Avenue. Jody took her to the junction where 23rd St. NW crossed, and let her out a stone's throw from the Lincoln Memorial, writing her mobile number on a scrap of paper.

"If you need anythin', jus' giv'us a holla…"

Sophie thanked Jody, and together they said their goodbyes.

That had been a good hour earlier. The solitude and the quietness had been a welcome relief from the hubbub of three excitable American teens talking constantly for one hundred and ten miles, but she soon missed them.

A glance at her watch confirmed that evening was close to moving way for night. 7:03 p.m. She had watched the sun set shortly before half-six and now the sky, clear of clouds, was peppered with many constellations, the names of which she'd never thought to learn.

She did a quick sum in her head, working out that it was 12:03 p.m. back in England. It was time she called Ryan she decided, pulling out her mobile. Using speed dial, Sophie called the man as he'd earlier instructed.

Ryan picked up on the third ring.

"'ello? Sophie?" He sounded weary.

"Ryan. I'm here."

"Are you in Washington DC?"

"Where else?" sounding abrupt. *Like, derr!*

"Whereabouts are you?"

"You know the place you see in all the movies with the obelisk and its reflection on a great rectangular pond?"

Ryan was quiet a moment whilst he pictured it. He knew the one. It was where Martin Luther King Jr. had famously delivered his 'I have a dream' speech to 250,000 supporters at the *March on Washington for Jobs and Freedom* political rally of 1963. As Sophie had pointed out, the landmark had appeared in countless movies, including *Independence Day*, *Forrest Gump*, *The Day the Earth Stood Still*, and more recently, and one of Ryan's favourites, *White House Down*.

"Let me see... Are you sitting on the steps outside the Lincoln Memorial?" Ryan asked, brightly.

"You bet-cha. I can see Abe looking down at me from over my shoulder." Sophie was peering behind her at the illuminated statue built in honour of the 16th president of the United States of America. He sat on his throne looking all serious, as though he had all the fears and worries of the whole nation pressing down upon his shoulders.

"Gives you goose bumps, doesn't it?"

Unseen by Ryan, Sophie shrugged. "Not really. It's just a statue, Ryan – made from white marble. Can't deny the view is something, though..."

"I'd love to talk tourist attractions with you all night but something pressing has come up."

"Have you found my father?"

"No, Sophie. But I'm working on it. Our contact in the agency must be close to something. Since I spoke to you earlier there's been some... developments."

"Such as?"

Ryan went silent for a moment. Sophie would have thought the line had been disconnected were it not for the heavy breathing sounds coming from the other end.

"Ryan?"

"I'm still here," he replied softly. *"My insider was targeted today."*

"Targeted? What d'you mean, targeted?" Sophie startled one or two passersby with the note of concern and her raised voice.

"His car was booby-trapped and exploded outside his home; his wife and two children were inside. They were about to go to a school fundraiser, apparently. He had just popped back in doors for his wife's handbag. The bomb detonated whilst he was returning back from the kitchen."

"That's... awful!" Sophie visualised this stranger and his family and the devastation of a car bomb exploding outside their home. "Were they all killed?"

"His wife is dead, as is his children. Agent Roberts survived, though not without sustaining serious injury. He is currently at Medstar Georgetown University Hospital. I have a representative over there as we speak. Hopefully Agent Roberts is able to tell us what he knows..."

"Is it wise sending someone to his hospital? Won't they be in danger too?"

"Relax, she'll be careful."

"She?"

"Yes. Emily. I thought you could do with a little help and she's keen to earn her keep. Plus she's always wanted to do some travelling."

Sophie shook her head. "You sent Emily into a hot zone... an analyst? Ryan, are you soft in the head? Do you think whoever tried blowing him up is going to stop there once they learn that he's still alive?"

"Emily's stronger than you give her credit... she was dead keen on getting her hands dirty."

"How is she against armed assassins? Is she keen to be dead?" Sophie railed, jumping to her feet. She grabbed her backpack and flung it carelessly over her shoulder, then reached for the sports holdall.

The answer wasn't positive. Ryan thought better to give a reply.

"Okay, Ryan. This is what I need." Sophie was striding down the steps, heading back towards the direction she had come. A few seconds later and she was jogging away from the memorial building. "Find out what you can about where your agency contact is in the hospital and ping me his location and room number. I know how fond of her you are, so if possible, get Emily out of there. I'll pick up things when I arrive. If it isn't too late."

Sophie ended the call with a sharp jab of a finger. In less than a minute, she was standing at the kerb a short distance from where Jody had earlier dropped her off on Constitution Avenue. She raised a hand and hailed a passing yellow cab. A small American man steered the vehicle to a standstill next to her. She climbed into the backseat, tossing her backpack and holdall ahead of her.

"Where to, doll?"

Sophie gave him his instructions. "Medstar Georgetown University Hospital please. And, can we be quick. I hope to see a patient there before they die..."

The taxi driver smiled. "You got it," he muttered.

CHAPTER TEN
EMILY

"**R**YAN? WHAT IS IT?"

"They killed her," he sounded distant and in shock. *"It's too dangerous. Our mission is over. I can't expect it to go on. Not now…"*

"What d'you mean, Ryan? What are you talking about? Is it Sophie? Is she… is she *dead*?"

Ryan composed himself at the other end. He was calling from his office deep within the building many referred to as 'Legoland'. Like all other telephones within the facility, the call was made on a secure line, but it didn't stop 'others' from listening in at the American end of the line.

"Sophie is fine… well, she was when I spoke to her earlier," he paused to compose himself. *"No, it's our contact from the agency; Spencer Roberts. His wife and children. A car bomb detonated outside their house. They were inside."*

"And Spencer?" Emily's voice sounded flat, almost unconcerned. She was sitting on the edge of the desk in the hotel room.

"Third degree burns over forty-percent of his body. He was lucky."

"Will he be all right?"

"He'll live," replied Ryan, *"but I guess, his life is all but over in other ways."*

"Why would someone do this?" Emily asked. She had an image in her head of Agent Roberts lying in hospital, despite having never met the guy or knowing what he looked like. She imagined burn victims all looked the same. After all, underneath the skin we all look identical.

"It's a bit farfetched to think this was a coincidence, Emily, happening within a day after I sought his help. No, someone targeted him. He probably knows something and was professionally hit to keep him quiet. Which means they're likely onto us…"

A subtle 'ding' sound came from her closed laptop, placed close by on the desk next to her.

"I've just sent you all I have regarding Spencer and his family, and details of the hospital," Ryan continued. *"I need you to pay Agent Roberts a visit and see what he knows. Be discreet. Be a distraught family member or something."*

Emily opened up her laptop, index-fingering the mouse and double-tapping to open up her email. "I don't know, Ryan. I'm just an analyst…" The subject heading was blank but the sender wasn't.

"Emily. I need you to do this. If not for me, for Sophie…"

The woman sighed. She knew she couldn't refuse his request. This was her job. This was why Ryan had sent her. Reluctantly, she opened up his email. A heartbeat later colour images of Agent Spencer Roberts and his dead family flashed up across the screen. Family portraits, private memories. She felt like an unwilling voyeur.

"Okay. I'm on it."

⸻ ⬖ ⬗ ⸻

Outside the Medstar Georgetown University Hospital, Emily stepped out of the metallic silver *Chevrolet Impala* the hotel had arranged for her on rental. Parking in one of the lots at the rear of the building (and paying for three hours at a nearby ticketing machine), she walked purposefully towards the main hospital (a building to her left identified only as *BLES*, named after the developer *Marcus J. Bles* who donated land to the hospital).

Back in the hotel room she had downloaded a copy of the hospital's map and called ahead for the location of Spencer Roberts. Giving out an alias of a distant cousin (provided by Ryan), she'd learnt that the agent was in a single ward within the critical care unit of the CCC building (Concentrated Care Centre). Visiting times were between 11:00 a.m. and 9:00 p.m... though the operator had indicated that Spencer Roberts was currently in surgery and not likely allowed visitors until the following day.

Emily had thanked the operator and said she would come and take her chances.

In the lobby of the CCC building, Emily read the signs for directions to the critical care unit.

"Can I help you?" An orderly wheeling a small cage containing medical supplies stopped close by. He was young and only friendly because Emily was an attractive woman.

"Ah, hi... yes," slightly flustered. "I'm looking for critical care. My cousin was brought in earlier today..." Emily adopted the part carelessly and heard a slight American accent creep into her voice without realising.

"For sure, it's this way. I'm heading up there myself." The orderly wasn't unattractive and clearly worked-out. Emily could tell by the finely defined musculature beneath his blue coveralls. She couldn't help but admire him.

A lift ride five floors up, a couple of corridors and some carefree small talk later, the orderly wished Emily a pleasant evening (after jotting his mobile number with a coffee invite on a slip of paper) before wheeling his trolley away down an opposite passageway.

Emily screwed the slip of paper into a ball, discarding it in a non-medical waste bin.

Across a small waiting area behind a reception desk, sat a big woman wearing oversized spectacles and a mop of hair that fell untidily in ginger ringlets about her shoulders. She watched Emily with disdain as she approached the desk.

"Yes?" the enquiry was abrupt and uninviting. Emily tried to keep calm and smile; instead she looked meek and fearful.

"I'm here to visit my cousin; Spencer Roberts?" Emily spoke softly, just above a whisper.

The woman behind the desk seemed to visibly melt in front of her, her hard demeanour evaporating like sea mist. "It was you I spoke to earlier?" she sighed. "Briony, was it?" she didn't wait for confirmation. "I did say 'no visitors' today. Doctors' orders…"

"I've travelled quite some way," Emily appealed, which, if you counted London, England, wasn't altogether a lie.

"I'll see what I can do. Take a seat over there by the drinks machine." The woman pointed across the corridor to a row of four vinyl-cushioned seats, standing up and making her way in the opposite direction. Emily watched her shuffle down the corridor, stopping at a room outside which, initially, she'd failed to notice was guarded by a uniformed policeman.

Doing as instructed, Emily crossed to the first seat next to the drinks' machine, and sat down. After a couple of minutes it became obvious that the receptionist wasn't in any urgency to return. She reached for a magazine lying askew atop a pile of others and flicked through its pages.

A phone began to ring from the reception area. No one appeared to answer it. After a very long minute an answer machine clicked on.

Shortly after, the receptionist returned accompanied by a tiny woman of five-foot-one-inches, her nurses' uniform doing little to give her any air of authority, though when she opened her mouth she was unquestionably in charge. Around her neck hung a lanyard with her ID badge attached, swinging pendulum against her chest. Emily made a mental note that the nurse was named Sarah Pooley.

"You've come to visit Mr Roberts?" The nurse had a loud voice for someone so small, which startled Emily. "Who are you?" No kindness was spared.

Emily stood up and smiled. "Briony; I'm Spencer's cousin," she lied, the American accent that she'd conjured with the orderly once again evident. "We were close…" The file Ryan had sent indicated Spencer and Briony *had* been close. But that had been sometime in the early nineties. They had actually grown apart and hadn't exchanged Christmas cards in nearly ten years.

The nurse bought the deception. "This way, Briony. Room five." The nurse headed in the direction she had come, taking large steps that belied her size. Emily felt almost the need to run to keep up. "Spencer is awake. The reception clerk said you are his cousin? He knows you are here. I warn you now though, his face, head and much of his upper torso is severely burned. Even without the dressings, your cousin will never be as you remembered." The nurse stopped just short of reaching the door that enjoyed twenty-four hour guard duty.

"Thank you."

"I should also mention – if you didn't know already – your cousin's wife and children all tragically died in the… *accident*. Try not to distress him any more than he already is."

Despite the warning, nothing prepared Emily for the sight waiting for her deep within the private ward.

A privacy curtain had been pulled across the room just ahead of the door, giving no view of the room's current occupant. Nurse Sarah Pooley guided Emily into the ward.

Electronic bleeps and the whining of machines filled Emily's ears as she followed the nurse in, bypassing the curtain partitioning and seeing Ryan's agency contact for the first time.

She couldn't help but gasp, stopping just short of passing the partitioning.

"Briony, we spoke of this..." Nurse Pooley voiced gently, galvanising Emily back into motion. She walked hesitantly to the near side of Agent Spencer Roberts' bed and took the only seat in the room.

"Hi cuz..." he spoke slow and hoarsely, with a dry, crackly rasp, needing to draw breath between every couple of words. "You look... differently... from when I last... saw you."

Emily tried to smile. "It's been quite a while. I've lost some weight."

Nurse Pooley laid a hand gently on Emily's shoulder. "I will give you ten minutes; Spencer needs to rest..." She removed her hand and quietly left the room.

Neither Emily or Spencer spoke until the sound of the door closed, signalling that the nurse was gone.

Spencer's face was bandaged with gaps for his eyes and mouth. Ryan had been right; the man's life was all but over. She became overwhelmed with pity for him.

"So... We both... know... you're not... Briony. Are you here... to... kill me?" he was wheezing now. The effort required to talk was frustrating.

Emily, dropping the American accent, looked aghast. She shook her head. "No, *God* no!"

"Then... Ryan... sent you." Spencer relaxed, closing his eyes. "Can I... trouble you... for some... water."

A jug of water sat on a nearby table, melting ice cubes tinkling against the glass inside as she lifted it. She poured half a glass full. With a straw, Emily lifted the glass closer to the man's bandaged face and guided the straw between his lips. He took a long, deep swig from the glass and gasped after.

"Thank... you. Who'd ever think... water would... be... so merciful..." almost a whisper.

"I'm Emily. Ryan asked me here... to see how you were."

"Cut... the... bull!" Spencer rasped. "Ryan sent... you here... for information..."

Emily looked down at her hands, feeling embarrassed.

"It's al'right... I know... this... game..."

"Did you get a chance to learn anything?"

"You look... too pretty... to... be a... agent." Spencer avoided Emily's question.

Emily couldn't help blushing. She didn't reply to the compliment; hell, she couldn't return it.

"Do you know where George Jennings is?" she asked gently.

"He... must be... someone... *special*... to... kill my..." he started to sob, "...family..."

Emily felt uncomfortable, fidgeting in agitation on the vinyl seat —a relative of the one she'd sat on in reception.

"I'm sorry..." she said awkwardly.

"Don't! Tell me... is he... *worth it*...?"

Emily looked at the broken man lying bandaged in front of her. In truth, George Jennings *wasn't* worth losing your wife and children over. And yet, the man had already tallied up a sizeable casualty list that kept on growing and growing.

"George Jennings is an asset; Ryan believes he's worth dying for."

Spencer sighed deeply. "Then... your death... won't weigh... so heavily... ... when it... happens..." His voice was ragged and almost spent. The ECG machine he was hooked up to was bleeping, a dancing white line flickering across a monitor in tandem; Spencer's pulse was quickening.

"Spencer..." Time was running out. The nurse would be back soon to chase her out – her ten minutes were almost up.

"In my... shoe..." he started, "you'll find... what you... want..."

"Your shoe...?" Before she could quiz him further the sound of gunshots echoed beyond the corridor, two in quick succession, followed by intermingled screams and incoherent shouts. A moment later an emergency alarm sounded – urgent and calamitous.

"Hidden... in the... bottom... *hurry...!*"

Emily jumped to her feet and crossed to a wardrobe – or what the Americans called a 'closet' – and found Spencer's shoes lying amongst the remains of his discarded clothing. Turning to face Agent Roberts lying in bed, she saw him nod slightly in confirmation.

"Good... luck..."

Emily barely heard him over the clamour of the alarm. Another gunshot sounded, this one closer. She mouthed 'thank you' and made to exit the room, disappearing around the curtain partition and pulling open the door.

She poked her head out into the corridor, then quickly jerked back, as though her nose had been touched by a naked flame.

Towering above the policeman, who was propped up against a wall, his bloodied hand held up in surrender, stood a stocky man in khaki fatigues with a black balaclava concealing his face. In his right hand, pointing down at the cowering man, a *Smith and Wesson Sigma* pistol.

Emily flinched on hearing the next gunshot. She didn't need her IQ score of 177 to know what had just transpired. Naively, she poked her head out through the door once again, repeating her 'jerk back' on seeing the armed man progressing towards her.

The policeman, only minutes earlier having been on guard duty outside Spencer Roberts' door, who'd left his post momentarily by walking towards the gunshots, now lay slumped against the wall, a gathering pool of blood spreading beneath him.

"Oh my God oh my God oh my God..." Emily had backed into the room, sidestepping the curtain partitioning and was close to hyperventilating. Held together in one hand were the size nine shoes belonging to the CIA agent.

"What… is… it…?" Spencer could hear the ongoing emergency alarm echoing outside his room, but all else was obliterated by the bleeps, hums, wheezes and whistles of the life support systems attached to his body.

"A man with a gun!" Emily was close to hysterical. "I told Ryan I wasn't cut out for this," she was whining, "I'm an analyst!"

"Don't… panic… he's… not here… for you… find… find somewhere… to… hide…"

Emily looked around the room. The cupboard? (or as in America, should that be *closet*?) The toilet? Under the bed? All these places were clichéd; if she was looking for someone, all three places would be hot on her 'check' list.

"Where?!"

"It… doesn't… matter! It's me… he… wants…"

"But… he'll kill you!"

"Without… my family… I'm… already… dead." Finding more strength, he shouted. "NOW GO!"

Emily raced across the room to the toilet (opposite Spencer's bed), pushed the door open – where it swung inwards – and entered, closing it (but not locking it) behind her.

No sooner had the toilet door closed, the man dressed in khaki and the black balaclava, stepped into the private ward from behind the curtain partitioning. He walked slowly, purposefully, towards the hospital bed and its severely burned patient.

Watching him approach, Agent Spencer Roberts lay in the bed, eyes staring, his breathing shallow.

The man sat down on the vinyl chair recently vacated by Emily, not noticing the seat was still warm. The *Smith and Wesson Sigma* was in his right hand. "You look a sight for sore eyes," he said. "Tell me. Does it hurt?"

Spencer Roberts chuckled. It sounded like the scrunching-up of a paper bag. "Smarts... a... little..." he rasped.

The assassin started to laugh sadistically.

"I'm sorry about your wife and kids. Collateral damage. You know how it is."

Spencer didn't reply.

In the toilet, Emily's ear was pressed up against the door, listening in.

"I had a dog once. Got hit by a car. A golden retriever. You remind me of her, the way you lie there, all broken and sorry-looking. Kindest thing I ever did was put a .38 into her brain." Without warning, the man in khaki raised the *Smith & Wesson Sigma*, aimed it at the agent's head and squeezed the trigger. The gunfire was explosive and deafening within the private ward. A mess of blood and brain spattered up against the wall behind the bed.

In the toilet, Emily vaulted back as though hit by the bullet herself, careening against the sink and clattering noisily to the floor.

Khaki man, alerted to the presence within the toilet, sighed regretfully. Releasing the magazine from the gun, he replaced it with a fresh one before standing up. Quietly, he crept around the edge of the bed and stopped, standing a mere foot away from the toilet door. For a long moment he stood there, deliberating on what he should do. Something didn't feel right.

He glanced around the room, feeling eyes on him, expecting to see that he'd missed a nurse or a doctor hiding in a corner; he could see no one.

That's strange, he thought. Spontaneously and without reason he kicked the toilet door open, splintering the frame where the catch had been engaged, but not locked.

"Please, don't!" begged Emily cowering beneath the sink. She'd never been trained for field work, so was never prepared against such scenarios. She barely knew how to fire a gun, only ever visiting a shooting range once.

"I'm sorry," he said, raising the *Smith and Wesson Sigma*. "It's nothing personal."

"I beg you," she whispered. Emily Porter closed her eyes and hoped death would be quick, and not too painful.

The gunshot was louder and more deafening than any sound she'd ever heard, seeming to emanate from within her head.

CHAPTER ELEVEN
DOMINIC

THE ADVICE GIVEN HAD been short and simple.

Lay low.

Jennifer never wasted a word when giving council. She hadn't even expressed for how long his exile should last.

Dominic Schilling had done as bidden, remaining off the grid, unseen, languishing and lazing about within the hideout Jennifer Ratcliff had arranged upon learning of his plight. The fact that he wasn't dead as initially reported came as no surprise to her; after all, she had been complicit with his plans. It had all been part of a wider scheme, one which had yet to completely run its course.

For Dominic, three months of lounging about, of waiting around, of being alone except for the cleaner (Polish and speaking no English), had taken its toll on the former military man. His appearance was changed from before. Weight gain and unkempt face hair had struck him down as barely recognisable, and his mood - melancholy at best - tainted every conscious thought.

Boredom had long since set in, and deep depression was eating away at whatever humanity was left within. He was lonely and filled with a rage that no one was there to dampen down – not even Jennifer who, apart from one fleeting visit shortly after arriving from Oban, maintained very little contact with her former *confidant*.

Would things have been any different had the *Whisper of Persia* been given to him, as promised? The reward for helping the CIA in their quest to capture George Jennings and his *oh so beloved daughter*, Sophie; compensation (which he claimed) for turning his back on a lucrative career in espionage…

Instead he'd been played the fool. Stitched up by the CIA, discarded like a piece of garbage on St. Kilda, lucky not to be dead. It was almost like they'd known all along that his intentions were duplicitous.

If he had felt unhappy finding himself naked on an almost uninhabited island, it was nothing compared to how he soon felt after being returned whole to his native England. His misery had truly dawned the day after his arrival at the stately home on the outskirts of London. Danuta, the Polish cleaner, had deposited the newspaper (that morning's issue of *The Daily Mail*) unceremoniously on the coffee table, an act she's repeated almost daily ever since.

The headline on the front page heralded the return of a priceless diamond, stolen less than two weeks earlier from an art and antiques exhibition in Chelsea. Careful examination had revealed the diamond to be the very one he'd courted and coerced George Jennings into getting his daughter to steal for him – all an elaborate trap at first, but one which had come with a promissory note that entitled him to keep the spoils.

Dominic had cursed in flagrant English, which even Danuta had little difficulty in understanding, physically demonstrating his grievance by turning the newspaper into confetti, which he'd then hurled around the room. Danuta had sighed and made for the utility cupboard where the *Dyson* was kept.

For three months, every waking moment was tormented by thoughts of 'what if' and self pity, subdued only by an increasing need for solace found from a bottle of *Johnny Walker* blue label – well stocked by his host who had grown distant of late.

Lying in bed, head pounding from the previous day's excesses, Dominic flinched from the sudden swath of bright light that cascaded into the bedroom. Initially he thought Danuta had overstepped her boundaries, intruding on his privacy and causing the incursion. Through bleary eyes, he could see that it wasn't the small, pudding-y woman who'd spent most of her life growing up in Lodz, a city found centrally in Poland. Instead, the silhouette shrouded by intense late-morning sunlight was taller, willowy, and somewhat familiar.

Dominic shielded his eyes against the glare. The light was adding to the hurt his hangover already caused him.

"I didn't agree to support you only for you to slowly eat and drink yourself to death." The woman walked away from the window and sat down on the edge of Dominic's bed.

"Jennifer?" Dominic spoke slowly. Within his head, he questioned his sanity. Was this woman actually here? In his bedroom?

Beneath Jennifer's steely gaze, behind the glasses perched on her nose, she was studying the former field agent. Half-undressed beneath the duvet, he certainly had changed in the three months since she'd last seen him. Three stone heavier, his face no longer clean-shaven. She'd seen tidier hobos slumming it on Earls Court Road.

"Go away Jennifer… I'm sleeping…" Dominic spoke breathily. He rolled to his side, his back to the brightness filtrating his room, and, more intentionally, to the CEO of Kaplan Ratcliff.

"You've slept enough Dominic. It's now time to get up. I have something I need you to do."

"Please… let me die…" he whispered. It was loud enough for Jennifer to hear.

"I believe we know where Sophie Jennings is."

Dominic sighed, rolling back over so that he was once again facing his uninvited guest.

"I thought that might grab your interest." Jennifer stood up from the bed.

"Where?"

"Clean yourself up and put on some clothes – if they still fit – and I'll tell you all about it."

<hr>

It had taken Dominic an hour to make himself presentable. His facial hair was thick and needed to be cut with scissors initially to allow the razor closer access to his skin. It had been so long since he'd shaved last that his skin was blotchy and red when finished, and applying two splashes of cologne brought tears to his eyes. He combed his shoulder-length black hair to the back of his head and tied it into a tail.

Still semi-naked (a towel wrapped about his waist) he appraised his reflection in the floor-to-ceiling mirrored wardrobe doors. He shook his head in disappointment and disgust. The image staring back at him made him think of *The Biggest Loser*. Opening the wardrobe door fully relieved his eyes of the hideous fat man who stood in front of him. He looked within for something comfortable to wear.

All that he found that would fit was a pair of sweat pants and an extra-large grey hoody that zippered up at the front.

Still hung-over, he made his way to the kitchen, the likely place where Jennifer Ratcliff would be waiting for him. It wasn't even great intuition that had led to that conclusion, but the strong aroma of coffee and frying bacon filling the whole house.

"So, what's this all about?" Dominic had made little or no noise as he'd entered the kitchen and had made the slightly older woman jump. She turned from the cooker, clutching her chest with her left hand; the right held a fish slice which she used to move the bacon within the frying pan.

"You startled me!"

"Surprised? Not bad for a fat man, hey?" He crossed to a kitchen counter and helped himself to a steaming mug of black coffee.

She ignored him. "No, no, no... that won't do." She appraised his appearance. "You look like you're going to rob an off-licence..."

"You try putting on forty pounds and see if *your* clothes still fit."

Jennifer ignored the sarcasm. "When I said 'lie low' I hadn't meant you literally lie around all day. We'll pick something up for you on the way."

"On the way?" Dominic quizzed. He sipped at the charcoal coloured liquid and winced. It was much stronger than he was used to, but it was what he needed for his hangover. "On the way, where?" He took a deeper pull from the mug.

Jennifer returned to the sizzling bacon. "The office."

Dominic almost choked on his next mouthful of coffee.

"You didn't think a man of your talents would be allowed to stay dead for ever, did you?"

CHAPTER TWELVE
GEORGE

GEORGE JENNINGS WAS SHACKLED like a common criminal – iron bracelets with thick steel chains enclosed his wrists and ankles, jangling heavily as he was escorted by four armed soldiers out of the industrial-sized elevator into the gigantic aircraft hangar that, to any who passed by or ventured inside, would believe long-disused.

"It's been a while since you've been above ground, hasn't it doc?"

Mechanically, the large double-doors began to bang and thrum as they slowly opened, controlled by a large green button positioned next to a red one on the wall to the left side of the hangar's door. A crack of sunlight cut through the gloom as George shuffled along towards the opening, the gap widening with each step, the brightness beginning to hurt his eyes. The intense heat of the Nevada desert could be felt, extreme compared to the air conditioning he'd grown accustomed to half a mile below the surface.

"Where are you taking me?" George had asked the question more than a dozen times since the meeting with Milo Calland had gone south. So far he'd not received a response, or at least a sensible answer.

The soldier nearest, and who happened to have been given charge over George, was Captain Will Hancote. He just smiled knowingly.

"All I can tell you, doc, is it ain't *Disneyland*."

Noticing that he'd slowed down, one of the soldiers shoved

George hard in the back with the flat side of his rifle. He stumbled forward a couple of steps before regaining his balance.

Outside the hangar, a *Humvee* was stationary, engine idling. The driver was standing beside the *Humvee*; he saluted the captain.

"Arrangements are in place for onward transportation, sir," the driver said. "*USS Princeton* is being prepared as we speak."

"Good."

"This here our prisoner?"

Captain Hancote just nodded.

"I'll take you to the helipad."

Two of the four escorts bundled George heavily into the *Humvee* whilst the driver and Captain Hancote climbed into the front. The last soldier slipped into the vehicle via the door behind the driver's seat. No seatbelts were worn and before anyone could get comfy the *Humvee* lurched forward.

A small *Learjet 85* aircraft was readying for take-off at the far end of the runway as the *Humvee* sped away from the hangars behind them, and came out onto a road that ran the entire length of the airfield. Through the right side of the vehicle, George watched the *Learjet* begin to accelerate from behind them, soon speeding past as it made for the optimum speed needed to attain flight.

"There goes the suit from Washington," declared the driver having ten minutes earlier driven the Deputy Director of the CIA out to his waiting aircraft. "At least he's got a nice home waiting for him at the other end; you-" indicating George with a sideward glance over his shoulder "on the other hand... I wouldn't like to speculate what your new home is going to be like."

George Jennings was none the wiser as to his destination, though if it needed a helicopter and a trip aboard the *USS Princeton*, he could only guess that it wasn't going to be some place pleasant. For a fleeting moment he wondered about his children, their whereabouts unknown, and about Sophie, before allowing thoughts to settle on Harriet.

Harriet. My wife…

It was impossible to comprehend life without her… and yet, this was the harsh reality. His wife was dead. How, why, when and where were all valid questions, but Milo's report had not been forthcoming with any of the answers.

Unfortunately, he was in no position to pursue the matter further.

Through a small window of the *Learjet*, Milo Calland peered through the toughened glass across the airfield towards the *Humvee* racing along the strip beside them. In the back of the vehicle he could just make out the silhouette of George Jennings. For a millisecond, George and Milo's eyes locked on each other. Then the moment was over and the Learjet climbed into the air, taking Milo and the small retinue of cabin crew back to Washington.

⸺⬥⬥⸺

The *USS Princeton* was named in honour of the Revolutionary Wars against the British that took place in and around the town of Princeton, New Jersey in January 1777. A *Ticonderoga*-class guided missile cruiser, the *USS Princeton* was berthed in California at the Long Beach Naval Shipyard, despite the fact that since 1997, Long Beach was a commercial container port on lease to *Hanjin Shipping*, and no longer chiefly the home port for the naval vessel.

No sooner had the *Sikorsky Seahawk* helicopter, one of two stationed on the missile cruiser, safely landed on the ship, the orders were given to ready for departure. Still manacled in chains and under armed escort, George Jennings was helped out of the helicopter and, entering the vessel via a steel doorway, led towards a cabin that for the duration of the journey would act as his cell.

Captain Will Hancote locked the cabin door and posted one

of the two remaining soldiers that had accompanied them on their journey from Groom Lake Airbase, on guard duty.

"Whatever you do, don't open this for anyone but me." The soldier saluted in reply and watched the Captain saunter away down the narrow corridor.

George, still cuffed and not yet coming to terms with the events that had transpired, sat on the end of the bed and looked out of the small portside scuttle window that gave views of the Pacific ocean. Despite repeatedly asking, details of where they were taking him were still not forthcoming; but he had a good idea.

He was an important man with a wealth of knowledge that, in the wrong hands, would be detrimental to the security of the United States of America. Now that he was surplus to demand the only move forward, short of having him killed, was incarceration.

Somewhere out of sight...

Somewhere out of mind...

He was being taken to a place where no court tried or passed convictions; a place where the Lord of the Manor had full say and swagger, beyond law and reproach; a place where even God had no sway. Instinctively, he knew what awaited him.

He was on his way to a place where its cohabitants were lost and forgotten, locked up, the keys all but thrown away.

There was only one place within US jurisdiction that fitted that ideology, and it was a place the President and federal government had sworn to cease using.

Within a matter of hours, the reality of his fears were confirmed. The bay of Guantanamo could be seen through the small window, the Naval base made famous for its military prison, the place *Amnesty International* had condemned as the 'Gulag of our times'.

After 9/11 pretty much anyone suspected of being linked to Al Qaeda was arrested and detained within one of its four compounds.

There had been more than 700 prisoners since 2002. Now, only forty-six people remained detained at the facility, deemed too dangerous to be moved to other prisons, destined to see out the rest of their days dressed in bright orange – forgotten by all except those who once considered them family; father, brother or son. They were all kept in *Camp Delta*, the largest compound and the only one still in use.

George sighed in resignation. This was where his journey would end. Once a CIA asset. Now a CIA liability.

The *USS Princeton* slowed as it approached, soon after gliding into the Naval dock. The sea was calm, the ship cut through the Pacific like a knife through warm butter. It came to rest alongside a hastily prepared quayside. Military personnel, looking small through the portside window, made haste like worker ants. A klaxon sounded giving a signal for something or other; George didn't care less. He watched as ropes were tied, mooring the ship ready for boarding. Readying the ship for his departure.

The jingling of keys were heard from outside the cabin – George's temporary prison. A lock clicked open and Captain Hancote stepped through the narrow doorway. Behind him, he could just make out the silhouette of the guard who'd been posted to keep the room secure.

"I hope your trip was comfortable." Hancote spoke with indifference. He didn't care much for the man's pleasure, he was just filling the air with small talk. "Come. Let's go see your new lodgings."

George stood up from the bed and shuffled awkwardly across the small room in the chains that hindered him from taking more than a half-step; anything more would have resulted in falling forward to his knees – a bit like trying to walk with a pair of trousers wrapped round your ankles.

"You must be a VIP Mr Jennings, or very lucky," continued George's chaperone. "Either that or you're deemed too dangerous to have contact with the other prisoners; you've got your own detention building all to yourself." Captain Hancote took the lead, with the soldier on guard duty joining an unseen other taking up the flank.

"Where am I being taken?" George spoke softly, downcast.

"A small compound called 'Penny Lane'. You've probably heard of it." George had and it had nothing to do with *The Beatles*. Between 2003 and 2006 it had been used by the CIA to house prisoners they attempted to recruit as spies against Al-Qaeda. He thought the place had been bulldozed years ago, but now guessed not. "I've heard that there's relative comfort with cable TV. There's even a pool table. Not too shabby. You'll love it."

"I doubt it," grunted George. It could've been *The Ritz* for all he cared.

Hancote shrugged. "I guess it will beat having a crudely made *shiv* stabbed in your throat or gut, the *Sunnis* don't take kindly to white folk... *for some reason*," he smiled. "Or perhaps an early morning wake-up call from a cellmate feeling particularly amorous. Gets kinda lonely in Camp Delta I should think. Some of them inmates have been without a woman for twelve years..."

Now Harriet was gone, George doubted he'd ever be with a woman again. That said, the advances from a male inmate could hardly be something yearned for. Unbidden, tears started to trickle down his cheeks.

On the quayside a black *Dodge Grand Caravan*, its windows tinted, idled patiently. The driver could be seen through the window, wound down completely; he wore the blue and grey working uniform of the US Navy, a matching baseball cap placed atop his head.

As they stepped onto the metal bridge that had been placed between the *USS Princeton* and the quay, the glare was intense and the heat of the Cuban sun scorched George's pale complexion – the average temperature for October was 31°C. It had been warm in Nevada, but being under ground for nearly four months meant he'd never experienced it; he'd almost forgotten what the sun felt like.

George still followed Captain Hancote, who had walked a good two metres ahead. Another shove from behind prompted George to follow. He took a tentative, shuffle-step and felt himself clawing to the side bars for support.

Maybe it was the heat, or the stress of the situation, or perhaps it could have been the fact that the geneticist had skipped breakfast and had eaten nothing since teatime the day before, he didn't know. Whatever it was counted for little at that precise moment. He came over suddenly peculiar, almost like he was no longer in charge of his body.

George Jennings' legs collapsed beneath him, propelling the man forward to flop down the remaining steps of the bridge leading to the quay, his face skidding on asphalt.

"Sir!" One of the soldiers leapt forward and was crouching beside George Jennings who was lying flat on his face, almost in parody of a penguin sliding down a slope on its belly.

Captain Hancote was on dry land when the hollering began. He hurried back to the fallen prisoner, stooping on the narrow causeway, close to where he'd fallen, feeling for George's pulse.

"Is he dead, sir?" asked the soldier who'd shoved George forward just before he'd collapsed.

The Captain didn't reply, but couldn't hide the answer from his face; he turned away and looked over his shoulder towards the driver of the *Dodge Grand Caravan* who'd jumped from his vehicle to offer assistance.

"Get me a medic!" Hancote called, before barking out the order more urgently: "I NEED A MEDIC RIGHT NOW!"

CHAPTER THIRTEEN
SOPHIE

Sophie gave the taxi driver his instructions.

"Medstar Georgetown University Hospital please. And, can we be quick. I hope to see a patient there before they die…"

The taxi driver had smiled before muttering: "You got it."

Ten minutes later she was handing the driver a crumpled $20 note.

The vehicle had pulled into a patient drop-off parking lot a short distance from the main entrance, having taken Entrance Two, gone all way around the roundabout before stopping next to an ambulance and an abandoned vehicle, a hastily written sign placed up against the windscreen advising: *Mother in labour with child.*

"Keep the change," Sophie said, hurrying out of the car with her backpack flung over her shoulder and her holdall just ahead of her, the contents of both representing everything she owned. She had little, and wanted little. Being invisible, finding what she wanted, including money, wasn't difficult – it was down to her conscience and knowing what was wrong and right. Although she could steal, she didn't like doing it.

From her backpack, she retrieved the tablet computer and opened up the email sent by Ryan a little earlier.

Details flashed up on the *Nexus* with directions on where she would locate Ryan's CIA contact, Spencer Roberts. She read the information, not realising that she was speaking aloud (although in hushed tones). It was of no consequence. There was no one in earshot or close by.

"...critical care unit... concentrated care centre... fifth floor... down the corridor... police guard..."

The hospital was well signposted, which made things much simpler. Before progressing, she concealed the holdall behind dense shrubbery, and a deep cloak of darkness. Then, she flung her father's tablet back into her backpack, and zipped it up as she started moving.

Skirting the building, she jogged towards the Concentrated Care Centre – also signposted as 'surgery centre'. She clattered through the doors and headed directly for the twin elevators situated past the reception desk, bypassing a room heaving with patients awaiting treatment. To any casually observing her, she looked a little dishevelled and distressed, a not too unfamiliar sight within those surroundings.

"Miss? Miss? Can I help you?" A desk clerk had hurried behind Sophie and had made a halting grab at her backpack, almost tugging it from her shoulder. The ID hanging around her neck gave her the name Cindy Harper.

"Hey!" Sophie pulled her backpack free from the desk clerk's grasp, slightly aggrieved; she continued towards the elevator. "I'm visiting someone in critical care." She jabbed the button to summon the elevator, and waited.

"Visiting hours are almost over. Perhaps you should come back tomorrow..." The desk clerk had raised a hand flagging for a security guard to come over. A bearded man in uniform approached confidently from a corner of the room, a serious look etched across his face.

"It'll be too late tomorrow," Sophie exclaimed. *I may be too late now.* She jabbed the button impatiently. "She'll be dead then!" Sophie regretted her decision not to will her genetic side-effect into play. At least then she would have been free to enter the hospital unseen and unchallenged.

"What's the patient's name? I'll go check her status…" The desk clerk was not giving up.

Before Sophie could argue further the elevator 'dinged' its arrival and the double-doors wheezed open.

From across the room a waiting patient started to scream, shrill, long and hard. A glance towards the screaming patient informed Sophie that she was staring past her, towards the elevator. Sophie turned her attention in the direction of where the screaming patient was looking, and jumped back in surprise.

"Oh my God!" The desk clerk had clapped a hand to her mouth, her eyes wide. "Oh my God!" she repeated.

The security guard, moments before summoned to escort Sophie Jennings off the premises, was no longer interested in the young woman. "Someone… call 911." Using a radio clipped to his belt he called for assistance.

In the elevator, slumped against the furthest wall, a doctor wearing surgical scrubs. A pool of blood was slowly spreading out beneath him on the elevator's metal floor. Sophie could see that the man had been shot in the chest from the heavy staining that had soaked into the front of his clothing. This had been very recent, she could tell from the continued flow of blood leaking from him. She could also see without the need to further inspect, that the doctor was dead.

"Is there another elevator? Or a set of stairs?" Sophie didn't think this desk clerk would be in any frame of mind to hinder her movements any longer.

The desk clerk's eyes were glazed over. She was deep in shock. "Oh my God," was all she said, repeatedly.

Not wasting any more time, Sophie turned her back on the chaos that had begun in the reception area, and headed for the double-doors just a short distance further into the building.

"Miss, wait…" The security guard had started to call her back but lost interest as the double-doors gently swung closed behind Sophie. She wasn't important; the chaos and shooting clearly was.

Immediately to her left she found what she was looking for. The staircase that would lead her up to the critical care unit.

After climbing five flights of stairs at a rush, most people would be dizzy through lack of breath; Sophie had barely broken into a sweat as she turned into a short corridor via another set of double-doors and followed the signs for 'Critical Care'. The truth was she was more than capable of scaling vaster flights of stairs than this before fatigue set in.

Stepping into a final corridor, she instantly knew something was amiss – even without the obvious visual signs, and the wail of the emergency evacuation alarm, she could tell by the sheer lack of people milling about the place. Blood spatters and a trail of crimson spots led a path towards a small room to her left; to her right she could see an unmanned reception desk. Slowly, Sophie followed the blood into the small room, a consultation room with a desk, a couple of chairs, an examination bed, and…

… a small woman in nurse's uniform, pressed up against a corner of the room as though trying to blend into the paintwork, a hand clutching her stomach where the gunman had shot her at close range. A hole the size of a plum had been torn into her centre, almost penetrating straight through. She was sobbing and shaking as quietly as she could, not wishing to draw undue attention to her plight; pain and fear competing for her consideration.

Sophie hurried to the stricken nurse. A glance at the ID around her neck established her as Nurse Sarah Pooley.

"Hi, Sarah… you're going to be all right. I am going to help you. But first, I need you to help me…"

The nurse winced and cried out as she tried to make herself comfortable. The movement caused her to bleed more profusely.

"How many were there?" Sophie spoke urgently.

"One… I think. He was here for a… patient." Sarah Pooley started to drift, her eyes closing. She suddenly felt the overpowering need to go to sleep.

"Stay with me, Sarah!" Sophie slapped her lightly on the face. The nurse's eyes sprung open. She felt so… so weak. "Where did he go?"

Sarah Pooley tried to raise a hand to point the way but found that she had no strength to lift such an immense weight – it was as though her arm was imbedded within a concrete block. "Room five… patient in… room…" The nurse mouthed another word but Sophie couldn't hear anything other than a small puff of exhaled air, despite leaning in close.

Knowing the young nurse had finished speaking, Sophie pulled away. Before she'd stood up, Sarah Pooley was dead.

Sophie sighed sadly. Would death confront her at every turn, everywhere she went? She turned away from the small woman who'd helped her with her last breath, and exited the consultation room.

Confidently, she strode past the reception desk, heading for the corridor beyond a further set of double-doors. Unseen, crouching behind the desk, was a large woman with untidy ginger hair and spectacles that anyone under the age of seventy would avoid wearing at all costs. Signage beside the doors indicated wards One through to Nineteen lay beyond the threshold; Sophie considered her next move, hands poised to push the double-doors forward.

The single gunshot from somewhere off the corridor ahead of her spurred her to action.

Behind the desk, visibly shaken by the sight of a masked gunman, and the shooting of Nurse Pooley only five minutes earlier, the reception clerk found that curiosity got the nudge over caution as she poked her head out from hiding and watched the brave, young woman walk towards what was most definitely going to be her demise.

As the young blonde girl thrust her palms against the double-doors, something bizarre and unworldly occurred.

The receptionist would later report that the Virgin Mary herself had descended from heaven to save her – the sweet Lord sent his chosen angel to deliver her from evil… for nothing rational could explain what her eyes had witnessed.

Sophie had palmed open the door with a forceful outward thrust and willed herself invisible – she'd done it so often that the transformation was almost instant.

Behind her, the large woman with messy ginger hair, kneeling with her head peering tentatively around the edge of the desk, felt her mouth drop open aghast, her eyes locked on the event playing out ahead of her; before the double swing-doors had had a chance to close, the young woman had evanesced into thin air.

⎯⎯⎯▰◆▰⎯⎯⎯

Room five was the third door along the left side of the corridor. Sophie knew this without the need of signage; the uniformed policeman sprawled across the floor was a few feet just ahead of it, the bullet hole to his temple and the resultant crimson mess was enough of a clue.

Hurrying to the door, the invisible woman's ears pricked up upon hearing a voice from within the ward. The door was open but everything within was shielded by a curtain that had been pulled across. Before entering, Sophie crouched down to the felled police officer and unholstered his *Glock 17* handgun from his belt, checking it was loaded whilst standing up. Like all *Glocks*, the *Glock 17* magazine incorporated ammunition windows, allowing at a glance assessment of how many shots are available.

It was fully loaded with seventeen 9mm bullets ready for action. Sophie heeled the magazine back into place and stepped into Agent Spencer Roberts' private ward. The emergency alarm still sounded but was less intense as she walked around the curtain partitioning into the room.

"I had a dog once. Got hit by a car. A golden retriever. You remind me of her, the way you lie there, all broken and sorry looking. Kindest thing I ever did was put a .38 into her brain."

The gunman was in the room sitting in a vinyl chair next to the hospital bed, its occupant covered from head to foot in bandaging and connected to a number of drips, wires and machines, monitoring and sustaining his life. The gunman was speaking softly, almost good-naturedly.

Sophie could see that he was military-dressed in khaki, his face disguised behind a black balaclava. In his right hand, cradled in his lap, a *Smith & Wesson Sigma*. Without warning or indication, and with adroit fluidity, he raised the weapon and shot the CIA agent in one swift movement.

The gunfire was explosive and deafening, the bullet slammed into Agent Roberts' head, giving him a third eye and ruining a perfectly well-decorated hospital wall.

A noise from the bathroom alerted both the gunman and Sophie to someone hiding within. Before standing he released the magazine from his handgun and replaced it with another slipped from a side pocket in his khaki combat trousers.

Quietly he crept around the side of the bed and approached the bathroom door. Silently, Sophie walked deeper into the room, matching the man's steps with her own, closing the gap between herself and him. Just a foot away from the door, he stopped. So did Sophie. She was two strides away from him.

For what seemed like an age the gunman just stood there, deep in thought, contemplating his next move; suddenly he jerked his head, looking about him in alarm, as though searching for something (or someone). Seeing nothing, and as abruptly as he'd shot the unarmed man lying dead in the bed behind him, he kicked the bathroom door open.

"Please, don't!" begged Emily. Sophie couldn't see her from where she was standing, but could hear the fear in her voice.

"I'm sorry," the gunman said, raising the *Smith and Wesson Sigma*. "It's nothing personal."

"I beg you…"

Knowing the gunman would likely act expeditiously and without remorse, Sophie raised the *Glock 17* towards the back of his head as she took two steps towards him. Coolly, indifferently, she gently squeezed the trigger.

The gunshot boomed, echoing within the bathroom. Emily had shrunk herself into a ball, pressed deep against the wall beneath the sink.

Crying, she was waiting for the immense pain to tear through her, or the absolute darkness that would signify the end to her life.

Surprisingly, neither came.

The gunman fell forward into the bathroom, his head colliding with the toilet with a heavy thwack! Had he not been dead already he would've been in serious need of medical attention.

"Emily?" The voice came as from thin air. Sophie stepped over the gunman's body into the bathroom and stooped down to where Emily was huddled. The *Glock* was still in her hand. "Are you okay?"

Emily couldn't see Sophie but she could sense that she was close. "I think I've soiled myself," she said by way of reply.

"Come. Let's get outta here." Sophie reached down to Emily, taking hold of her hand. It felt strange to Emily being pulled by an invisible force. She could feel Sophie's warm, strong hand grip her tightly and hoist her up onto her feet. The feat was almost without effort.

Above the sink beneath which she'd been huddled, Emily glanced at the mirror, seeing the reflection of her saviour – an unexplained side-effect of the genetic modifications made to Sophie's DNA before she had been born. She looked almost like she had the last time Emily had seen her, except... a bit older.

Emily guessed her age was somewhere around twenty now.

Being led from the room Emily almost forgot. "Wait!"

Sophie stopped. "What's wrong?"

"Agent Roberts' shoes!" Emily broke free from Sophie's grasp and turned back to the bathroom. Trying to ignore the dead gunman, she stepped over his lifeless body and returned to the sink. Beneath were the CIA agent's discarded size nine shoes she'd dropped whilst hiding.

"What are you doing?!" Sophie hissed, looking in after Emily.

"There's something hidden in the bottom of one of his shoes. Agent Roberts said it had everything we wanted to know." Emily retrieved them and hurried back out of the bathroom.

"Okay. You've got the shoes. Let's go..." Once again Sophie took hold of Emily's hand and guided her forward, almost like she was leading a person with impaired sight.

Emily couldn't help taking one last look at the agent who Ryan had enlisted to help, and who'd paid the ultimate price, sacrificing his life and his family in doing so.

How many more would have to die? She couldn't help wonder. Then she was being led around the curtain partition and back out into the corridor, past the body of the dead police officer (which she hardly noticed) and back towards the reception area, all whilst the emergency alarm continued to reverberate all around them.

CHAPTER FOURTEEN
DOMINIC

THE CONTROL ROOM WAS exactly how Dominic remembered it. A big dingy room with three dozen desks awash with papers, large LCD flat-screen monitors and manned by clean-shaven, bespectacled nerds with more qualifications than he'd had hot dinners. Some had letters after their name. Still on the wall, a large flat-screen television dominated. Nothing was on display, just a screensaver with the Kaplan Ratcliff company logo merrily dancing about on an endless loop.

One or two gasps were uttered as the chunkier-than-remembered Dominic Schilling was led into the room by the Corporation's CEO, Jennifer Ratcliff. Having taken a detour to *Harvey Nichols* and now dressed in an *Alexander McQueen* black suit, white open-collared shirt and a pair of *Valentino* black leather shoes, Dominic looked close to his former-self – if you ignored his escalated weight gain and long, tied-back hair.

Dominic heard a weasel-faced analyst whisper: "I thought he was dead…" to a neighbour who chose to remain quiet but did nothing to hide the smirk that had appeared on his face.

"This way." Jennifer directed Dominic up the metal staircase to the mezzanine floor, towards the Director's office, which was currently in darkness.

Heavier by three stone, Dominic climbed the stairs noisily, each footfall clanging around the control room drawing additional attention to his portly size. From the balcony, Jennifer pushed down the door handle to the office, opened the door and entered. Motion activated fluorescents burst into life overhead, immediately washing the room in a clinical white glow. "Come. Take a seat…"

Dominic reluctantly followed Jennifer in and took a seat in front of Samuel Jackson's desk. The room felt strangely empty without the Director's larger-than-life presence. In fact, a quick glance around the room revealed that it wasn't just the Director's ominous absence that made the room feel empty, it was the lack of any of his possessions too.

"What's going on Jennifer? Why am I here? I'm supposed to be dead…"

"No one as resourceful as you can stay dead for long… not even Ryan Barber."

"Ryan Barber?" After the trauma of St. Kilda had passed and he'd settled under the care of Jennifer Ratcliff, she'd kept him up to speed with regard to all developments relating to George Jennings, Sophie Jennings, his wife, children and others related to or involved in his case. Ryan Barber was dead, so she'd claimed. But that was three months ago.

This was now.

"Director Jackson was played a fool by the man. After he betrayed us, Jackson claimed to have had the man killed. The sick fool boasted about keeping Ryan's heart in a jar as a trophy." Jennifer shook her head in pity. "It could hardly be his heart in the jar when confirmed reports came up expounding that Ryan is not only still alive, but alive and working for MI6."

"How?"

Jennifer continued, exhaling exasperatedly. "A security guard, Richard Cullum. But it doesn't matter. My father used to say 'there's no point wasting energy dwelling on the past'. We should focus on the future."

"Okay. I guess there's a reason for you bringing me here, then."

Jennifer smiled deviously. "Ryan and MI6 are seeking to recover our former asset George Jennings, and his research. The CIA currently have him locked up someplace; all the groundbreaking discoveries made with us at Kaplan Ratcliff are now in the hands of the Americans."

"Sounds convoluted."

"It's going to get worse. I want George Jennings, and all that information that he keeps locked-up in his brain, here at Kaplan Ratcliff. It's ours by right. We invested millions in George's research, we've paid for it in both money AND blood; he owes us. It's ours and I want it back." She paused, before adding, "all of it…"

"I still don't see what any of that has to do with me…" In truth, Dominic wasn't the slightest bit interested.

"I'm giving you a chance for retribution." The vague look on the field agent's face was frustrating. She spoke again, a little aggressively. "Dominic, Jeez!" It was like talking to a three-year-old. She was blunt and spoke slow and clearly. "I'm offering you the keys to the kingdom. I want you to head the unit and bring me back what is rightfully mine."

Despite noticing the former Intelligence Director's absence, Dominic asked the obvious question. "What about Jackson? Shouldn't this be his gig?"

Jennifer shook her head. "Sam's gone. You don't need to know the specifics." Her eyes glazed over for a moment as she remembered the look on Director Jackson's face before he had died, his image was as clear in her mind as Dominic was in front of her. She blinked the thoughts away – temporarily. "Well. Are you my new Intelligence Director?"

Dominic looked about the spacious office. The blinds hanging from the ceiling along the full length of the glass wall were half-open to allow observation of the control centre below. A dozen or more analysts flitted around the room like worker-ants scurrying to collect food. He exhaled in resignation. "I guess it's time to get my fat-ass off the sofa and do something," he said. "I could do with a new challenge."

"Good. Welcome to your new office."

"When do I start?"

"You just did. Here..." Jennifer Ratcliff tossed an A4 manila envelope onto the desk; it landed with a heavy thud, then skidded to a halt just in front of the new Intelligence Director.

Dominic looked up enquiringly, making no move to reach for the envelope. He was reluctant to open it. The act – in his mind – meant that he was committing himself, accepting the job.

"This is everything we have on Jennings and his associates' current whereabouts. Him, his kids, Ryan..."

Dominic raised his eyebrows, still making no moves towards opening the envelope.

"We've been quite resourceful whilst you've been away." A long pause developed between them, with it an uncomfortable silence. "Well? Aren't you going to open it?"

It was Dominic's turn to smile. "I don't put much credence in information that I've not learnt first-hand." With a sweep of his hand he brushed the envelope across the desk back towards the CEO. "Besides... I doubt there is much in there that I don't already know. I may have become fat and lazy, but I've not grown stupid." He stood up and made to leave. "Like you, I've been quite resourceful whilst I've been away..."

"You didn't know Ryan was still alive..."

Allowing the door of the office to swing closed gently behind him, Dominic Schilling stood on the balcony of the mezzanine floor and looked over the control room as a General might, assessing his army for the battle ahead.

CHAPTER FIFTEEN
MILO

NO SOONER HAD THE wheels of the *Learjet 85* touched down, Milo Calland had been summoned to the White House.

A black *Cadillac* was parked up alongside the taxiway, its chauffeur standing to attention as the Deputy Director and his personal assistant clambered down a short flight of steps from the private aircraft.

President Avery Harrison had cleared his schedule, demanding an audience with him. Despite a tiring return journey from Groom Lake Airbase, an awful decision weighing on his shoulders regarding his old friend George Jennings and a long-standing dislike for the current president, Milo was never going to ignore a request from the Commander in Chief.

Half an hour later he was seated within the Oval Office opposite the President, a silver-haired man with a deep golden tan, in his mid-fifties and who, many claimed, was just keeping the president's seat warm until the next election when the Democrats were likely to win.

Narrowly gaining the presidency, his popularity had sunk deeper than the Titanic after making a u-turn with regard to public spending, increasing taxes and implementing budgetary cuts across all federal departments, most significantly Milo's own department, the CIA. President Avery Harrison had few friends in government, but this did not change the fact that he was the most powerful man in the world.

"So, I gather your trip to Groom Lake went well?" The President was leaning forward on the cream-coloured leather sofa, one of a pair situated off-centre in the room. Milo sat in the matching sofa opposite President Harrison. An oval-shaped coffee table was placed between them, atop which was a silver tray with cups, a jug of tea, a jug of coffee, milk and a sugar shaker. Alongside the tray was a bowl of fresh fruit and a plate full of sweet pastries and cake.

"It was satisfactory, Mr President," Milo replied. "It wasn't easy, but I achieved what I set out to do…"

"Good. Here, help yourself to some Pound Cake…"

Milo reached down for a hunk of cake, helping himself to a side plate and a serviette.

"I had your boss in here earlier. I was most perturbed to hear that you had a canary in the company; someone was asking about your George Jennings."

"I had heard, sir…" Milo replied hesitantly.

"Yes… terrible shame. I understand the problem has been dealt with?"

"Indeed. The individual was neutralised. Also, on learning the threat I personally saw that George was moved somewhere safe – for protection."

"Of course… protection," a note of cynicism slipped into the President's voice. "His…? Or our own?"

Milo shrugged. It was one and the same in his book.

"What of his work…? How's Project *GYGES* progressing?" It was pronounced *jhay-gees*.

Not wanting to be drawn into discussing George's work at any great length, Milo shrugged and said. "It's good. Work on the second batch is underway. We should have a viable product by the end of next year, with more to follow."

"Good… good… that's excellent. They may be operational and

reaping rewards before the next election." The President bit a large mouthful from his cake. "But, there is something troubling me…"

"What's that Mr President?"

"Some loose strands. You said the canary had been 'neutralised' but you've made no mention of what happened to the 'neutraliser'." The silver-haired man did not hide the fact that he was already privy to the answer to this. "Tell me, what fate befell this… man?"

Milo set aside his cake, returning it to the coffee table. He suddenly lost his appetite.

"Our agent was found dead at the hospital. A shot to the back of the head. Looked professional. On the plus side, before he died he'd completed what he was sent to do."

The President took a moment to consider Milo's response. "Doesn't sound much like the situation has been 'neutralised' to me," he guffawed. "Tell me, what do we know of his killer? Was it law enforcement? Do we have a handle on the situation? What are the facts?"

The Deputy Director fidgeted uncomfortably under the barrage of questions. He wasn't a politician and was unused to dealing with such people. The facts were simple:

They didn't *know* who'd shot their agent in the back of the head.

"We looked at the CCTV footage and are following one or two leads…" Milo started. "Eye witnesses indicate our target had a visitor shortly before our agent shot him; the receptionist said she was his cousin. She intimated the cousin was still with him when our agent entered his room, and saw her leave shortly after the gunshots stopped.

"The woman babbled on about another thing; a further woman arriving a little after our agent. She said her eyes had played tricks on her, though. She swore that this newcomer vanished as she entered the corridor leading to our target's private room – poof, just like that! – like a ghost… She went on to say, she couldn't have been a ghost, because if she were, she wouldn't have had need to open the doors. She could have just gone through them."

"Stressful situations are apt to make you hallucinate," the President said. "She probably just imagined it."

"Possibly. But I don't think she did."

"No? What are you suggesting?"

"Seems a strange coincidence that the person who our target had been asking questions about – *George Jennings* – also happens to be the pioneer behind a genetically enhanced super human who just so happens has the ability to make themselves invisible at will…"

"But, you said we won't have a viable product until end of next year…" The President was a little puzzled.

"We won't," replied Milo. "There's another, call it a *prototype*. Sophie Jennings, George's daughter. George tested on his own gene pool before making his research available to us. I would bet all the dollars in the BEP that this other woman at the hospital was her." The BEP or the *Bureau of Engraving and Printing*, was where all denominations of US currency was produced.

"Is this going to be a problem?"

"We did give her immunity; George's only condition for coming back to work for us, was that we left his family – including Sophie – alone."

The President sat back into his sofa and finished off his piece of cake. "Tell me… does that still apply now that she's on US soil and killing US citizens?"

Milo smiled. The agent, a skilled assassin sent to kill Spencer Roberts hardly qualified as a 'US citizen', but he liked the President's candour. "Not if she poses a clear and present danger to national security. Besides, her father's work is finished. He is in no position to bargain for her safety."

"Well, it's settled then. I'll leave you to… carry out the *executive orders*." President Harrison reached for a second slab of pound cake.

"And what exactly are the *executive orders*, Mr President?"

"The same ones we gave for Osama Bin Laden…" Taking a bite from his cake, he added (with mouth half-full), "Mmm, it's good being the President…"

On leaving the Oval Office, Milo Calland was escorted away from the West Wing of the White House by two presidential aides, and through the labyrinthine corridors that led towards the exit of 1600 Pennsylvania Avenue. Parked outside the building was the black *Cadillac* that had brought him. Climbing in, the driver, a clean-shaven young man in a regulation black suit, black tie and matching *Ray Bans*, peered over his shoulder, peeping through the opening of the partitioning that separated him and the rear passenger section.

"Where to, Deputy Director?"

"Langley," he replied, glancing at his watch. It was close to six and he still hoped to be home for tea, wanting to see his two young children off to bed. As always, it was a fantasy; work came foremost, and like most nights, what he 'hoped' and what he 'did' always had a gulf between. It was a rarity for Milo to be home with his family before ten o'clock. "Occupational hazard," he often reminded Charlene, his wife. She knew what she was marrying into when she agreed to say the vows. She dutifully stood by him, the model wife – both in looks and temperament. Besides, she enjoyed the lifestyle that accompanied a high-ranking official who had regular contact with the President.

Before arriving at 1000 Colonial Farm Road, McLean, Virginia – or Langley, now officially known as the *George Bush Centre for Intelligence* – Milo started formulating the plan that would bring George Jennings' daughter to heel. He would give it a catchy operation name, something like *Geronimo*. Everyone knew that a successful mission needed a strong name to refer by – it helped aid the drama in any spinoff book or film adaptation. Milo thought he'd call it *Operation Shakespeare*. You couldn't get a more quintessentially British reference point without it threatening to sound like a cliché. The full might of the CIA would be deployed in finding this young woman. Maybe the NSA and Homeland Security could lend a hand. Within the hour her name would be inserted within the country's Top Ten Most Wanted Fugitives list, and an image of her 'visible form' would be sought and distributed soon-after to all law enforcement agencies, stepping up the hunt.

It's not going to be easy, Milo thought. If she was invisible, how could you realistically find her in a country as vast as America?

"At least it gives us a chance to see how good an invisible soldier could be out in the field," he answered himself aloud, thinking about Project *GYGES*. Every nut had a shell. Shells could be broken.

This situation, and *Operation Shakespeare*, were no different.

CHAPTER SIXTEEN
EMILY

Emily Porter felt like she'd barely had time to take a breath as she followed Sophie's voice at a run through the corridors, down flights of stairs and eventually out of the hospital.

Armed police heading into the building gave her little notice, assuming her haste was due to fear and the continuing racket of the alarm system. An invisible hand occasionally grappled with hers, leading her in directions less obvious.

Street lighting illuminated the paths surrounding the hospital buildings. Running to the left of the Critical Care Centre, passing the *Lombardi* Comprehensive Cancer and the *Pasquerilla* Health Centres, Sophie brought her to a stop outside the garage entrance of the Georgetown University Hotel.

Out of breath, Emily doubled over in her standing position, trying to recover. She looked up to where she imagined Sophie was standing, just a step away from her. "I guess..." she started, "... I owe you one..." Her words were punctuated by gasps for oxygen.

"What were you and Ryan thinking?" Sophie scorned. "You could've died in there!"

"I..." Emily couldn't think of an excuse. She stood upright. Her heart was still pumping fast. Instead she said: "I know. We are *trying* to help you!"

"And I appreciate that." Sophie sounded quite the opposite. "Just do it from the end of a phone. I can do without these… *distractions*…"

"I think you are forgetting something." Emily held up Agent Roberts' shoes. "Without me we wouldn't know how important these are."

"Size nine brogues… Classy."

"He hid something in the heel of one of them." Emily turned the shoes over to inspect the soles. Not seeing anything obvious, she put one shoe down and paid closer attention to the one still in her hand. With a finger she probed the inside, feeling the lining for any signs of a secret compartment. She turned it back over and tapped the sole with the nail of her index finger. It sounded solid. She discarded the shoe in favour of the other.

"It's beginning to look like you nearly died for nothing…"

Emily repeated her actions from the first shoe. Probing the lining inside the shoe again, she turned it over and ran the flat of her hand over the surface of the sole. The treads were rough for the most part but worn smooth in others.

"Just ditch the shoe and let's go…"

Emily tapped the sole with the nail of an index finger once again. Solid… until the heel. The sound of the tapping changed pitch slightly – more dull, hollow.

"You were saying?" Emily noticed a very minute line of an indentation just above the surface of the flat of the heel. She tried prying it off with her nail but it seemed stuck down fast. "Do you have a knife?"

"Do I look like someone who carries a knife?" Sophie countered.

"Um, yes… actually you do!"

Sophie ignored the comment. "Here. Give it to me."

Emily held the shoe out. It abruptly disappeared into thin air as Sophie snatched it away.

"Hmm. I see," Sophie made a few more noises of affirmation. "Yes. Got it." She placed the shoe back into Emily's hand where it suddenly reappeared.

"A sliding compartment," she grunted satisfactorily. "Should have guessed that." A thin piece of hard rubber at the base of the heel had been pushed from the centre outwards to the back, to reveal a small square compartment big enough to hide any object the size of a small matchbox. Whatever was hidden in the secret compartment was steeped in shadow. Emily upended the shoe and gave it a gentle tap with the flat of four fingers. A small flat piece of plastic the size of a thumbnail came dislodged and fell out into the palm of her hand. Carefully, she examined it under the soft light of a neighbouring streetlamp.

"A flash card," she said with an air of bewilderment, turning it over one handed with her thumb. In her head she heard Agent Spencer Roberts:

"In my... shoe... you'll find... what you... want..."

———◆———

"I can't believe how easy that was," exclaimed Emily.

The two women were sitting in Emily's hotel room at the Hyatt Regency. A now visible Sophie was perched on the edge of the double bed; Emily was sitting in a chair positioned beneath the desk. Her laptop was open and booted up in front of her. She slipped the SD flash card into the thin narrow socket to the front of the laptop.

"If you think five people getting killed PLUS nearly getting shot yourself is easy, then yes," Sophie shrugged, "I agree." Within the *Chevrolet Impala* on the way to the hotel they'd heard the news reports regarding the mass shooting at the Medstar Georgetown University Hospital on the radio. Although sketchy, the reporter indicated that police were not looking for anyone in relation to the incident, that the perpetrator had been found dead at the scene. No further details were made available and the incident would soon be forgotten, absorbed into the mainstream like so many other reports – seemingly daily – of gun crime, so desensitised the American people were to such events.

"Here goes everything." Emily used her thumb to slip the flash memory card into the slot until it clicked home.

A little green light flickered on as the laptop registered its presence. A moment later a new window popped up on the screen with a list of options. Emily selected *Open folder to view files*. The window was swiftly replaced with a new window, this one presenting a list of files, mostly word documents. The topmost one, though, was a video file. Emily double-clicked on the small icon and waited for the media player to kick in.

Sophie stood up from the bed and stooped beside Emily, leaning in as the video file began to play.

A man that wasn't Agent Spencer Roberts appeared on the screen. He was older, in his late forties with short, black hair, parted at the left side. Although not overweight, his face appeared round, his nose seemingly too large and his eyes deep-set. He spoke a little nasally.

"If you are viewing this it is most likely that myself and Agent Spencer Roberts are dead, or soon will be. It's possible that our deaths are being reported as accidental; let me assure you that they are anything but. My name is Paul Lebrock. I am a senior analyst within the CIA with direct contact with the Director, Deputy Director and POTUS.

"I had arranged to meet up with Agent Spencer Roberts with the intention of helping a young woman find her father. It is for her I have made this video message." He stopped to take a drink from a disposable plastic cup.

"Until recently, my directive was to ensure that work regarding Project *GYGES* remained top secret; the nature of the work, the where and how, and the people involved, were all strictly classified. I was led to believe the work undertaken was for the benefit of the nation, for the peace of all free men, and for the good of mankind. How naive I was." The figure looked down solemnly into his clasped hands. "I fear that we are at a crossroads, and that our leaders are about to take us down a path that will have serious consequences for all of humanity – all under the guise of fighting terrorism.

"For this reason I give you all the information we have regarding George Jennings and the project codenamed *GYGES*. It is all here within this flash drive: reports, blueprints, schematics. Everything that will help you locate George Jennings and his research. But it comes with a condition, and I would beseech you personally, if I could. You need to close down *GYGES*. No good could ever come of it no matter how it's packaged.

"Sophie, I know about the diamond, and that you returned it; I know I can trust you to do the right thing…" For a moment his eyes seemed to lock onto Sophie's. It was almost as though he was able to see her standing there. "Good luck." The lone figure on the video then leant forward and manually turned off the video camera, ending the message. The screen went black as the media player window shrunk to a third of its size.

For seemingly a long time neither of them spoke, the only noise the gentle whirr of the fan in the laptop. Emily was the first to break the silence. "Wow."

"Are you being sarcastic?"

Emily shrugged. "I guess we should get this over to Ryan to take a look, see what he makes of it all." Her face took on a puzzled expression. "What's all that about *GYGES*?"

Sophie sighed. "I don't care about *GYGES*. It's my father I'm after."

"I know, that's a given. But this *Paul Lebrock* wants us to pursue it. He's given us everything and probably died because of it…"

Sophie shook her head. "For all I know he's given us nothing. I'm tired," she said, yawning. "Do what you want to do, but I need to sleep. Is it okay if I crash here?"

"Be my guest…"

CHAPTER SEVENTEEN
DOMINIC

THE TRUTH OF IT was, the new Director of Intelligence at Kaplan Ratcliff *had* wanted to accept the file Jennifer had offered him. Call it vanity or pride, he'd begrudgingly turned it away. She'd done enough for him for one day. The next turn would be for her to offer to wipe his butt.

Besides, he did have a bit of a grasp for what was going on, and what he didn't know could easily be gleaned from one of the worker ants out on the floor. *Look at them*, he thought, peering over the balustrade, *all rushing about like puppies competing for a bone. Fools.*

Not wasting a moment longer he turned and clattered down the metal staircase.

"Okay ladies," he bellowed as he descended, despite more than half the bodies in the room being male. "Listen up. I don't know if you got the memo but I'm now in charge." The thirty-odd analysts stopped what tasks they were doing and jostled for a better view. "Thank you, thank you." Dominic perched himself on the edge of a desk once occupied by Emily Porter. By the absence of clutter it was safe to assume she hadn't been replaced.

"So... I'll keep this short." Dominic looked around the room slowly, assessing his audience.

Satisfied he had all of their attention, he started: "I don't know what your objectives have been thus far, but whatever you are doing,

I want you to stop. Admit it to yourselves; it's *not* working. George Jennings took K R property and we were this close…," he raised his hand and intimated a small measure with his thumb and index finger in front of him, "… to catching him and getting it back."

Someone in the room nervously raised a hand. He was seated and in his forties. He had a 'mummy's boy' appearance and a face only a hard-pushed parent could love. Over the years he'd earned the respect of the control room, for despite his timid disposition, he had the audacity to vocalise what everyone else was usually thinking.

"Yes…?" Dominic turned his head to the apprehensive man, the look he gave seeking an introduction.

"It's Ja-Jason, sir…" he stammered. "Am I right in th-thinking that… um…"

"Spit it out Ja-Jason… we're not sanctioning overtime."

Finding some courage and slightly annoyed by the comment, Jason steadied his voice. "Wasn't it you who defected to the CIA, faking your death and helping THEM in capturing George Jennings?"

Dominic stood up making himself taller than everyone in the room. It was already quiet in the room but suddenly a heavier silence settled about the place, and an ominous tension thickened in the air.

"You know, " Dominic started, "Jason is right. It's good to get things out in the open. Clear the air. That's the only way we're going to trust one another to see this job through to the end." Dominic sat back down on the desk's edge. "I didn't defect to the CIA, as some of you believe. I was working covertly on Jennifer Ratcliff's instructions," he smiled. "You see, sometimes you need to do things out of the ordinary to get results." He didn't expand further. His audience didn't need to know the full facts. Not even he knew everything.

When George Jennings had surprisingly contacted him with a strange request of help, initially he'd balked at the idea – after all, he had been hunting the man and his family for near-on two years. He refused George's invitation – and his offer of money – hanging up on him.

He had a change of mind almost an hour later when his eyes fell upon an article about a diamond on display at a London arts and antiquities exhibition.

He had called George back and agreed to do it… on one condition.

Dominic's temporary alliance with George was just a means to an end.

The *Whisper of Persia* had been promised as his reward for helping George with an elaborate plan designed to maintain George's civilian cover, whilst getting him back to America.

Fantastic! he'd thought. His retirement fund. How easily it had seemed that he'd been bought. George had left it with him to instigate contact with the CIA, and further to plan whatever measures necessary to keep his true allegiances silent.

The only time he spoke further with George was the day his son, Charlie, was admitted to hospital after breaking his arm. A stroke of luck that set things in motion, providing him with the first move in what was to become an eventful two days. Regretfully, the move resulted in him wrapping his prized silver *Mercedes* around a tree, and a day later – not so regretfully – in the death of George's wife.

Had he been honest, he would have admitted that he HAD defected to the CIA… just for those forty-eight hours, but how would admitting that have helped his newly acquired position or the task at hand, or gained the respect and assistance of the workforce clustered around him?

Besides, that alliance truly ended when he awoke butt-naked on one of the St. Kilda islands. The deal with George was rendered null and void when his daughter posted the *Whisper of Persia* back to its owners; but he could hardly blame her after what he'd done to Harriet.

"So," Dominic started, "our objectives are simple. To locate

George Jennings and retrieve all information and data pertaining to the *CHAMELEON* project. Team leaders, I want you to collate all your information and leads, and meet with me in the…" it sounded strange, "in MY office… at five this afternoon…" Dominic stood up. "In the meantime," speaking to no one directly, "I am going to 'think outside the box' and see if we can enlist some help…"

Dominic had formulated the plan whilst addressing the control room. It was simple really. It had something to do with what Jennifer had said about Ryan Barber.

The man who'd aided George Jennings was still alive.

What's more, he was working for one of the world's leading intelligence agencies. MI6 had a wealth of resources that Dominic could only half-dream about. If Ryan had been helping George back then, it stood to reason that he was still assisting him now. With his help and the support of MI6, achieving their objectives could be made easier.

It wouldn't be easy contacting Ryan, though. It wasn't as though his telephone number was listed with Directory Enquiries. And his whereabouts were even less locatable.

But there's a proven adage; you are six people away from speaking to anyone in the country, no matter who they are. You know someone who knows someone who knows someone who knows someone who most likely knows the person you most likely want to speak to.

In the case of Ryan Barber, Dominic didn't need a long chain of people. He just knew 'someone' who would in all likelihood be the guy who could help him out; and it just so happened that he was still in the employ of Kaplan Ratcliff Biochemical and Life Sciences, Intelligence Division.

Returning to his office, Dominic secured the door behind him and marched across to the telephone. He sat down behind the desk, and using the inbuilt directory, called the 'someone' who was likely in contact with Ryan.

There were two people with the same surname in the Directory. He selected the dial button alongside the one he wanted.

Richard Cullum ('Ricky' to his mates) picked up the call on the third ring.

"Security Desk, Cullum speaking."

"Hi Ricky, long-time-no-speak…" he spoke in a casual, off-hand way.

"Dom Schilling. I'd heard you were back from the dead."

"I'm not the only one." Dominic skipped the preamble. "Listen, Ricky, I need a favour from you. I need a meeting with Ryan…"

The phone line went silent. Cullum was a slow thinker and took an age to answer the newly appointed Director of Intelligence.

"You still there?"

"Dom, Ryan's dead…"

"Try again Ricky. He's alive and well and working for MI6."

"I-I-I-," Ricky stammered before ending the call.

"Damn it!" Dominic slammed the receiver into its cradle with force, throwing his hands up in despair. He swept them through his pony-tailed hair, pulling it loose from the band.

Before he had time to re-tie his hair the phone on his desk began to ring. The display identified the caller as Cullum. Dominic scooped up the handset, allowing his hair to fall to his shoulders scruffily.

"Go on."

"Okay, Dom. He's not going to be pleased, though."

"I'm not asking you to arrange a date for me. I just want to talk business with the guy."

Cullum was silent once again which struck Dominic as odd. What was there now to mull over? After seemingly taking a long time,

Cullum spoke in a clipped tone before disconnecting once again: "I'll be in touch." The dial tone was quick in its arrival.

"Don't take too long," Dominic muttered into the mouthpiece of the receiver knowing that Cullum was already gone. He returned it to the cradle, this time less aggressively.

CHAPTER EIGHTEEN
RYAN

THE EMAIL HAD COME shortly before the phone call. Ryan was still in his office having worked late and had been finishing the last mouthful of a *Subway Melt* that had been laying in its packaging since early evening. He had been skimming through the first of a dozen encrypted files attached to the email sent by Emily Porter from Washington, deciding part-way to put together a team to work through its significance.

When the phone call came, Ryan checked the clock on the wall, its round face enclosed within a chrome-effect casing. The hands pointed to Roman numerals. The time was 2:23 a.m. Ryan worked out that it was 9:23 p.m. in Washington DC. They were five hours behind.

"Hi, Ryan? It's Emily…"

"Thank Christ you're alright! We've been getting reports of a shooting at Georgetown University Hospital and conflicting details about fatalities, but nothing concrete. What happened?"

Emily brought Ryan up to speed, explaining that Agent Spencer Roberts had given her a flash drive containing a number of files (which she'd earlier emailed him), and that a gunman had taken him out whilst she was cowering beneath a sink in the bathroom.

"He would have killed me too had Sophie not arrived when she did," Emily concluded in a tiny voice.

Ryan exhaled noisily, relieved that both Emily and Sophie were unharmed – but he knew that he'd been careless in sending Emily into the field.

"I'm sorry for putting you at risk. It was ignorant of me."

"Don't bust your balls over it," Emily urged. "Had I not gone in, Agent Roberts would have died for nothing. Have you had time to look at the files yet?" she swiftly changed the subject.

Ryan sighed, glancing at the document appearing on the centre of the large flat screen in front of him. Idly, he jabbed a finger at the keyboard, scrolling down the document. "Not really," he said. "I've barely had time to eat a sandwich, but I'm looking through one of the files now. Something about a classified project called *GYGES*…"

"From what I can gather," Emily interjected, "*GYGES* is what the Americans are calling their work into genetically engineered super soldiers, picking up from where *CHAMELEON* left off… only on a much grander scale."

"*GYGES*…? isn't that something mythical?"

"It's interesting you should think that; whoever named the project had a sense of humour. I looked it up. *GYGES* was a shepherd in the service of a king who, after an earthquake, came across a dead body from beneath the earth; he wore nothing except a ring of gold. Taking the ring he discovered that upon wearing it he turned invisible…"

"I see… a bit like the ring in the *Lord of the Rings*…"

"Yes, a little bit… without the wizards and Orcs*! GYGES* was a good person but, upon wearing the ring, he used his invisibility to seduce the queen and together they killed the king. The story suggests that, no matter how righteous a person and his beliefs, if given an opportunity to do something where there was absolutely no chance of reprisal, temptation to do it would eventually become too great.

"Theft, rape, murder; all deeds easily succumbed to by those who face no risk of consequence. I think George gave the project its name because he has a conscience. He knows – and believes – that no matter how good the intentions are, nothing good could ever come of being invisible; these *super soldiers* being no exception. Like *GYGES*, the risk of enticement from the guarantee of no punishment will be there for the taking... and all too easy."

"If that is true, surely George must think the same of Sophie?"

Emily gave pause to think, turning to look at the young woman asleep on the bed behind her. "Potentially," she said, subtly.

⸻ ❧ ⸻

A short time before Emily's email, Ryan's mobile phone had vibrated deep within his pocket. It was on silent so not to audibly interrupt his meeting with the Chief of SIS. They had been discussing the progress of his American operation (or lack of it).

Using the call as a reason to excuse himself, Ryan sauntered out of the large room and into the corridor, closing the door behind him.

"*Hi Ryan, it's Ricky Cullum...*"

Taken aback, Ryan darted into a private office to take the call. "Ricky... what do I owe the pleasure?"

"*Someone wants a meeting with you,*" Cullum skipped the pleasantries.

"Oh?"

"*Dominic Schilling.*"

Ryan sounded subdued as he grunted: "Oh..."

The conversation had continued to its conclusion in a curt and stunted manner. That had been more than four hours ago. Since then he'd spoken with Emily, had a further meeting with the Chief of SIS, had a chat with three agents (whereby he delegated the task of reviewing the files Emily had sent via email), and had a final meeting with the Chief of SIS, before he'd left the clandestine world of the MI6 building overlooking the Thames for a rendezvous point agreeable to both him and the new Director of Intelligence at Kaplan Ratcliff.

It was over a regular sized black coffee at a familiar setting that he entertained Dominic Schilling and his intriguing request for a meeting.

Dominic was already seated in the corner of the small coffee shop, nursing an iced smoothie, when he arrived. A lime green straw bobbed up and down within the tall glass. Dominic removed it, dropping it to the table.

"So, why this place, Ryan?"

The small coffee shop was situated between a newsagents and an empty old shop that was boarded up and graffiti-painted just how Ryan remembered it. It was quiet with just one other customer.

The coffee shop was where he'd committed career suicide, back in July with his call to George. His mobile had been tapped, and so it was he'd been caught red-handed as the mole within the corporation.

"I don't know," replied Ryan. "Nostalgia, maybe. Or it could be I just like the coffee..."

Dominic smiled humourlessly. "No one likes the coffee..." He sipped the smoothie. A Blueberry Banquet, a very tasty and nutritious choice, favoured by many as an alternative to breakfast. Lowering the glass, he wiped away a frothy purple moustache with the back of his hand.

"So, does Jennifer Ratcliff know that it was you who helped repatriate George with his American buddies?"

"Ryan, we all make mistakes, but this one... Jennifer and I were reading from the same page. When George contacted me for help with his plan, we saw an opportunity to flush him out."

"You meant to double-cross him?"

Dominic smiled deviously but did not answer the question. After a swig from his smoothie, he continued. "We agreed to assist George... and the CIA... but the Americans must've suspected something and played me for a fool. I nearly died because of it."

"I heard you took a holiday to the Outer Hebrides…"

Dominic grunted. "Huh! Wasn't exactly *Hoseasons*."

An awkward silence settled over the pair. It was Ryan who spoke next: "You know, it wasn't altogether surprising to get the call from Cullum today. Tell me, Dom, why the meeting? Your first day in the big chair and all?"

Dominic was slow in his response. He looked away from Ryan and stared through the plate-glass window out towards the road, where passersby strolled along, oblivious to his gaze.

"There's something I want and you can provide a means to an end."

"I'm guessing you mean Sophie?"

"No, not Sophie," Dominic replied, hesitantly. "It's George."

Ryan snickered. "Haven't we done that angle already?" He sipped his coffee. It was hot and he winced, scolding his lips. "Besides, I want George… for my own reasons."

Dominic smiled. "I know your reasons for wanting George. I know about Clara and your relationship with her. But Ryan," his tone turned serious, "this thing is bigger than all that; bigger than us and potentially bigger than anything the world has ever seen."

"But Dom, he *killed* Clara and those other people." Ten others, to be exact. Thomas Mundahl, though alive and well, was still listed as one of the dead and intended to maintain a low profile. "He should be brought to justice…"

"Justice? By who? *You*?" Dominic mocked. "What makes you so high and mighty?" He took a deep gulp from his smoothie, once again backhanding the residue from his lips. "I'm not saying you can't have George… ONCE we're finished with him. Just let us have him first."

Ryan nursed his coffee, turning the cup round in its saucer, the handle slowly pirouetting away from him. "I don't work for Kaplan

Ratcliff any longer Dom, I work for MI6. What makes you think what I want and what my employer desires is any different?"

"Because, Ryan," he started, "Kaplan Ratcliff can give them something better."

"And what's that?" Ryan asked, curiously.

"With George alive... and *CHAMELEON* reinstated... we can have what the Americans wanted. An invisible army. Besides, we just want back what's rightfully ours. If we work together we could both get what we want."

"I think you need to adjust the tense in your statement there, Dom. What the Americans wanted, the Americans now have."

"What?" A look of concern appeared on Dominic's face.

"George wasted no time in giving up his secrets." It was Ryan's turn to smile. Changing the subject, Ryan leaned forward. "Okay, say I agree to work with you on this, what's to come of Sophie? What about her, seeing as Kaplan Ratcliff invested so much in trying to reclaim her?"

Dominic shrugged. "She's flawed. You can keep her. Except..." he said with a smirk and a wink, "she does owe me a diamond."

CHAPTER NINETEEN
SOPHIE

THE WASHINGTON POST REPORTED very little of the events that took place the night before at the Georgetown University Hospital. Shootings were so frequent around America that they barely got an inch of coverage (unless they involved numerous fatalities, or took place within a school or a cinema complex).

On page six of the newspaper, a journalist had offered a brief outline of events taking place at the hospital, citing that a masked gunman had killed a patient and three staff members before killing himself. Nothing had been mentioned of Emily or Sophie visiting the hospital, or the obvious oversight – the gunman had not killed himself, instead dying from a gunshot wound caused by a different weapon.

So it was that Agent Spencer Roberts had died, but the earlier killing of his family in the car bomb received no column space at all; neither did the death of Paul Lebrock.

Suspiciously, Lebrock had died in a car accident somewhere remote in Glenmont, his body discovered within his upturned vehicle alongside a quiet road. Ryan had learnt of his death from sources within MI6 and had shared his discovery in a call with Sophie and Emily shortly before breakfast.

It was an hour later. Sophie and Emily had accepted the video conference call and were sitting at the desk in front of the laptop computer in the hotel room; on the screen was Ryan, and just out of view sat Dominic. Had he actually been in the same room as Sophie, she would have ripped his throat out for what he'd done to her mother.

Ryan had earlier explained to them that MI6 were working with Kaplan Ratcliff, and Dominic was now their Director of Intelligence. The fact that he'd killed her mother and gotten away with it did not appear to register with the MI6 man.

Sophie could barely comprehend how Ryan had just accepted him back into their lives without recrimination or reproach, yet he was quite prepared to pursue her father for the death of Clara. Seemingly, the man had double-standards.

"So, we've had time to read the files you emailed over to us, Emily, and reflect upon their importance. Unfortunately, a couple of the files are corrupt, but what we've been able to view so far..." he paused, "has been very useful."

Emily and Sophie were quiet. Ryan continued:

"Most of it, as you know, revolves around Project *GYGES*. As feared, the Americans are well-ahead with their development of genetically enhanced super humans. Further than we thought, I suspect.

"From the intelligence provided by Paul Lebrock, we've learnt that their research is taking place within a sizeable laboratory deep underground below the secret military site of Area 51 in the Nevada desert. Phase One of Project *GYGES* is complete, which means they are no longer at foetus stage and are progressing through infancy at a growth rate similar to that experienced by Sophie. It's truly remarkable; allow me to explain..."

Sophie recalled from her earliest training, her father had explained the various things that made her different to other children. In addition to the obvious ability (or curse) of invisibility, there were four other key improvements to her *abilities*: Strength, Intelligence,

Endurance and Longevity. The longevity bit meant she would live for a very long time, but only because she would age more slowly now that her body had reached maturity. Physically, she appeared to be twenty-one, but without George's interference her birth age was actually just three-and-a-half-years old.

Ryan continued. "…there are four stages to the subject's growth. Up until age two, the physical and development cycle is approximately three times the speed of a normal infant. After this, things take an amazing turn. The body then ages approximately a year every two months until it reaches the physical age of thirteen. After that it ages about a year-and-a-half every month. This continues until the subject reaches the physical age of twenty-one. After this, maturity slows to about one tenth of a normal person, allowing the subject to appear at their peak for a very, very long time."

Sophie's physical age had only recently reached twenty-one. It was hard to fathom that she would look this way for several generations.

"Okay, much of this we already know. How does this actually help us?" asked Emily.

"Well, we know that the subjects at Area 51 are likely around nine months old, give or take a few weeks. Which means, they aren't yet viable and give the Americans no advantage at all."

"What Ryan means," interjected Dominic, still in the background out of view "is, yes, they are genetically manufactured with give-or-take the same capabilities as Sophie, but they're too young to be of any real use."

"Well, they're not *exactly* like Sophie," interrupted Ryan. "That's to say, they are, except for one thing. Well two, actually. Emotion… and, they're all boys," his eyes bored through the screen and seemed to drill into Sophie. "None of them will show, feel or be capable of emotion. The intel suggests, it was felt that subjects possessing it were inherently weaker. Therefore, it was eradicated from them."

"But it's emotion that makes us human! They'll be monsters!" It was Sophie making the outburst.

Dominic leant over the desk, his head poking into view on the LCD monitor. "If they're monsters, Sophie, you'll have no qualms with doing what needs to be done."

"Dom, let's not get ahead of ourselves…" unenthused Ryan.

"What's he saying, Ryan?" asked Emily.

"Well, um…" Ryan was squirming. "It's not so simple…"

"First and foremost, it's felt that the best course of action would be to recover the stolen intelligence and, what we can't retrieve we destroy. All traces of its existence over in America is to be removed, and their Project, *GYGES*, is to be indefinitely suspended," explained Dominic with no hesitation.

"What exactly are you saying? You mean? Murder them?" The increased pitch of Sophie's voice demonstrated that she did, indeed, exhibit emotion.

Ryan sighed, almost as though he was struggling with what he was about to say. "Not really. You see, George has been playing God, making all manner of unethical decisions, whether willingly or under duress. What we would be terminating are not… technically, babies… but *clones* of babies. He's used DNA from himself and created embryos artificially. We cannot, in good conscience, allow them to grow into adulthood."

The rooms at both locations, brought together by the power of technology, went silent. Emily and Sophie, eyes downcast, looked at each other gloomily.

"How many are we… dealing with?" Emily, ever pragmatic, asked the question that Sophie didn't want the answer to.

"The first batch…" Ryan made a show of looking at a hard copy of the report, flicking through the pages. "…is 250. It's suggested more batches are to follow…"

"Great. Genocide…" Sophie spat the word out, sarcasm thick in her voice. "Thanks Dad."

"I wish we could do this mission without you, Sophie," said Ryan. "The truth is, with your abilities you're a shoo-in for the job. Area 51 is a military base and heavily guarded. It's almost impenetrable… but with you… we have a chance…"

"Do I have a choice?"

"Well…" Ryan didn't complete the sentence.

"Okay… what about my father? You've said nothing about him."

"Um…" Ryan went quiet once again.

"What's happened to George?" Emily pressed.

"Honestly, we don't know," replied Dominic. "Paul Lebrock's files indicate that George was fired from the programme; his involvement in Project *GYGES* has ceased. Unfortunately, the file which may shed some light as to his current whereabouts is corrupt and cannot be opened."

"Great… just perfect! He could be dead for all you know." Sophie stood up from the desk and stormed out of the hotel room in frustration. Had she stayed she felt like she may have smashed something – perhaps the laptop itself, ridding herself of the ugly sight of Dominic Schilling, sitting there smugly indifferent, as though he hadn't murdered her mother. The door slowly closed after her.

"Maybe, Emily, if you send us the flash drive, our computer forensic guys might be able to do something to retrieve the lost data…" Ryan offered a glimmer of hope.

"I'll Fed-Ex it; you should get it tomorrow."

"In the meantime, take a day off," suggested Ryan. "Take Sophie out, go see some of the sights…"

<hr>

Sophie wasn't too hard to find. Emily found her sitting in the main lobby, the staircase and ascending escalator situated a few feet behind her. The seats were luxurious black leather and very comfortable. The lobby was quiet, just a couple of patrons dotted about reading newspapers and drinking coffee. The smell of breakfast hung in the air. Emily sat in the chair facing the girl.

"I'm sorry," said Sophie. She looked like she'd been crying. "I couldn't listen to it any more. Or look at that man. Talk about *GYGES*... Huh! It's as though... they've lost sight of our true objective."

"You know that's not true. Ryan wants to find your father..." Emily smiled, trying to reassure her.

"Only because he wants to kill him!" Sophie retorted, vehemently.

Emily ignored the comment. "I'm going to Fed-Ex the flash drive to London. Ryan says MI6 have some computer guys who can pull stuff off corrupted discs... it's not over yet."

"You don't get it... I NEED my father!"

Emily turned away from the young woman, aware that the people in the lobby were watching them. Sophie's outbursts and obvious agitation were drawing unwanted attention.

"Shoosh... keep it down!" Emily hissed, her eyes darting around the room to see if anyone listening looked suspicious.

"We're running out of time," Sophie spoke in a hushed, serious tone. "I am using five vials of serum a day. I don't have an endless supply of the stuff."

"How much have you left?"

Sophie shrugged, trying to make light of it. "A couple of boxes..."

Doing the maths, Emily quickly calculated that Sophie only had enough serum to last ten or so days.

"Before he was taken, my father was working on a more effective antidote, maybe something even permanent, I don't know. He never got to finish his work... that I'm aware of."

Emily reached forward and took hold of Sophie's hands. "Sophie, the solution to this does not end at your father's doorstep. There's likely to be serum at the laboratory where he was working on Project *GYGES*," she smiled, adding with enthusiasm, "don't you see…? Our missions are aligned."

Sophie sighed, conceding. "Okay. I'll do this, but promise me: no-matter-what, whether he's dead or alive, you'll still help me find my father?"

"No matter what," Emily was still holding her hands. "I promise."

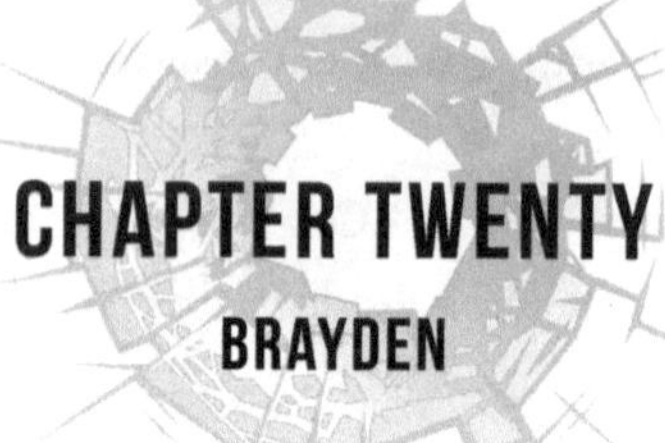

CHAPTER TWENTY
BRAYDEN

A T SIX-FOOT-TWO-INCHES, BRAYDEN SCOTT was the tallest in the room. Deputy Director Milo Calland and a commander from DEVGRU (also known as *Seal Team Six*) were in attendance. DEVGRU was a special missions unit within the Navy, often called upon by the CIA for armed support when missions needed some specialist fighting power.

The room they occupied was situated deep within Langley and large enough to host both sides of an American football team – including their cheerleading support and a sizeable portion of their away fans. The three men were seated at the large desk that filled the centre of the room; Milo and the DEVGRU commander on one side, Brayden opposite them, like they were conducting an interview. The two senior men had brown nondescript files closed in front of them. Nothing on the outside hinted at their contents; no legends or insignia, not even a 'Top Secret' rubric stamped across a corner.

Brayden wondered why he'd been summoned. He'd seen the memo issued the previous evening referencing Sophie Jennings, complete with an artist's impression of how she might appear.

A blank piece of paper would have been a more accurate portrayal, he'd mused.

The text within the memo didn't elaborate on why she was being sought; however it warned that she was armed, dangerous and high on the CIA's Most Wanted list.

"You had dealings with Miss Jennings earlier in the year, didn't you?" Milo started, his hands steepled in front of him; he was talking matter-of-factly. "Tell me, what d'you make of her?"

Brayden shrugged. "I never saw her," he replied, deadpan. She *had* been invisible at the time, so as far as he was concerned, their paths never crossed. "My mission was to extract her father. I understand she was at the warehouse when we collected him, but I never laid eyes on her. My then partner, on the other hand, got up close and personal with her. She laid him out cold during the rescue attempt of her mother..."

"Who you were holding as bait?" The DEVGRU commander interrupted. He radiated the authority of a heavily decorated war veteran. Having served tours in Iraq, Somalia and Afghanistan, he deserved every ounce of respect and attention. His hair was silver-grey and his skin deep-tanned. He looked like he spent most of his days sunbathing on Daytona Beach.

"It had been George's idea, to make his extraction look like we'd taken him prisoner; it was to preserve his cover for if – and when – he was returned."

"The mother died, didn't she?" The commander pressed.

"I later learned that, yes. It's regrettable. She was a fine lady." Brayden sighed heavily. "She was shot by someone working for us – it hadn't been sanctioned. Military police discovered her body outside an American airbase in England after she'd escaped."

"Not exactly going to George's plan, hey?" The commander grunted, turning to face the man next to him.

"We could reminisce and in a minute get our holiday snaps out, but let's skip all that. Why am I here?" Brayden spoke testily.

"Agent, I'll be frank with you," began Milo, unsteepling his hands.

"I'm promoting you to SOG. I want you to work with DEVGRU in finding Sophie Jennings. The President has issued an executive order authorising whatever force necessary in apprehending her. Dead or alive..." SOG was the abbreviation for the CIA's elite Special Operations Group, heavy hitters in covert military operations with a formidable success ratio when dealing with high risk personnel and hostage extractions, including many who fell under the 'war on terror' umbrella. This of course, included Bin Laden himself, the most high-profile target in the agency's history.

"Well, Agent Scott... are you in?" The commander was itching to get things started, hands stroking the cover of the brown folder in front of him, tantalisingly.

"I must admit, I'm interested," replied Brayden, weighing up the enormity of the situation. "But, where would we start?"

"Well, Washington is as good a place as any," answered the Deputy Director. "Just say two words and you can take a look at what the commander has beneath his fingertips."

The intrigue was too much. "I'm in," Brayden said. "On one condition... You don't saddle me with Mitch Youngs or anyone like him."

The commander didn't know who he was. "Say the word and he won't bother you or anyone else again." Getting no reply, he pushed the brown folder forcefully across the desk, watching it slide like a puck on an air-hockey table.

Brayden used his left hand to drag the file so that it was fully in front of him and slowly lifted open the cover. Immediately he was taken aback by the photo printed on the first page within.

"Is that...?"

"Yes. The first image of Sophie Jennings. In the flesh, so to speak." Milo had a copy of the picture in front of him as he spoke. The picture had been lifted from CCTV footage taken at Georgetown

University Hospital on the night of the shooting. The woman was looking almost directly at the security camera which had been placed in a corner above the entrance to the reception area. The image had been enhanced through specialist software, enlarged and airbrushed so that her identity was unmistakeable. "We followed up on a lead from an eyewitness claiming that they saw 'someone disappear into thin air'. Detectives on the scene took her statement but assumed she was in shock or delusional, and of course dismissed her statement outright. Who in their right mind would believe such a story? For us, it was our first bit of good fortune..."

"She's beautiful..." whispered Brayden, captivated.

"She's a killer," countered the Deputy Director.

"Only adds to her charm," Brayden replied, half-smiling.

Milo chose to ignore the comment. "Using face recognition software and searching the city's closed circuit surveillance feeds, we've been able to track her movements," he continued.

"So... we've been able to see where she's been," Brayden wasn't easily impressed. "Hardly cutting edge."

The commander, quietly listening to the exchange of words, leaned forward and smiled. "Agent Scott. We don't just know where Sophie's been. We know *exactly* where she is right now... *and* what she ate for breakfast."

⚊⚊⚊◆⚊⚊⚊

It was now several hours later. The day had given way to dusk and all he was waiting for was the signal so that he could give the order.

He had spent most of the day assembling his team, making and renewing acquaintances and, after formulating a plan, briefing his unit on the details of their assignment.

The last time Brayden had led a team into a mission with a goal linked to capturing Sophie Jennings, things hadn't quite gone to plan.

Even with thermal goggles and the ability to 'see' her, nothing could be taken for granted against a foe who had more in her arsenal than just invisibility. Enhanced strength, speed, and intelligence, as well as being stunningly beautiful; she was a very adept adversary.

She'd evaded capture before – at London's *Masterpiece Art and Antiques Fair* during the summer – and she hadn't even been at her physical peak. Things had changed in three months. She was now 'fully grown', and likely an even tougher opponent.

Also, Sophie Jennings wasn't alone.

Within the brown folder, beneath a couple of sheets of A4 paper, a photograph of her accomplice. Deputy Director Calland had given a brief outline of the other person, which was to say, he had learnt very little.

Brayden was looking at her image, holding the photo like it was a playing card at a high-stake game of poker. A slightly older woman with delicate features; quite bookish. The image had been taken covertly from CCTV footage from within the lobby of the Hyatt Regency earlier that day. She had been sitting close to Sophie at the time. Currently, the CIA had been unable to identify her.

He was parked opposite the hotel on New Jersey Avenue; the Capitol Building could be seen in the distance. Three other vehicles were stationed behind; government issue black SUVs, each with a retinue of four armed DEVGRU and SOG agents.

The agents wore black and had thermal imaging eyewear strapped to their heads. All of them were male, mean looking and itching for action.

Static crackled in his headset, followed by a voice: *"I have a visual on the mark."* A sniper was positioned on the roof of the building where the *West Wing Cafe* was located on the ground floor, adjacent to where the SUVs were parked. From his vantage point, Brayden could see that only a handful of customers were inside – potential witnesses, he thought.

Brayden pressed a button on his communications device and spoke into the mouthpiece which was attached to his thermal eyewear. "Standby, squadron." He flicked the switch so that he was only addressing the sniper. "Are you sure?"

"Positive. I have their photos in front of me. It's them alright…"

"Okay. Where are they now?"

"Coming down from Capitol Hill passing Upper Senate Park; just the two of them… just like you said." The sniper's voice was surrounded by hiss and crackle and a little electronic whistling.

"Are they armed?"

The sniper went silent for a moment whilst he peered through the telescopic lens of his long-distance rifle, then replied, confidently: *"That's a negative."*

"Good. Let me know when we are close. Keep them in your cross hairs and be ready should anything go wrong." Brayden switched the communications device button, changing channel to address the squad waiting with him in the SUVs. "They're coming towards us and we're not expected. Let's move…" Brayden gestured for the driver seated next to him to start, an assertive stab of his index finger pointing towards where he knew the two women were approaching. "Remember your orders, men. This comes from the White House; take her alive – if you can – but under no circumstances is she allowed to escape."

The convoy of black SUVs pulled out into the gentle stream of traffic and moved purposefully up New Jersey Avenue almost as one, the Capitol Building imposing in the near-distance, the Japanese American memorial on their left. Not far ahead was Upper Senate Park.

"You are one hundred yards from target." The sniper on the roof alerted through Brayden's earpiece.

"Copy that."

Thirty seconds passed.

"Fifty yards…"

"I have them in my sights," he spoke to no one in particular; the driver nodded in agreement. Brayden spoke into the communication's mic. "Twenty seconds…"

"Twenty yards…"

"Ten seconds…"

"Ten yards…"

"Eight seconds…" Brayden continued to count down. He was itching to go. He could see the young women, oblivious to their approaching, deep in animated conversation, one swinging a souvenir bag, the other laughing like a school girl.

"Six seconds… five… four… three… two… Now! Move in! Move in!" The driver of Brayden's SUV deliberately drove past the two women, turned onto the sidewalk, and mounted the kerb, tyres screeching, abruptly blocking the exit path. Behind them two of the SUVs had pulled up alongside the women and the fourth and final SUV had mirrored Brayden's manoeuvre and parked across the walkway, only ahead of the girls, creating a pen, cutting off any escape routes.

All the inner doors of the SUVs burst open and a phalanx of men charged in a semi-circular line towards their marks.

The young women clung to each other like a pair of cowering kittens.

"Take no chances!" shouted Brayden into his microphone – though he needn't have done as he was close enough for all to hear in the flesh. "Use the tranks!"

One of the SOG agents unholstered a sidearm, levelled the weapon at the younger woman and fired, quickly adjusting aim to shoot the other target. He shot them both at close range, a tranquiliser dart hitting one in the chest, the other in the shoulder. The effects of the drug (*sodium thiopental*) immediately incapacitated them.

Still clutching each other, they collapsed into a heap without so much as a murmur, completely unconscious.

Well-practiced, the agents acted quickly, binding the unconscious women's hands and feet with plastic ties and placing black hoods over their heads, before bundling each of them into the back of separate SUVs.

Brayden was back in the lead vehicle. With a glance out of his side window he watched as the last of his squadron closed the door of his vehicle, the convoy once again ready to move. "Okay, that was easy," he said, mildly satisfied. "Let's quickly get them in. I want them singing in time for supper."

CHAPTER TWENTY-ONE
DOMINIC

NO SOONER HAD RYAN disconnected the video conference call, his secretary had knocked on the door and hastily entered. Dominic was still sitting at the table.

"Sir Marty Heywood for you. He says it's urgent." Sianna Clemence, a woman in her mid-thirties with the skin and complexion of a twenty-something, stepped aside to allow a portly man in an ill-fitting off-the-rack black suit to enter. His Oxford University tie was hastily knotted and hung lopsided. He didn't look like a senior MI6 operative; more like an insurance salesman with a poor track record.

"Let him in," said Ryan grudgingly; Marty hadn't waited for an invitation and had already walked into the room, identifying a chair next to Dominic, and, flapping non-existent dust off the seat with the edge of a closed file. Sianna's eyes momentarily locked on Ryan's; she smiled as she left the room, closing the door behind her.

"Ryan," Marty acknowledged, sitting before opening up his folder. "I'm sorry for busting in on you like this, but I am privy to some intel that you may be interested in."

Though not in service to Ryan, Marty Heywood itched to be on his team, having once worked with him at Kaplan Ratcliff. Of late, he had been a loose end within SIS. A bit aloof with his colleagues with no direct reports of his own, and very few cases warranting merit. He was a floating handler, someone who acted as a contact within MI6.

Many questioned his value to the agency, but his past record kept him on the payroll, plus he controlled a large network of sleeper-spies reporting in from all over the world.

One such spy was highly placed within the White House, minutes earlier feeding Marty a piece of gossip that Marty knew would gain him some favour with his former colleague.

"Go on, Marty." Ryan spoke with the air of impatience, though couldn't stop himself from gazing at the file opened out in front of the handler.

"There's a whisper of a covert operation taking place in Washington later today. Something to do with *Sophie Jennings...*"

Ryan's face dropped. Within SIS, only Emily, Dominic and the Chief knew of her existence. Not even the team working on the files emailed over by Emily knew about Sophie – you needed high-level clearance.

"Oh Ryan, don't look so shocked..." Marty was smiling. "We worked together at Kaplan Ratcliff, we were practically made from the same cloth. Besides, I still have my sources within their corporation. When Sophie's name came up, and the nature of the operation, it wasn't hard for me to put one and one together..."

"Okay Marty, tell me what you know."

Marty closed the file in front of him, no longer offering any chances of a further peek. He attempted to speak, then paused, hesitating. Looking as though he was building up courage to say something big, Marty finally spoke. "I will tell you everything. But first, I want in."

"What?"

"Let me join your unit. We were good at Kaplan Ratcliff, we worked well together. And we were *friends...*"

"That was before... you left." Ryan laced his fingers together in front of him, resting them on the table. "Besides, how could we trust you?"

"Trust? I'm not the only one here with trust issues!"

"Touché!" Dominic assumed that Marty was implying Ryan's own subterfuge at the corporation, which, incidentally, was far worse than any wrongdoing that Marty had ever done, but he could well have been having a dig at Dominic with his own history of chicanery.

"Besides," Marty continued, "we're spies. Deception's in our DNA."

Ryan ignored both men. "Okay, Marty. What've you got?"

Marty smiled. "Do I get your agreement in writing?"

"Just give us the damn information already, Marty!"

Marty reopened the folder and started to read from it.

A little over two hours later, Dominic stepped through the security scanning machine at London's Heathrow airport. A small alarm sounded as something metal was detected on his body.

"Step this way, sir." A large security officer guided Dominic to one side and started waving a portable metal detector across his body, guiding it the length of his torso, before migrating south to his legs. While hovering an inch above Dominic's left knee, a beeping commenced. The security guard raised an eyebrow.

"A souvenir from Iraq," Dominic said by way of explanation. He rolled the leg of his grey flannel trousers up to reveal his bare knee. It looked no different to anyone else's, not bearing the slightest sign of scar tissue.

Accepting the reason, the security guard urged him to continue forward. Dominic rolled the leg of his trousers back down, careful not to dislodge the length of cheese wire taped within – he never travelled without some form of protection – and collected his hand luggage clogging up the conveyor belt at the end of the X-ray machine. Half a dozen steps further, he proceeded into Heathrow's departure lounge.

Marty Heywood's revelation had initially stunned Ryan. He'd slumped into his chair, accepting defeat. Like a carefully planned game of chess, he'd felt like his whole strategy had fallen apart after just one unforeseen move.

"Are you sure this is good intelligence?" Dominic had asked, unsure whether he could trust the information, or the man sitting in front of him.

"My man is within the President's security detail. He's perfectly placed and not so loyal to their cause... An executive order was given..."

And so Dominic Schilling, despite vocally protesting against travelling to America, was booked on the 16:20 *United Airlines* flight to Washington DC with barely half an hour to spare.

Stepping into Business Class within the *Boeing 777*, he admired the comfort and space afforded the higher-priced ticket holders. He walked a short distance along the aisle and found his seat – a nice, big chair that reclined into a bed. He was accustomed to Economy Class, so the upgrade courtesy of MI6 was something of a luxury. The foot-space in front of the seat was plenty big enough to sit cross-legged – he was more used to having his legs wedged between the seat in front and his own, threatening deep vein thrombosis.

He stowed his hand luggage in the overhead compartment above his seat, closing the fold-down door. As an air hostess made to walk by, Dominic took her by the arm, preventing her progress.

"Can I make a quick call on my mobile?"

The air hostess looked towards the closed door of the cockpit, weighing up her options. "Go on, but be quick. Once the Captain begins take-off procedures you'll have to end your call..."

"Thank you." Dominic keyed in a number and waited for the ringing tone.

Ryan answered after two rings.

"Ryan, it's Dom… I'm on board *UA925*… I should be landing in eight-and-a-half hours…"

Two late passengers – American – one a small man, the other a raucous large woman, bustled onto the aircraft talking loudly amongst themselves, oblivious and unsympathetic to others seated around them. The man, quite young and handsome, tripped over and fell onto Dominic. "Sorry, dude…" he said, hands held out apologetically.

Dominic ignored the acknowledgement, swapping the mobile to his other ear to better hear Ryan, failing to notice the lingering look the large woman gave him.

"The girls know you are coming…"

"Get them to meet me shortly after landing. Don't let them return to their hotel… and don't forget all the arrangements."

"Dom… everything is covered. Emily knows what we're doing."

An electronic voice sounded over the *Boeing*'s Tannoy system. *"This is your pilot speaking. We are now going through final checks before take-off. Can you ensure all electronic equipment is turned off, your seats are in an upright position and your seatbelts are fastened. On behalf of United Airlines I thank you for choosing us and wish you a comfortable and pleasant flight…"*

"Ryan, I've got to go. I'll speak to you from Washington… just ensure everything is ready." He disconnected the call and switched off the phone.

The two Americans, receiving a warning from an air hostess to quieten down, settled into their seats and made little further noise.

⸻ ❖ ⸻

The *United Airlines* flight landed on time, the pilot taxiing to the designated docking point. Within minutes he gave the cabin crew permission to allow passengers to alight.

Upon retrieving his luggage, a black diamond-quilted wheelie suitcase with gold-tone hardware, Dominic entered the gents toilets to relieve himself and for a quick wash – a ritual he carried out after any flight, domestic or international.

He placed the suitcase and his hand luggage at the back of the small room and went about his business. A moment later he was stood over a small sink, testing the taps. Both functioned adequately, running uninterrupted. He hated those spring-release taps, the ones which needed you to maintain pressure in order to release the tiniest flow of water; it all but negated the effectiveness of its function when removing a hand to wash it.

With hot water sluicing into the basin, Dominic leaned over and, using one hand, scooped up the warm liquid to wash his face. It felt good; refreshing.

The door into the toilet opened behind him; he glanced through moist eyes at the mirror above the sink; it provided a reflected-view of the washroom. The American from the aeroplane ambled in, catching his eyes in the mirror.

"Whatssup, Dude?" The American strode across to the basin alongside Dominic. There were five in all, with two free to the left of the one he chose.

What the hell? There's plenty of room in here, why use the sink so close? Dominic didn't reply, instead continued to wash, hiding his irritation at having his space invaded.

"Flying's a bitch ain't it?" The American continued, simply standing next to Dominic, making no move towards using the sink, content on making conversation.

Dominic grunted, hurrying with his wash. Finishing up, he stood and crossed to where a paper towel dispenser was screwed into the wall, alongside it was an electric hand dryer. His back now towards the American, he chose the less environmentally friendly option. He pulled a wad of light-blue paper towels and dabbed at his glistening, wet face.

Behind Dominic, the American turned a tap on but didn't touch the steady stream of water falling to the basin. He was watching Dominic, studying him.

Dominic glanced at the mirrored button of the electric hand dryer, seeing a condensed version of the room behind him. He dropped the soggy paper towels into a bin and edged over to the hand dryer, pressing the button to activate a surge of heated air from the electrical device. Placing his hands beneath the heat-stream gave him a plausible reason for standing there; all the time watching the American in the reflection of the dryer's big mirrored button.

"Is this… your first time… here in America?" He spoke casually, almost genuinely interested.

Dominic watched the American pull out a gun from behind him, hidden beneath his jacket, probably stowed beneath the waistband of his jeans. Deftly, he was attaching a silencer to the weapon, screwing it on clockwise, making absolutely no sound.

"No, I've been here before…" replied Dominic, playing out the scene, giving no hint that he was aware of the situation unfolding behind him.

"Too bad it's your last!" The American aimed the pistol at Dominic's back and fired.

BANG!

The bullet exploded loudly from the gun. All a silencer does is make a big gun sound like a small gun (120 decibels instead of 140), and in a built-up area, confuse the origin of the noise.

Seeing the American raise the gun towards him, Dominic made a split-second decision, throwing himself heavily to the floor as the gun boomed and the bullet punched a hole the size of a golf ball into the wall beside the air-dryer. Within a roll, he picked himself up and charged at the American as he brought his weapon down to bear on his advance.

Shoulder-slamming into the American, Dominic propelled him like a fullback at the *Super Bowl*, charging him across the short distance of the washroom to pummel into the furthest wall. The American, whose finger was still pressed against the trigger of his weapon, fired again; this time the bullet pulverised one of the washbasins. Water began to geyser up into an arc. A third shot punched harmlessly into the ceiling.

Grabbing hold of the American's gun arm, Dominic repeatedly smashed it down hard against the floor, crushing his fingers to a bloody mess until he released the pistol; it skidded across the wet tiling, ending up in a puddle beneath the shattered sink.

The American smacked Dominic hard with a karate-chop against his neck, the blow missing any vital pressure points, the strike barely causing a problem. Dominic retaliated by squeezing both hands around the American's throat, applying maximum pressure with strangulation his intention.

Not to be overcome, the American kicked Dominic hard in the groin, the shock and sudden pain causing him to loosen his stranglehold and sending him wheeling backwards; clutching himself and winded, he crumpled to the floor.

The American, seeing the gun laying in the puddle, dragged himself slowly across the room, sliding through the expanding pool.

"No... you... don't," Dominic growled, breathlessly. Recovering enough, he reached absently beneath his left trouser leg and tugged the cheese wire loose.

Just as the American's bloodied hand scrabbled with the butt of the wet gun, Dominic staggered up behind him and fell onto his legs, the ends of the cheese wire held as a garrotte. Crossing his arms to form a wire ring, he added to the American's struggle by bringing the wire over the man's head and pulling the loop closed; effortlessly and effectively compressing his windpipe. For several moments, the American flailed in the expanding puddle like a fish out of water, his hands frantically clawing at the wire tightening around his neck, all whilst he moaned and whimpered the strangest of guttural sounds.

The American's body relaxed before his mouth did, and as the man died beneath Dominic's weight, a groan escaped his lips with his final exhalation. Releasing the garrotte, Dominic allowed the American to slump forward, his face hitting the slick tiles.

Standing up, catching his breath, Dominic considered the scene in front of him. The still-gushing water from the leaking washbasin, the bullet holes in the ceiling and the wall next to the air-dryer, and the dead body lying across the floor.

"This is why I hate coming to America," he sighed, before retrieving his suitcase and hand luggage, and vacating the washroom.

CHAPTER TWENTY-TWO
EMILY

DUPLICITY ONLY COST **$200**. Their resemblance was not exact, but for a casual observer or someone looking for them from a distance, the two girls were a good-enough likeness to match their description.

Blame it on the economic downturn, but Emily had no trouble finding two willing participants to take part in her elaborate plan. What was surprising was how quick and easy the transaction was. On two separate tables in a small coffee shop within which Emily and Sophie were resting, they found their doppelgangers. American teens were so malleable, it beggared belief!

Of course, the reason Emily gave the two young women for impersonating her and Sophie, wasn't exactly the truth. Had she shared the real reasons, neither of them would have been willing to take part and most likely would have run to get the first policeman they could find. Instead, Emily concocted a story about being pursued by an ex-boyfriend who wouldn't accept that their relationship was over, and that he was following her and her sister (Sophie masqueraded as her younger sibling for the purpose of the tale); Emily pleaded for their help, offering each woman $100 as a reward for their assistance. All they needed to do was swap clothing and walk down New Jersey Avenue to their hotel. They would re-swap the clothing, Emily had assured them, at the hotel a bit later.

From a safe distance, Sophie and Emily watched their doubles heading towards the hotel through a cheap pair of binoculars they shared. Dressed in their clothing and wearing sunglasses, even Emily couldn't tell them apart.

"Do you think Ryan was right?" asked Sophie, referring to the warning received during his call earlier that day. She looked away from the two girls and started scanning the area to the front of their hotel through the magnified lenses.

Emily trained the binoculars on the roof of the *West Wing Cafe*, turning the knob at its centre to focus.

"Yes, he was right," Emily replied, matter-of-factly. Through the binoculars she made out the small, prone figure of a man in black clothing, a rifle pointed ahead of him. Further scrutiny revealed others in situ, waiting in cars, loitering on corners or sitting in restaurants. It was clear that an ambush had been prepared.

A minute later and three black SUVs pulled out into traffic and headed towards their replacements. Sophie focused on the two girls masquerading as them, both talking excitedly, one swinging the souvenir bag Emily had given her.

"Here we go," whispered Emily, now watching the spectacle unfold. With the Upper Senate Park on their right, the three SUVs pulled up alongside, behind and in front of the two young women, boxing them in. A swarm of men surrounded them, brandishing rifles.

"Will they be all right?" enquired Sophie as they watched one of the men remove a firearm and shoot the two women, point blank. She gasped, flinching from imagined gunshots before turning away.

Emily was slow in her response, still watching the drama play out. Truthfully, she didn't know. She was unused to fieldwork; until recently she had never been exposed to violence or peril. She felt terrible and nauseous, tasting bile at the back of her mouth. When she finally spoke she feigned confidence, more to reassure herself. "They'll be real pissed. Otherwise, they'll be fine... eventually," she sighed, hoping it wasn't a lie. She added: "They've been neutralised with tranquiliser darts."

Sophie returned to looking at the spectacle once again, watching as four men restrained their body-doubles, tying their hands and feet, before covering their heads with black bags.

"Should we help them?"

It felt wrong, but after giving it some thought, Emily replied: "No. We need to use them to buy us some time. Let's make the most of it to go get our things. It won't be long before the Americans realise they've been duped."

--- ---

Half an hour later, Emily was dying her shoulder length blonde hair over the sink in the hotel bathroom. With a bottle of *L'Oréal* hair dye in one hand, she applied the dark orange liquid liberally all over with the other. The instructions, and the corresponding model on the box, indicated that the end result would give a natural, red-head look. A glance in the mirror returned an image that wasn't what she expected. Her hair was neon-orange; small beads of dye streaked down her forehead and the side of her face.

She walked into the hotel room. Sophie was hurriedly packing.

"How do I look?" Emily asked, seriously.

"Is it supposed to be the colour of a pumpkin? I thought the idea was to NOT get noticed!" Sophie was laughing.

"It will change, you'll see." Twenty minutes and a phone conversation with Ryan later, Emily had rinsed her hair and was now almost unrecognisable.

Tied in a tail, her hair was now a deep auburn colour. A little of the dye stained her skin around the edges of her face, however it was barely noticeable.

"I think I might keep this colour." Emily crossed the room and assessed the luggage that Sophie had packed. "Is this everything?"

Sophie nodded. She'd opted for a less-drastic disguise; a *Washington Capitals* baseball cap, beneath which her hair was tied-up into a bun. As she could make herself invisible quite literally at the drop-of-a-hat, she didn't think it necessary to colour her hair.

"It might be better if we go separately," suggested Emily.

"Where are we going?"

"Somewhere safe. Off the grid," replied Emily, grabbing the small purple suitcase she'd travelled with and another case supplied by MI6 containing the laptop, a handgun, bullets, and various other items that she'd had no time to check or inventory.

Sophie picked up her sports holdall and backpack. "Good, I guess we should go. They've probably figured out those two girls they grabbed aren't us by now..."

"There's another thing..." Emily spoke as she led the way out of the hotel room. She didn't know how to tell Sophie that Ryan had sent Dominic over to assist them.

"Go on," urged Sophie, seeing the torment on the older woman's face. She closed the door behind her.

Emily was standing still, just ahead in the corridor. "Well... you're not going to like it," she said.

CHAPTER TWENTY-THREE
GEORGE

THE MEDICAL FACILITY WAS deep within Guantanamo Bay, and George Jennings had been drifting in and out of consciousness for four or more hours. A saline drip was attached to the back of one hand, the cannula taped over four times with *steri* strips; another bag of fluids was being transfused via his other hand. There were a number of wires attached to his body and head, all leading to electronic machines whirring and bleeping behind him.

He was lying in a regular hospital bed in a private room that overlooked the bay. A glance through the window gave George a spectacular view of the dock not too far in the distance, and the clearest of blue skies above. It wouldn't be difficult to imagine being on holiday on a tropical island.

George chuckled hoarsely. He guessed he was half-right in his musings. He just wasn't on holiday. A peep to his left confirmed it.

An armed guard stood sentry outside his door dressed in the blue and grey working uniform of the Navy. Beyond him bustled medical staff dressed in scrubs.

George tried to talk, but nothing escaped his lips. Just a burst of empty air. His mouth felt desert-dry and his throat prickled with razor blades. He attempted to speak again, this time with a bit more gusto: "He-llo?" he rasped.

The guard at the door half-turned, acknowledging that he'd heard him. He said something to someone out of view and a moment later a plain-looking nurse in a pale-blue uniform stepped in. The badge pinned above one breast gave her name as: Nurse J. Hanwick.

"Mr Jennings? Do you know where you are?" The nurse stood next to him, reached for a temporal thermometer and ran it across George's forehead. The gadget bleeped and the nurse recorded the reading on a chart.

"Guantanamo Bay," George croaked. For the first time he noticed the drips, the lines and all the medical equipment placed about him. "What happened?"

"Let me take your blood pressure," she replied, feeding a cuff around his arm (careful of the intravenous tubes and wires), fastening it tight about his left bicep, and then pressing a button on the blood pressure monitor. The cuff ballooned and seconds later the monitor began to buzz and warble, numerals flickering on the LCD screen before settling on his results. The nurse jotted the systolic and diastolic readings upon George's chart.

"Nurse? Why did I black out?" It came out as a whisper.

"At first, we thought it was *neurovascular syncope*, a fancy way of saying you fainted, which is a result of the heart slowing down, the blood vessels widen instead of narrowing and blood pressure falls, thus depriving the brain of full blood supply. It's quite common. Usually, it takes less than a minute to recover."

"So, nothing serious then... can I get some water?" George sounded gravelly.

"I said 'at first we thought'... You were unconscious for more than an hour, and have been slipping in and out of consciousness for four hours since." The nurse poured George a plastic beaker of water from a jug on a side unit. Ice-diamonds chinked and sparkled within the translucent liquid of the jug as she placed it back down. George accepted the water and drank deeply.

"So, why did I black out?" he repeated.

The nurse made to reply but shook her head subtly. "The doctor will answer all your questions," she replied, but her eyes told him something else. They looked deep and remorseful.

George finished the water and offered the empty beaker back. The nurse refilled it and placed it on a rolling table, so that it could easily be wheeled above or away from the bed.

"The doctor knows you are awake so will be with you shortly. We're just waiting for some test results."

"Test results?" George probed.

The nurse smiled, almost apologetically, but did not reply. She placed George's medical chart at the end of his bed, turned away, then exited the room.

———— ⬥ ————

Dr Beckerman was standing in an office adjacent to the ward where George was lying. The overhead lights were off and the room was lit only by the glare from the large VDU screen hanging on the wall. Beckerman was staring at the MRI scans – half a dozen images of George's brain from differing angles, appeared alongside each other on the forty-two-inch monitor.

The nurse walked into the room and stood next to the doctor who continued to study the electronic representations.

"Is that George's scan?"

Beckerman sighed. "Yes," he replied. "See the dark mass there…?" He prodded an index finger at a dark circle at the centre of what was George's brain. "That's the reason Mr Jennings collapsed earlier, which is an altogether bizarre occurrence. It's surprising that he's not experienced any more obvious symptoms before."

"Unless he did, but thought nothing of it… or was too scared. You know what *men* are like!"

Beckerman ignored the slur, but agreed with the sentiment.

"What type do you think it is?" the nurse asked, hoping to distract the doctor from dwelling on her statement further. "Could it be benign?"

Beckerman shrugged. "By its shape and the ring-enhancing lesions, I'd say it's a glioblastoma… and a well-fed one at that; Christ, it's a beauty." After a moment of silent admiration, he added: "A biopsy would certainly confirm what we are dealing with, then we can start planning how best to treat it. I'll need to have an O.R prepared."

"I can arrange that," offered the nurse.

"Sure, thanks. I probably ought to give Mr Jennings the *good* news…" Beckerman muttered, sarcastically.

⸻ ⬥ ⸻

His head pounded like there were half a dozen pneumatic drills smashing the inside of his skull. He didn't know what was worse, though. The thumping headache, or the itch from beneath the bandage. It was three hours after the biopsy and just five minutes since Dr Beckerman had crept into the room, a cold draught following after him; he was like a harbinger of death.

"And you are sure you never experienced any of these symptoms? Headaches? Seizures? Nausea? Vomiting? Memory Loss?"

George had said "No," to each of these in order.

"George. I'm sorry… it is cancer. Glioblastoma. Very aggressive, and a bit like my mother-in-law at Christmas; a hell of a pain to get rid of."

George had smiled at the doctor's wit. The joke about having cancer, that was a hoot.

"I'll let you take it all in and pop by a bit later. I'm sure you'll have plenty of questions. Jennifer will check in on you periodically."

No sooner was the doctor gone, George reflected on the events of the past thirty-six hours. Before then, life was so vastly different. Working on Project *GYGES* deep below Area 51, his wife had still been alive (he believed), and, least of all (in his order of priorities), he didn't have cancer.

Why?

Why me?

The two questions most asked by those afflicted with a terminal illness. He felt the tears before he knew that he was crying, and found his thoughts were wandering to his children; Meredith, Stanley and Charlie. And of course, to Sophie.

He didn't know it, but he would never see them beyond his dreams again.

"Where are you Sophie?" he wondered aloud. She would come for him, he didn't doubt. Together they'd gone for Harriet. She would rescue him from imprisonment, George was certain; but the cancer? No one could rescue him from that death sentence.

Dr Beckerman hadn't needed to feed him all the info relating to the glioblastoma; he already knew about it. He was a geneticist and had done many studies relating to cellular growth, including cancerous ones. Glioblastoma was one of the nasty ones with a zero cure rate and a life expectancy of just fifteen months (with treatment) – or four months (without).

The nurse – Jennifer – stepped past the guard (still on duty) at the door, and walked in.

"Are you okay, George?" she spoke softly.

George tried to smile but found that his emotions betrayed him, his face creased up; he blubbered uncontrollably, tears rolling down his cheeks like transparent ball bearings. Some would assume that George cried because he'd just learnt of his overwhelming fate, that he grieved for his own mortality; Jennifer was no different. She sat on the bed beside him and placed a comforting arm about his shoulder, absently pulling him to her chest. She was feeling pity for the man, regardless to the crime which saw him placed within Guantanamo Bay.

The truth of it was, he wasn't crying for himself. He was crying over the realisation that his wife was dead, that he would never see Harriet again, and that his children were far removed from him.

There was also the stark reality of not being able to remember when he'd last seen her, or now even being able to recall what she looked like.

Harriet Jennings' face was now just a blur.

CHAPTER TWENTY-FOUR
RYAN

TRUE TO HIS WORD, Ryan had accepted Marty Heywood into his trust and rewarded him with a place in his unit. The Chief of MI6 had merely raised an eyebrow when Ryan informed him later that day. At first, the most senior man in MI6 said nothing in the grand office that overlooked the Thames. They were sitting opposite each other, a large, ugly antique desk between them. There was no one else in the room, though the Chief's secretary had presented a tray with glasses and a fresh jug of water a moment before.

"I suppose he'll be wanting a raise?"

Ryan shrugged. "We didn't talk money," he replied. "The only topic discussed was the imminent danger posed to my assets Stateside."

"And what have we done to counter the threat?" the Chief queried.

"I sent Dominic Schilling on the first flight to Washington and warned Emily of the immediate danger."

"You know you can't trust him," the Chief cautioned. "The guy's a mercenary."

"I know that, but you've heard the old saying, 'keep your friends close, but your enemies…'"

"…closer," the Chief interrupted. "Yea, yea… I know all that," bored of the quote.

"I'm doing just that," Ryan continued, pausing briefly, as though reflecting. "Besides, I have someone else on hand in DC should I need it. Dominic has his uses, so I think we can give him some credit; plus, he reported in a short time ago with news that he'd been attacked at the airport."

The Chief showed no surprise. "What happened?"

"Someone on the flight followed him to Washington and tried putting a bullet into his back in an airport washroom. He's fine, a little banged up I guess... more than can be said about his dance partner."

"And what of our two assets?" quizzed the older man, reaching for a glass from the tray on the desk and pouring himself some.

"They used deception to evade capture and managed to clean out their hotel room of anything incriminating. They're meeting up with Dominic somewhere safe as we speak."

<hr>

Ryan was back in his office and on his third cup of coffee when Marty Heywood rapped knuckles to his door. A quick glance at the clock on the wall confirmed it was late (or early): 12:45 a.m. Ryan was looking at the newcomer as he entered the office.

"Haven't you got a home to go to?" Ryan asked, disinterested.

"You can hardly talk," Marty slung back, sitting without waiting for permission.

"Yea, well... I hardly have family to go home to," Ryan said, sadly. "But you do."

Marty smiled, "Did: past tense. My wife left me, taking the kids."

Ryan chuckled. "I'm sorry... two lonely old farts with nothing but work to keep us company... I owe you my gratitude. Your intelligence allowed Emily and Sophie to employ measures to counter the planned attack on them."

"Glad I was able to earn my dinner today," Marty replied, humbly.

"So, what grand news are you here to present me with this time?"

Marty waved a hand casually in front of him. "I've been familiarising myself with the material Emily emailed over to you… there's some amazing stuff in there."

"Yes, I know. Analysts have been picking at it all day." He didn't know whether it was Marty's voice, or the effects of the coffee wearing off, but Ryan was feeling very tired.

"Project *GYGES* is all very exciting, don't you think?"

"Yes, yes, very exciting," he replied dismissively with a yawn, "what of it?"

"Well, I just wondered what our true objectives are? I mean, an invisible army? How cool would that be?"

"Marty. You've been given all the info, you've read my memo – we're on the same page. Our remit is simple: find and liberate all research and data that was stolen from Kaplan Ratcliff, and destroy everything else relating or pertaining to Project *GYGES*."

"Sounds stellar," mocked Marty. "But, what I really want to know is: how broad is our stance on 'liberating all research and data'? Does that include live specimens?"

"If you've familiarised yourself with what's been learnt from the files sent over by Emily, you'll know that what the Americans have created is far removed from what George Jennings and Kaplan Ratcliff envisioned."

"Okay… so, what's the answer?" pushed Marty.

"We have no use for their live specimens, so the answer is quite self-explanatory."

"But, Ryan… they're just children." Marty sounded horrified.

Ryan sighed, closing his eyes. "I didn't say I liked it," he said, "but we can't let the Americans have these super soldiers; what do you think would happen to the world if they possessed such a weapon?"

"Okay, but if it's not the Americans, one day it'll be someone else,"

Marty emphasised. "Maybe the Russians or the Chinese, terrorists, or perhaps, someone worse!"

"Maybe," agreed Ryan, thinking over what Marty said. "But then, if someone is going to have it, why not us? After all, the science was developed here in England… it is ours by rights."

"And what about the mad scientist?" Marty asked, almost hesitantly.

"What d'you mean?" Ryan raised his eyebrows.

"Shouldn't we take care of him also…?"

"No." Ryan was quick to respond, the word punctuated by an air of finality.

Marty ignored the man. "Won't they just get him to start over? They still have him on their leash…"

"I guess… but finding him isn't so simple. The Americans have moved him… but it's not your concern… I have my own plans with dealing with George Jennings," said Ryan firmly.

"I guess, then, we need the location of this Project *GYGES*." Marty appeared to move on from George Jennings but was still mulling this obvious problem over in his head.

"We already have that," said Ryan, smugly.

"Really? It wasn't in the files emailed over by Emily."

"It was," asserted Ryan. "I just removed that information before passing it on to the analysts."

A look of surprise flashed across Marty's face. "Seriously?"

"You betcha."

"Ok… look, see that… I'm intrigued," he was pointing to his face. "Where are they?"

Ryan stroked his chin thoughtfully, as though contemplating his response.

Seeing the reluctance on his boss' face, Marty spoke again:

"Come on, Ryan. I can help…" Marty's look was imploring. "Remember our days at Kaplan Ratcliff?"

Ryan sighed, nodding slightly. "Groom Lake, Nevada."

"Area 51?" inquired Marty.

"Well, you know the Americans don't officially recognise the existence of the place… but yea, Area 51. Deep below ground beneath a large aircraft hangar. There's a secret laboratory."

"So, what're we going to do next?"

"Next?" asked Ryan, incredulously. "We're already doing something now." Seeing the other man's inquisitive look, he added: "Why d'you think I sent Dominic to Washington in the first place? It wasn't a vain attempt at rescuing Sophie and Emily. Ha," he laughed. "They can take care of themselves."

━━◆━━

Closing Ryan's door behind him, Marty pulled out his phone from a pocket in his trousers and used a speed dial to call his contact in the White House.

Talking as he walked, the veteran MI6 agent spoke swiftly in a hushed tone into the handset pressed tightly against his face. The recipient's side of the conversation was contained within Marty's ear.

"Can you help me with a problem? It's George Jennings… uh-huh, yes… he's the problem… yes… You know where he is? Okay… I'm sure… yes… because *GYGES* needs to be terminated… that's affirmative." With no valediction, Marty ended the call.

He looked about him nervously, his eyes falling upon a CCTV camera. Quickly he turned and headed away down the corridor in the direction of his office.

CHAPTER TWENTY-FIVE
DOMINIC

HALF EXPECTING A TAIL, Dominic scuttled out of the washroom, dragging his suitcase along on overworked wheels and carrying his handluggage over his shoulder – he appeared as a passenger late for a flight, though one who was wet, dishevelled and a bit bloody; plus he was travelling in the wrong direction, away from the terminal.

A backward glance confirmed his fears. The woman accompanying the American who'd tried to kill him was following, matching him stride-for-stride, and not encumbered by any luggage.

Dominic cursed.

Dodging dozens of slow-moving people and others just standing about, Dominic made to exit Dulles International Airport via the electronic doors marked as 'Door two' on the map. Rushing through, jostling and barging past anyone blocking his path, ignorant to the many exclamations and expletives, he hastened towards a 'Taxi cabs' sign to his left.

Turning the corner he faced a queue of yellow cabs waiting patiently for fares. Thankfully, there were more cabs than there were people in proximity.

Feeling the extra pounds gained since returning from St. Kilda, Dominic ran the short distance to the first taxi.

"Are you for hire?!" Dominic asked, breathless and anxious.

"Sure…" The driver was about to climb out. "Let me help you with your…"

"No time." Dominic squeezed his suitcase into the back seat ahead of him, piling in beside it, tossing his hand luggage carelessly atop the case. Slamming the car door behind him, he barked: "Just drive… quick! There's a hundred extra in it for you if you can get me outta here, no questions asked."

"Okay, boss." The taxi driver was dark-tanned and wore a garish, Hawaiian shirt. Dominic saw his eyes dart to and from him as he steered the yellow cab away; probably wondering what trouble his paying customer was running from.

Daring a look behind him, Dominic watched the woman who'd clearly been following him since London appear at the taxi rank. Hunkering low, he was pleased to see that the woman looked frustrated, her body language telling him what he wanted to see; she was too late, she had lost him. Comically, he thought he saw her stamp her feet.

Pulling out of the airport, taking the Dulles Access Road, the driver dared to speak: "So, boss… where're we headin'?"

Dominic was hoping to speak with Ryan before leaving the airport. It was Ryan who knew his destination. Dominic had relied on MI6 to make all the arrangements, source a location to bring him together with Emily and Sophie. Because of events outside of his control, he was a bit in the dark.

"Um…" Still catching his breath, Dominic tried to think. "Capitol Hill," he instructed. It was as good a place as any, and the last known place where Emily and Sophie had been staying.

Reaching into his pocket, Dominic retrieved his mobile phone and called London. He was conscious to the time, but Ryan had made it clear that he should call as soon as he arrived.

The plane had landed more than an hour earlier, and most likely the MI6 man had expected a call sooner. The time locally was 10:35 p.m. In London it would be 3:35 a.m. He hoped that Ryan was still awake. Dominic didn't delay any further.

Ryan picked up on the fourth ring.

"You made it… I was beginning to get worried."

"They know that I am here," said Dominic, skipping the verbal foreplay. He took a moment to fill Ryan in on the details; the brash Americans on the plane, how one of them had tried to kill him in a washroom, and then being pursued by the other across the arrivals lounge. "I managed to lose her at the airport." Curiously, it hadn't been difficult, he reflected.

"Okay, Dom. I'm going to tell you exactly what I told the girls earlier…"

"Are they okay? We weren't too late, or anything?"

"No, no, they're fine. They played out an elaborate plan that will embarrass our counterparts across the pond. But listen: Washington is too hot for us now. They will already know that we fooled them with our body-double stunt, and with knowledge of your arrival too, they will no doubt be suspicious as to what our intentions are."

"Surely they won't think that we are all working together?"

"Dom. They maybe CIA, but they are not entirely stupid…"

"Entirely…" Dominic chuckled at the subtle use of humour.

"Listen, Dom: they'll know that you are working with MI6, trust me. And they'll know Sophie is there looking for her father. So, you're all going to have to be extra careful. I've arranged for you to stay somewhere low-key."

"So, I guess I'm not booked in the Hyatt Regency, then?"

"No."

"Don't tell me you've put me up in one of those hicks-ville motels out in the sticks."

The line went quiet for a moment, before Ryan returned with an indecisive, *"Um... It was Sophie's idea..."*

"That's just perfect."

In the dark, the dilapidated single storey motel standing in the foreground looked like something from a slasher-movie, possibly belonging to *Norman Bates*.

The cab pulled into an almost-empty car park and stopped just a short way from the entrance to the reception. A tatty 'vacancies' sign hung from the door, moth-eaten and uninviting, and an old neon light confirming room availability, glowed brightly In the window, though two of its neon letters flickered on and off.

Dominic paid the taxi driver the fare plus a hundred dollars, as promised. Dragging his luggage out of the back of the car, he sneered at Sophie's choice of hotel; it made a *Travelodge* look like the *Ritz*. Before he was able to change his mind, the taxi sped back in the direction they had come.

"I guess no expense is being spared, Ryan," Dominic muttered under his breath. He picked up his hand luggage and pulled up the handle on his suitcase, dragging it behind him as he entered the motel reception.

A small bell jingled as the door opened.

The reception area was almost as uninviting as the motel's facade. The service desk was littered with papers and coated with a thick carpet of dust, and the man appearing through a narrow doorway behind it was just as tidy. Wearing a dirty-grey T-shirt and a buttonless black cardigan, he stopped just short of the desk. Unfortunately, his smell didn't. Dominic wrinkled his nose at the stale odour that assailed his nostrils and could not stop himself from gagging.

"Can I help you?" He had a croaky voice.

Dominic tried to ignore the smell as he considered the motel's owner standing before him. He looked terrible – much worse than he smelt; a long rectangular face, yellow-skin, and sunken-in eyes, he was bald with big, dark liver-spots. Patches of stubble grew around his face, chin and neck, a poor relation to a beard.

"I have a reservation," replied Dominic through gritted teeth. He'd never forgive Ryan for this. The taxi driver had driven them past a Holiday Inn just down the road; hell, they'd even driven by a burnt-out shell of a building; anything would have been better than this.

"And you are?"

"John Virgo." Ryan had booked the motel using aliases for Dominic, Sophie and Emily. For Dominic he'd picked a name famous in the sport of snooker.

"ID?" wheezed the motel owner.

"I'll pay you extra if we go without," said Dominic.

"Whatever…" The man disappeared for a moment through the narrow doorway and came back with a key on a fob. He walked around the service desk and out through the hatch. "Your friends arrived earlier. This way. I'll take you to your room, it's next door to them."

Dominic followed the ill-looking man out of the reception, the bell on the door jangling excitedly as it closed behind them.

"Here," they stopped outside room number eight. The motel owner unlocked the door and led Dominic in.

Taking him by obvious surprise, and failing to hide it, Dominic appraised the room; it was clean and smelt fresh (threatened by the owner's lingering presence).

"There's towels and toiletries in the bathroom, and cable TV, but you need to pay for that separate. If you and your friends can keep the noise level down, myself and the other guests would appreciate it…"

Other guests? Dominic raised an eyebrow but said nothing.

"Enjoy your stay."

"What about food?" queried Dominic. The only meal he'd had since London, was a child-sized microwave meal served during his flight to Washington, DC.

"There's a shack down the road that does steak, cooked how you like. Tell 'em Ray sent you and he'll throw in a slice of warm cherry pie for free..."

The smell, which Dominic had started to grow accustomed to, left as swiftly as the motel owner did.

CHAPTER TWENTY-SIX
BRAYDEN

EVEN CLOSE UP, THE two girls had looked identical to the photograph taken from the CCTV footage earlier that day at the Hyatt Regency hotel. Plus, with wearing the same clothing, it stood to reason that the women – held separately within the interrogation rooms – without a hint of doubt, were Sophie Jennings and her accomplice (the still-unidentified blonde girl wearing glasses).

"I told you, you've got the wrong girls!" insisted the older girl with a passing resemblance to an unknown Emily Porter. She had a strong American accent, itself a good indication that she was telling the truth.

The fact that neither girl had resisted arrest or given any hint of a struggle had initially surprised Brayden; but it hadn't set any alarm bells ringing.

Now, two hours later, Brayden started to believe the girls were telling the truth. Not long after, he would be totally convinced. Had he asked to see their identification sooner, the whole embarrassing episode could have been curtailed.

Instead, after two-and-a-half hours of ruthless questioning, sight of their individual driving licences and an ID check through a database, their story was corroborated.

After that debacle, the least Brayden could do was offer the girls a ride home. As he closed the car door on the young women seated in the back of a black government issue SUV, Brayden's mobile started to ring. A glance at the screen gave no indication as to the caller. He accepted the call.

"Y'ello?"

"Brayden Scott?" A confident, female voice filled his ear.

"Speaking," he replied.

"Please hold for the President…"

A moment later and President Avery Harrison was on the phone. News had reached him regarding the botched attempt at seizing Sophie Jennings.

Cutting short all attempts at pleasantries, President Harrison spoke with a harsh, impatient tone. *"I was hoping to be calling you with congratulations on a successful mission. Instead I find out that you were duped by a couple of schoolgirls."*

"They looked the same," bemoaned Brayden, sounding meek and unconvincing. "They were also wearing exactly the same clothing."

"Yet, DEVGRU," the President interrupted, *"had no problems accurately identifying Bin Laden in Pakistan the other year in the middle of the night…"*

Brayden knew better than to defend himself further. "I'm sorry, Mr President. I'll tender my resignation with immediate effect."

President Harrison started to laugh. *"Don't be such a martyr, Brayden. We all make mistakes. I only ask that you learn from it and make good."*

"Am I still on the case, sir?" Brayden asked, hopefully.

"Yes… for now. But, Brayden; no more foul-ups."

"Thank you, Mr President."

"Oh, one other thing. I think you need a partner on this. Someone with… more experience."

"Okay… any help is better than none."

"I'm glad you think so. Anyway, I think you've worked with him before and I want you to work with him again."

"Sir?"

"Mitch Youngs. Milo Calland said you'd relish the chance to work with him again!"

"Mitch Youngs...?" Brayden had unequivocally insisted never to be saddled with him again.

"Do we have a problem?"

Through gritted teeth Brayden thanked the President. Upon concluding the call, Brayden cursed and hurled the mobile phone into the road where it smashed into half a dozen fragments.

Mitch Youngs!

Not Mitch Youngs, he considered angrily. Anything but Mitch Youngs. A bullet to the head was preferable to another stint with that old fool as his partner.

A short, fresh-faced agent appeared next to Brayden having crept up behind him once he felt it was safe to do so.

"Sir, Deputy Director Calland wants to see you in his office."

"Okay."

"He says it's urgent," pressed the agent.

"I'll get to it when I return!" Brayden shouted, bustling over to the shattered remains of his mobile phone. He picked through the pieces of plastic and electronic detritus and retrieved the SIM card, discarding the rest. Swiftly, he crossed to the black SUV in which the two young women were patiently waiting. The agent followed him with his eyes, watched as Brayden drove out of the compound and sighed in resignation as he realised he had to now go and report to the Deputy Director that Brayden had ignored his direct order.

CHAPTER TWENTY-SEVEN
SOPHIE

FROM WITHIN ROOM NINE, Sophie and Emily had heard Dominic's arrival. The walls of the motel weren't thick and the owner's croaky voice was easily heard from outside; as was Dominic's.

"I don't see how having my mother's murderer here will benefit us," said Sophie, sullenly, adding: "It's an insult."

"Ryan knows what he's doing," soothed Emily. "I don't like him any more than you."

"Did I mention, he killed my mother?!"

"He's here to help," continued Emily, matter-of-factly.

"Help Ryan, you mean. He's not here to help me find my father."

"Sophie!" Emily chided. "You know we aim to find your father."

"But, not before we find his sons of *GYGES*... yea, I know..."

"It's all part of the same mission," insisted Emily. "We don't know where your father is – yet, but we DO know where to find the research and everything relating to Project *GYGES*."

It transpired that Ryan was already in possession of the most important piece of information regarding Project *GYGES*: the location of the secret laboratory where George Jennings had been taken to continue his research in genetically-enhanced embryonics; the home to America's first batch of super soldiers.

At first, Ryan hadn't been forthcoming with his reasons for sending Dominic over to meet them, using a ham-fisted rescue mission excuse for his hasty departure, but when Emily accurately pointed out that owing to the time difference and the flight time, Dominic would be too late to be useful, Ryan was forced to fess up.

"In a little over twenty-four hours, Dominic will be leading a task force into the hot zone of Project GYGES... if we're to be successful, we need Sophie to go in too..."

Ryan had disclosed the location of Project *GYGES*. Emily had gasped on hearing it, exhaling a breath of dismay.

"And my father?" Sophie asked the man, a steely tone to her voice.

"No longer there, I'm afraid..."

Sophie had exchanged some heated words about what she thought of his idea and abandoning her father before he terminated the call.

A short time after, he followed up his call with an email to Emily, attaching schematics of Area 51, the exact location of the secret laboratory (beneath a hangar that had no identifying marker, but close to another marked as '17') and details of all security measures taken.

Through the motel wall, rushing water could be heard from the neighbouring room, followed by muffled singing. The internal walls seemed even thinner than the external ones. It was ten minutes after they'd heard Dominic arrive, and he'd wasted no time, luxuriating in taking a shower.

"*GYGES* is a distraction," Sophie further griped. "We should find my father first..."

"It's important we find George, I agree. But you've got to understand that *GYGES* poses the greater risk."

"Well... I can't promise I won't kill him," Sophie said, sullenly. Meaning Dominic.

Sophie went silent for a while, which was more noticeable when the sound of gushing water stopped. It highlighted the tension in the room.

Five minutes had passed when a knock at the door alarmed both women. Emily was sitting at a folding table, one drop-leaf pulled open upon which was the metal case supplied by Ryan along with the laptop. She looked up from the LCD monitor, the schematic emailed over from London filling the screen; Sophie sat bolt upright on one of the two single beds.

A second rap sounded, defiant, more urgent. Sophie reached into her backpack and pulled out the *Glock 17* handgun she'd taken from the policeman at the hospital the night before. Automatically, she checked the clip. The magazine was almost full. She'd only dispensed one bullet.

"Open it; I'll cover you," Sophie calmly aimed the weapon towards the door, swinging her legs gently out, over the bed's edge.

Emily stood up from the table and crossed to the door. Before lifting the latch, she engaged the security chain – a flimsy, brass sash that hung from the door frame and slotted into the limiter on the door – a pointless measure which did next to nothing for added protection.

Emily looked towards Sophie for reassurance. Sophie, holding the gun with barely a breath of movement, nodded.

Emily opened the door a crack, the chain pulling taut and allowing just enough of a crevice to see the dark silhouette of a man standing a couple of steps ahead.

"Are you going to let me in or is it your plan to continue acting like a couple of school girls?" He spoke with little patience. With his long wet hair dankly hanging down to his shoulders, black jeans and an XXL *Aerosmith* T-shirt that barely covered his torso, Dominic looked like he might've been auditioning for a part in an unsuccessful heavy metal band.

Not speaking, Emily closed the door enough to allow her to remove the security chain, then stepped aside to permit admittance.

Dominic didn't wait for an invitation, following Emily in. Sophie was still perched on the edge of her bed, the *Glock 17* aimed at Dominic as he entered the room.

"Woh… hold on there…" Dominic raised his hands defensively, stopping at the threshold.

"Sophie, put… the… gun… down…" urged Emily, slowly.

Ignoring her, Sophie spoke to Dominic. "You've got some nerve, I give you that." Her face was stony-hard and determined-looking.

"Sophie…" He spoke softly. "I…," he started, he didn't know what to say. "It was an accident. It was dark… and… the gun went off…"

Sophie shook her head, dismissing his reason. "You knew what you were doing. I saw you. You shot her in the stomach… she died slowly – painfully!"

"I'm SORRY…" the apology sounded forced through Dominic's gritted teeth.

"She died on a road in the middle of nowhere," Sophie continued. "Because of you, there are three children out there without a mother." She stood up, the *Glock* pointing menacingly ahead of her as she closed the gap between herself and Dominic, her index finger coaxing the deadly promise the trigger offered.

"Sophie, listen to me," Emily was trying to reason with her. "You don't need to like him. He's here to help us. Ryan sent him, remember."

Sophie pressed the barrel of the gun against the side of Dominic's head. "I dare you to struggle with me, Dominic," almost a whisper. "Who knows, maybe I'll have an 'accident' as well."

Sweat or a bead of water from Dominic's wet hair rolled down his forehead and trickled past his right eye. For several hurried heartbeats he was sure she was going to shoot him, then Sophie released the pressure against his head and lowered the gun. He sighed heavily.

"I'm truly sorry, Sophie," Dominic offered. He still didn't sound like he meant it. Sophie walked away, back to her bed. She tossed the *Glock* onto her pillow.

"Maybe you are," Sophie replied, pensively. "Just don't think for a moment this is over..." Turning her back on both Dominic and Emily, she lay down, her head next to the gun, curled up into a foetal position and closed her eyes.

Dominic sighed as he considered the young woman lying there on the bed. It was almost hard to believe that this young woman was so special. Turning, he saw that Emily had placed herself in front of the laptop at the table. She was quietly watching him.

"Are those the blueprints of Groom Lake?" he asked, swiftly getting over the embroilment with Sophie.

CHAPTER TWENTY-EIGHT
WYATT

The joint operation between MI6 and Kaplan Ratcliff had been put together almost immediately upon Ryan receiving the location of Project *GYGES*.

Less than twenty-four hours later, the *Boeing C-17 Globemaster III*, one of eight operated by the RAF, sat idle on the only runway in operation at RAF Northolt. Situated to the west of London in South Ruislip, RAF Northolt was home to No. 32 (The Royal) Squadron, the British Forces Post Office and No. 600 (City of London) Squadron. Today, it played host to the large military transport aircraft drafted in by Ryan Barber; an hour earlier the plane had taken off from RAF Brize Norton, the pilot and his co-pilot oblivious to their final destination.

Two plain white coaches and a black *Hyundai Sante Fe* arrived into the RAF base a short time later, pulling up alongside the *Boeing* aircraft one behind the other, the black vehicle in the lead.

Ryan Barber and Marty Heywood climbed out of the *Hyundai* (Ryan was driving) and walked around to the metal staircase that led up to the aircraft's passenger door.

Electric doors opened simultaneously at the front of the coaches and a stream of armed men dressed in nondescript military fatigues with black body armour and stern faces, piled out and made for the aircraft.

Ryan counted fifty men. Elite operatives from Kaplan Ratcliff and MI6 clambered up the metal staircase and into the aircraft.

"Impressive," Marty was looking each of the men over as they passed. None of them met his gaze.

The final operative came up behind one of the lines and stopped in front of the two MI6 men.

"Ryan." Jack Wyatt acknowledged the senior agent standing in front of him. Since Tom Kaplan's death in July, Wyatt had progressed within the corporation. No longer a team leader, he was Head of Covert Operations.

"Jack," replied Ryan, seriously. Until then, neither man had had a reason to talk to each other since the events of the summer.

"So, what's this all about? Where we going?"

"I'll brief you en route." Ryan gestured for Wyatt to lead the way up the staircase and followed him up. Marty Heywood clambered up close behind.

<hr>

It takes approximately eleven hours to fly from RAF Northolt to Nevada, USA – eighty-three miles north-northwest of Las Vegas. Ryan had timed it so that they would arrive after midnight, deep under the cover of darkness. It wasn't until three hours into the flight that Ryan called Jack Wyatt over to brief him on the task force's mission.

Marty Heywood had vacated the seat next to Ryan, making space for Wyatt. He wandered down the line of the craft, making use of the moment to help his blood circulate.

The inside of the plane looked like the interior of a spaceship, was dimly lit and not nearly as opulent as a passenger plane, but no one, not even Ryan, was inconvenienced by the lack of in-flight comfort. The interior of the *Boeing* had space for 134 passengers, fold-up seats were fixed against the walls along each side of the plane facing the opposite side, with extra seating available at the centre of the craft when required (currently folded down and concealed beneath the floor). Owing to the vast open space, sound echoed throughout, including the drone of the engines.

Ryan handed the younger man a file that had 'classified' stamped across its centre in red ink.

"I gather you're aware that Sophie Jennings is in America… searching for her father."

A fleeting memory of the night when Tom Kaplan died came to mind. Jack had led Bravo Team that ill-fated night in July. He remembered feeling uncomfortable, almost sensing something not right, but that had been overshadowed by the adrenalin rush as he'd readied himself – and his team – to mount a surprise attack on the warehouse where Harriet Jennings had been held captive. Only, it didn't play out that way; instead, they were taken by surprise by armed forces belonging to the CIA, and Tom, who foolishly thought to escape, took a number of bullets to his back, halting his progress, in addition to his life.

"I'd kept tabs on her, sir."

"Good," continued Ryan. "In addition to finding her father, we've tasked her with locating – and destroying – her father's work. Inside that folder, you'll see the coordinates of where we know it to be; you'll also see schematics of the base, the exact location of the laboratory and details of onsite security measures."

Wyatt opened the file and rifled through the pages. There were aerial photographs, detailed maps and black and white diagrams.

"Are you serious?" A perplexed look crossed Wyatt's face, quickly replaced by a maniac's smile. "Impossible." He closed the file up and swiftly handed it back to Ryan.

"I never mentioned anything about it being easy."

"You never said that it was a suicide mission, either."

"We'll have ground support and we'll be taking them completely by surprise," Ryan opened the folder. "Yes, it is well defended," he studied the aerial photograph of Area 51, "but their main defence is the vastness on either side of it, or what they call 'restricted area'."

"What about military presence?" Wyatt held out his hand for the file. Ryan folded it and handed it back.

"A couple of squadrons and some private security detail patrolling the perimeter, nothing sinister." Ryan offered back the file.

Wyatt flipped through the pages, studying the map. A highlighter pen had been used to circle the exact location of the secret laboratory. It was beneath an aircraft hangar, unmarked, but close to another noted as '17'.

"The Americans will see us on radar, but even if they don't, where do you propose we land?"

"Radar isn't going to be a problem. We're masquerading as a commercial flight to Los Angeles; our flight number, identification signals and everything, are all cleared to enter American airspace."

"Landing in Los Angeles is quite a distance from the target zone. You don't think we'll be able to access the base via the road, do you?"

Ryan started to laugh. "Of course not. Who said anything about landing?"

It slowly dawned on him. "You mean?" Wyatt almost couldn't believe what he was about to say: "We're parachuting in?"

"You've done it before, haven't you?" Ryan stood up and clapped Wyatt on the back. "I'll leave it to you to prepare your team. Might be an idea to get some sleep. We'll be meeting Dominic there."

"How's he getting in?"

"That, Jack... you don't need to worry about; but it's not going to be quite as easy."

CHAPTER TWENTY-NINE
DOMINIC

IT WAS AFTER MIDNIGHT when the Director of Kaplan Ratcliff's Security and Intelligence Division thought it prudent to leave Emily, retiring to bed. Sophie had kept her back to them and made little sound, not the slightest of snores and barely a breath.

Closing the door to his motel room, Dominic sighed. Next to the door was a switch. He pressed it and two dingy lights flickered into life; one at the centre of the room, the other in the bathroom.

This time tomorrow, we'll be joining up with Ryan's task force... then... show time...

Kicking off his shoes, pulling off his T-shirt and slipping out of the black jeans, he crossed the room in just his boxers and wristwatch, glimpsing himself in the mirror.

"Jeez, you need to lose some weight," he said as he threw himself onto the single bed.

Springs in the mattress boinged and squeaked and dug uncomfortably into his back; the pillow was hard, like, he imagined, lying on a sandbag. He raised himself up enough to fluff up the pillow (which made little difference). On the wall just above his head, was a switch he assumed, correctly, turned off the lights. He pressed it and blackness enveloped the room.

As there was little street lighting around the motel, darkness was total.

After half an hour of tossing from one side to the next, turning from his front to his back, flailing his arms, kicking his covers off, pulling them back on, and repeating the sequence two dozen times, Dominic accepted that he wouldn't be getting any sleep that night; probably wouldn't get any tomorrow night either.

Reaching for the bedside lamp on the table next to him, he fumbled with the bell-press switch hanging from the cord, then, with a modicum of light, he climbed out of bed and padded over to the table where a small clutter of coins, his wallet, four different passports, a box of *tic tacs* and his mobile lay. Securing the mobile in the palm of his hand, he returned to his bed.

Keying in a long number, he waited for the call to be connected. A glance at his watch and a quick conversion indicated that it was 6:00 a.m. in London. Although the control centre wouldn't be fully staffed at this hour, Dominic knew that at least four analysts worked overnight.

After ringing for an indeterminate length of time, the call was answered.

"*Hel-lo?*" The voice sounded even more tired than Dom.

"Hi, who's that? Is it Mike?"

"*Yes...*" Mike Davro, a ladies' man. Boy band good looks and a razor-sharp personality. In the short time Dominic had been at Kaplan Ratcliff as Samuel Jackson's replacement, he'd taken a distinct dislike to the man.

"Mike, it's Director Schilling." Dominic imagined the little man shuffling up straight and trying to make himself look taller in his seat.

"*Sir... I guess you got to Washington okay...*"

"Um, yea... listen, I need you to help me source some things in the Los Angeles locale."

"*Sure, whatever, man...*"

Dominic ignored the flippant remark and started to reel off a long list of specific items he needed. Half-way through he felt Mike

Davro was slipping away; if he'd been sitting opposite him, Dominic imagined that his eyes would have glazed over and he'd have been making a sweeping hand movement in front of his face.

"Okay... Mike, scrub that. Just help find somewhere I can get my hands on a good selection of light arms, heavy arms, grenades, flash grenades, combat clothing, knives, signal flares, night-vision glasses, an armoured vehicle..."

"Anything else...?"

"Well, glad you asked Mike... see if you can find somewhere to buy *Planters Cheez Balls*. They come in a tin; I used to eat them all the time, practically lived on them when in the States... I've not been able to find them anywhere..."

"Give me two hours and I'll get this for you..."

Four hours later, Dominic was trying to pound some life back into his neighbours' door. Both Emily and Sophie stirred in their room, but only Emily responded to their unrequested early wakeup call.

Bleary-eyed, she opened the door. It was 5:10 a.m., and two hours away from sunrise. Pale light from a single streetlamp allowed Dominic to see the eldest of the two women. She was dressed in a nightdress that allowed Dominic sight of too much flesh.

"Good morning," said Dominic cheerfully, taking pleasure from the view.

Subconsciously, Emily folded her arms across her chest, at least concealing part of her body from unwanted attention. "What... time... is it?" Emily spoke groggily, yawning and rubbing at her eyes. Behind her, Sophie was still lying on her bed; not that Dominic would've been able to see her. Like most nights, the serum that enabled Sophie to sustain visibility had worn off. To any who casually glanced into the room, the bed would appear empty and stripped bare to the bottom sheet. Except, on closer inspection, one may have seen 'pitting' within the mattress where Sophie's weight was distributed.

On the pillow, unseen, the *Glock 17*, exactly where Sophie had tossed it the night before. A hand wrapped around it, a finger teasing the trigger:

Soon, enough… she thought.

"It's time to get up," Dominic chirped. "We've got a plane to catch."

"Since when?" Emily was waking herself up, self-consciously pulling at the fabric of her nightdress to cover up her cleavage.

"Since Ryan booked us on the 8:15 a.m. flight to LA… Freshen up ladies and get your crap together, we need to leave within the hour."

"Los Angeles?" Emily sounded puzzled. "Aren't we needing to be closer to Vegas?"

"Yep… but we need to go on a little shopping trip first."

Abandoning the silver *Chevrolet Impala* within the long-stay parking area, together with their luggage (excepting a few personal effects which they carried in shoulder bags), Dominic led Emily and Sophie (fully visible) into Dulles International Airport, towards the terminal where their *American Airlines* flight to Los Angeles was due to depart.

Having eaten very little since arriving in America (the shack *Ray* had recommended the night before at the motel had burned down a week earlier, so he'd had to satisfy his hunger with a couple of bags of pretzels), Dominic had suggested breakfast, and after arguing as to where to go, they sauntered into *The Great American Bagel Bakery*. Sophie and Emily selected scrambled egg and cheese with bacon bagels, whereas Dominic went for a *Jalapeno Breakfast Sandwich*, which he would appear to regret on account of the perspiration he frequently mopped away. All three ordered large Café Lattes, needing the caffeine to help keep them focused.

"We should split up." After finishing his bagel and emptying the cardboard beaker of coffee, Dominic was keen to get moving. "They'll be looking for two women together, and with knowing I'm in the country, likely be expecting me to be with you also."

"He's right." Sophie hated admitting it and thought she saw a flicker of satisfaction appear on Dominic's face. "We should expect our descriptions to have been circulated."

Despite dying her hair, Emily couldn't help but feel exposed. Simple things like hair colouring and easy changes of appearance would be expected. Only Sophie had the best disguise; in a game of 'rock, paper, scissors', invisibility would come up trumps every time.

An announcement on the PA system indicated that the *American Airlines* flight to LA was boarding, the saccharine-sweet announcer requesting all travellers make their way to gate thirty-nine.

"We'll split up at the newsstand," suggested Dominic, getting up from the table, "let's get moving."

At the newsstand a grey-haired man with a flat cap and a four pocket money belt that, at first glance looked like a skirt wrapped about his waist, sat on a bar stool reading a paperback.

Dominic, closely followed by Emily, with Sophie a little behind her, stepped up to the newsstand and helped himself to a copy of that morning's *Washington Post*. Paying the attendant with loose change, he folded the newspaper in half and slipped it beneath his arm.

Turning to Emily, Dominic smiled and said, "I'll see you on the plane."

A moment later he was taking purposeful strides in the direction of gate thirty-nine, easily viewed from the newsstand.

"Are you ready?" asked Sophie, a little apprehensive.

"One moment. Let's allow a bit of a gap between us," picking up a copy of *Cosmopolitan* from the stand as she replied, then paying the attendant.

———◆———

At the entrance to gate thirty-nine, a security desk was placed barring the way. A little fat bald man of indeterminable age – due in part to his lack of hair, and owing equally to his round chubby face – stood behind it. Wearing bifocal glasses and a ginger moustache and goatee-beard, he looked imposing despite his contradicting size. On his crisp-white shirt was a gold name badge pinned to his pocket; Herbert Smicer engraved across it.

"Boarding pass and ID," the security guy drawled, his hand held out like a child waiting for sweets.

Dominic handed over his passport. The boarding pass acted like a bookmark, allowing Herbert Smicer to check his details easily.

"So, *Eric Nichols*, what's the purpose for travelling today?" All three of them were travelling with false passports. Dominic had arrived in the States with four, as had Emily. Sophie had travelled invisibly without documentation, but Ryan being the pragmatist, had sent hers over with Emily.

"Oh, you know… doing the American tour… always wanted to see Hollywood…"

Herbert Smicer studied Dominic's face, comparing it to the photo in the passport. He closed the passport with the boarding pass still inside and was about to hand it back to Dominic when he noticed the *Washington Post* propped beneath the man's arm. Dominic's hand was poised to accept the passport on the other side of the desk.

Before Dominic had folded the newspaper in half at the newsstand, he hadn't noticed the headline on the front page:

AMERICA'S MOST WANTED!

A picture of Dominic was clearly on display, and another

photograph, less clear and more grainy of two young women (as though lifted from CCTV footage), was hidden beneath Dominic's arm.

Realising something was turning sour by the hardening of the airport security man's face, Dominic glanced at the newspaper. Even from upside down, he was able to see that his photograph stared out brazenly.

I'm such an ass! he thought.

Slowly, Dominic stepped back from the desk, his eyes holding Herbert Smicer's in a stare. The security desk operator hesitated for just a moment before hitting a button on the desk.

An emergency siren started to blare, alarming some travellers in close proximity to throw themselves to the ground; most people stood around like sheep and gaped in fear.

Galvanised into action, Dominic dropped the newspaper and turned away from gate thirty-nine, sprinting away towards an exit on the other side of the terminal. Within seconds, airport police were charging into the terminal building from all corners, some brandishing handguns, others waving for people to move out of the way.

From the newsstand, Emily and Sophie watched Dominic run across the airport until he disappeared from view. Half a dozen policemen charged past them, joining in with Dominic's pursuit, but none paid the two young women any notice.

Dominic clumsily hurdled a security barrier and charged, out of breath, towards a fire exit. The months of inactivity in Jennifer Rattcliff's house was adding to his exertion. Policemen were pounding hard behind him, gaining ground, and close to catching him. One or two were shouting at him to stop; others were threatening to shoot him. He didn't doubt they meant it; this was America post 9/11 after all. Had he read the *Washington Post* news report accompanying his photo and that eye-catching headline, he would have learnt that he, along with Emily and Sophie, had been named as terrorists, and all of a sudden linked to a number of atrocities, including the deaths of CIA agents, one unsurprisingly named as Paul Lebrock.

At the fire exit, Dominic made to push down on the lever of the door. As his hands came in contact with the bar, a final warning was screamed at him from behind:

"HALT OR I WILL SHOOT!"

Dominic closed his eyes as he pushed down on the bar securing the door, and waited for the pain of a bullet and the sound of gunfire.

CHAPTER THIRTY
MILO

PRESIDENT AVERY HARRISON WAS pacing the White House Situation Room in the basement of the West Wing. Within the Conference and Intelligence Room was his Chief of Staff, two advisors, the Director of Homeland Security, the National Security Advisor, the Director of the CIA and his deputy, Milo Calland. They sat in comfy leather chairs around a long mahogany table that filled the centre of the room.

The mood was oppressive and especially tortuous to Milo.

A live audio feed was being communicated over a set of speakers from Dulles International Airport. The most senior officer at the scene was reporting, breathless and exasperatedly, details of the events that were occurring within the domestic departures terminal.

"…we don't know what happened! It's like a ghost attacked us. One minute… we had Dominic Schilling pegged down; the next… chaos. Officers being knocked down, some getting shot. Regrettably, one of our officers got spooked and took pot shots taking out his own men." Muffled gunfire could be heard over the speakers.

"Thank you officer. Keep us updated…" The audio communication ended and the conference room became immediately quiet. A moment elapsed before President Harrison spoke again.

"Did we not have any intelligence regarding this?" The President had stopped and was directing the question at Milo.

Calland turned visibly white. "I... I... I don't know," he stammered. He looked at his boss Director Montgomery for support, who, until that morning, had been completely oblivious to what Milo Calland had been tasked with.

"With all your resources you've been unable to catch ONE girl." President Harrison shook his head in disappointment. "You told me you'd found her. I gave you an executive order to eliminate the threat. This is getting out of hand."

"We underestimated her," Milo said, defensively. "But, with due respect, somehow she knew we were coming."

"I somewhat doubt that. You telling me she's got mystic powers as well? Has she got the ability to see the future?" The President started laughing scornfully.

"No, sir. But, we're thinking she may have had insider help. I think we have a mole; someone is feeding information to MI6."

"Limey bastards!" President Harrison slammed the flat of his hands down on the table making all but his Chief of Staff jump. "I want the treasonous son-of-a-bitch apprehended and charged; I want this girl found!"

"I know I'm late coming into play with this Mr President, but we think that Sophie Jennings is over here to get her father." Director Thawn Montgomery, a thickset former American Football player, Navy Seal and a writer of heroic fantasy novels, swivelled agitatedly in his chair. Milo had briefed him in the limo en route, and he was not at all happy with his deputy's cloaked escapades over the past twenty-four hours.

"Okay, that's as it may. Why was Dominic Schilling boarding a flight to LA?" President Harrison was pacing the room again. Dominic Schilling was travelling under the name *Eric Nichols*, and had been positively identified by airport security. Of Sophie Jennings and her companion, there'd been no sighting.

Milo Calland was the only person in the room who offered to speak. Everyone else sat in silence like a bunch of kids being reprimanded for throwing a firecracker into a busy crowd. "We don't know. Maybe he had nothing to do with Sophie Jennings; he did kill her mother, after all.

"Two of our agents followed him from London yesterday and, as far as we can tell, he's not been in contact with her."

"Wasn't one of the agents found dead in a washroom?"

"Err, yea, Mr President," Milo replied, sheepishly.

"And the other agent lost him at the taxi rank! And now a whole squad of policemen claim to have been attacked by what their senior officer claimed was, a ghost…"

Milo shrugged.

"We don't need CIA to know that Dominic Schilling has been in contact with Sophie Jennings, regardless of their frosty past. We know it. But why's he travelling to LA? Sophie's father isn't in LA… if that's who she's here in the States for…"

"LA could be a diversion?" ventured the Chief of Staff, the eldest man in the room with thinning grey hair and round spectacles. "Clearly they know we are looking for them."

The President walked a circuit of the room making little thought noises as he went. Motion helped him think. After circling the room twice more, grunting to himself a couple of times and making a little humming sound at the back of his throat along the way, he stopped at the head of the table, finally taking his seat.

"And when was I to be told about Dr. Stacy Monaghan?"

"Stacy who?" Milo raised his eyebrows quizzically.

"The Director of the FBI mentioned to me this morning that Dr. Monaghan was found dead in Washington this morning. She was an assistant at George Jennings' research lab in Nevada. Don't tell me that her death is unrelated?"

"Honestly, Mr President, I think we're digressing here. It's likely a coincidence regarding this Dr. Monaghan turning up dead in Washington… but, I'll have someone look into it."

"Good. You do that." President Harrison turned to face away from the table, deep in thought for a long moment and sighed. He swivelled the chair back to face his advisors. "Okay, this is what we do." He leaned forward and clasped his hands together. "Step up the search for Sophie Jennings at the airport, that's a no brainer; she can't be far. If she eludes us, as she's done before, expect her in Cuba. If she knew about our trap yesterday, no doubt she'll know Guantanamo Bay is where her father is being held. Send reinforcements to the base in full battle-readiness; alert the prison, tell them something like, I dunno, we expect Al Qaida to attack them imminently, that will put them on heightened alert. I want it locked tighter than a nun's chastity belt."

"That's good, sir," smiled Milo, nodding his head.

"Glad you think so, Deputy Director. Before you go, though, I want you to know that once this fiasco is over, you'll be relieved of your position."

Milo's smile dropped off his face faster than the blinking of an eye. "I understand… Mr President."

CHAPTER THIRTY-ONE
SOPHIE

"**W**HAT SHOULD WE DO?"

Emily was just an analyst, not a field agent. She wasn't used to being chased or shot at, and already within three days she'd faced more than had she been enlisted into the army and stationed in Kabul.

Dominic was still in their eyeline, sprinting across the airport. Probably, Sophie considered, drawing the police away from them.

Slow in her response, Sophie offered Emily an answer. It wasn't what Emily expected.

"We should continue with the plan. Ryan needs us…"

"What about Dom?" Emily asked, doubtfully.

Sophie had no allegiance to Dominic Schilling. Her thoughts, when she answered was: *He killed my mother.* "He's a big boy; he can take care of himself."

"No," Emily said, stubbornly. "We're not leaving him."

Dominic had now run out of sight, but policemen continued to charge past, individually and in pairs.

"There's too many," insisted Sophie. "We can't save him."

"WE MUST!" Emily had grabbed Sophie by her clothes and drawn her up close, faces almost touching. The newsstand attendant, still reading his paperback, was trying to ignore the spat playing out in front of him, but raised his eyebrows at the sharp rise in Emily's voice.

Sophie gave Emily a stern look but did nothing to disengage Emily's grip on the clothing beneath her neck. "What do you think I can do?"

Emily relaxed her grip and withdrew her hands. "You know… your thing?"

"My thing?" Sophie sighed, closing her eyes for a moment, thinking or composing herself. When she opened her eyes again, her stern look still remained. "Okay. I'll do this… only because I want to kill him myself."

"Thank you…" Emily sounded relieved, almost as though the act had already been done.

"But, I tell you now. Once this is all over, and when I've got my father back, you, me and Ryan… we're done. I don't care what you've promised MI6 or Kaplan Ratcliff… I won't do this anymore. None of it!"

Like a stroppy teen, Sophie turned away from Emily before she could reply further, and stormed off in the same direction as the cops were still heading.

The newsstand attendant had seen it all before; he assumed it was a lovers' tiff, or one of them was having their 'period'. He had two daughters; he knew the drill.

Emily stood watching the blonde girl lope away until she disappeared from view – not through using her ability – around the same internal building Dominic had; the copy of *Cosmopolitan* she'd rolled up like a truncheon and nervously tapped it against the front of her right leg.

———— ◆ ————

"HALT OR I WILL SHOOT!"

Dominic had no place else to go. He was surrounded by more than two dozen policemen. Hell, it looked to Sophie like the whole of Washington PD had turned up. Before turning the corner that led to the fire escape, Sophie had summoned the change to her appearance, fading to nothing as she ran between a number of people milling about, voyeurs to the police action carrying out before them.

Sophie watched in slow motion the twenty-two policemen (she counted), who had stopped five metres behind Dominic, level their handguns (*Glock 17*s, the same as the weapon she'd taken from the dead policeman in the hospital) towards Dominic's back, and saw the Intelligence and Security Director of Kaplan Ratcliff ignore the order, applying pressure to the metal bar securing the door, an act of defiance which almost certainly meant his death sentence.

"Stupid fool!" she hissed under her breath as she reached the first policeman. Although the corridor was wide enough to drive an airport trolley-car through, it wasn't wide enough for more than ten people to stand in a line, so policemen were thronging in a bottleneck. The mass of bodies between her, the lead-policeman and Dominic, hindered her chances of getting to her uninvited companion in time, but she knew she had to try.

Not for her, but for Emily.

"Mother, don't let me die," she whispered as she charged thoughtlessly into the herd.

The first policeman slipped to the ground unconscious from a hard blow to the neck; Sophie pulled his *Glock* from his loose hand and fired three times into the legs of three policemen. The men crumpled to the ground, guns clattering to the tiles, hands clasping at their bleeding legs, screams of pain filling the air.

Before the three had hit the floor, Sophie fired a further three shots, taking the legs out from three more policemen immediately in front of them, opening up a path of writhing bodies for her to wade through.

By now, attention on Dominic had shifted to the unseen shooter taking out police officers from behind. The lead policemen had turned to look over his shoulder.

A moment was all Dominic needed. He slammed the bar down and shouldered hard out through the door to make his escape. The lead policeman, realising Dominic was about to get away, squeezed the trigger of his gun twice, one bullet slamming into the closing door, blasting a small hole the size of a fifty-pence piece into the wood; the other passing through the small opening, disappearing somewhere outside.

Before the lead policeman was able to give further chase, something hard kicked him off his feet. He landed on his back, winded.

Sophie, seven policemen lying at her feet and fifteen others gathered around her in a stunned pack, hit four people with the butt of the gun, felling them before taking two others down with carefully placed punches and somersault kicks. In the chaos, a trigger-happy cop fired five random bullets into the melee, unwittingly killing a colleague, seriously injuring two and wounding two others.

At the door through which Dominic had seconds earlier vacated the building, Sophie looked back at the carpet of bodies. Three policemen were still on their feet, including the one who'd shot five of his fellow officers. They were blockaded by the groaning, writhing men bleeding about the floor.

Satisfied she'd done enough to slow them down, Sophie opened the exit door and ran outside.

Dominic wasn't far ahead. He was limping away. The bullet fired by the policeman had hit Dominic high up the back of his left leg, hitting him in the buttock.

"Wait!"

"Sophie? Where are you?"

"I'm here." Sophie had closed the gap and was now standing alongside Dominic. She placed an arm around his shoulder and felt Dominic drape an arm over hers; she tried to help him walk. To any observers it would look like Dominic was walking awkwardly on his own, his arm bizarrely raised at shoulder-height beside him.

"We need to get outta here," Sophie said, guiding Dominic around the side of a building. Ahead of them they could see one of Dulles airport's four runways. Aircraft were taxiing close by and a domestic flight was making speed and about to take-off.

"Why did you do that? Why didn't you just let them kill me?" The roar of turbine engines was deafening and Dominic needed to shout to get himself heard.

Although he couldn't see it, Sophie smiled. It was conveyed within her voice, but did not lessen her hard, certain-tone as she answered him. "I won't lie to you Dominic. I want you dead... more than anything. But no one... I mean NO ONE, is going to take the pleasure of killing you away from me."

CHAPTER THIRTY-TWO
BARRY

THE AMERICAN AIRLINES FLIGHT to Los Angeles was going to be delayed, which was inevitable in view of the incident occurring at the airport that morning. By how long was a factor that could have implications further down the line; this concerned Emily. She was the sort of person who lived by carefully laid plans and hated deviating from a set path.

With her *Cosmopolitan*, she made her way to gate thirty-nine, hoping to obtain details relating to her flight and some indication as to how long the delay was likely to be. A few minutes had passed since Sophie had charged off to help rescue Dominic. By the sound of sirens and the number of EMTs (Emergency Medical Technicians) running in the direction Sophie had headed, she assumed Ryan's granddaughter had been successful.

The security operator, Herbert Smicer, was still on desk duty, unfazed by the earlier excitement. It was just another day at the office.

"Excuse me, can you help?"

"Yes, ma'am, I'll try..." Herbert Smicer wore a smile that stretched from ear to ear.

"Do you know how long this flight will be delayed for? It's... I have a meeting to attend in LA." Emily had her passport and boarding pass in one hand but made no attempt to hand them to the man.

"Ah, sorry ma'am… there's been a security threat…" he tried to sound authoritative.

"Really?" Emily feigned surprise. "Is there a danger?"

"Ah, no ma'am. The police are currently dealing with it," adding, upon seeing her concern, "I'm sure it's nothing to worry about."

Emily smiled, *yeah right*, she thought, before thanking the security operator. She turned and walked away, feeling Herbert Smicer's eyes undressing her from behind.

Across the departure lounge, a young guy in jeans and a brown leather jacket watched Emily Porter make her way from gate thirty-nine to a bank of five payphones. A moment earlier the sirens had stopped, making the airport seem unnaturally quiet, even with the number of people rushing about. He checked his watch for the time. 8:10 a.m. It didn't matter what time it was, though he had his own schedule to keep.

With her focus on making a phone call, the man in the brown leather jacket walked towards Emily, passed her and took up the payphone to her left. He picked up the handset, placed it against his right ear and pressed a few buttons on the keypad, making it look like he was making a call.

He wasn't. Instead, he craned his neck and focused his hearing, turning his ear slightly. He listened.

"… *our position has been compromised… I don't see how we can get to LA, let alone our rendezvous time… I know that… I don't know… I guess she is okay… there's loads of injured policemen…*"

The man in the brown leather shifted slightly, risking a sideward glance towards Emily. She looked flustered. Emily looked up and for a split second their eyes locked. He shifted his gaze down and pretended to speak into his handset.

"*... why didn't you tell me? ... Okay, but you should have said we had an alternative... I know that! ... oh, whatever! Bye!*" Emily replaced the handset on the cradle forcefully, venting her frustration.

"Are you okay?" He spoke with an English accent.

"Hmm? Oh this..." Emily gestured offhand, implying the phone call, "I'm fine. Just my father," she lied, "you know how it is."

"Oh?"

"I was supposed to get the eight-fifteen flight to Los Angeles to meet with him, but... you know... delays."

"Yea, quite. There's been some sort of... *incident*. Though, if you ask me, the Americans jump at their own shadow these days."

Emily forced a smile, her eyes meeting his. They were nice eyes, she thought. Piercing blue. He was also handsome, but young... too young. He was close to Sophie's age, well, her genetically increased age... not her birth age, obviously.

"I'm Barrington, by the way. I know, it's a ridiculous name. My mum thought it would help toughen me up at school. It did. I'm 'Barry' to most people, though." He offered out a hand. Emily shook it.

"Listen, I don't mean to be rude... but..." she looked around nervously, "... I need to... you know, go." Although Barrington seemed nice enough, the casualness of the encounter seemed overfamiliar.

"Oh, okay... Before you go though, you may be interested to know that I'm going to LA too."

"Bye, Barry..." Emily turned away, misinterpreting the comment as a chat-up line.

"I have my own jet," he said, hastily.

"Now you're starting to sound creepy." Instinctively, her eyes were darting from one side to another, searching for a means of escape were she to require it. There were a number of options she considered.

"Wait, hear me out," urged Barry, a stray hand reaching for

her arm and momentarily pulling her back. "I know who you are... *Emily*."

Emily stopped, fully attentive. She shook her arm free from Barry's grip. "Okay, I'm listening. You've ten seconds." She didn't attempt to hide the contempt from her voice.

"It's you that's all over the news, right... with that other girl and the guy called Dominic. I've been looking out for you..."

"I don't know what you're talking about." Concern started to ring at the back of her mind.

"Yes you do. I saw you arrive together."

"Time's up Barry." Emily turned her back to him and started to leave.

"Which I guess sounds even worse," Barry muttered to himself. "I'm with Ryan!" he blurted a little too loudly, the words halting Emily, her back still turned to him. Because of the ongoing drama taking place the other side of the airport, no one paid attention to him. "I've been looking out for you..."

Emily wasn't convinced. "Why didn't Ryan say anything? I was just speaking with him."

"Oh, I thought you were speaking with your father?" Barry wore a puzzled look, then smiled, applying the charm.

"He IS my father," she replied without humour. It wasn't altogether a lie. Ryan had been the closest thing to a father she had had since as far back as she could remember.

Barry considered his reply for a moment. "We weren't supposed to meet... not yet at least. Ryan suggested I lend a hand if things turned ugly."

"It should've been expected. Sophie would say everything involving Dominic Schilling tended to turn ugly... one way or another."

He returned a blank look before going on. "Emily, you need to trust me, we don't have much time."

"I don't know you, so how can I trust you?"

"Ryan said you might say that. He said I should mention *Penshurst Place…*"

Penshurst Place held dear memories for her. It was the place where Ryan had first taken her with his Clara, when they were kids. Since then, it had unofficially become a codeword that Ryan occasionally used when needing to prove the reliability of information provided, and its origin.

Misinterpreting scepticism on Emily's face, Barry sighed in resignation. "I am cleared to take-off once the jet is refuelled. You're welcome to a ride."

"Okay, okay! But, were you really going to LA?" It all seemed too contrived, too good to be true.

Barry's eyes sparkled as he spoke. "Yes. My work here in DC is done. I've got a… *package* to deliver. My boss called me from London a short while ago giving me instructions," he said enthusiastically. "Come, let's go… let me help a fellow Brit."

"Okay, Barry." *Things might work themselves out,* she thought. "I just need to find my friends first…"

◆

The engine of the *Bombardier BD 700 Global Express* business jet was rumbling as Emily made herself comfortable in one of the butter-cream-coloured recliner seats, one of ten passenger seats within the small aircraft. Barry had seen her safely through security and out onto the tarmac, escorting her the short distance to the waiting jet.

Once she was safely inside, he'd jogged away in search of Sophie and Dominic.

Looking around the customised aircraft, Emily couldn't help but be impressed. Modified for a businessman on the go, the cabin included a desk with a computer workstation, phone, fax and internet

221

facilities, and a small kitchenette with sink, fridge, electric hob, microwave and an agglomeration of crockery and cooking utensils. A large TV dominated the wall closest to the front of the plane, behind which were toilet facilities, and a little further, just before the cockpit, the door that opened down to become a set of steps.

At the back of the plane was a private room which Emily guessed contained a small sleeping section. In fact, not only did it include a bed and a fitted wardrobe (behind a mirror), it also included a private washroom.

Within the cabin was another passenger. A big man in his mid-twenties, with bulging muscles over-accentuated by a khaki-green T-shirt a size too small; appearing to be asleep, his chair was reclined so that he was supine, facing the ceiling. The black eye mask with elasticised straps wrapped around his head allowed little daylight to breach his senses. Unable to resist, Emily appraised her fellow-passenger further.

He was wearing dark green combat trousers and a pair of black *Alt-Berg* combat boots, the sort Emily – remarkably – knew were worn within the armed forces; they were laced up to above the man's shin. Half-hidden beneath the sleeve of his tight T, a black tattoo; just a word, or a name… Emily could make out the first letter. C. The rest was obscured.

"I know you're watching me!" The man had a gruff, *WWE* wrestler's voice, though positively English.

"Err, sorry." Emily averted her eyes, feeling like she'd just caught the man stepping out of a shower naked.

"It's all right. I guess I'm too pretty." In truth, he wasn't. A scar down the right side of his face, just beneath his ear, marred his appearance, a souvenir of a past skirmish outside a bar in Liverpool. The scar was hidden from Emily's view as she was sat on the opposite side of the plane.

"I... I wasn't," she stammered, looking back across to the man.

He had sat up a bit and was slipping the eye mask above his eyes, blinking and half-squinting as the light flooded his senses. Emily waited for the man to become accustomed to the light, allowing him to focus before speaking further.

"Barry hadn't mentioned there were other passengers, is all."

The man pulled the eye mask off, swept a hand through his short, cropped black hair and winked. "Life's full of surprises, love." He made no attempt to explain his presence, instead he stood up and walked to the kitchenette, stooping down to the small fridge. Opening it, he reached in and removed a bottle of water. "Do you want one?"

Before the man had closed the fridge door, the engines of the jet roared louder and the business aircraft lurched forward, unbalancing him. He stumbled, arms flailing out to stop himself from falling.

"Johnson, damnit!" he blasted, his voice carrying through to the cockpit.

"Sorry, my instructions are to prepare for take-off," the pilot said through the cabin door from the cockpit. Emily's companion struggled back to his seat.

Glancing through the small window of the *Bombardier* aircraft from her seat, Emily watched the two familiar figures of Dominic Schilling and her new acquaintance, Barry, sprinting towards them. A small band of policemen were giving chase, but the gap between them was impressive.

The pilot of the *Bombardier* spoke over the PA system. "Okay, boys and girls, time to buckle up your seatbelts. We are cleared for take-off." The jet trundled towards the two running figures, gaining momentum, closing the gap between them as the door started to close; it remained open enough to allow access, but only with a little leap and a large AMOUNT of faith.

Deathly white and sweating profusely, his face a mask of pain, Kaplan Ratcliff's Security and Intelligence Director was running awkwardly with a limp, like he was being half-carried.

"Oh my God… Dominic's bleeding," exclaimed Emily, noticing the dark stain spreading around the left side of the man's lower half.

CHAPTER THIRTY-THREE
DOMINIC

S OPHIE CONTINUED TO SUPPORT Dominic away from the terminal building, but not before first applying a makeshift blockade, jamming a length of scaffolding against the fire exit door, wedging it in against the concrete paving. The door was held fast.

We have to get out of the airport, she thought, panting through exertion. Despite her enhanced strength, Dominic was three stone heavier than he should have been, made heavier by the fact he was injured. Trying to run with him over your shoulder, wasn't easy.

A short distance from the first runway, shielded by a mobile staircase, Sophie stopped.

Where do we go?

On her own, escaping from the police and bypassing security wouldn't pose a problem. She'd already established how advantageous being invisible was. With Dominic literally anchoring her down, getting away was going to prove almost impossible.

"Sophie... it's no use. I appreciate you coming back, but seriously. Just leave me..." He spoke in a pained voice.

"Dominic. I'm not leaving you behind!" Sophie started walking again, half-dragging Dominic with her. In her right hand she continued to hold the *Glock* she'd liberated from the policeman she'd knocked unconscious.

In the distance a small dark silhouette approached from the

runway, too far to see that it was a 'he', and that 'he' was running flat out; behind him, a small jet aircraft could be seen in the distance. Both things seemed insignificant to Sophie. The danger, in her mind, remained behind her, endorsed by the sudden clap and thunder of semi-automatic gunfire, and the jangle and thumps of metal and wood as the door she'd moments earlier secured was blasted open, the scaffold clanging aside.

"COME ON, DOM… RUN WITH ME!!"

"I…*can't!*"

"YOU MUST!!"

Dominic gritted his teeth and took more of his own weight despite the pain in his left leg that sent stars and blinding light to coalesce behind his eyes; he suddenly felt the world shift beneath his feet. He felt faint, felt like he would not be able to carry on. *This is it,* he thought. *My time to die.*

Sophie risked a look over her right shoulder, supporting Dominic with her left. The first of three uniformed policemen came into view running hard, closing in on them. They were all brandishing firearms. They looked like 100m relay runners at an Olympics, pumping arms, exhaling hard, their guns outstretched batons, pushing themselves on towards gold – only Dominic was the reward they sought.

The small silhouette ahead of them was closing in. Dominic saw him coming, running almost as hard as the police behind them, but Sophie didn't.

"Sophie…" Dominic panted. He was good to drop. "Sophie… it's… it's… over… we're surrounded…"

"No!" Sophie raised the gun. With unbelievably good accuracy, she squeezed off two rounds. The first bullet lifted the lead policeman off his feet; he crumpled to the ground, dead or alive, Sophie couldn't tell. The second bullet winged the next policeman, who dropped his gun and lost his balance, tripping over his feet and skidding to a halt on his chin. The third uniform hurdled over the second man and continued to give chase.

"Dominic Schilling?!" The voice came from ahead of them, a young, friendly, English-accented articulation, shouting to get heard above the audible rumble of a nearby jet engine and the general noise of Washington's busiest airport. The dark silhouette was now more visible. Wearing a brown leather jacket and jeans, and, Dominic realised, unarmed, he quickly worked out that this man wasn't working with the uniforms giving chase. Certifying that, as he caught up with them, the newcomer added, "Emily sent me to find you."

The policeman still chasing shouted at them to stop, levelling his gun and firing just as Dominic began to speak.

"That's goo-uh!" The bullet skimmed across Dominic's arm, ripping a chunk out of his shirt but barely grazing him. *That was close*, he thought. A small amount of blood peppered the fabric around the bullet hole.

"What's... going... on?" Sophie wheezed, turning her attention away from the policeman following, seeing Barry who was now running beside them.

Not seeing Sophie, but knowing of her and her 'unusual' abilities, Barry replied: "Come on... this way... we'll fix Dominic up on the plane." He reached into a pocket of his leather jacket and pulled out a small radio transmitter that fitted snugly in the palm of his hand. "Time to go," he barked into it as he increased his jog into a run.

The *Bombardier* business jet roared into greater life ahead and began to roll towards them.

"Is... that... yours?" laboured Sophie, Dominic's large form beginning to relax even further, becoming increasingly difficult to carry. She felt him begin to slip from her grasp, but just before collapsing to the ground, the jet drew up beside them, and Barry took hold of Dominic from the other side. The door-hatch on the jet lowered a bit, just enough for Sophie and Barry to help Dominic on. Barry, stepping up the ladder, pulled Dominic up the steps and into the jet.

Sophie quickly followed, feeling a bullet whistle past her right ear seemingly miss her by a margin; the gunshot sounded twice, but she soon gave it no mind as the door of the aircraft closed automatically behind her.

The remaining policeman continued to give chase, running alongside the *Bombardier* jet as it began to increase speed along the runway, soon falling away as optimum speed for take-off was met. The policeman emptied his *Glock* towards the fast-disappearing jet, but to no avail.

Dominic Schilling had escaped.

Sophie passed the toilet facilities, invisibly entering the jet's cabin, unaware that a few droplets of crimson trailed behind her. Just ahead, Barry dropped Dominic to the floor with a heavy thump. The man grimaced and a loud moan accompanied with a curse escaped his mouth with a sharp exhale of breath.

Emily unbuckled herself and was kneeling at the man's side. "My God, is he going to be okay?" Through the windows behind her, the ground fast disappeared as the jet climbed up towards the clouds.

Dominic was crying from the pain. "I'm dying," he whispered, followed with some theatrical coughing that baited sympathy from Emily but garnered only disdain from everyone else in the cabin.

Barry quickly assessed the injuries, applying pressure to Dominic's wound, causing the man to cry out pitifully before passing out; Barry continued to probe. The bullet that had shredded his shirt had barely nicked his arm.

"The wounds are nothing," he said, offhand. "The blood makes it look worse than it is. An *Elastoplast* should fix this," indicating

Dominic's arm, "and the other…" he looked up to address Emily, "is buried deep… within his ass."

Emily clasped a hand over her mouth to stifle a whimper or a cry, or possibly a laugh. No one could tell.

"Do we need to get him to a hospital?" It was the other passenger on the plane dressed in combat trousers and khaki T-shirt. He was standing a little out of the way and spoke with a deceptive note of concern. He didn't care for the man bleeding on the floor of the jet aeroplane; his worry was for their schedule.

Barry shook his head. "No. There's no need, besides we have a rendezvous time to adhere to. Let's get him into the bedroom, I'll find a first aid box and some pain relief. There's some vodka somewhere in one of the cupboards, try the kitchen."

Feeling forgotten, Sophie crept across to the kitchen and began searching the cupboards.

⎯⎯⎯◆⎯⎯⎯

Dominic was lying on his front when he awoke two-and-a-half hours later. Remembering little, he tried to turn over to his side. Pain flared in his left buttock, shooting up his side and slamming deep into his head; it felt like a defibrillator had been jabbed against his face and a thousand watts released into him. The shock brought it all back, the airport, the security operator setting the alarm, the police chase, and being shot in the rear. After that, everything was a blur.

Lifting his head up and turning from one side to the other, the Intelligence Director correctly assumed he was lying on a bed in a plane, the whirr of the *Bombardier's* engine vibrating throughout the aircraft. The room was sparse with just a wardrobe set behind a mirror in the corner beside the entranceway. Opposite was another door that led into a washroom.

"Welcome back."

229

Dominic jolted from the unexpected voice that came from beside him. Sophie – still invisible – was sitting beside him, keeping watch. A glance towards the mirror, turning slightly to gain the precise angle, afforded him sight of the young woman perched on the bed.

"How are you feeling?" Sophie asked with surprisingly genuine interest.

Dominic paused before replying. "Alive, I guess."

"Barry managed to dig the bullet out of your butt. He stitched you back up too, and stuck a plaster on your arm. The bleeding has stopped."

"Will it scar?"

Dominic caught Sophie shrugging from the reflection in the mirror. "Probably," she said. "Barry's not a doctor. To be honest, he made a bit of a mess of it," she laughed. "But, on the other hand… it's still prettier than your face."

Dominic ignored the insult. "I see you got hit."

"What?" Sophie was confused.

"Your ear." In the mirror, Dominic saw that Sophie's left ear had been bleeding, though it looked in one piece; dried blood caked the lobe and stained the side of her face and the shoulder of her pink T-shirt.

Sophie instinctually touched her ear, wincing from the slightest probe, making a hissing sound.

"Stings?"

Sophie nodded. "A little…"

"Now you know how my butt feels." Dominic closed his eyes and went quiet. For a long moment, Sophie thought that he'd passed out or gone to sleep. Then he spoke again, his voice low, forlorn. "You shouldn't have come back for me. If the role was reversed, I wouldn't have."

No longer inspecting her clipped ear, an image of her mother lying dead next to her father's car three months earlier flashed in her mind. She took in a deep breath, cleared her thoughts and looked down at her mother's killer.

"I know," she whispered.

CHAPTER THIRTY-FOUR
BRAYDEN

BRAYDEN HAD DRIVEN THE decoy girls home, verbalising his sincerest apologies for the frightening experience and making an offer of tickets to a *Redskins* game of their choice.

The fact that neither girl lived close to Langley – or each other, come to that – meant that it was late into the night when Brayden was ready to return to the office. At 10:33 p.m., the CIA agent was exhausted, hungry and disinclined to receive a further dressing down from Milo Calland that night, so called it a day, returning home to his nondescript condo where his wife had retired to bed.

Climbing onto the bed, Jordana, his wife, stirred.

"Hi…" she spoke softly, her eyes thin slits and her huge smile genuine. Brayden kissed her on the forehead, stood up and started to undress for bed. "Your boss has been calling you all night. Says it's important." She yawned.

Brayden shrugged, his back to the bed.

"Is everything okay?" Jordana sat up, pulling the duvet up with her, maintaining her modesty.

"Hmmm, yea," Brayden replied, distractedly. "Just a tough day at the office." Wearing boxer shorts, he climbed into bed. "Worse still, I'm going to be back working with Mitch again."

"Oh dear God, no!"

"Yep…"

The conversation carried on deep into the night and, despite President Avery Harrison's refusal to accept his resignation, Brayden had concluded that leaving the CIA was his best course of action. Being duped by Sophie Jennings was one thing, working with Mitch Youngs again was another.

With a predetermined course of action in place, Brayden settled down for the night next to Jordana and sleep came fitfully.

At CIA headquarters early the following morning, he sat outside Milo Calland's office waiting for the Deputy Director to summon him in. It felt like he was waiting for a job interview, and to any passing glances, he was dressed for the part; grey suit jacket, matching trousers, white collared shirt and royal blue tie set off by his shoes that sparkled under the artificial ceiling light. After an hour, Milo's receptionist informed him that Milo had left through a back entrance for the White House and that he would be indisposed until further notice. Brayden thanked her and cursed inwardly as he made his way to his office.

A TV in the reception area was on and *Fox News* was broadcasting live footage of events occurring at Dulles International Airport.

"What's going on?" Brayden asked. Marcy, his assistant, looked up from a computer. She was tall and skinny with a complexion as pale as a glass of milk. And very attractive.

"One of those fugitives tried to fly out this morning. Police are on the scene and there's been shooting, but he's yet to be apprehended."

"He?"

"Dominic Schilling," stated Marcy. "Airport security formally identified him. It's surprising he's not been caught, the size of him…"

"What about the girls?" Brayden raised an eyebrow quizzically.

"I wouldn't know," she replied. "Word is the invisible one is there… but… no one has been able to see her." Marcy was grinning. Brayden laughed with her. It was infectious. Laughing with Marcy was natural, and easy.

Too easy. The two of them often flirted with each other, it made working within the world of clandestine operations a little more exciting.

"You wanted to see me, sir?"

Brayden had been requested shortly before 12:00 p.m. Milo Calland had arrived an hour-and-a-half earlier but hadn't called upon him until now.

"I wanted to see you yesterday, Brayden. Today, this is altogether a different thing. This, I'm afraid, is not just us 'seeing' each other, it's us having a 'meeting'." Deputy Director Calland spoke in a strained tone. He was standing up behind his desk and had the poise of someone suffering with severe haemorrhoids that no cream could sooth.

"I'm sorry I missed your calls…"

"And messages?" Calland was perplexed.

"Yes… and messages. I had an accident with my phone and didn't get home until late last night."

Calland sat down. "Sit," he told Brayden. The CIA agent did as told and waited for the dressing down. "I understand the President called you yesterday."

"Yes. Yes, he did."

"Well, we don't need to harp on about the past. We've been given an opportunity to redeem ourselves…"

"Sir… I don't know if I can do this anymore. I've given it a lot of thought and think it would be for the best if I seek opportunities elsewhere…" Brayden stood up and reached into his jacket pocket. He pulled out an envelope.

"Shut up and sit down, Brayden! Put that away. If I'm going down, I'm taking you with me."

"But, sir… *Mitch Youngs?*"

"Quit bitching and suck it in. We've been given a unique opportunity, as I say, to redeem ourselves. Together with the President, we think we know where Sophie *et al* are heading."

Brayden reluctantly slipped the envelope back into his jacket pocket.

"Okay, I'm listening…"

"Guantanamo Bay," said Calland. He liked the taste of the words in his mouth. "I had George Jennings moved there."

"With due respect, I don't think so… sure, yesterday I would've agreed… with Sophie on her own, but… I hear *Dominic Schilling* is here. That changes things…"

"Nonsense! It changes nothing." Calland spat.

"He killed her mother! Sure, she wants to find her father, but this is more than that… this is something else. Trust me!"

"Like what, Brayden?"

The CIA agent shrugged, lacking commitment. "Maybe they're going for something more important… like… I dunno… George's work, perhaps." It sounded flippant and his tone was too weak.

Milo Calland snorted back laughter. "That would be impossible – insane even!" he boomed. "No, Brayden, no, no, no. The President himself agrees, Guantanamo Bay is where they're likely heading. Which is where I'm assigning you and Mitch."

"But, Deputy Director…"

"No buts, you're going. My *Learjet* is refuelling as we speak ready for your trip to Cuba. At least if there's any further foul-ups, it's not far for us to dump and forget you."

CHAPTER THIRTY-FIVE
EMILY

HER DWINDLING SUPPLY OF serum, her change of clothing and all her other personal possessions (including *Flopsy* the bunny and the *Glock 17* obtained from Georgetown University Hospital) were stashed within her holdall in the boot of the silver *Chevrolet Impala* in the car park to the back of Dulles International Airport. Ryan had made arrangements for her holdall to be collected, but for now, everything she owned, including the means to make her visible, was beyond her reach.

In the compact washroom annexed to the private room on the jet, Sophie washed the blood from her face, inspecting the damage to her ear in the mirror above the small sink. Her earlobe had a slight nick in it and cleaning had restarted the bleeding; apart from that, there was hardly any damage. This was surprising considering the amount of blood. She applied a plaster from the first aid box next to Dominic's bed, moulding it from one side over to the back of the lobe, stemming – or at least concealing – the blood-flow.

I was lucky, she thought. A couple of inches to the right and the bullet would have killed her. The officer taking the shot hadn't seen her. He had been firing blindly and had hit her by sheer chance. It was a wake-up call. Despite all her engineered abilities, she was not immune to injury or dying. *Don't get complacent*, she warned herself. Her father needed her. She was no use if she wasn't alive.

After little less than five hours flying, the *Bombardier* started to descend as it approached a small airfield twenty-five miles east of Palmdale, California.

"Ladies and gents, please buckle up and prepare for landing." The pilot, Johnson, spoke over the internal speakers.

"Where are we going? This isn't LA?" Emily was peering out of the window closest to her.

"L-A-X is too hot for us," said Barry, meaning it was too dangerous. He strapped himself into the seat next to Emily. "We've been given clearance to land at a private airport normally used for developing and testing unmanned aerial vehicles for the US military."

"Drones?"

"Yea..."

"Isn't that sorta dumb?"

Barry smiled, his mouth suddenly appearing full of teeth. They were brilliant white. "Bold, yes... dumb, not really."

The asphalt airstrip quickly came up to meet them as the jet suddenly dropped fast, the pilot deploying the landing gear in readiness for grounding.

"Is this right? We're going too fast!" Emily sounded panicky, her hands tightly gripping the armrests of the recliner seats.

"Try to relax. Johnson knows what he's doing. It's a short airfield."

The *Bombardier* landed hard, the wheels bouncing twice before settling on the asphalt, continuing to surge forward. Johnson applied the brakes firmly and everyone, though strapped in their seats, was flung forward with tremendous force.

The jet came to an abrupt halt.

Emily had never experienced such a landing and felt her stomach lurch and acid reflux bubble at the back of her throat.

"You okay?" Barry found a folded paper sick bag beneath his seat and handed it to Emily. "Here."

Emily opened it quickly and shamelessly vomited her breakfast of scrambled egg and cheese with bacon bagel up into it, tears streaming down her face. "Sorry," she said, indifferent. "I'm the same on roller coasters."

Barry handed her a handkerchief. "Remind me not to take you to *Cedar Point* in Ohio. They've got a ride that'll have you hurling for days..."

"Thanks."

The jet, still in motion, but significantly slower, taxied away from the short runway and rolled towards a designated spot to where a ramp agent holding a pair of orange flags marshalled the pilot in.

Two silver SUVs were stationed a short distance away, their drivers climbing out. Both wore mirrored sunglasses and casual clothing. The weather in California was bright and sunny. The temperature was currently 19°C, and would go as high as 23°C later in the day, warm for October.

Sophie unbuckled her seatbelt before the aircraft had come to a complete stop. The internal speaker crackled on followed by a little shrill static feedback.

"Ladies and gents, that concludes this flight from Washington DC. I hope you enjoyed the landing as much as I did! If you want to set your watches, the local time is currently ten thirty-six a.m."

The time difference between California and Washington highlighted how vast North America was. The time in Washington was 1:36 p.m. Sophie quickly calculated that the time in England was now eight hours ahead of them. It was 6:36 p.m. It could get easily confusing.

For a moment she wondered what her brothers and sister were doing right then. *Probably around a television in Grandpa Theo's house.* Around the cabin her travel companions were unbuckling their belts and beginning to ready themselves to leave.

By the time the exit door of the *Bombardier* had opened out to reveal steps leading down to the asphalt, the drivers of the SUVs had headed over to meet the disembarking passengers; one was deep in conversation on a mobile phone that had an antennae sticking up.

The first passenger to step out of the jet was Barry, followed by Emily. A large gap appeared between her and the next traveller. Sophie was inconspicuous in the absence of a visible body. The unnamed man in dark green combat trousers and khaki T-shirt stepped out. The scar down the right side of his face looked menacing in the harsh sunlight. Behind him, Dominic limped out, taking each step with slow and measured determination, trying to dismiss the pain and humiliation.

"Is he okay?" the first SUV driver asked Barry, nodding up towards the wounded man.

Not getting a chance to reply, the second SUV driver stepped forward. "Sir, a call for you."

Barry took the handset. "Hello?" He stepped away for privacy, wandering over to the first of the SUVs, leaning up against its silvered bonnet.

Emily and Sophie stepped off the ramp, followed by the man with the scar. They were soon joined by Dominic.

"You know, Dom, it'd be no shame if you were to sit this out," professed Emily. "We can't carry you there."

"Sit? SIT? You being funny? I doubt I'll be *sitting* for months." He half-smiled. "Don't sweat it, Princess. I've had bigger pains in the ass than this." Bizarrely, he knew where to look when Sophie felt his gaze upon her.

After a lengthy conversation, Barry sauntered back, the mobile still in his hand but no longer pressed up against his ear. "Emily. Ryan wants to speak to you…"

Emily accepted the proffered phone, giving Barry a serious look; she pressed the phone up against her face. A dozen questions suddenly filled her head, all vying for dominance, all concentrated on what Barry had to do with all of this.

"Emily? Thank God you are okay!" He sounded distant, the connection crackly and a thick droning sound filling the background.

"Ryan… what's going on? When were you going to tell me about Barry?"

"Emily – ah yes, Barry. I'm guessing an explanation is in order. Barry's with us. It was felt safest for all concerned that your missions were handled independently; with the heat growing in Washington, I asked Barry to keep a check on things and lend a hand if needed. You didn't think we'd not have a contingency plan, did you? It's just a happy coincidence that he was in DC at the same time… Listen," changing the subject, *"has Dominic told you the operation?"*

"Hardly. As far as I'm aware, we're here to shop and sightsee."

"Forget that, your vacation is over. Dominic is leading a task force to close down GYGES, and you and Sophie are there to add whatever assistance he needs."

"Ass-istance? Was that a pun?"

"Err, hey?"

Emily explained Dominic's injury.

Ryan started to laugh at the Kaplan Ratcliff man's misfortune.

"What about Barry and the other… the *guy* with the scar?"

Ryan's laughter subsided. *"They're MI6, both ex-military. They'll stay with you as long as you need them."*

"Would've appreciated a heads-up about them. Could've avoided the whole airport farewell party and Dom and Sophie wouldn't have been shot."

"Barry and Liam weren't assigned to us before then, but… Sophie's been shot?!" Emily's flippant remark dawning on him, he sounded suddenly alarmed.

"It's nothing. She's fine. Just a graze to her ear, she'll live… She's a bit cranky though, and not at all happy about leaving her serum behind." Emily was walking slowly about in a circle. Whilst she talked, the others were climbing into the two SUVs.

"*Being invisible is the least of her problems. Tell her not to worry. She'll have her serum in no time.*"

"It's not like she can go into a *Boots* and get some more!"

"*Your luggage is on its way to you. I had it collected three hours ago. It'll be with you – including the serum – tomorrow.*"

"Ryan, look I have to go. We're about to pull out of here."

"*Okay. We'll catch up later. We've just left the UK. Our ETA is approx. midnight.*"

"We?" Emily quizzed, hurriedly.

"*Dominic's task force.*"

"And you're comin' too?"

"*We'll meet you there. And Emily…*"

"Yes?"

"*Don't do anything heroic. You're not a field agent. Leave all the fighting to the others… and Sophie. I've already lost a daughter… I can't lose you.*"

Emily pressed the disconnect icon on Barry's phone as she climbed into the second SUV beside the MI6 agent, handing it back to him. She assumed Sophie was in the other vehicle with Dominic and the other MI6 man Ryan had called 'Liam'.

"Dominic says we're going shopping," Barry said, "we've got quite a few hours before the rendezvous time; perhaps we can go grab a bite to eat as well." Emily raised an eyebrow, prompting Barry to add quickly, "Not just me and you… all of us!"

The SUV in front started moving. The driver of the car in which Emily and Barry sat, revved the engine and soon followed.

"I guess we could do with stopping off somewhere. After that landing, I'm famished. My stomach must be empty."

CHAPTER THIRTY-SIX
SOPHIE

AFTER FILLING THEIR STOMACHS with traditional American cuisine of gigantic portions of burgers, hot dogs and fries, followed by 'small' cups of *Pepsi*, the SUVs carried them for about half an hour before stopping alongside a busy shopping district in spaces usually reserved for the disabled.

"And that place will have what we need?" Sophie's voice filled the back of the lead SUV. She sounded doubtful. Behind them having conversations of their own, Barry and Emily were waiting for instructions via a comms-link. They all wore them, buttonhole microphones with small in-the-ear speakers the size of a large peanut. They crackled to life upon voice activation.

Across the carriageway, cars charging by on either side, a row of shop fronts and restaurants no different to what you'd expect in any town or city the world over. Nestled between a grocers and a hardware store was a large outlet that was heavily barricaded with a thick steel grille. A similar security feature that usually protected the entranceway was pulled up, allowing access for business.

"This is the place, yea," said Dominic drowsily, suffering the side-effects of a painkiller recently administered. "Well, that's what they told me..." Implying his contact in London.

The signage above the door was old and faded and gave little doubt about the type of business the proprietor was in.

"*Combat Zone*. Guns and Survival specialists," said Liam in the front passenger seat, reading the dilapidated sign. "Every town in America has got to have one. It's their constitutional right…"

"And they love to do a bit of hunting…" the SUV driver added dryly.

"Yea… plenty of game roaming the streets," Liam continued, sardonically.

Ignoring them, Sophie cut in. "Well, we can hardly stroll in there and buy the stuff we want. There's protocols they follow… and err, ID checks… besides, we're *British!* We're the folks they armed themselves against in the first place," Sophie reasoned.

The SUV driver glanced at the rear-view mirror, seeing Sophie leaning forward in the seat behind him. For a moment he just studied her reflection, thinking it almost impossible for someone so young and so strikingly-*attractive*, to be such a threat. Before leaving the *Bombardier*, she'd changed her bloodied clothing and was now wearing grey combat trousers and a black crop cami that hung loose over her shoulders, her posture exposing a lot of cleavage that Sophie hadn't grown used to, and that the SUV driver couldn't help focusing on.

Dominic had stretched out and was leaning his head back, eyes closed. When he spoke, some of the lethargy had left his voice. His eyes popped open. "This is where you come in, Sophie."

Sophie sat back and turned to face Dominic. "Uh-uh, no way. I stole a diamond for you remember, and look how that turned out."

"Yea, well… I'm still waiting delivery of that diamond. Have you ever stopped to think that maybe, just maybe, had you and your father done as I'd instructed, things might've turned out differently?"

"Stealing the diamond was a trap, try denying it. For all I know, this is a trap also…"

"What's she talking about?" Liam asked, puzzled.

Dominic sighed, shaking his head. "Just a misunderstanding," he said quietly. He turned back to where he knew Sophie was. "Look, I know things went south in July, I'll shoulder my share of the blame, but here, today, I'm with you a hundred percent. Help me and Ryan close down *GYGES* and I'm with you in getting back your father. Trust me on this."

Sophie couldn't trust him, he was beyond that. But Ryan did and that counted... just a little. "Okay," she finally said. "What do you want me to do?"

"Here..." Dominic reached into a breast pocket of his collared shirt, removing a folded piece of paper. "I wrote down what we need."

Sophie snatched it making it disappear into thin air.

"I so love it how she does that," said Liam in awe.

"You should see my Vegas show," Sophie said sarcastically as she unfolded the slip of paper. Once open she placed it on the back of the seat in front so that it would reappear. Upon it, in Dominic's untidy scrawl, was a list of two dozen items. "I bet your parents hated Christmas," she said, glancing at the inventory.

"What can I say... I was an only child. My parents loved to spoil me."

Sophie read down the column, stopping at one item. "An *M61 Vulcan?*" The *Vulcan* was a hydraulically driven, six-barrelled *Gatling*-style rotary canon usually attached to fixed wing aircraft. Not something you'd lug about with you. "Who've we got in our task force, *Arnold Schwarzenegger?*"

"Ha-ha. Just get the damn gun, will you!" Dominic settled back into his seat. He was too sluggish to argue.

"Okay... let's get moving. Dominic... you can stay here." Liam was climbing out of the SUV and didn't care to notice him wave him off half-heartedly. Sophie and the SUV driver followed him out.

Barry, Emily and the other SUV driver met them on the sidewalk beside the two silver vehicles. "Gentlemen… Sophie," greeted Barry as they came together almost in a ring. "This is what we are going to do."

***

The fact that anything Sophie touched became invisible was one of the enigmas surrounding the young woman. A side-effect of the genetic enhancements made to her DNA, and one which defied the laws of physics, it had its disadvantages (like not being able to see the things she was holding). However, when entering a store with the sole purpose of stealing many items, it definitely proved a blessing.

Sophie went ahead, entering *Combat Zone* on her own. Walking around, she found the store was quite small – a fact that initially confused her; from outside the place appeared the size of a moderate supermarket. On closer inspection, she realised that much of the 'hardware' must be stored in a backroom, concealed behind the sales counter and a door marked with a sign: *Authorised Persons Only*. Only small calibre hand guns, camping equipment, combat clothing and cross-terrain footwear was on sale in the immediate shopping area.

Shortly after, Barry and Liam walked into the store together with the intention of causing a distraction, Barry walking towards clothing and Liam heading directly to the sales counter. A guy wearing a faded denim sleeveless jacket and a bright-white T-shirt stood at the counter flicking through a copy of *American Handgunner* magazine. A quick scan of the room confirmed that there was no one else about. It also provided Liam with a couple of reasons to draw the store owner out from behind the counter.

"Can I help you with somethin'?" The sales guy looked up at Liam, whose size and build would be a little intimidating to most people. The fact that the store owner kept a loaded shotgun beneath the counter helped his confidence; he was not like most people.

"I'm looking for a…" Liam looked over his shoulder. "…a shooting jacket."

"Shooting apparel is over there in the corner." The guy returned to perusing his magazine. Liam had to do better than that.

"I was rather hoping I could get some advice?" Sounded lame.

The guy raised his eyes and flashed Liam a look of annoyance before allowing a cheesy smile to fill his face. "Certainly, sir. This way…"

Liam felt Sophie brush past him just before he followed the sales attendant to the corner of the store. Barry was lurking near to where the footwear was.

With the sales counter unattended, Sophie slipped through the access-way and headed towards the door marked: *Authorised Persons Only*. Peering towards where Liam and the sales guy had headed, she saw the way was clear. She pushed down on the handle and quietly pulled. Unexpectedly, the door swung open.

This is too easy, she thought. Stepping through the doorway she discovered that she hadn't entered a room but a short, narrow corridor approximately three metres in length. She closed the door discretely behind her and stepped forward. At its end was another door, this one steel, the type you'd expect in a bank's vault. Sophie could see that it was secured by an electronic keypad combination, the small numbered panel glowing a soft light-blue.

"Great!" she exclaimed to herself, activating the comms-link. "Guys?" speaking quietly, "we have a problem. It's like frigging Fort Knox in here."

CHAPTER THIRTY-SEVEN
GEORGE

GEORGE WAS SITTING IN a large wheelchair designed for a bigger man within the dayroom of the Naval hospital. The nurse had positioned him so that he was facing outside. The view was of a deep blue sea and an azure, cloudless sky. The sun was bright, but on the other side of the building, behind him.

Alongside the wheelchair was a medical infusion drip stand on castors. An IV drip was attached via a cannula to the back of his hand, the tubes leading up to a bag of fluids hidden beneath a black veil, hanging from the stand. An electronic pump connecting the plastic tubes to the chemotherapy drug, administered them specifically over a set period of time. A timer counted backwards and the pump made a small groaning noise as it operated.

Captain Will Hancote walked casually into the dayroom, George's back to him. Under his arm, he carried his peaked cap. Half a dozen strides into the room and he was standing to the right of George.

"Fantastic view," Hancote exclaimed, sounding genuinely impressed.

"Is it?" George asked. He hadn't noticed. He had been staring into nothing, deep in thought. He focused for a second on the shoreline outside before letting out a deep sigh. "I suppose it is Captain. But…, I prefer the Bahamas…"

Conversation ended for a moment as Hancote struggled to think of something to say. He settled on: "I'm sorry George…"

"For what? For imprisoning me, or for my getting cancer?"

Hancote pondered the question for a moment. He walked a little ahead of the wheelchair, turned and rested his body against the windowsill so that he faced George. "For both, I guess…"

"It's not your fault."

"True, but, I am responsible for your continued incarceration. If it were up to me I'd let you go. Let you live what's left of your life… with a little dignity… with your family."

"Excuse me if I don't say thank you," George said, sardonically.

"Alas, it's not up to me, however. You're a very important person, George. What you have done, what you CAN do, and what you know… it's just too dangerous. There are others out there, even as we speak, seeking to find you."

George's ears pricked up. "Who?"

Captain Hancote shrugged. "I couldn't tell… suffice to say the President himself takes the threat of an attempt to *abduct* you very seriously… he's sending in two intelligence agents and ordered an immediate increase in the number of personnel guarding this facility. Five thousand, to be precise."

George laughed. "I doubt five thousand would be enough," he said. "You won't know, let alone *see*, what you are up against."

Hancote ignored the comment. "Just thought I'd let you know, George… but don't worry. If anyone, including your friends, do attempt to free you… they'll be keeping you company real soon." He stood up from the windowsill, making ready to leave, placing his cap on his head.

"We'll see," grunted George. They were the final words on the matter as Hancote swiftly left the dayroom.

CHAPTER THIRTY-EIGHT
SOPHIE

"SOPHIE, DON'T DO ANYTHING... *we'll find a way to get you in."*
Emily had been the one to respond to Sophie, but all six of her companions had heard the distress in her voice as she'd revealed that the room where *Combat Zone* kept its serious military hardware was not going to be easy to get into. Sophie had explained in detail the type of door she faced and Emily, using a tablet computer, had researched the model.

"A Diebold Titan vault. It has a unique locking mechanism," Emily continued to read it in her head. *"No... there's no way you're breaking into that thing... we'll think of something else."*

"Great."

Five minutes stretched into ten and within the confined, unventilated space, Sophie was sweating profusely and beginning to feel nauseous and claustrophobic. Propping herself up against a wall, she felt uncharacteristically weak. When the urge to lie down seeped into her mind as heat overwhelmed her, the sudden opening of the entrance door startled her back to attention.

"It's just through here..." Sophie heard the sales attendant say as he entered the narrow corridor. Liam and Barry followed him in. How they'd persuaded the guy to take them into the fortified room, she couldn't guess. Instead, another thought panicked her.

Oh crap!

Not only was the corridor quite short, it was also narrow – just wide enough for one person to walk through single file.

Invisible or not, Sophie standing just ahead of the keypad-secured door, was obstructing the way forward. Her presence was about to be discovered.

Think!

There was absolutely no time to think. There was just three metres between the beginning and the end of the corridor. Sophie glanced about her and did the only thing possible. Using both walls of the narrow walkway, stealthily she leapt up high and pressed herself up against the ceiling, her lips almost kissing the plasterboard, her legs scissor-split against the two opposing walls, her arms stretched out in symmetry and balance, the heel of her hands tight, her whole body taut to control and maintain the position. Spread-eagled against the ceiling, she held her breath as the sales guy walked beneath her, his head just two inches away from her bottom! Unconsciously, she pulled her midriff up closer to the plasterboard. Sweat coated her face and forehead and a bead gathered just beneath her chin, dripping to the floor. In slow motion it fell, narrowly missing the sales guy passing by.

"Okay, no peeking!" *Combat Zone*'s sales assistant was standing at the steel door, Sophie poised above him. Using his right hand, he keyed in a six digit number, waited a moment, then smiled. A soft thud sounded as the locking mechanism retracted within the door. The man reached for the handlewheel and turned it anticlockwise, releasing a series of internal bolts, before pulling the heavy door open. A moment later the large whitewashed room with motion activated bright fluorescents flickering on above, came into view.

"Follow me."

Liam and Barry walked beneath Sophie. Owing to his large

size, Liam unavoidably felt his head rub against Sophie's back and posterior. He dipped his head abstractedly.

"You keep it well and truly secure," observed Barry disappearing into the room.

"You can never have too much security…" the sales-assistant said cheerfully.

Silent and nimble, Sophie dropped down behind Liam and crept after him. All around her she saw handguns, machine guns, rocket launchers, boxes of ammunition, grenades, military uniforms, bulletproof vests, silencers, and knives. Lots of knives. Big knives, some as long as machetes. And others, smaller, throwing knives.

"It's the law. Sure, us Americans love our guns, but this stuff… some of it you can't even get a licence to own."

"You've got enough hardware here to start World War Three…" Barry's eyes were wide and he couldn't contain the note of excitement from entering his voice.

"Well, I don't know about that. But, we've supplied local law enforcement before; LAPD and their SWAT guys."

"Impressive. Very impressive," Barry was still doing the speaking. The way Liam viewed it, Barry was the boss. Liam knew his place.

"Anyway, I don't usually let normal folks back here. But, as you are ex-military and fellow members of NRA, thought you'd appreciate our collection." Barry had handed the store attendant an NRA membership card, a prop he carried with him when masquerading as an American. The guy still held it in his hand, like it was a security or some such.

"Absolutely."

"D'you have any questions?"

"Um, do you have a '*M61 Vulcan*'?"

The Californian laughed. "You bet'ya… it's over here." Barry and Liam followed him almost to the back of the room. A large metal box secured just by a couple of clasps was presented for inspection. The store guy opened up the box to reveal a large rotary gun. "I can't say I've ever sold one, but I keep one in stock just in case. Ammo too," inclining his head towards a wall full of shelves containing boxes and boxes of ammunition.

"Thanks, err…"

"Brian."

"Thanks Brian. I think I've taken enough of your time."

"You're welcome to try out some of our guns. We've got a fully equipped shooting range in the basement…"

"Some other time, maybe."

"Okay, but you must see my decommissioned *Abrams* tank…"

The store owner led Barry and Liam back out of the secure room. Just before the door was locked, Sophie heard Barry ask another question.

"For big orders, do you have a back entrance…"

"Oh, no. The only way in is through this door." The steel door shut with a loud clang followed by the sound of the locking mechanism and all its bolts clicking home as the round handwheel was turned clockwise.

"Just perfect," muttered Sophie. Getting in apparently wasn't the problem. She spoke into the comms-link. "Um, did anyone give any thought to how I'm supposed to get out of here?"

"I'm on it. Just get everything you can on the list. Leave getting you out to me." Dominic's voice filled her ear and then the comms-link went silent.

"Forgive me for not feeling *too* confident," Sophie whispered to herself. In the corner of the room was a fold-up flat bed trolley. Sophie crossed over to it and opened it up, placing it down onto its four wheels. "I suppose I've got nothing better to do…," she muttered, placing the list Dominic had given her onto a clear work surface. She quickly re-read it, then walked around the room beginning to 'shop' for what Dominic needed. In no time a pile of rifles, machine-guns, handguns, knives, ammunition, and not forgetting the *M61 Vulcan*, weighted down the trolley to the point it could barely move.

When she found everything on the list, Sophie couldn't help seek some supplies for herself. She slipped into a black double-gun shoulder-holster, then secured a tactical belt complete with pouches, sheaths, pockets and an additional holster attachment around her waist; she had plenty of places to carry her weapons. Crossing over to a wall filled with handguns, Sophie selected three to fill her holsters. Two *Glock 19*s (which she placed in the shoulder holsters) and a *Sig Sauer P226* pistol.

"That'll do nicely," she said, slipping the *Sig Sauer* into the holster to the right of her waist.

Within the pouches, pockets and sheaths remaining about her belt, she stowed ammunition clips, throwing knives, and a folding, double-bevel, serrated combat knife.

Not satisfied that she had enough ammunition, she filled a heavy duty canvas rucksack with as many *Glock 19* magazines as she could carry. Each magazine held thirty-three rounds. With the rucksack on her shoulder, and her hands on the trolley, everything she touched disappeared; nothing out of the ordinary could be seen on the CCTV video being recorded.

"Right, Dom... I'm done."

Nothing but dead silence answered her.

"Dom?" She began to wonder whether Dominic had betrayed her again and started to feel panic well-up inside her. A sudden burst of static filled her ears.

"I heard you," he said. *"Find some place to take cover. And cover your ears!"*

The earth beneath her feet began to vibrate and a distant

rumbling, too long and constant to be thunder, sounded through the brickwork. Boxes of ammunition clinked and jangled on the shelves and guns and knives began to rattle around the walls.

"Guys? Guys, what's happening?"

In answer to her question the rumbling progressively intensified until it was deafening and the wall at the back of the secure room cracked open loudly and imploded.

Sophie dived for cover as debris rained down on her.

A large armoured vehicle burst through bricks and steel girders, causing part of the ceiling to collapse and the lights to suddenly flicker out. Exposed cables within the remains of the wall spat sparks like indoor fireworks. The *Abrams* tank came to a halt in the centre of the room, its decommissioned gun turret battered, the replica gun barrel sheared clean off.

A thick, hazy cloud of dust filled the room.

The hatch on the tank lifted open and Dominic poked his head out. "Sophie?"

In the corner of the room, a little bruised but mostly unscathed, Sophie pulled herself invisibly up from beneath a pile of rubble wearing chunks of plaster and a thick coat of dust. She stood and started coughing. "I'm here," she said against her left arm, shielding her airway from the dust; it came out muffled. "You nearly killed me!"

"But I didn't, did I?" Dominic disappeared back into the tank and the hulking armoured machine began to reverse; bricks, mortar and other parts of the structure rained down as he slowly backed out to reveal a gaping hole that replaced much of the back wall, allowing Californian sunlight to burst in.

Through the haze, Sophie watched the approach of four men; Barry, Liam and the two SUV drivers. The drivers were armed with handguns.

A moment after, Dominic limped into view having discarded the

Abrams tank away from the building, allowing access for the SUVs. Wincing and a little strained, he spoke: "Gentlemen, let's load up and clear out. We've got two minutes before we have company…" Almost as though highlighting the point, sirens could be heard keening in the background.

Unseen, Sophie walked past them all, clambered over wall debris and padded over to the nearest SUV within which Emily was sitting and waiting.

Watching the young woman's reflection in the rear-view mirror as she climbed into the back of the vehicle, Emily observed how dusty, bedraggled and beat-up she appeared. "The way you look, I bet you're glad no one can see you.,,"

"Just another perk to add to the list," Sophie said stiffly, slamming the car door closed behind her. "I guess once my batch of serum runs out, I have that as a bright side. It'll save hours in applying make-up and doing my hair."

CHAPTER THIRTY-NINE
RYAN

ALMOST TEN HOURS INTO flying and after four-and-a-quarter hours' sleep, Ryan woke to find the cargo hold of the *Boeing* aircraft in almost complete darkness; a red safelight glowed in various places, offering the barest luminance, but enough to see the huddled forms of his task force seated about the plane. The noise of the turbine engines still boomed, but having acclimatised to the sound, he barely noticed it.

Adjusting his eyes to the gloom, Ryan soon made out the figures of Wyatt and Marty Heywood positioned at opposite ends of the plane. Wyatt's team were seated around; most were asleep or resting their eyes.

Ryan unclasped the seatbelt and walked the tiredness out of his legs, heading for the front of the plane. A moment later he checked his chronograph wrist watch, pressing the backlight button. Having set the watch to Las Vegas local time earlier in the flight, Ryan checked the time; 11:23 p.m.

Using an internal phone situated in a corner near to toilet facilities, Ryan lifted the handset and called the captain piloting the airplane just by pressing one of the preset buttons. The cockpit was situated above him up a flight of steps, but the connection quality was crackly and reminiscent to ringing someone on the moon. He could have easily been on the other side of the world.

"Alby, it's Ryan. What's our ETA?"

Almost immediately the captain replied. *"We're pretty much on schedule. Twelve-O-five. Flying conditions have been good to us."*

"Any problems entering American airspace?"

"That's a negative. Our flight plan has not been challenged."

"Good. Good. Thanks, Alby. I'll ready the men." Before disconnecting, Ryan quizzed the pilot further. "At what altitude will you be dropping to for the jump?"

The captain did not hesitate in his reply. *"To avoid too much scrutiny, we'll need to stay pretty much where we are, approx 13,000 ft. It's what we call a HAHO – high altitude, high opening jump. The advantage is we'll avoid detection. Owing to the speed we're travelling at, you'll have ten seconds to get you all out... so no dawdling. You'll then need to drift for a couple of miles to reach the LZ."* The captain knew that a change in his altitude would not go unnoticed, even though a low jump would be more accurate and require less time in the sky. This way necessitated a lot more skill, and vastly more time free falling through the air.

"We'll be ready. Just give me the signal." Ryan disconnected, flicked half a dozen switches activating the interior lighting and watched the overhead fluorescents flicker into bright milky light.

Jack Wyatt squinted at the sudden glare.

"Men... gather round," started Ryan. He was standing in the centre of the aircraft. A bit of turbulence made him sway slightly, as though drunk, but he maintained composure. Once all the men of the joint MI6 and Kaplan Ratcliff task force were surrounding him – Wyatt and Marty Heywood flanking him either side – the MI6 officer reiterated the mission, leaving nothing out and highlighting the importance of destroying all evidence of Project *GYGES*.

When the briefing was over, the plane's interior became a blur of activity as men geared up, strapping on body armour, squeezing heads into helmets with built in speakers and microphones, and attaching night-vision eyepieces. They fitted parachute packs to backs, and checked and rechecked the safety features on them, before doubling-up and checking each other.

Safety was of paramount importance.

Once satisfied, the men armed themselves, holstering weapons (guns, knives), attaching miscellaneous items (grenades, flash lights, radio equipment), gathering up rifles and machine guns, and finally, stocking up on clips and magazines of ammunition.

Similarly attired, including Ryan, Wyatt and Heywood, they were all groomed for the battle ahead.

"*Gentlemen… we're almost entering the target zone. Get ready.*" The *Boeing*'s captain spoke over the internal PA system, his voice steady and tinny.

"Ten minutes!" shouted Wyatt. The interior of the plane went dark as the lights were all turned off. Red safety lighting guided the way to the aircraft's exit. Soldiers, dark shadows in two columns, began to shuffle towards the rear where the cargo ramp was being prepared for opening.

"Are you sure you're not getting too old for this?" Ryan asked Heywood. They were to the back of the column of men psyching themselves up for the jump, and were to be last out.

"You can talk, Ryan!" Marty said. "Besides… I'm an adrenalin junkie; I wouldn't miss this for the world."

⎯⎯ ⬥ ⎯⎯

At exactly 12:05 a.m. the pilot of the *Boeing Globemaster III* signalled that it was mission go. The cargo door was fully distended and the first six paratroopers ran out into black nothingness. The night sky was void of light; not even the moon was in sight to highlight the descent of their plummeting bodies.

Scrutinising his chronograph watch, Ryan counted down ten

seconds – the available time allowed for the jump so that the task force weren't too far apart and all on course for the designated landing zone.

A second ticked by and the next six paratroopers leapt from the back of the plane, followed by another, and another. At eight seconds the last four paratroopers jumped leaving Wyatt, Heywood and Ryan Barber standing watch.

"After you…" said Wyatt.

"No time!" Ryan grabbed Wyatt with one hand and Heywood with his other. The three men leapt off the cargo ramp as Ryan's watch flashed '00:10:00'. Ryan thought he heard Alby wish them "*Good luck*," over the PA, then it was gone. The *Boeing* sped away from their freefalling bodies, pulling away fast, the roar of its engines fading gradually as distance and gravity separated them.

All fifty-three men were in the night sky, the thrill of the fall at 120 mph and the adrenaline released through anticipation of the mission overloading their senses. Hearts were pumping as they flew through the sky; some, acting like they were on a pleasure excursion, linked hands with colleagues and formed mid-air lines or circles, though most concentrated on the job of locating their landing zone and fell solo.

Throughout the drop, expletives, exclamations, whoops of joy and tears of laughter could be heard through the built-in speakers of their helmets. The experience was exhilarating and something that would stay with them for the rest of their lives – unfortunately for some, this wasn't for very much longer.

Owing to the darkness, their falling bodies could not be seen from the ground; in the air, they were just dark shapes floating on a less-dark background. Earth, below them, was just as dark; a blank canvas. Ryan imagined he was floating in space, the thought weirdly cathartic.

After what seemed like forever – which in actuality was just fifty-eight seconds – the first jumpers pulled the cords dangling from their parachute packs, their freefalling suddenly halted as large squares of canvas sprung open and dragged them back skyward for a stomach churning moment, before they started to glide down more gracefully.

They had descended to 3,000 feet above ground.

Ryan pulled his cord and felt like he'd hit a wall as the parachute opened, halting his plummeting body with such force that he felt his head snap back and stars begin to dance in front of his eyes.

I wish I had stayed on the plane. It wouldn't be the only time this thought would surface that night.

As his parachute dragged him skyward, the silhouette of Marty Heywood shot past him fast. Ryan recognised him by the size of his frame. He was the fattest agent – including Dominic – on the mission.

"Pull your cord, Marty," Ryan instructed, his head clearing. His eyes followed after him and nothing seemed untoward; but, then it was dark and a bit of distance soon grew between them.

"Ryan… my cord. It's not working…"

"Pull the backup cord. You're running out of time."

"I'M TRYING!" Heywood's voice was thick with panic. "It's not working. Ryan… Ryan… my chute… my chute's failed."

"Don't panic, Marty… it's probably just stuck. Try again…"

"Thanks Ryan for… giving me a chance on your team…"

"Marty, try the cord again," insisted Ryan.

"There's some correspondence in my drawer back in the office. Can you see that it gets delivered…" Heywood wasn't listening to Ryan. He'd already accepted the inevitable. "I hope you can forgive me for what I have done. I did what I thought was best…" These were his last words.

Far beneath him, Ryan could just make out Sir Marty Heywood's frame; he watched as something became detached and fell away to his right side. Heywood had removed his helmet. There was no further way of communicating with him.

"No, Marty. Noooooooooooooooooooooooooooo!!!"

Marty had dropped so far, so quickly, that Ryan could no longer see him. In less than eight seconds, without a parachute, Sir Marty Heywood hit the ground. It's not unheard of for people to miraculously survive a freefall from 3,000 feet, albeit injured with multiple fractures and broken bones. Marty wasn't one of those people. His body fell from the sky with such force that it exploded on impact, in just the same way, and equally as messy, as a watermelon.

The airwaves went quiet as they all reflected on what had just occurred. Death had an uncanny way of putting things into perspective, making things scarily real.

After four minutes floating down in eerie silence and a seemingly endless void with nothing but one's own thoughts for company, the built in speakers of their helmets crackled into life.

"*I see the LZ,*" an unidentified voice announced loudly in all of their ears. "*Follow me in.*" The speaker activated a small white guide light which flashed slowly, revealing his position in the night sky.

Skilfully, the fifty-one paratroopers glided up behind the soldier, following the flashing beacon like it were the star of Bethlehem.

After a minute, the lead soldier landed gracefully, almost running when he hit the ground. Behind him, one after another, each soldier landed with varying degrees of skill. Some landed hard, falling onto their faces, scuffing knees and colliding with others; some floated down like they were suspended in the air from a safety cord tied to a crane.

None of them plummeted to the ground like Marty Heywood had.

Ryan was the last to land, hitting the earth most awkwardly, twisting his ankle on impact. It took all his effort not to scream out. He sat on the ground nursing it. After a few seconds he looked about him. No one paid him any notice, too preoccupied with their own preparations.

All about, dark shadows were detaching parachutes and making themselves ready for onward movement; guns were being checked, loaded, held in position and double-checked.

Beyond the immediate area, the terrain looked rugged, dry and inhospitable. In the distance were some large buildings obscured by the blanket of darkness that provided them with continued cover.

Without a shadow of doubt, Ryan knew they had arrived. The place politicians and the military, for so long, had denied existed. The fabled Area 51, home to many of America's UFO and alien conspiracies, and the place where top secret research and aviation testing was carried out.

It was also the place where George Jennings had been seized to undertake his work on producing an army of genetically-enhanced super soldiers. This was the home of Project *GYGES*.

Using a satellite phone that was three times bigger than his mobile and as chunky as a house brick, Ryan keyed in a number and waited for an answer. Whilst he waited, he unclasped his helmet and pulled it from his head.

"Ryan? Where are you?" Little time had passed between ringing and speaking.

Ryan lifted the phone to his ear.

"Dom. We've just landed."

"Good."

"We didn't all make it…" Ryan relayed details of what had transpired with Heywood.

"That's too bad," he said, disinterested. *"Listen. Focus. We're nearly there; we're coming in from State Route 375. Be ready for action in fifteen minutes. I expect a welcoming committee at the perimeter. Can I rely on you to remedy that?"*

"Copy that."

"Any ideas how we get in once we're clear of the border guards?"

"Improvising is a good starting point. See what happens and what our girl does. Also, Barry might have an eye on a way in…"

"I don't like it, Ryan… not a jot."

Ryan sighed. He could understand Dominic's reservations. Until 2005, Area 51 didn't officially exist. Since then, despite numerous accounts being made public, the US government kept information regarding the place highly classified. MI6 had secured maps of the base and schematics of the underground research facility, but as far as security was concerned, he was about as knowledgeable as any of the many thousands of UFO enthusiasts that descended on the place each year. "I know Dominic. I never said the mission didn't come without its risks."

"Okay… just secure the perimeter for me… And Ryan?"

"Yes?"

"Watch out for yourself. I know you've grown soft and prefer the safety of the office desk, but there's no room for complacency. This isn't going to be pretty." With that, the line went dead and the brief communication ended.

You can talk, Dominic, he reflected, thinking of the weight Kaplan Ratcliff's Director of Security and Intelligence had gained. A glance at his watch told him it was 12:15 a.m. Replacing the satellite phone at his waist, Ryan limped across to Wyatt. Placing a hand across the man's shoulder, Ryan reiterated the operation to the task force leader, much of which he'd already stated back on the *Boeing* early on in the flight.

CHAPTER FORTY
BARRY

BARRY, LIAM AND THE two SUV drivers loaded up the vehicles with the trolley of weapons and supplies selected by Sophie. Dominic stood by watching and dishing out orders, his hands unsullied. The injury to his backside was making him cranky, especially as the pain relief had worn off.

The *M61 Vulcan*, designed for military aircraft, was loaded first and made the vehicle the young women sat in, rock from side to side.

"What on earth are we going to do with that?" asked Emily, glancing at the large metal box placed behind her.

After a minute, the last of the items were stowed in the silver vehicles. Dom, Barry, Liam and the two drivers climbed into their vehicles hastily, slamming doors behind them as engines roared to life.

Barry climbed into the passenger seat in front of Emily and Sophie. Dom and Liam took the other SUV.

As they pulled away, the first police cruiser, tyres screeching, lights flashing and sirens wailing, came into view on the carriageway behind them, too far to cause immediate concern, but not alone. Dozens more weren't far behind it. There was one thing the Americans could do well, and that was organise a spectacular car chase if given half a chance.

"Nicely timed," Barry sighed. "Now the easy part."

"Don't get too comfortable. We've got more than an eight hour drive," said Emily pointedly.

"In the presence of two fine looking women, it's not going to be all that bad." Barry had noticed Sophie behind him through the reflection of the rear-view mirror and found himself unable to tear away his eyes, his gaze making her feel a little uncomfortable. He'd heard of this crazy phenomenon, but hadn't believed it; not until then. He didn't understand how it was possible, but then, no one did. Even George Jennings couldn't entirely comprehend it, and he'd committed hours of research trying to assimilate it.

"Can I help you with something?" Sophie asked coldly, feeling Barry's eyes on her for way too long.

It wasn't the fact that she was invisible and yet he could actually see her in the mirror that made him stare; it was how attractive she was that captivated him.

"Um, no… it's just… has anyone ever told you… how beautiful your eyes are?"

Sophie felt her cheeks flush red, a reaction she'd never before experienced. "Shut up," she said quietly, turning away to look through the window as California passed them by.

⬛◆⬛

They crossed the State line into Nevada leaving California behind them via Interstate 15 north, taking a route that would lead them through the bright lights and the razzmatazz of Las Vegas. Owing to time limitations and an urgent desire to get business out of the way, there would be no excursions or opportunities to gamble in any of the casinos. The journey time to Rachel, the closest documented town to Area 51 with a population of just fifty, was eight-and-a-half hours, excluding stops or delays.

They had pulled away from *Combat Zone* just after 1:00 p.m. They would roll into Rachel approximately 9:30 p.m., barring any issues along the way.

Surprisingly, nothing untoward met them on Interstate 15, which, after driving past lavish hotels and world-famous casinos in Vegas, they exited north of the city after five-and-a-half hours and, just as the sun was setting, joined Great Basin Highway, also signposted as US-93.

The journey had been hot, and long – tediously so, to the point that Sophie had resorted to playing 'count the road kill' along the highway, sharing her progressive count with her travel companions as and when a new carcass presented itself.

"Eighteen… nineteen…" were counted in quick succession; a pair of coyotes, likely part of the same pack. They were small, probably young. Sophie felt a little sadness overcome her. Soon, failing light made it impossible to continue entertaining herself in such a way.

Ninety miles north of Las Vegas, they drove past a sign for Alamo, a small town. The sign indicated a population of 1,100. Neither car stopped or showed signs of slowing down.

One hour forty-five minutes after passing *Caesar's Palace*, *MGM Grand, Excalibur* and many others along the Las Vegas strip, the driver turned left onto a road that took them onto State Route 375 – a road famously dubbed as the *Extraterrestrial Highway*. Barry glanced at his watch. The time was 8:45 p.m. They were making great time despite making one stop for fuel, but that had been way back at a service station just before exiting Vegas. For the past hour the strong need to go for a pee had overcome him; he held it in and tried to focus on something else.

A short distance along State Route 375, they passed an unpaved, dusty road leading south-west, just wide enough for a single car to travel. Under the cover of darkness, it could easily be missed, except the driver of the SUV had been looking out for it.

"This here, is 51 Road," said the driver of Sophie's vehicle, his left hand leaving the wheel of the car to point out towards the road.

"We'll be returning here a bit later. It's the one we take to the army base."

The next road they passed, also unpaved and dusty, was known as Mailbox Road on account of the lone mailbox placed at the road's edge a short way in. The mailbox wouldn't garner any attention were it not made famous as a prominent meeting spot for UFO sightseers. The driver, like a veteran tour guide, killed the silence by giving a brief history of the spot, voicing the many theories associated with the area with such enthusiasm you could be mistaken for thinking he was a local expert on the subject.

Driving past Mailbox Road, it was too dark to see what all the fuss was about. Sophie did all she could to ignore the driver; she closed her eyes and ears and gave no thought to the alien conspiracy nonsense. It was short-lived. Every time she opened her eyes there was a subtle reminder of how serious the locals took the UFO thing.

At 9:20 p.m. they passed a sign that read: *Welcome to Rachel, Nevada. Population: Human: Yes; Aliens: ?*

A short while afterwards, they pulled into a small parking lot with a large signpost marked as 'Restaurant, Bar, Motel: EARTHLINGS WELCOME, LITTLE A'LE'INN.'

"Hey... this place is famous," declared Barry. "I remember seeing it in the film *Paul*, with Simon Pegg."

The SUV following parked up beside them and Dominic and Liam climbed out. Sophie, Emily and Barry joined them.

"I'm thinking we should freshen up, take a bite to eat and wait it out here." Dominic was still limping and looked tired, even with just the small amount of light emanating through the windows of the LITTLE A'LE'INN.

"Do we have much choice?" asked Sophie who'd crept up behind Dominic, making him jump from speaking in such close proximity.

Dominic shrugged. "You've always got a choice, Sophie. Life's simple like that. Come on... let's see what gourmet is on the menu..."

At 12:05 a.m., Barry's mobile phone rang. Country music played loudly, so he excused himself from the table at the back of the LITTLE A'LE'INN restaurant, answering the call as he rushed from the building.

"Hello?"

He continued moving until he was standing between the two silver SUVs, away from any eavesdroppers.

"*Barrington?*" There was a lot of background noise competing for attention, the drone of an engine most prominent.

"Yes, I'm here."

"*It's time… the Kite is flying…*" Barry had been expecting the call. Alby, the pilot of the *Boeing*, spoke in code, just as Ryan had prepared him earlier that day.

"Thank you."

"*Good luck.*" The line went dead and Barry took a deep breath. For a moment he didn't move, enjoying the peace and serenity offered by being in the middle of nowhere; a blanket of dark sky and lack of road lighting giving the terrain an ominous, empty atmosphere. It was eerily quiet and the air was still. For a moment, despite the abundance of space, he suddenly felt asphyxiated, almost claustrophobic, like the sky had become heavy and was crushing down upon him.

Only a handful of customers graced the hospitality of the LITTLE A'LE'INN, most having retired for the night within the twelve bedroomed motel placed at the back of the restaurant. When Barry walked back in, the waitress had turned the lights off over the serving counter and was giving meaningful hints that it was time to go. Closing time was, she'd already informed them, 10:00 p.m. They'd already overstayed their welcome by over two hours.

Barry stepped up to the table occupied by his travel companions at the back of the room. The only other customers stood up and made for the door leading to the motel, one wearing a Stetson and walking with a cowboy's swagger.

Dominic and Emily looked up at Barry, eyebrows raised enquiringly.

"The kite is flying," Barry relayed. "It's time to doff our hats gentlemen and mount our steeds."

"Kite? Hats? Steeds? What's he talking about?" Liam looked puzzled.

"I think he's saying, it's time to go," replied Emily, standing up. Sophie was already on her feet, not that anyone had noticed. She'd said little or nothing since arriving. At times, it was like she wasn't there at all, completely forgotten by Dominic, Emily and the rest. Her plate of food had gradually vanished, one bite at a time, but no one commented on it.

The waitress, a delicate girl with a slight tan, came over and started clearing the table. "I hope you folks have got somewhere to go tonight," she said, sweeping food waste onto one plate, then stacking a tower of plates atop each other for ease of carriage. "All our rooms are taken."

"Thank you, but yes... our plans are all mapped out," replied Barry, smoothly, his accent very English against the waitress's. "Here," he pulled out two folded hundred dollar notes deep from inside his trouser pocket and handed them to the waitress, a smile charming his lips. The dollars were warm to the touch. "This should cover the bill," he said. "Keep the change."

Bereft of lighting and the moon, the SUVs looked dull grey on State Route 375 illuminated by their own dipped headlights; they were the only vehicles moving in any direction for as far as could be seen. Just after half an hour, the driver of the lead vehicle pulled off the road, followed closely by the second. The SUVs came to a halt soon after near a copse of weirdly-shaped trees and the occupants all climbed out, moving slowly, almost reluctantly, into the glare of one of the vehicle's headlights.

Dominic's mobile began to ring, the sound seeming to be magnified out in the wide open space and probably heard for a good distance around.

Dominic quickly answered it, ending the noise.

"Ryan? Where are you?" Without realising, he was talking in a hushed tone.

"Dom. We've just landed."

"Good."

"We didn't all make it…" Ryan informed Dominic that Marty Heywood's parachute had failed.

"That's too bad," he said, unconcerned. "Listen. Focus. We're nearly there; we're coming in from State Route 375. Be ready for action in fifteen minutes. I expect a welcoming committee at the perimeter. Can I rely on you to remedy that?"

"Copy that."

"Any ideas how we get in once we're clear of the border guards?"

"Improvising is a good starting point. See what happens and what our girl does. Also, Barry might have an eye on a way in…"

"I don't like it, Ryan… not a jot." Dominic hated going into the unknown. In his experience success was dependent on three things: preparation, preparation and more preparation.

Ryan could be heard to sigh. *"I know Dominic. I never said the mission didn't come without its risks."*

"Okay… just secure the perimeter for me… And Ryan?"

"Yes?"

"Watch out for yourself. I know you've grown soft and prefer the safety of the office desk, there's no room for complacency. This isn't going to be pretty." Dominic ended the call and stowed the mobile back into his trousers. He turned to the small gathering.

"Okay. Ryan and his task force are in place. We'll go in via 51 Road. Ryan is going to help limit the resistance we meet along the way, but..." he paused for emphasis, "there's likely to be some, so we're going in prepared. Guards are stationed all along the perimeter of the base. Usually, anyone who happens on, or heads towards the roads leading into Area 51, is swiftly intercepted and met by a less than hospitable welcoming committee."

Dominic released the catch on the boot of the first SUV and lifted up a black blanket hiding the cache of weapons concealed beneath. "They won't be expecting what we have in store for them." Dominic lifted out a machine gun and chambered a round. "Take as much as you can carry." Turning, Dominic faced Emily. "This is going to be too dangerous for someone without field training. One of the drivers will take you to Alamo. I'll call you when it's over."

Emily didn't protest. Before climbing into the second SUV, an invisible force embraced her, arms encircling her body. The hard protuberances of Sophie's holstered guns dug into Emily's chest, and at her hip. She gently released Emily. Behind them, Liam was helping himself to body armour, weapons and night-vision goggles from the boot of the SUV.

"Wish me luck," Sophie whispered, the slightest tremor in her voice. Nerves rarely affected the young woman, but precisely then, despite the genetic alterations and military programming, a strange feeling overcame her.

"You don't need luck, Sophie. Just do what you need to do and get out. Think of the endgame. Once this is over, we'll find your father."

Although Emily couldn't see it, Sophie smiled falteringly. "Yea. My father..." it came out as just an exhalation.

"Right... we'd better move. Dom, you ready? Cinderella wouldn't want to be late for the ball!" Barry called out as he closed the boot on the second SUV. He wore body armour and night-vision goggles (pushed atop his head) and carried an assault rifle over his shoulder.

Dominic was positioning the *M61 Vulcan* on a stand in the back of the first vehicle, its six barrels pointing through the open boot.

"Nearly… there," grunted Dominic, inserting an ammunition belt into the machine gun, aligning the first bullet ready for dispensing. "Done!"

"I was wondering what you had planned for that…"

"This thing can fire off six thousand rounds in a minute. I figured we might be needing it for our getaway."

Barry raised his left eyebrow. "If it's all right with you, I'll hope that we won't."

"Bye," Sophie said towards Emily, her voice sounding a little distant as she climbed into the back of the first SUV. Liam was already inside. Not wanting either Dominic or Barry to sit on her lap, she scooted over into the middle.

Dominic climbed into the front alongside the driver; Barry took the final seat beside Sophie. Closing the door behind him, the small interior light just ahead of the rear-view mirror faded off leaving just the soft lights of the dashboard to glow.

"Okay gentlemen… *and* Sophie. Safety's off. Let's take what is rightfully ours." Dominic was holding the *Kalashnikov AK-12* assault rifle in his lap, the barrel pointing up towards the ceiling. An array of other weapons were holstered and strapped around his body.

Emily stood with the second SUV driver, her arms folded, and watched her companions drive away until distance and darkness obliterated them from view. She sighed resignedly. "Come on," she said, "there's little point staying here."

CHAPTER FORTY-ONE
BRAYDEN

THE LEARJET HAD DELIVERED Brayden Scott to Cuba eight hours after his meeting at Langley with the Deputy Director. The two-and-a-half hour flight from Washington to Guantanamo Bay would have been comfortable were it not for the company. Mitch Youngs had joined him on the private aircraft shortly before take-off and had tried to engage him in conversation. Brayden cared little for the older man and made no pretence about it.

"Excuse me, Mitch… I have something I need to do." Brayden turned his head away from the man (who'd taken the seat next to him despite there being six other empty seats spaced around the cabin) and pressed two ear bud earphones into his ears, pressing play on his iPod. *Erasure's A Little Respect* drowned out any further words spoken by Mitch; closing his eyes, Brayden could almost believe he wasn't there.

Milo Calland's private plane landed within the naval airbase at Guantanamo Bay shortly after 8:00 p.m.

Will Hancote led the welcoming committee, together with the Bay's most senior officer, Admiral Jefferson-Price. Both men wore the blue and grey Naval uniform with matching baseball-style peaked caps. The only thing setting them apart were the insignia badges stitched into their shirts.

"It's been quite an eventful few days," started the Admiral in a gruff, authoritative voice; he offered his hand, "Guantanamo takes in its first prisoner since *Said Rafique Abbabas*, an Al Qaida terrorist responsible for over nine hundred deaths, including thirteen US citizens; then we get news of a large deployment of men from 38th and 40th Infantry Divisions – five thousand men in all – for heaven knows what. And now, here you are; the CIA's best… or so I'm told." He didn't mask the contempt in his voice, or the corresponding look.

Brayden shook the Admiral's hand. "It's just a precaution, sir." Behind him, Mitch clambered down the ramp from the *Learjet*.

"I've seen precaution, chief… and this ain't it. Initially, we went into 'Nam (he pronounced it Na-rm) with less men… I know – I was an eighteen-year-old grunt with more hair than I had brain-cells back then, and most of it round my nut-sack. It's like you're preparing for an all-out invasion. I hope someone's going to tell me what's going on?"

"Of course, Admiral. I'm sure it's nothing… just, as I said, *precautionary*. The President himself has given the order… based on up-to-the-minute intel – although, personally I think it's a little extreme." His own theory that the base was under no immediate threat, he kept to himself.

"Hmpf. Well, I guess I'd better offer you a little hospitality. Captain Hancote here will take you to the digs for your stay. There's a galley-room where food is still being served – nothing grand, usual military slop. I think spaghetti bolognaise is on the menu. If you're real lucky there may even be some Boston Cream pie, though I'm not sure it's up to much. The chef's on loan from 38th Division. Make yourselves at home."

George Jennings was lying on his bed. It was after ten and Chemotherapy was over for the day. He felt physically sick and emotionally drained.

His dinner was untouched and pushed to the side of the room on the trolley table. Spaghetti bolognaise had congealed and looked like sun baked cat vomit. George considered the dish, when freshly cooked, a kid's meal and would have left it untouched, even were his appetite to have been normal. US television was being beamed into the room via satellite and George had been flicking through the channels to pass the time. *The Walking Dead* flashed on the twenty-two-inch LCD screen affixed to the wall for a moment before being replaced by *Downton Abbey*, followed by *Falling Skies*. After flipping a dozen more channels he settled on a news channel that was in the middle of a broadcast.

"...is becoming an internet sensation with over three million hits on *YouTube* since this morning..." A shaky image of an airport scene was appearing beneath the female reporter's voice. "... this eyewitness's recording clearly shows a number of police officers in pursuit of one of the terrorists and, seemingly, have him cornered, when... something... strange happens..." The grainy video footage showed the group of policemen, their backs to the camera, and the terrorist – seemingly cornered – when suddenly the policemen started falling down to the ground, some buffeted over by some invisible force, the others felled by an officer shooting aimlessly, hitting some of his own men. "... the terrorist got away with the help... and you heard it here first... from the invisible man..." The video image changed to a shot of the news anchor and her co-worker, both laughing at their apparent joke.

George turned the television off as the uniformed figure of Captain Hancote appeared through the doorway. He was accompanied by two suited men, one older, fatter and unrecognisable, the other George easily identified. Comically, they reminded him of Laurel and Hardy.

"I'll be in my quarters if you need me." Hancote nodded and left the room to George and the visiting CIA agents.

"I know you," George said, accusingly. He recalled the night in July when he'd last seen Sophie. The warehouse and the attempt to rescue Harriet, all part of an elaborate scheme to protect his true identity.

This man had played a part in his fabricated capture. He'd assured him Harriet was going to be safe, that nothing bad would come to her. It had all turned out to be a lie.

"Hello George," said Brayden Scott, walking around the bed and stopping just beside him. He made himself comfortable in the vacant chair placed next to the bedside drugs cupboard, and faced George. "I was in the area and heard you'd been taken ill; thought I'd drop by and see how you were. Plus, I thought you might like the company… I don't expect you'll get many visitors…" Brayden turned up his nose as though a bad smell had wafted by, "… not here."

Mitch offered no greeting, instead wandered over to the window and looked out at the darkened sky and the scenery enveloped in murk and shadow. Brayden had noticed a marked change in the older man. He seemed preoccupied, withdrawn and ill at ease; it was as though he was shouldering a burden that tore at his conscience. Brayden dismissed any concerns from his thoughts.

"Amazing coincidence you showing up here… the same time as the news is reporting strange goings-on in Washington."

Brayden smirked but gave no response.

"Tell me, is it customary in America for visitors to turn up at a hospital without fruit or flowers? In England I'd have enough of both to open a market stall."

Brayden reached into his trouser pocket. "I've got a stick of spearmint gum…" He offered out a loose stick from the crumpled pack.

"Keep it," George replied tiredly, before adding tersely: "So, the President has sent you two here to babysit me… and five thousand men. Do you think that's enough?"

"Honestly?" asked Brayden. "Too many. If it were up to me I would've just put a bullet in your brain and cut out the hoopla and expense. Someone, though, thinks you are worth keeping alive... at least, for as long as can be. Plus, there's the incentive of your daughter... sure, we have our own group of Top Secret freaks, but they're only children... it'll be a while yet before they are operational. Sophie is already viable... despite her... flaws. They believe you are the perfect bait."

"I doubt you or all the armies of the world would be able to take her. She's far cleverer than you – or even *she* – realises."

"Well... that she may be... but, like as not, it's a waste of time. My hunch is she's not coming here any way... not yet at any rate."

"No?"

Brayden ignored any further questioning, making no offer to expand on his flippant remark. He stood up. "It's good to see you again."

"Don't make a habit of it."

Brayden was joined by Mitch who had remained at the window looking out to sea. So quiet he had been, that George had completely forgotten him.

"Oh, before I forget," Brayden turned his head back, peering over his shoulder, "Milo sends his regards." It came out almost as an afterthought, despite Brayden having already rehearsed the comment in his head a moment earlier.

As they left the room, George heard the two agents engage in a brief conversation before they were no longer in earshot, their voices hushed.

Brayden: *"You could've at least said hello."*

Mitch: *"I don't like hospitals."*

Brayden: *"I don't like you but I..."*

George sighed as once again silence descended upon the room.

He flicked the television back on using the remote lying by his side. The news channel was still on but a different story was being reported. Something about a robbery using an *Abrams* tank at a weapon store in Los Angeles.

CHAPTER FORTY-TWO
DOMINIC

SQUASHED UP BETWEEN LIAM and Barry in the back seat, Sophie felt terribly uncomfortable. Both men were wearing full military body armour and carrying more weapons than she could count, their bodies pressed up against her small frame.

In the rear-view mirror, despite the gloom, the driver could view Sophie's discomfort, her arms dangling between her legs, hands laced together as there was no room to keep them at her side. Unlike Liam, Barry and Dominic, she'd not bothered with body armour. The added weight and the restricting material would hinder her movement and agility, she reasoned. She hoped her natural camouflage would be enough to shield her.

"Nearly there." The driver slowed the vehicle to a crawl and turned off the headlights, immediately shrouding the car and the abutting surroundings in total blackness. He slipped his night-vision goggles into place and turned them on.

Ahead, they could just make out the border – no fencing or barbed gates as you might expect, just orange posts spaced fifty yards apart and the occasional signpost giving grave warnings should you pass beyond that point. In fact, to the unsuspecting, there *was* no border (an error many tourists had made over the years); unfortunately, ignorance was not an acceptable excuse to the American authorities.

Beyond the posts, just behind a small hill, bursts of bright light seared the darkness, first from one side (the left) and then from the other (their right), almost like some bizarre communication exchange was in progress.

It didn't take long to translate. Evidently, a gun battle was taking place in the foreground.

"I think we're early," exclaimed Dominic. "Ryan was meant to take care of the welcoming party."

"Not afraid, are ya?" the driver asked, flooring the accelerator. The SUV shot forward.

The exchange of light-bursts continued frenetically ahead of them as the SUV crossed the non-existent barricade.

"Do you intend for us to drive into the thick of it?" Dominic exclaimed, his right hand gripping the passenger-assist-handle fixed into the ceiling to calm his nerves.

"I hate being late for a party," the driver said. Driving around a bend, the hill beyond which the battle raged, the occupants of the SUV steeled themselves ready for the conflict.

"You're not even invited!" Dominic moaned at the driver.

"D'you bet?" An automatic handgun appeared from nowhere in the driver's left hand and as the vehicle turned into the thick of the gunfire, he began squeezing off shots at armed guards dressed in combat clothing (through his open window). Suddenly, he slammed on the brakes and the SUV screamed to a halt. Before the momentum had even completely finished, Liam had opened his side door and was on the ground next to the vehicle.

Sophie jumped out after Liam, leaving Barry to come to his senses a few moments afterwards. He hadn't been prepared to take part so suddenly and was only energised into action when a side window shattered beside him, glass crystals showering his face. He slumped to the floor of the SUV as though he'd been hit, and crawled out after Sophie and Liam. A small line of blood curved a trail down the side of his face where a splinter of glass had nicked his skin, but no other injuries were present.

Dominic climbed out of the SUV and crouched down beside Liam, Barry and, he assumed, Sophie, using the vehicle for cover. All three men had slipped their night-vision headgear into place and could now see what they faced.

Handguns, rifles and machine guns were cocked and loaded, barrels pointing at the ready, though none were being fired – other than the driver's; he appeared to be taking potshots out of his side window into the darkness.

"I expected Ryan to have cleared the way. We need to end this," shouted Dominic over the echo of machine gun fire being volleyed between two different dunes, muzzle flashes lighting each side frequently and fervently, but not long enough to indicate how many soldiers were fighting on either side. He retrieved his phone from a small leather pouch attached to the military belt clasped at his waist, and called Ryan. A moment passed and his MI6 ally was talking into his ear.

"What the hell's going on, Ryan?"

"*We're coming up against a bit more resistance than we expected,*" Ryan replied. Gunfire threatened to drown him out.

"How many are there?" Dominic asked, agitated. A bullet ricocheted off the roof of the SUV and whistled above his head.

"*At a guess… about a dozen left. We've taken out twice as many…*"

Beside Dominic, Liam had decided he'd had enough of crouching in fear and stood up, firing off half a magazine of bullets from his *M60* machine gun in the direction of the perimeter guards.

"See if they've got any flares!" Sophie's voice was close to Dominic's other ear, but even so she needed to shout to be heard over the deafening clatter of Liam's gun. Dominic relayed the message. In almost immediate answer, a small ball of light whooshed into the air and popped like a defective firework sending a number of phosphorescent spheres raining slowly down, brilliantly illuminating the entire area.

"Tell them to cease fire," Sophie instructed loudly. She tapped Liam on the shoulder, making him jump. He stopped firing the *M60*. "I'm going in," she said, unseen.

"Ryan… tell your men to stop shooting and fall back. It appears our girl wants to rush into the action and hasn't the temperament to fight this battle your way…"

"Hold your fire!" Ryan could be heard over the telephone line, followed by, *"STOP SHOOTING, DAMN IT!"* after one of his team squeezed a couple more rounds off.

"If you've got the drinks I'll bring the popcorn. This, I reckon, is going to be good…" Dominic pressed a small button on his night-vision glasses that turned the infrared function on allowing him to view heat signatures and see Sophie's form; he looked over towards where she had momentarily stood. The ghostly figure appeared before his eyes, slight of frame, with her back towards him. She walked like a Goddess, moving calmly into the field of battle, both her hands clutching *Glock* handguns, a machine gun hanging over her shoulder, draped across her back.

With the abrupt gunfire ending on Ryan's side, the American perimeter guards ceased their shooting also, a couple prematurely thinking the attack was over, standing up from defensive positions, exposing themselves as easy targets. Small talk and anguished moans from the injured could be heard, the wide open space and night-time acoustics amplifying their voices.

Sophie needed little prompting. With no effort she ruthlessly picked the two soldiers off, firing double shots from her *Glock* at each, bullets taking them in the chest and head, muffled thuds and gasps of shock sounding after each impact. They fell to the ground amongst their colleagues, dead.

Before the remaining Americans had time to realise that they were under attack from close quarters, Sophie had walked unseen around the dune behind which they were hiding, and was picking each uniformed guard off clinically, her twin guns exploding shot after shot at a multitude of angles, her hands automatically taking aim with the barest of movement and the slightest of thought.

She stopped shooting when just one guard was left; though clueless to what was going on, he'd thrown down his weapon and had raised his arms in surrender after seeing all his companions die around him. Although he couldn't see her, he felt the warm barrel of a *Glock* press into the back of his head. The muzzle was hot to the touch.

"Please...!" Fear resonated in the guard's voice. "I beg you." He involuntarily emptied his bladder. He was thankful that it was dark and that his trousers were black.

"Come with me..." she said, impassively.

From start to finish, it had taken Sophie less than thirty seconds. After another twenty seconds, she'd swept the entire area and marched back to the SUV, her prisoner ahead of her. Only Dominic saw her; the others could only see the guard shambling forward, his arms raised above his head. Liam turned his *M60* on the prisoner, a finger lightly teasing the trigger, itching to press it.

Dominic, the phone still pressed to his ear, started to gasp. In the half-minute that had passed, he'd forgotten to breathe, totally mesmerised by how, like a ballet dancer, Sophie had moved gracefully and with purpose about her business. He knew of her abilities, but seeing it... it almost brought a tear to his eye. "She's..."– catching his breath – "... incredible..." Dominic had forgotten Ryan was on the other end.

"Now you see why it's important we put a stop to the Americans," replied Ryan. For the first time since skydiving into Area 51, his voice sounded clearly, no longer competing with the noise of gunfire.

"Here…" Sophie said, "I've brought someone who might prove useful… I'm a little disappointed, though. You know, I was expecting a bit more of a challenge." With the guard now under Liam's watchful eye, Sophie stepped away and released a magazine from one of the *Glocks*, replacing it with a full clip. She chambered a round.

Dominic was still awestruck. He shook himself to regain composure and smiled. "Ryan… it appears the threat has been neutralised… also, you know you said improvising was a good starting point on getting into the base? I think Sophie's handed us a solution."

"Might you explain?"

Dominic mentioned the guard who had surrendered to Sophie. "I think we should use him; who knows, he may get us in closer than we expected. Let's move in."

"Copy that…" The line went dead and Dominic, standing up, returned the phone back to his military belt. Turning to Liam and Barry, he spoke: "Okay, we're on the clock, guys. The base and underground research facilities are approx. fifteen miles from here. We need to get moving. They'll likely be expecting us, but, if they're not, we want the job done before they call in reinforcements. Sophie's gifted us an opportunity," – he nodded towards the prisoner – "I think we should capitalise on it." Climbing back into the passenger seat of the silver vehicle, Dominic groaned. "Ah, Jeez…" He'd forgotten about the driver. He stepped back out of the SUV, shaking his head.

Slumped against the driver's door, half-hanging out through the shattered window, the driver, a bullet hole the size of a ten-pence-piece in the centre of his head. Gore coated the inside of the vehicle and was spattered across the seats and stained the ceiling.

"What's…" *wrong*? Barry had peered in after Dominic. He didn't need to finish the sentence, instead exhaling in exasperation. "WHY didn't he take cover like the rest of us?" A sudden wave of anger flashed in his mind. He dismissed it almost as quickly as it had come. "Did anyone get his name?"

Dominic and Liam shook their heads simultaneously.

Barry sighed. "Too bad," he said. "… no one should be without a name when they die."

"Come on… give me a hand. We'll grieve for him later." Dominic opened the door and allowed the dead man to fall unceremoniously and heavily to the dusty road.

━━━◄◆►━━━

Sophie had pinpointed the three white *Jeep Wranglers* and the armoured military transport vehicle parked a short distance from where they'd battled the perimeter guards, keys all in their ignitions and suitable transportation for Ryan and his foot soldiers for the remaining distance to the research facility. Although Ryan and his small army of twelve had fought for nearly half an hour, the number of guards providing resistance amounted to more than three times that amount; Ryan's paratroopers had killed two dozen and Sophie had neutralised the rest – bar one. The remainder of Ryan's task force – all thirty-eight paratroopers – had been ordered ahead to surround the base and find suitable places in readiness for the attack. They had landed closer to the airfield with Jack Wyatt leading the way.

Taking up driving the SUV, Liam sat behind the wheel doing his best to ignore the blood stains on the upholstery and ceiling, and also splashed across the dashboard. Dominic was beside him. Sophie and Barry were in the back seat; Barry was checking a handgun. Like before, Sophie was quiet. Preparing or reflecting, none of them could tell.

The terrain was rugged and bumpy, but despite the lack of light, the convoy of five vehicles moved swiftly without incident, a cloud of dust billowing in their wake. They were led by one of the *Jeep Wranglers* within which Ryan and two of his paratroopers sat, guns pointed at the prisoner who was driving; moments before setting off, Ryan had instructed him to radio into the base with a plausible reason for driving a convoy in. He relayed the conversation via satellite phone to Dominic in the SUV, the third in the five vehicle procession. The armoured transporter, like a conventional single-decker bus, albeit built with toughened steel and bulletproof glass, trundled along furthest at the rear.

"The way's clear, Dom. Base commanders are expecting our vehicles to return transporting a number of prisoners from a border breach. Turns out they're unaware of the gun battle... or so they claim."

"You'd think they'd have seen the fireworks," asserted Dominic incredulously.

"That's what I said, but our prisoner was adamant that they'd not called in, other than to report a border breach. Turns out it's not unusual for them to let off a few rounds once in a while. Besides, they're private contractors and didn't want to be seen as being unable to handle things themselves..."

"Glad to see that worked out well for them," sniggered Dominic.

"It sounded like he regrets it, now..." Ryan added.

A full twenty minutes later and they pulled up just before the final hill that allowed them cover before the world's most secretive military base came into view, a mere half a mile away.

Ryan climbed out of the *Jeep Wrangler* and walked past the second *Jeep*, stopping at the passenger door of the SUV. He peered in through the open window.

"Okay, Dom... you're in command from here-on-in. Good luck!"

"Are you not coming with us?" Sophie's voice floated through from the back.

"Uh, no... this is as far as I go. As Dominic so rightly pointed out to me earlier: I've grown a bit *soft*. I much prefer the safety of an office desk these days. Besides, I've twisted my ankle." It sounded lame.

"Too bad," sighed Sophie. Up until then her respect for the MI6 man had swelled; now he was ditching them on the cusp of battle, foregoing the threat of danger.

"We'll come and get you when it's over," said Dominic, not hiding the contempt from his voice. Liam was leaning out of the shattered window away from them. "I hope you know how we're going to get out of here after… when it's done. I'd hate for us to get stranded…"

"It'll be fine," Ryan replied. "Trust me."

CHAPTER FORTY-THREE
SOPHIE

"**S**o… how do we get in?" It was a legitimate question, one which was on all of their lips, yet only Sophie cared to voice it.

Barry had a ten-inch tablet computer out in front of him; a schematic of the base helped pinpoint the whereabouts of the hidden research facility. It flashed up in front of him, white lines on a black background. A finger swipe across the screen highlighted where the secret labs were hidden. A couple of taps with the pad of an index finger revealed the exact location. Deep below an unmarked hangar a short distance from one labelled as '17'.

"I guess Ryan failed to share that with you too," grumbled Dominic. He was still feeling morose from the dull throbbing pain flaring in his rear-end. He removed the night-vision goggles that had been resting on his head and lay them down for a moment whilst he re-tied his hair.

"Oh," Sophie exclaimed disappointedly. Nothing was ever straightforward. Barry remained quiet seated next to her.

"Okay… we're nearly there." Liam slowed the SUV in tandem with the two *Jeep Wranglers* ahead of them.

Having driven off a dusty, bumpy track, it was comforting to drive on smooth road surface again. Although noticed by the passengers, the transition was ignored, too absorbed and mentally preparing for the operation ahead.

The road swiftly expanded into a long runway, obscured by darkness before its end. Along the right side of the runway (as they approached) a host of buildings and aircraft hangars cluttered the foreground and the skyline. Floodlighting washed over an area of the runway in front of what Sophie assumed was the control tower. A contingent of soldiers and security personnel waited to welcome the convoy; *Jeeps* and other military vehicles sat stationary close by.

"Okay, Wyatt... d'you read me?" Dominic spoke into a hidden mic. In his left ear was a small, discrete earphone he'd moments earlier inserted.

Wyatt's voice crackled in response. "*Copy.*"

"Be ready to meet any resistance. We are good to go. Repeat, we are good to go... over."

"*Roger that...*"

The two *Jeeps* came to a standstill a short distance past the eight armed men sent to meet with them. The SUV, clearly not a regulation vehicle, drew curious glances, but none of those waiting thought to make issue of it or expected anything untoward as it too drew to a halt, thinking it likely belonging to the prisoners. The *Jeep* behind and the armoured transporter were the last to stop, their tinted windows hiding their passengers, all of whom were readying weapons for lethal use.

"Men... on the count of-" Before Dominic had finished his sentence, the driver's side door of the lead *Jeep Wrangler* burst open and the driver – the perimeter guard who Sophie had taken captive – stumbled out, ran around the front of the vehicle screaming "Help!" and charged towards the welcoming committee like a distraught toddler to a parent.

Dominic swore. "Take them out. All of them."

Through opened windows gun fire rat-a-tat-ed and exploded from all five vehicles, bullets punching holes into the waiting soldiers, none able to respond as hands flailed uselessly at holstered weapons. The fleeing captive took three rounds in the back and another to the side of his head, pulverising his right ear and the idea of escape. In a matter of seconds the welcoming committee were on the ground.

Up in the control tower, the three officers, one commanding, the other two assistants, heard the gunfire. At first they mistook it for high jinks by a group of over-exuberant officers, too engrossed on trivial matters and light-hearted banter. When the shooting hadn't stopped, they took stock and did a double take, initially too stunned to understand what was occurring below them.

"Barry…" Dominic turned to look at the younger man behind him. The pain in his ass momentarily forgotten. "Organise Ryan's men. Make sure we have a clear path out. When our work is done we won't want to dilly-dally."

"Right you are… here. Take this." Barry handed Dominic the tablet computer. "Full schematics of the research facility, including security detail. MI6 were able to scramble some info from the *GYGES* file sent over to them. Oh, and this…" he patted his trouser pocket, reached in and pulled out a security key card on a lanyard that had been wound tight. "And, not forgetting this," he located a small, leather-coated box that looked like it could contain an item of jewellery, sealed by a sprung hinge. "Don't open this until you're on the laboratory level… and, no questions on how I got them. It should help you get in." Barry placed the security key card and the box into Dominic's palm. Like Ryan, he had contacts within US government. He sometimes used blackmail and promises to get what he wanted; in this instance, he'd bypassed both and blatantly stolen the coveted items from a well-placed female whilst she'd slept; one item she would miss more than the other. Her trust and his duplicity came with just a dinner date price tag.

"When were you going to tell me?"

"Right then," Barry replied, smiling. He climbed out of the SUV and slammed the door behind him. Liam put the vehicle into gear and pulled out of the cavalcade, speeding down the tarmac towards the end aircraft hangar – numbered '17' on the schematics; Barry and Ryan's task force members quickly disappeared behind them.

<hr>

The aircraft hangar was larger than anything Sophie had ever seen in her life. Even without any overhead lighting, she could see that the enormous room was completely empty. In one hand she held a torch, the swath of light visible ahead of her even though the source of its glow was not. On her shoulders she carried a bag and the rifle she'd yet to use.

"Are you sure this is the right place?" Sophie asked. Liam, a little way ahead, swept a powerful torch beam around, highlighting nothing but dust motes. On his shoulder he carried a heavy bag, which moments before he'd stuffed full with explosives and ammunition.

"Barry's schematics led us here correctly. Let me see... if I..." Dominic started muttering to himself as he tapped the map on the tablet's screen and watched the image flicker as it changed. A profile of the facility appeared, showing the architectural design from its top – the hangar – to the bottom, the research laboratories, situated below ground level. "Okay... now I get it..." he said.

"What?" Liam was getting agitated by the man's talking to himself. Dominic ignored him.

Sophie glanced at the ten-inch screen. "How do we get to it?" she queried.

"Your guess is as good as mine," replied Dominic, looking about towards sheer darkness. The night-vision goggles were in the SUV where he'd left them to tidy his hair. "There must be a hidden entrance. Liam... sweep the torch all around. It's got to be here somewhere."

Liam aimed the torch towards the ground, searching for a hatch leading downwards. He walked a few paces, sweeping the torch beam side to side, then moving a bit further.

"Anything?" Dominic called, his voice echoing within the large open space.

"Does it look like it?" Liam replied, his tone belligerent.

"Try over there…" Dominic pointed uselessly in a different direction, but owing to the gloom and his positioning, Liam didn't see which way he meant.

Sophie had taken it upon herself to search as well, wandering towards a dark side within the hangar.

"This is hopeless…" muttered Dominic in frustration.

"Guys… I think I've found something." Sophie could be heard loud and clear. The acoustics within the empty hangar made her sound as though she were talking from all around.

"Where EXACTLY are you?" called out Dominic. Even had she not been invisible, she would not have been seen owing to the absolute darkness.

"At the wall… ahead of where we came in. I've found what appears to be… a hidden door." Sophie lifted her torch highlighting the way. The sound of feet pounding resounded and a few moments later both Liam and Dominic were standing close to where Sophie stood. "It's here… look!" Sophie directed her torch towards the outline of a large door set into the brickwork.

Liam aimed his powerful beam towards the wall, moving it steadily along, stopping when something caught his attention. "There… look… see it?" Liam settled the torch beam over one place. A small rectangular metal plate affixed to the wall was painted the same colour, camouflaging it to blend in. At its centre was a narrow slot, two inches wide.

"Looks like some sort of key card slot," said Sophie quietly.

Dominic delved into a trouser pocket and pulled out the key card Barry had passed him, lanyard first. Without preamble, he limped over to the illuminated spot and confidently inserted it. A thin line of sapphire-blue light appeared from within the slot as Dominic took a step back.

From behind the wall a mechanical groan could be heard. Gears, pulleys and levers rumbled and squeaked as machinery sprang to life in response to the activation key. Instinctively, Liam and Sophie followed Dominic's lead, taking large backward steps to join him. All three took comfort from holding handguns or rifles at the ready; safeties off, bullets chambered, fingers poised on triggers.

A line of light grew into prominence ahead of them, a thin wisp of luminance outlining the base of what clearly was a set of double-doors discretely built into the wall. The mechanical sounds, still grinding and screeching, came to a jerky halt, replaced by an electric buzz as an ingress appeared within the wall, the doors sliding open with a whisper.

Like Milo Calland had before them, it was impossible not to be impressed with the sheer size of the elevator's interior. Initially, Dominic thought all the double-doors had to reveal was just another empty room. It wasn't until he spied the electronic LCD touchscreen on the far wall that he realised what confronted them.

"You could live inside this thing," ventured Sophie, stepping through the wide entrance. Liam followed her in. Dominic withdrew the key card from the slot and stepped in last.

"If you're fascinated by this, I guess you'd be blown away by a complete tour of this place," aggrandised Dominic. "According to Barry's schematics, the underground facility goes down half a mile and spreads out beneath the base for near on a mile around. There are fifty floors in all... most of which unoccupied..."

"Jeez," exclaimed Liam, thinking about the task at hand.

"Oh… don't worry. Our intel indicates George's lab and Project *GYGES* took up only the second from bottom floor. Level 'negative forty-nine'." Dominic walked across the large floor-space to the touchscreen, keyed '4' then '9' and waited.

"Please insert your security pass to complete this action." A female voice without accent filled the void.

Dominic inserted Barry's key card into a slot to the left of the keypad and rekeyed the floor number.

"Thank you," responded the elevator without emotion, following it up with the automatic closure of the double-doors. A motor from above the lift's ceiling began to whirr and the floor began to shift and vibrate slightly beneath their feet.

"You're welcome," mumbled Dominic.

"I guess it's too late to change our minds," reflected Liam in an attempt at humour. Two minutes later the slight quake beneath their combat boots suddenly stopped, followed by a lacklustre 'ding' sound, announcing the arrival of their floor.

"That was quick," exclaimed Liam sarcastically. "You sure this thing goes down half a mile, and not a couple?"

Dominic shrugged. "Do I look like a bloody tour guide?" He stepped towards the double-doors, and turned to face Liam and, where he hoped Sophie was standing close by. "Remember what we're here for. Project *GYGES* needs to be totally destroyed," he spoke with the gusto of a battle-general. "They took what was rightfully ours. Now to pay them back… with interest." Dominic stowed the tablet computer in Liam's bag and started forward, drawing his weapon, both hands clasping it like he was an action-star in an eighties movie; he carried it at an angle, pointing downwards.

The double-doors of the elevator smoothly slid open to reveal a short but wide corridor, at the end of which was a sealed security door guarded by two soldiers in regulation khaki fatigues and wearing aviator sunglasses despite it being night and indoors. In their hands they carried *M16* rifles at the ready. If the 'ding' of the elevator's arrival took the guards by surprise, they didn't demonstrate it, which was their pitfall. As Dominic stepped purposefully out from the lift, he raised the gun to eye level and squeezed-off two shots. The two guards fell to the floor in a jumble of limbs, matching bullet holes to the centre of both their foreheads, their aviator glasses shifting slightly-askew on the bridge of their noses.

"Nice..." complimented Liam as he followed Dominic into the corridor towards the security door. "Did your intel indicate there being guards at the first set of doors?"

"No... but I had a hunch," Dominic approached the end of the corridor cautiously. "Barry's schematics revealed there are three sets of these security doors before reaching George's laboratory. I figured... if you take security that seriously, it wouldn't hurt to have guards as well."

"Any thoughts on how we get through the doors?" Sophie had rushed ahead and, stepping over the dead guards, was studying the ten-inch scanner screen to the left of the steel-reinforced entrance. A key card reader was alongside it. "It's an iris scanner," she said matter-of-factly.

"Great... perfect." Liam started to curse obscenities.

"I..." *haven't a clue*, Dominic absently scratched his head. "Explosives?"

"I don't think *Semtex* is going to penetrate these doors," said Liam. He was up close to the entryway, scrutinising the security barricade. "It's designed to withstand bomb blasts."

"What about the box Barry gave you?" asked Sophie, hopefully. "He did kind-a suggest opening it once at the laboratory level."

The box.

Dominic had forgotten about the small leather box Barry had

handed to him with the key card back in the SUV. It was squeezed into one of the utility pockets on his military belt. He opened the press stud securing the pouch and removed the tightly wedged small box with a grunt. Opening it on its hinge, Dominic gasped, shaking his head. "Oh, that's gross." His initial reaction was to hurl it across the room in revulsion, thinking Barry had played a sick prank.

"What is it?" Sophie demanded, a note of concern in her tone.

Dominic slowly turned the opened box towards the sound of Sophie's voice, a grimace etched across his face. Within the small receptacle was a small, orb-like item. Someone, somewhere, was missing an eye and likely dead. "Barry said that this should get us in… but I don't know, seems a bit barbaric and primitive to me."

"I think I'm gonna be sick," exclaimed Liam, a hand clutching his mouth.

"There's no time for weak stomachs, big man," taunted Sophie. "Come on, let's keep moving before we're discovered."

Dominic stepped over the commingled guards and stopped at the scanner screen mere feet away, becoming very aware of Sophie close by, having brushed past her. He swiped the key card, activating a small green light – part one of security clearance. From the small leather-coated box, he gently scooped out the eyeball, sticky vitreous liquid clinging to the inside of the box, fibrous and stretching as he pulled it free. The eyeball was surprisingly warm to the touch and at its back stringy optical nerves and thin cords of sinew dangled like the roots of an onion. Dominic turned the eye so that the iris was forward facing and aligned with a designated spot upon the ten-inch screen. A green line of light floated in front of the eye and took a retinal image, comparing it against others stored within the security database. Faces flashed up on the screen, flicking through fifty in a couple of seconds. An instant later and a picture of a young woman appeared on the small display screen, accompanied by her name and credentials. Dominic didn't recognise her, but she was someone important.

Dr. Stacy Monaghan, FRS, FRCOG.

A word in bright neon green flashed up:

MATCH

Followed by the door instantly gliding open, as if it were a curtain made from silk, revealing another short, wide corridor, brightly lit and smelling like a hospital. Another pair of soldiers guarded the security door at the end. Unlike the first guards, these two were alert.

"Halt!" Soldier One raised his *M16* rifle and looked ready to use it. Discarding the eyeball, Dominic reached for his gun; too slow. Soldier One's finger was poised on the trigger and about to fire, when –

BANG! BANG!

Sophie's *Glock* emptied two shots, both hitting Soldier One, a brief look of shock preceding his almost instant death; one to the chest, the other to the head. Before Soldier Two could react, Sophie was standing behind him with the muzzle of her gun pressed into the side of his head.

"I don't think you want to be doing that, do you?" Sophie whispered into the soldier's left ear. The soldier released the grip on his rifle and raised his hands. With large strides, Liam entered the corridor and liberated the weapon from him.

"It's no good… you won't be able to get through *this* door. And if you do, there's the next…"

Dominic trained his gun on the soldier and Sophie removed the *Glock* from the side of his head. She turned away and checked the lock mechanism used on the second door. "Vocal recognition," she said. "I don't suppose Barry gave you a recording of Dr Stacy Monaghan's voice as well, did he?"

The soldier started to chuckle, looking directly into the barrel of Dominic's gun. "Looks like you're out of luck, you sphincter… ha, ha, ha…"

CHAPTER FORTY-FOUR
WYATT

BARRY LED THE MEMBERS of Ryan's task force into the cover of darkness beyond a group of well-lit buildings and a very large hangar that dwarfed even the one beneath which the entrance to the secret underground laboratory was situated. First, he'd ordered the removal of the welcoming committee. Task force soldiers scuttled about, dragging uniformed bodies away, hiding them from sight using makeshift camouflage. Then he gave instructions for the men to fall into their prearranged 'teams', deal with the control tower operators, and to take up strategic positions around the base.

Through night-vision binoculars, Jack Wyatt had watched the young agent as he'd alighted the silver SUV and organised the perimeter contingent who had returned to the frontline in readiness to engage with the enemy.

"*Set watches for one hour,*" Barry's voice spoke into Wyatt's right ear. "*Let's follow the plan to the letter.*"

"Copy that." Through the binoculars, Wyatt watched the SUV with Dominic, Liam and Sophie disappear behind a row of buildings and sighed. It seemed, no matter what his rank, he ended up sitting in the background, watching, and waiting. *Always the bridesmaid; never the bride...*

Fifteen minutes slowly passed. Snatches of conversation played over the airwaves which he half-listened to. Dominic and Sophie, or Dominic and Liam. Occasionally he'd focus on what they were saying, but without visuals little of what they said made sense. When Dominic wasn't talking, other conversations between Ryan and Barry were transmitted. All the while, he sat scanning the area for enemy movement or for signs that they'd been compromised.

After Forty minutes an old air raid siren sounded, long, deliberate and extremely loud, reminding Wyatt of an old WW2 movie he'd seen as a kid. Soon after, more modern alarms began clanging, reverberating and braying, from all around the base. Almost immediately, American soldiers started streaming out of a number of buildings like ants escaping a hovering foot poised above their nest.

"What's happening?" Wyatt was frantically looking through the binoculars from one side to another, searching for any immediate danger.

"*My guess… our presence has been announced,*" said Barry studiously.

Wyatt then heard Barry again, only this time directing his words to his colleagues deep underground: "*Dominic… time's up. Your work on level forty-nine is compromised. They've found us… a little sooner than I'd hoped! Blow the floor and get out of there!*"

In the night sky, three dots of light fast approached. Wyatt aimed his binoculars upward, making adjustments to the night-vision focus dial so that the three beacons gained clarity, and, more importantly, shedding some light on their occupants.

"This isn't good…" Wyatt muttered to himself as the image of three *Boeing Chinook* transport helicopters grew into recognisable form. He spoke louder into his mic: "Guys. We've got company coming from above, due east… and it doesn't look like Santa…"

Barry swore over the airwaves as the first of the *Chinooks* landed swiftly. Already open, the doors spewed forth a platoon of dark, shadowy figures; soldiers, jumping out in pairs, their rifles pointing ahead of them, all eager for action. Wyatt counted twenty-two in all, battle ready and dressed in full body armour. The second and third helicopters landed and a similar number of heavily armed personnel exited.

Wyatt watched as a large number of soldiers headed towards the group of buildings the SUV had disappeared behind. Others fanned out and looked to be forming a perimeter.

"*What's happening? What's going on?*" Ryan filled their heads. He was watching from a safe distance. From where he was kneeling he was blind to the action.

"*Um… I think we've been discovered,*" Wyatt heard Barry reply. "*Teams A to E… engage. The rest… stand by.*" The task force had been split into teams before the jump. Wyatt was leading teams F and G Each team consisted of six or seven former Special Ops, marines or SAS. Without preamble, shots were fired. Snipers, hidden in various vantage spots, took aim and picked off American soldiers one after another, like they were hitting ducks in a shooting gallery at a carnival fairground. Before their commanding officers knew what was happening and were able to regroup, twenty-one Americans lay dead or wounded.

Machine gun fire sounded in the distance, coming from where Dominic, Sophie and Liam were currently working. Wyatt guessed the other team – Team H – was now in action, placed in a defensive position a short distance from the secret underground laboratory.

Through the binoculars, he continued to watch. Heavy gunfire exchanges were taking place ahead of him, the clatter and bang of weapons was deafening, white flashes of light oscillated between locations as weapons emptied their deadly loads, taking life after life. Grenades were being tossed into enemy lines and explosions soon followed, the detonations causing the ground to vibrate.

Wyatt could see casualties falling on either side, agonised voices filling his head over the comms-link. He didn't want to think of the number of his own men who were dead, dying or going to die that night.

"*Wyatt... send in your... reinforcements. We have... Yankee on the run...*" Barry was out of breath and his speech was punctuated by the sound of his handgun going off in quick bursts.

"Copy that," said Wyatt. "Teams F and G... you heard the man... Let's go, let's go..." Around him men stood up and advanced, darkness providing a continuance of cover until the last second.

Startling eight Americans who'd taken refuge beside a building just a stone's throw from Wyatt's position, men from Team F aimed their automatic rifles and mowed them down in a hail of bullets, some emptying their guns over-enthusiastically, continuing to fire well after the battle was ended.

"Conserve your ammo, damn it!" Wyatt yelled. "Come on... the party's not yet over." Taking the lead, he ran out into the open and guided his two teams towards the thick of the fighting. Now flanking the Americans, they didn't stop to allow their enemy to regroup, instead shooting dozens of men in the back before they knew what hit them. In a matter of minutes, the encounter was over in the main, with just skirmishes taking place on the fringes.

Wyatt strode across to where Barry was standing.

"You're bleeding," Wyatt said spotting dark crimson down the side of the young man's face and the shredded remains of his left ear flapping by the side of his head.

"My mum always said I had big ears..." Barry smiled. As though prescient, he added: "Manoeuvre your men into defensive positions; it won't be long before the Americans realise what's happened here and unleash hell on us. We want to give Dom and the others a fighting chance."

On cue and proving Barry right, a number of very small dots of light appeared on the western horizon. Wyatt counted eight. Barry followed his gaze.

"Oh, Jeez." Wyatt raised the binoculars but the dots of light were too far in the distance to be identifiable.

"Dominic… time's up. We'll soon be outgunned. Get out. GET OUT NOW!" Barry did nothing to hide the trepidation in his voice.

Wyatt shook his head. He figured the US military reinforcements would arrive in five minutes. Taking the number of dead or mortally wounded out of the equation, he was left with just thirty-one of his task force, a paltry figure comparative to what was likely heading their way. He didn't consider the odds very favourable.

The radio crackled in Wyatt's ear as Dominic replied to Barry's order with a request. As if things weren't bad enough, the Director of Kaplan Ratcliff's Security and Intelligence Division had to give them an extra challenge, something else to worry about.

Wyatt started to laugh uncontrollably.

CHAPTER FORTY-FIVE
SOPHIE

"**L**OOKS LIKE YOU'RE OUT of luck, you sphincter... ha, ha, ha..."

A small buzzer sounded behind the soldier, and door two glided open. On the other side, a deathly-thin man in wire-framed glasses, with wispy-blond hair, a white lab-coat and matching complexion waited to exit, his mouth falling open upon seeing the dead soldier on the floor and the other soldier being held at Dominic's gunpoint. Behind him, in the background, a final pair of soldiers guarded the last internal security door.

As yet they hadn't noticed anything suspicious at the opposite end of their short corridor.

"I guess not," replied Dominic. "But you are..." Before the Director of Kaplan Ratcliff's Security and Intelligence could shoot the soldier, Sophie had brought the heel of her *Glock* down onto the man's head, knocking him unconscious. Dominic glared angrily towards the place he imagined her to be standing.

"Haven't you killed enough people?" she asked him, poignantly.

The man in the white lab-coat stood transfixed in the doorway – not sure whether to carry on forward or to just stand stock-still. A dark patch had appeared at the front of his trousers and a small pool of liquid gathered about his feet.

"No... have you?" Dominic briefly lowered his gun, turned his head and walked towards the nervous man.

"She's…" *one of them?* The lab technician looked bewildered and started to talk gibberish. "But… they're…" his eyes were wide, "… it can't be…"

"Yes, yes, yes… We have one of our own… Now, if you value your life, you're going to help us get all the way in," Dominic interrupted impatiently. As he drew parallel with lab-coat man, the gun was up again and two rounds exploded past his head. Without the slightest resistance, the two soldiers guarding the final door slumped to the floor.

⸻ ✦ ⸻

Maurice, the lab technician, stood by the doors awaiting his fate. He'd given Dominic, Sophie and Liam access to the research facility using his fingerprints and breath to clear the final obstacle.

"There's another security door," announced Liam, having wandered past a conference room, a kitchen and a store cupboard. There were other doors leading off the passage beyond the third high-security entry point, but these were unlabelled.

"That's just an internal door," said Maurice, timidly. "Key cards activate those. They have them on the toilets too," he smiled nervously. "Even the cubicles…"

"I'm not here to take a dump," spat Dominic. He wandered over to the card reader and swiped Dr. Stacy Monaghan's key card down through the narrow slot. A small double bleep sounded, followed by a dull, muted click as the door unlocked. Dominic laid his hand gently on the handle. "Maurice… I'm feeling sort-a generous tonight and will let you live… but you need to be honest and tell us everything we need to know."

"Erm… okay," he replied, his voice cracking.

"Come… come with us." Dominic opened the door and entered into the largest room he'd ever been in. Directly ahead, and from one side to the other, were row upon row of racks, each containing five large polyethylene bags suspended hammock-like from side to side, all containing liquid – and something else, something more *physical*. There were literally thousands of these bags suspended in the air, Dominic observed. A lab technician dressed in a bio-hazard suit turned around, startled. Before he could question them or object to their presence, Dominic had fired a bullet into his brain, the sound of the gunshot absorbed by the drone and hum of compressed air machinery.

All about were control centres – electronic monitoring equipment and laboratory apparatus that assisted the miracle of life; wires and IV drips were connected to the pods administering essential nutrients and recording growth development. A handful of other technicians dressed in white lab-coats or sealed within hazmat suits flitted about, absorbed within their work, monitoring the equipment, ensuring George's work continued flawlessly, even without him. Owing to the time of day, the majority of the facility's employees had retired for the night, solving one concern Dominic initially had regarding the mission.

"This is…" Sophie spoke as though deep in thought.

"I know," Maurice said. "Amazing, isn't it. Batches two to twenty. Four-thousand-seven-hundred-and-fifty souls… all genetically enhanced at varying stages of foetal development. George Jennings – our *God* – created these beautiful creatures based on his original work."

"…monstrous," Sophie finished.

Maurice smiled and carried on, haughtily. "Of course, all *her* flaws have been eradicated in these subjects. George was quite adamant not to repeat his earlier… mistakes!" Sophie's invisible fist connected with the lab technician's abdomen, taking him unawares, doubling him up and rendering him to the floor where he clutched himself like a small boy.

"Feel better, Sophie?" asked Dominic.

"Come on… let's get this over with. If we split up, we'll get it done quicker."

"Whatever, as you wish… you start here, I'll take the other end. Explosives on each control unit should be adequate," Dominic said. "We've got less than an hour."

Liam man-handled Maurice up from the floor and urged him forward with the muzzle of his rifle; Dominic, still limping slightly from his earlier injury, headed off towards a number of lab-coats milling about oblivious to their presence. To their detriment, that wouldn't last.

Sophie stood for a moment, contemplating her next action. She knew what she had to do but found it abhorrent and against her good conscience.

You can do this, she thought, *it's what you're here to do.*

But I… I can't. They're just… children.

Who'll grow up into men with abilities similar to your own.

What gives us the right to kill them…?

What gave THEM the right to give them life?

On and on… she argued with herself until a voice crackled in her ear… "*You don't need to set the bombs off… just place the detonators and we'll do the rest,*" and, as though sensing her reluctance, Dominic added, "*it's not good what we're doing, but it's necessary.*" The voice went silent in her ear, as did her own internal monologue, as she was spurred into action.

"Okay," she replied. From her shoulder bag she removed a small explosive device with a remote detonator. Sophie crossed to one of the control centres that a myriad of tubes and wires sprouted from, all connecting to the array of pods within which life was contained; she placed the explosive to the rear of the electronic unit, flicking a small silver switch to 'on' once secure. A red LED began to glow below it. For several minutes Sophie continued, one rack at a time, attaching and activating an explosive detonator to the back of each control centre until she came to the last.

"*Sophie… where are you?*" Dominic hissed into Sophie's ear, the earpiece crackling into life. "*Have you finished, yet?*"

"Just about done," she replied.

"*Good. Liam's collected all the hard drives from the research room and everything's good to blow. There's just the matter of batch one.*"

"Batch one?"

"*The pods contained batches two to twenty… that's what Maurice said. The first batch are in what he called the 'nurture' room. Two-hundred-and-fifty children all undergoing their intense 'programming'.*"

An image of her own 'programming' flashed into mind; hours sitting in front of VDUs where images flashed up in front of her, subliminal memories had been planted into her brain.

"And where is this 'nurture' room?" Sophie asked, placing her final detonator to the back of another control centre. She flicked the silver switch and waited for the LED lamp to glow.

The 'nurture' room was situated on level forty-two. With Maurice continuing to be their unofficial guide, Dominic, Liam and Sophie left the breeding ground of Project *GYGES*, setting further explosive detonators in the conference room and along the corridor. In the gigantic elevator, Dominic inserted Dr. Stacy Monaghan's key card into the slot next to the touchscreen before tapping '4' and '2'.

"This level has restricted access," the voice of the lift intoned. "To avoid detainment, please ensure you have the correct credentials before entering this level." The double-doors into the elevator closed behind them before the floor beneath them started to vibrate as pulleys and motors whirred into action and the lift began to climb again. Eighteen seconds later and the 'ding' sounded, announcing the floor's swift arrival.

"So, Maurice… what's going to be waiting for us when these doors slide open?" asked Dominic.

The lab technician shrugged. "I wouldn't know for sure, I don't have level clearance," he said. "Although, I've heard that a whole company of soldiers patrol the floor. Gets the kids used to interacting with military personnel."

"A company?" Sophie queried, "that's what… a hundred men or more?"

Maurice smiled. "Give or take twenty," he said.

The large double-doors glided open like the curtains to a grand stage play. Over the threshold, men and women dressed in the operational khaki camouflage pattern walked about in what appeared to be a large entrance room, like that to a grand hotel, Sophie thought. Guns holstered at belts and *M16* assault rifles were flung over shoulders.

Sophie counted at least thirteen soldiers standing about. None had given the elevator's arrival, or its occupants, any notice.

"Where on this level will we find batch one?" asked Dominic in hushed tones.

"At this hour, probably asleep in their dormitory. It's towards the end of the hallway, past the reception… but look around, it's quite impossible for you to sneak in. There'll be military personnel around every turn, and others in the dormitory itself. You should leave this place whilst you can." Maurice sounded almost happy.

"Impossible maybe for you, my friend Liam here, or even me. But not for Sophie…" Dominic wanted to knock the tall, thin man down to the floor and give him a good kick to the solar plexus. It took every ounce of restraint from doing so.

"True… but-" before Maurice could finish his sentence, the four of them jumped from the deafening siren that started to warble from the foyer outside the lift.

"Dominic… time's up. Your work on level forty-nine is compromised. WE'VE BEEN DISCOVERED! Blow the floor and get out of there!"

Barry was talking frantically over the comms-link, punctuated by sporadic gunfire and chaotic screams and shouts around him. Liam and Sophie heard the conversation through their own small earphones.

Outside the lift, soldiers were running back and forth, many disappearing down the corridor towards the dormitory, no doubt having received their orders to protect the children.

"We're not finished!" Sophie heard Dominic shout into his mouthpiece behind her as she left the elevator and entered the foyer. She ran past soldiers unaware of her presence, and followed a stream of military men and women piling into a large room at the end of a long aisle, where overhead lights were being flicked on, and 250 children were climbing sleepily out of their beds, all dressed in uniform grey pyjamas, bleary-eyed and terribly afraid.

As Sophie entered the room, forty soldiers were ushering young children up and towards the furthest corner of the room where a human barricade was being formed. Rifles were held in dangerous fashion, and a hubbub of conversation competed with the continuous drone of the intruder alarm. An order had been given: protect the infants at all costs, but no word had been given as to the threat, or where it would come from.

"What the…?" Sophie exclaimed, seeing the children. How could it be? Ryan had indicated them to be no older than nine-months-old?

"You have five minutes before we remote detonate the bombs," said Barry over the comms-link. *"Ryan has learnt that the US have reinforcements and air support on its way."*

"In a minute!" hissed Dominic over the airways.

"Guys… I see them! I'm in their room… they're…"

What?

Older!

"…surrounded."

"*Sophie?*" Dominic hadn't realised she was no longer in the elevator by his side.

"*Good… then put an end to it,*" ordered Barry. "*You've got four minutes…*"

"Dom… there's too many soldiers… I… I… I…" *don't know if I can do it.*

"*Sophie… this should be easy for you. This is what your training was for…*"

"Is it necessary to kill them?" She'd never killed a living thing until July when an intruder at Willoughby Rising had threatened the lives of her brothers and sister. Now, killing was becoming too easy, like life was expendable and did not matter.

"*Yes, they may look like babies… but they're not,*" replied Dominic without hesitation.

"You're right, they're not," Sophie said, without elaborating.

"*Don't think about it!*" Dominic hissed. "*Soon, it'll all be over. Liam and I'll clear the foyer for you for when you're done…*" Almost immediately gunfire could be heard from beyond the corridor behind her, barely loud enough to compete with the siren braying all around and the hubbub of talking emanating from the corner of the room.

Without further words or thought, Sophie ran deeper into the room after the stream of soldiers she had followed. They had now formed a wedge in front of the children, battle-ready; she gripped her two *Glocks* tightly, fingers coaxing the triggers.

She approached the human wall, her arms outstretched. Unconsciously, she began firing her weapons in unison, her aim was with sniper precision; shot after shot, bang after bang.

The *Glock 19* took magazines with a capacity of holding fifteen, seventeen, nineteen and thirty-three rounds. Naturally, she'd opted for the largest capacity magazines and fired the gun without fear of running out, although, there was also the rifle strapped across her back and the *Sig Saur P226* pistol holstered at her waist, both fully loaded with plenty of ammo easily found on the utility belt strapped tightly above her slender hips.

Unable to see the threat, the soldiers forming a barrier around the children gave little resistance, falling like dominoes as Sophie ruthlessly cut them down two at a time. By the time one of the soldiers had squeezed off only a few rounds towards where he thought the aggressor – Sophie – approached (bullets peppering the wall and punching holes into the ceiling), he too succumbed to a lethal projectile to the centre of his head.

Taking less than eight seconds, the last of the soldiers guarding the children crumpled to the floor. Without the body-barricade, the children – roughly five-years in appearance – clutched each other, trembling and crying, eyes darting this way and that, their whining and moaning, being pitiful to witness.

Sophie climbed over a stack of bodies and stood in front of the throng of children pressed up against each other, so close that it was hard to distinguish where one child started and another finished; wearing the same uniform pyjamas, it was almost as though they had merged together and were appearing as one.

Sophie levelled her two *Glocks* towards the pack of children and made ready to fire.

It would be easy, she thought. They couldn't see her. Death would be swift and sudden. They were burdened with the same curse her father had bestowed upon her. She'd be doing them a favour, she reasoned.

One of the small boys seemed to look directly into Sophie's eyes, could almost see her; unknowingly, they pleaded with her and begged for mercy. Without realising, she lowered her guns slightly.

With his dark hair, pointed chin and delicate cheekbones, he looked almost identical to her youngest brother, Charlie. The last time she'd seen him he'd had a broken arm. She expected it had healed by now and that he was back to climbing trees, probably exploring the oaks and cedars out back at grandpa Theo's.

She shifted her gaze away from the boy to land on another set of eyes and a face whose likeness to the first was exact. He too seemed to be looking directly at her, as though her invisibility did not work on him.

A quick scan over all the children – all boys – made her quickly realise that George had created all of them in the same likeness.

Sophie cleared her mind and lifted her now-heavy hands so that the guns were aimed ahead again, her fingers touching the triggers but not applying any real pressure.

There's too many to kill, she thought. A quick calculation confirmed she had less than twenty rounds left in the *Glocks*. Swiftly, she reholstered the weapons and pulled the rifle over her shoulder, an *M4*, smaller and lighter than the *M16*'s that the Americans were using, its magazine holding twenty cartridges. She released the clip, checked it was full, and heeled it back into place. Taking a deep breath, Sophie aimed the rifle on the first boy (who still looked at her), closed her eyes and tried to compose herself. For the first time she noticed that she couldn't hear the sound of the siren braying in the background. Instead, her heartbeat thumped loud within her head. Her throat was suddenly scratchy and dry.

Sophie opened her eyes again, readjusted herself, opened the hand that clasped the trigger mechanism, and readied herself to fire.

The boy whose eyes held her gaze looked imploringly at her.

Sophie shook her head. *I can't do it.* She slowly lowered the rifle.

"Sophie, are you done yet? We're out of time..." She ignored

Dominic as the overpowering need to vomit forced her to keel over and empty her stomach onto the floor.

Dominic crept into the room holding a machine gun he'd appropriated from an American he'd killed, having spent all of his own ammunition.

"I guess you're not done ye…" he didn't finish the line, his gaze falling upon the mass of children huddled together. Just as Sophie had a couple of minutes earlier, Dominic stepped over some bodies so that he was face-to-face with the 250 children, who still cowered into the corner of the large room.

"How's this possible?" Dominic could see that the children were much older than the expected nine-months.

"I guess my father has improved the genetic formula," Sophie said. "Who knows what else he's done to their DNA."

Theatrically, Dominic chambered a round and aimed his weapon at the mass of moving bodies. "Probably for the best that we don't find out."

"I… I couldn't. I tried. But… they're just children," said Sophie. "Look at them. LOOK AT THEM!"

Dominic looked at the little faces staring up at him. "We have our orders," he said. "Destroy Project *GYGES*. I wouldn't have any problems sleeping at night."

"They are innocent," Sophie insisted, "the victims of circumstance. They don't deserve to die."

Dominic sighed, lowering the rifle. "They maybe victims Sophie, but they are still the sons of *GYGES*." He looked at them in pity. "They will all be like you, but without emotion. They'll be soldiers who'll kill with little thought and with no regret. It's better to put an end to it before it's too late."

"I know," Sophie said simply. "I know," she repeated, "but, Dominic, I don't think they ARE without emotion." Almost on cue, a couple of the children burst into tears whilst others sniffed and snorted. "Look at them. They're afraid."

"*Dominic... time's up. We'll soon be outgunned. Get out. GET OUT NOW!*" Barry spoke urgently over the comms-link, his voice filling both Dominic and Sophie's ears, left and right respectively.

Dominic came to a decision fast. A thought entered his head and a sly smile appeared on his lips. He'd later call it divine intervention.

"Okay... we're done here," he was speaking to Barry. "Call Ryan. Tell him we're on our way. Tell him we need transport for 250 children... and not babies either. 250 infants, approx five in age..."

"*What?*"

"What?" Sophie spoke in unison with Barry, a note of disbelief in her voice.

Dominic addressed them both, but his response was directed more to Sophie. "If we're not going to kill them," he said, "we can hardly leave them behind."

CHAPTER FORTY-SIX
GEORGE

THE NIGHT WAS STICKY and warm, the sort better suited to summer vacations in underdeveloped countries where luxuries such as air-conditioning, poolside cocktail bars and mosquito repellent, weren't available. The air-con in the room was off and George thought that maybe this extra level of discomfort was another form of torture he was forced to endure, as though suffering the side-effects of a further course of chemo wasn't bad enough. Despite pressing the call button for the third time, no one came to his aid.

After Brayden and the other CIA agent had left, George had turned off the television and tried to sleep. For two-and-a-quarter hours he tossed and turned in the hospital bed, sleep close, but his over exertive mind keeping it at bay. Thoughts of all that had happened that past forty-eight hours kept creeping into his head, playing back over-and-over. He couldn't help also wondering at the news story of the Washington airport incident. Was Sophie truly going to attempt a rescue bid? Together they'd plotted to rescue Harriet. Despite it being staged, that hadn't turned out well – even the best laid plans weren't foolproof. George worried that any attempt to break him out would be met with a similar kickback.

He sighed. It wasn't long after that an idea sprung to mind. Some might call it inspiration. He couldn't guarantee that he would live to see his children again, but, were this to be the case, there was something he needed Sophie to know.

When the night nurse finally did step in, twenty minutes after being buzzed for a fourth time, she apologised with a warm smile and said she would fix the air-con. The ID card pinned to her dress informed George that her name was Katherine. She'd replaced Jennifer from 11:00 p.m. and seemed nice enough, though not as attentive – or as *attractive* – as Jennifer was, disappearing for long periods of time (as she had just then).

Katherine poured George a glass of water and placed it alongside the jug on the cabinet beside the bed. Any ice that had been scooped into the jug had subsequently melted within the heat of the room.

"Apart from the heat, are you comfortable, George?"

George nodded, closing his eyes. "I can't seem to sleep, though," he said.

"I thought as much. Here, let me rough-up your pillows." After making George comfortable, Katherine carried out a number of routine checks; temperature, blood pressure, heart rate. She jotted down the results on the chart at the end of George's bed.

"What happened to Laurel and Hardy?" George asked, alluding to Brayden and his partner, an original odd couple. Truthfully, he didn't much care for them but had nothing better to say to fill the noticeable emptiness; seeing the nurse coming to the end of her routine checks, he thought it might be nice to engage in some conversation to maintain her presence. Plus it suddenly occurred to him that he wanted to ask her something.

"The suits from Washington?" she asked, eyebrow raised. "Oh, they're about." She sat on the bed uninvited, narrowly avoiding George's left leg. "In fact, I just saw one of them outside whilst having a smoke."

Unconsciously, George wrinkled his nose.

"I know… I know. I'm a nurse; I should know better. Causes cancer." Katherine realised how insensitive that sounded, "Sorry. Anyway, as I say, I saw one of 'em outside. The tall, hot one. He was on the phone and didn't see me. Mind, I was hanging back out of the way. The guy was out of sorts and flapping about all agitated-like."

"Oh…?" George's interest was piqued. He sat up slightly.

"Yea, he looked a bit flustered. At first I thought there was trouble at home… if you know what I mean; but then he started babbling about 'being right', that he 'didn't expect Sophie to come here', and that he was just 'wasting' his time." Katherine used her fingers to further illustrate when she was quoting Brayden.

"What do you think he was talking about?" asked George quietly, trying to sound only mildly fascinated.

"Funny you should ask that," Katherine replied in hushed tones. "I followed him back into the building. He met up with the other, older guy, where he had a long chat, which is why I wasn't able to answer your call. Well, I know I shouldn't have done, but I got real close – not close enough to be seen, mind – and listened to their conversation. It turns out there's been a military attack on mainland America… the first of its kind. I couldn't get much more of the conversation, but the tall younger man was speaking excitedly, like he'd won a bet or something."

"Did he mention where this attack took place?"

"Yes, in a fashion; some place I've never heard of. *Dreamland* or something… or I might've misheard and he'd said *Disneyland*… I don't know. Who'd want to attack *Disneyland*?"

It wasn't *Disneyland*.

Dreamland.

A nickname for the base, one of several George knew. *Paradise Ranch*, *Home Base* and *Water Town*, amongst others. Its correct name was Homey Airport or Groom Lake, but it was commonly referred to as Area 51. It was a place George was very familiar with, and, until two days earlier, he'd called his home.

"Do you think it's terrorists, like those who did the World Trade Centre?" Katherine asked. "I'd hate for that to happen again... there's been enough innocent blood spilt."

George placed a reassuring hand atop the young nurse's and smiled. "It's not terrorists," he said.

"You sure? How do you know?"

"Oh, I just know," George said with a mischievous twinkle in his eye. "Call it a hunch. Now, can I ask you for a favour?"

"Depends," Katherine replied, suspiciously.

"Oh, it's nothing too onerous. We both know that this cancer," he indicated a spot towards his head, "is going to kill me... whilst I'm locked up in here... eventually. If I write a letter to my daughter – call it my will – could you see that it gets to her when I'm gone?"

Katherine smiled. "Sure."

"But only when I'm dead. You must keep it safe until after my funeral."

"Okay."

"However... should I get out of here... alive...," he did not elaborate any justification to this, "I would want you to burn it and forget you ever knew me. Promise me..."

"Fine... whatever."

"Good. Could you get me a pen and some paper, I'd like to get this done before the dynamic duo make a reappearance."

CHAPTER FORTY-SEVEN
RYAN

FROM THE VANTAGE POINT atop a dusty knoll, half a mile away from the twin runways and the various buildings that dotted the US Military base, Ryan watched through powerful night-vision binoculars. Accompanying the visuals he heard the chatter of conversations over the airwaves through his earpiece, sporadic, sometimes nonsensical, but mostly informative.

Things had gone close to plan for the first thirty minutes.

He watched as his team dispatched the welcoming committee and tidied the area after. He saw Dominic and Liam (with Sophie) drive off in the direction of the hangar beneath which the underground research facility was located. He heard them communicating with each other as they planted explosives strategically within George Jennings' former laboratory, exchanging verbal confirmations as detonators were primed for activation.

When alarms started to warble and clang, Ryan knew that it was just a matter of time before his task force would engage with the Americans. He watched as soldiers flowed out of buildings dressed in military fatigues and holding automatic rifles, looking relaxed as though all that was occurring was a military drill.

Three *Chinook* helicopters quickly came in from the west, surprisingly swift, and dropped like stones from the sky, landing hard on the asphalt of one of the runways. Men jumped down in pairs from each aircraft, tightly organised and eager for action. Ryan removed the binoculars from his eyes, rubbed them with his free hand, turning away.

It'll be a massacre, he thought, negatively. *I've led them all to their deaths…*

Ten seconds later and the sound of distant machine gun fire reached his ears, soon followed by punctuating booms as grenades were thrown.

As the battle played out on the airfield, snatches of conversation came through on the comms-link from deep beneath the ground, intermingled with shouts and urgent calls from those fighting above ground level. The words, tumbling through the airwaves, were a babble and almost incoherent.

Taking less time than it felt, the encounter between his task force and the Americans seemed to be over. Ryan lifted the binoculars up once again and risked a glance towards the air base. In clear view, Wyatt and Barry were standing chatting. Ryan wished he could hear what they were saying; their microphones were turned off. One was gesturing frantically whilst looking into the distant sky.

Ryan lifted the binoculars and aimed them up, towards the direction where Wyatt seemed to be pointing. Some small dots of light floated in the distant sky.

"*Dominic… time's up. We'll soon be outgunned. Get out. GET OUT NOW!*" The voice belonged to Barry.

Refocusing the binoculars on the young agent, Ryan watched as the man ordered Wyatt to round up what remained of the task force.

Dominic's voice replaced Barry's within Ryan's ear. "*Okay… we're done here. Call Ryan. Tell him we're on our way. Tell him we need transport for 250 children…*"

"What?" Ryan did not mask his intoned shock.

That wasn't the plan, Dominic… you had orders!

Dominic did not speak further. Instead, an uncomfortable silence filled the airwaves and a discernible stillness settled about Ryan.

"Ryan? We ne-"

Ryan interrupted Barry. He was still watching him through the binoculars. Wyatt had wandered away towards a group of men, one injured and being supported by another. "Yes, yes, I heard... through the comms-link. What the HELL'S going on? *GYGES* was to be destroyed in its entirety!"

"Can we have the confab later, things are more pressing?"

Ryan sighed audibly. "Why can't we follow the plan... just for once?" The question rhetorical, quietly spoken to himself. Ryan sighed again. "Well, calling for our ride home is not an option," he muttered. "There's no way Alby is going to turn the bird around. There's a flight plan, and an agreed rendezvous point. We need to find another way."

"You were responsible for sourcing our way out. How did you think we were getting out of here?" asked Barry anxiously.

"Honestly," said Ryan, "I didn't figure there'd be many survivors. Before we landed I didn't have a clue... but when we expropriated those vehicles from the border guards... I kind-a thought we'd use them and drive our way out."

Barry laughed uncontrollably and maniacally into Ryan's ear.

"Look. I didn't say this mission was without its flaws. Our objective in the main was: destroy *GYGES* – anything else... well, nothing else mattered. I thought we could use our imagination."

"Perfect!"

"I guess the vehicles we have won't be enough," Ryan was thinking aloud. Over his thoughts, he could hear Barry making disgruntled sounds through his earpiece. "Barry... get a grip. I didn't pick you for this mission based on your looks or charisma. You can do this. You were top in your class at problem solving..."

"Problem solving... Yes! Miracle working..." Barry trailed off.

Ryan sighed again, dropping the binoculars for a moment as he tried to think, then repositioning them. "Look, I know. I'm sorry."

"We need an escape plan. I'm guessing we've got less than five minutes before... well... before things get REAL."

Ryan was looking about the airbase, and stopped. "What about the *Chinooks*?" he asked excitedly. His focus was on the three helicopters sitting stationary and empty on the asphalt, their pilots having run to the hills when it became clear Ryan's task force was winning the battle.

"I don't know... maybe... even with three, I'm not sure there's capacity to hold so many people."

"Barry, they're kids. How big d'you think they are. Besides, it's only to get away from the base. I can source other means of transport once we're safe."

"Safe? I don't think we'll be able to fly them to London..."

Ryan chuckled. "Let's not get ahead of ourselves. Do we have anyone who can fly them helicopters?"

"Yes... I think so, unless they've been shot." Ryan watched Barry look about. *"We've got a lot of people been shot,"* he said.

<hr>

BOOM! BOOOM! BOOOOM! BOOM! BOOOOOOOOM!

The explosions were muffled and came from beneath the ground, but powerful enough to shake the foundations of the buildings scattered about the base; glass shattered in several window frames and at least one building collapsed like a house of cards, spewing up a small mushroom cloud of dust and smoke. The deserts of Nevada weren't unaccustomed to underground explosions. 828 nuclear devices were tested up to 5,000 feet below the surface between 1951 and 1992. But they took place at the Nevada National Security Site located in south-eastern Nye County. Underground explosions never took place in these parts, not at Area 51. 51 was a testing site for advanced aircraft.

"Any sign of Dominic or the others?" Ryan was still watching from his safe distance. Five minutes were up and the dots of the approaching aircraft – *Chinooks* or *Sikorsky Black Hawks*, he couldn't tell – were no longer dots but growing spheres of light that obliterated the inky blackness of the night sky. There were six of them. It was just a matter of a couple of minutes before they were close enough to land.

"*Negative*," replied Barry.

Communication with Dominic, Liam and Sophie had ceased just before Wyatt remotely detonated the explosives they'd placed around George's laboratory. They'd waited as long as they dared, but waited no more. The after-effects of the explosions continued to ripple underfoot. Ryan silently prayed they'd managed to clear the building before it was too late.

"*They're nearly upon us!*" Wyatt's voice cut in desperately, stating the obvious. "*We need to go!*"

Ryan searched the distance through the binoculars, hope beginning to slip. Resignedly he agreed. He turned away. "Okay. Clear out… Get your men to the rendezvous… we'll debrief back in London. Over…"

"*Wait! I see something.*" Between a hangar and a small brick building, Barry spied the SUV crawling slowly out into the open. Beside the vehicle a large mass of bodies were shuffling forward, huddled together in fear or from cold, blankets draped around their shoulders making them look like little old men. It was the first time these kids had stepped foot outside and some wore bewildered expressions.

"*Ryan… do you have my transport?*" Dominic spoke urgently. Ryan had shifted his gaze from the sky down to where Barry had indicated.

"Barry… get the *Chinooks* over there. Make haste… we're running out of time." Almost immediately the first of the three helicopters lifted off the ground, made an about turn, and glided placidly towards the slowly approaching group of children. The other two followed soon after.

As the first helicopter landed, dust billowed from the down draught caused by the rotor blades; Dominic drove the SUV around it so that he was parked between the *Chinook* and the enemy coming in from the west. Tyres screeched as Dominic did a handbrake turn, spinning the vehicle 180 degrees so that it faced the grounded chopper, the rear of the SUV aimed out towards the twin runways stretching behind.

"What are you doing Dom?" Ryan watched Dominic leap out of the driver's side, and run to the boot to release the catch, pulling up the rear-facing door, before promptly climbing into the back of the SUV.

"*A bit of rear-guard defence*," said Dominic, hidden deep beneath shadow within the back of his vehicle. "*And they laughed at me when I picked out this baby.*"

Ryan watched as the six-barrelled tube of the *M61 Vulcan* Gatling-style rotary cannon poked out through the opening at the back of the vehicle. Dominic cranked it up so that the big gun was pointed skyward.

Ahead of the SUV, the first helicopter was preparing to take off. Children were being hurried into the second and third helicopters, unceremoniously being bundled in by Barry, Liam and other soldiers who had gathered close by, weapons hanging from their necks, swinging by their sides.

"I mean, with the children? Bringing them with us wasn't part of the arrangement."

"*I have done many things over the years. Despicable things, Ryan.*"

Things I'm not proud of," Dominic paused for a moment to think, also to concentrate on loading the military aircraft gun. Clicks and clacks came through Ryan's earpiece. *"Adding 'killing children' to my list isn't something I'm ready to do. Not yet."*

"Okay, I get it. You've got a conscience. But what are we to do with them, assuming we manage to escape?"

Dominic was quick with his answer, as though he'd had much longer than ten minutes to think it through. *"We'll take them to Kaplan Ratcliff,"* he said.

"Then what?" Ryan persisted.

In answer, Dominic fired off a few rounds from the big gun, streaks of light projecting into the sky towards the six American helicopters that were now descending from the night, bullets sparking as they ricocheted from their undersides. The *Vulcan* was deafening as Dominic continued to fire it. He shouted to be heard, dismissing the subject: *"We'll talk more when this is over!"*

The second *Chinook* left the ground and glided away into the east, followed a moment after by the third, which Wyatt and six of his team jumped aboard just as it readied for flight; sitting themselves on the floor near the rear doorway, one or two dangling their legs overboard, assault rifles pointing ahead of them. Of Ryan's task force, eight remained behind to lend support to Dominic's current single-handed defence mission. Through the binoculars, Ryan picked out Liam and Barry joining the fight with Dominic.

The American helicopters, with their reinforcements, landed close on the asphalt and under heavy artillery fire. Soldiers jumped down and started engaging with the remnants of Ryan's force, some killed or injured immediately, others running in a line towards the SUV. Dominic didn't stop, continuing to feed belt after belt of ammunition into the big gun, mowing advancing soldiers down mercilessly, knocking them down like bowling pins at a *QubicaAmf World Cup* tournament, laughing wildly as he pressed the trigger.

It didn't take too long for the Americans to realise their disadvantage; helicopters floated back up into the sky taking their marines out of harm's reach. They hovered at a relatively safe height, search lights bathing the area, pinpointing the enemy.

"Dom… Barry… there's only one way this is going to turn out if we stay here. Let's get going whilst we've got a margin…"

"*I'm on it*," said Barry. He climbed into the front of the SUV. Liam was getting into the driver's seat again.

"And Sophie?" Ryan enquired.

"*Sophie? Why, didn't you see her?*" Barry was chuckling to himself. The joke never got tired. "*She's fine. She went with the first helicopter.*"

The sonic boom of a jet aircraft sounded across the sky as a *USAF F-15 Eagle* joined the American's cause in pursuit of the three appropriated *Chinook* helicopters transporting the liberated sons of *GYGES*. With a speed limit of up to 1,650mph – depending on altitude – the helicopters were no match for the superior fighter aircraft, offering a measly 196mph in comparison.

Ryan followed the sound of the jet, turning away from the airbase and looking up into the eastern sky, his gaze following the sound.

"Are you sure she's okay, Barry?"

Shocked into silence, Barry had no words to respond.

CHAPTER FORTY-EIGHT
SOPHIE

WITHIN WHAT COULD POSSIBLY have been the world's largest elevator, Sophie had stood to one side closest to the right wall; Dominic and Liam stood opposite. 250 children were huddled in between them, wide-eyed and terribly afraid, further evidence that their emotions had not been inhibited.

Sophie had tried talking to them, but that just made things worse. Unable to see her, her voice had freaked them out. It turned out that discussions regarding their genetically enhanced abilities had yet to take place, a fact that made killing them even more incomprehensible.

Subdued, Sophie quietly reflected about her own plight and the moments just earlier. After requesting transport for the children, Sophie had sought desperately for the other item Emily had led her to believe would have been in bountiful supply at her father's research lab.

Serum.

The antidote to her condition. Her current supplies were dwindling fast and, without her father, the facility promised the next best thing.

A mad dash around the room had revealed nothing. The laboratory had drawn a blank too.

"Sophie! We don't have time. This place is going to blow!"

Reluctantly, Sophie had given up her search and followed Dominic, escorting the kids away from their dormitory.

With the kids huddled around, Sophie close to Dominic, she

remembered the lab technician who'd been helping them. "What happened to Maurice?" she asked.

"Dead," replied Dominic. "He got in the way of a few bullets."

"You killed him?"

"No."

"But you didn't save him either."

"True. But he did save me."

Before the elevator had completed its journey, the bombs placed at Level forty-nine, her father's former laboratory, were detonated. A dozen explosions rocked the underground complex, making the elevator judder and rock and the lights flicker on and off. For a terrifying moment the whirr of the motor stopped and the lift came to a sudden halt. She dared not think what might have happened had the motor not started cranking again and the elevator not continued its ascent.

As fire engulfed her father's former laboratory deep below her feet, destroying Project *GYGES* and all its future sons in the process, the elevator stopped at Ground Level. Once again arrival was announced by a ridiculously tiny 'ding'. No one gave it a second thought. They would have felt relief, but not knowing what dangers they faced next kept that in check. The large twin sliding doors slipped open smoothly to reveal the empty aircraft hangar that Dominic, Liam and Sophie had left only a short time earlier.

"Let's go. We'll stay close to the buildings. I'll lead; you two flank…" Dominic motioned for the children to follow him like an overweight Pied Piper. Leaving the hangar, he spoke into the comms-link: "Ryan, do you copy?"

Nothing. No sounds, not even whistling or interference. The chitter-chatter of conversations had ceased immediately after the bombs had detonated. Dominic could only guess that the explosion had caused something to block the radio signal, maybe an inadvertent electro-magnetic-pulse. He cursed inwardly to himself.

Streaming from the hangar, Dominic led the children out into the open. "I'll drive and provide a shield." He climbed into the SUV and started the engine. Sophie said nothing about her plan. Ryan's mission was over. All that was left was escaping in one piece and returning to the real reason she was in North America.

Finding my father.

Evidence of a battle was everywhere to see. Bodies from both the American and Ryan's task force, were strewn, bullet-riddled and bloodied, all over the place, though Sophie counted more of the American soldiers. In disdain, she shook her head. *What a waste of life.*

Walking out from the cover of the buildings, Sophie heard Dominic through her earpiece. The comms-link was working once again. There was no explanation for the brief radio silence.

"*Ryan... do you have my transport?*"

Ryan instantly replied by issuing instructions: "*Barry... get the Chinooks over there. Make haste... we're running out of time.*"

Ten seconds later a *Chinook* helicopter landed a couple of metres from where they were gathered, the rotors kicking up grit and an almighty wind that buffeted their clothes and threatened to blow over some of the small children. Dominic drove the SUV off like a maniac, around the helicopter, tyres screeching and leaving a looping mark on the ground. He positioned the SUV behind the helicopter, rear-facing the twin runways.

"Okay, let's be quick. Let's load them up!" Barry jumped down from the door leading into the back of the helicopter and ran over to the first line of children. "Liam, give us a hand!" Together, they bundled the children in two and three at a time. The way they handled them, it was like they were stowing sandbags or sacks of grain. As the children were small, it took little effort and in no time a third of the children were squashed in the back of the helicopter.

"It's close to the maximum loaded weight. Much more and the bird won't fly…" Barry was about to give the order to close the door.

"Is there room for one more?" asked Sophie. She had sauntered around the gathering of children and was standing close to Barry. Even so near to his ear, she needed to shout over the sound of the helicopter: "I think the kids need a chaperone, someone to watch over them…!"

"I guess it won't hurt," said Barry, "go on, clear out. I hope to *see* you at the rendezvous point."

Sophie climbed into the *Chinook*. "You will," she murmured. "Okay Barry, I'm in."

"Good luck!" Barry closed the door and the helicopter floated up from the ground, banking slightly so as to head in an easterly direction, climbing higher and gradually gaining speed.

Through a round window, Sophie watched the ground move away and the people she'd fought alongside slowly disappear. It was cramped in the cabin so she moved into the cockpit. Inside, two task force soldiers sat behind the controls of the helicopter. One was speaking over a radio whilst the other handled the avionic instrument panel, pressing buttons and pushing and pulling levers. There were two empty seats in the cockpit, one of which Sophie manoeuvred across to and buckled herself in. Hanging from the wall was a pair of aviation headphones. Sophie pulled them down and, after hooking out the earpiece of her comms-link, she slipped them over her head. In addition to allowing her to hear the pilots, the headphones suppressed some of the helicopter noise, loud, beating and deafening from all around.

Conversation immediately filled her head between the pilot and co-pilot of the *Chinook*, and also with those piloting the other two helicopters. Sophie was surprised to hear confirmation that all three *Chinooks* were in the air almost before she'd had a chance to get comfortable in her seat. Conversation continued in stereo from one ear to another as pilots and co-pilots exchanged comments regarding their flight position, or sharing pleasantries now that the stress of combat was over. Ryan joined the conference having changed radio frequency to interrupt and communicate with them.

"Alpha, Papa, Tango... this is Group Leader, you copy?"

Three voices chimed in concurrently.

"This is Alpha, go ahead..."

"Papa, over?"

"Tango here..." Sophie recognised the last voice as Jack Wyatt's.

"Okay boys, listen. Keep at a low altitude to avoid radar and ditch the birds in Alamo. My associate will converse with you directly when you are close. I've arranged for onward transport to be waiting for you there."

"And what about you?" asked Wyatt, a note of concern.

"Don't worry about me, Jack... I'll be following by road with Dominic... just a couple of hours behind. I suspect you'll have company soon, so be careful. Just make sure you get to the rendezvous with your cargo intact. I'll meet you there."

"Copy that," replied the pilot of Sophie's *Chinook*, concluding the conversation between the four parties.

Radio silence followed for the next three minutes. Sophie was peering ahead through the front windscreen though saw nothing but total darkness. The co-pilot reached and tapped the pilot's arm, drawing his attention to a screen built within the avionics operation panel. A combined moving map display with roaming radar highlighted the two other helicopters flying close behind, and another aircraft travelling much faster in pursuit.

"Uh, we have a bogie coming up fast due west." The co-pilot spoke calmly into the radio whilst simultaneously activating a computer programme on a touch screen to the left of him, fingers prodding gently, selecting words and images as they flashed up across the display. Sophisticated software, combined with radar and satellite technology, ran an aircraft recognition procedure which almost immediately settled upon a make and model aircraft.

Sophie leaned over for a closer view.

"Appears to be a *USAF F-15 Eagle* on our tracks." The co-pilot pressed some more buttons in front of him. He appeared to know what he was doing.

"*Could it be coincidence that they're in the air?*" asked someone over the radio, possibly Wyatt.

"Unlikely. Be prepared for evasive manoeuvres." The pilot of the *Chinook* banked sharply and took the helicopter down lower, hoping to avert detection. The helicopter was so low eddies of dust were being sucked up from the ground, creating a sand cloud vortex that followed incessantly below them.

A warning alarm began to bleep constantly in their ears, loud, urgent, insistent. Sophie removed her headset. The alert sounded through the radio and not within the cockpit of the helicopter.

"The *F-15* has a lock on the rear chopper!" The co-pilot was staring at the fire control radar screen. The two following helicopters were clearly on view – as was the *F-15*; the *Chinook* furthest behind had a red triangle appearing around it, an indication that it's laser warning system had kicked in. Along with the continuous clamour from the alarm, both factors confirmed the American fighter jet was not only tracking them, but was engaging for an imminent attack.

"That's Wyatt's, isn't it?"

Sophie slipped the earphones back on and tried to ignore the noise of the warning system being transmitted from the third helicopter. Desperate radio chatter filled her ears.

"*… it's no good. I can't shake it…*"

"*Take the helicopter down as low as you can…*" Ryan was trying to offer advice.

"*I AM DAMMIT!*"

Even with the deafening sounds of the helicopter and the desperate shouts from the pilots, plus the fact she was wearing earphones that blotted out much of the background noise, Sophie heard the mid-air explosion as the *F-15* fired one of its four *AIM 120 AMRAAM*s, or simply known as air-to-air missiles.

An upsurge of air buffeted Sophie's helicopter, causing turbulence to rock and shake the *Chinook,* and for Sophie to unconsciously grip the edge of her seat. A moment passed and the aircraft started to settle again. The alarm that had been transmitted through the airwaves, together with Jack Wyatt's panicked voice, was no longer heard, instead replaced by unearthly, dead silence.

"Jack? Jack? Are you there? Jack?" Against certain truth, the pilot spoke into his radio hopefully, his voice the only sound registering. No one responded, not even Ryan.

Jack Wyatt was dead.

All those children were dead too. Sophie felt numb from the sheer horror of what had just happened.

The co-pilot had seen the small marker on the radar screen disappear and shook his head slowly when the pilot looked to him for reassurance.

Before either of the pilots had a chance to compose themselves to the reality that some of their number had just died, the warning sirens started to whoop and chord in their ears. Surprisingly loud, once again Sophie clawed off the earphones.

The co-pilot glanced down at the radar and then back up to the pilot. Before either of them could react the *F-15* discharged another of its four missiles.

The second helicopter blew up, this time much closer than the first, trailing just fifty metres behind and flying at a similar height above ground level.

As before, Sophie was flung forward in her seat as the *Chinook* was battered by a fresh wave of hot air, the turbulence this time more violent and more startling.

"Hold on!"

Lights started to flash red and white on the instrument panel accompanied by a small, intermittent, buzzing sound.

"Are they dead?!" Sophie shouted over the discord in the cockpit, oblivious to the difficulties the pilot and co-pilot were experiencing bringing the helicopter back into control.

"YES!" shouted the co-pilot wildly, not turning to see who it was who had spoken, an act that would not have been any more enlightening. He gave her no further attention. Instead, his eyes were fixed on the radar screen. Only one aircraft was present and it moved quickly towards them. "The *F-15* is closing in on us."

A warning alarm, the same as that which had preceded the attack on the two other helicopters, began to resonate around the cockpit.

"He's locked on us…!"

A more strident electronic tone sounded as the *Chinook*'s built in missile warning system was activated. Sophie found herself looking out through one of the side windows, eyes searching the darkness for something bright projecting towards them.

The pilot cursed to himself. "HOLD ON!" he shouted as he pulled up on a control lever, forcing the helicopter to climb skyward, almost vertically, before levelling it off and shifting it to one side as he made a sharp change in direction, taking the *Chinook* on a course opposite to their original path. "Get ready to deploy countermeasures."

The co-pilot flicked a couple of switches in front of him and waited, his right hand poised for action. On the radar screen in front of him a small dot accelerated from the chasing *F-15* and headed straight for them.

"Now!"

The co-pilot pressed a button releasing a number of infrared missile seeker flares, each launching with a small explosive sputter. Creating a much stronger heat signature than the *Chinook*'s engine, the counter-step had the desired effect. The *AMRAAM* exploded harmlessly behind them but not without swatting them hard with a thermal current.

Sophie bit her tongue from a sudden jolt of turbulence, her heart skipping a beat as the helicopter dropped a few feet before regaining flight momentum. Through the door separating the cockpit and the cabin, frightened children could be heard sobbing.

"We've got a few seconds before he locks onto us again," said the pilot, flying the helicopter back down to an even lower altitude. He followed the landscape as it climbed up a steep hill, before suddenly shifting the aircraft down into a valley behind a sheer bluff. The descent was sharp and akin to an extreme white-knuckle rollercoaster. The helicopter nosedived down the other side of the hill, the pilot straightening up at the absolute last moment and bringing the aircraft almost to a halt.

The pilot turned to his colleague. "Quickly… get everyone off…"

The co-pilot unbuckled. "What about you?"

"There's no time. Just do it Pete!"

Sophie unbuckled her own straps and followed the co-pilot into the large cabin of the helicopter. As he ordered everyone to their feet, Sophie pulled up the lever of the door and opened it out. She jumped down onto dry, arid land and was followed by one of Ryan's task force soldiers who had been on guard duty, hitching a ride in the cabin. A further two were on hand to expedite the evacuation. One had an injury to his head, a bloodied bandage was wrapped tight around his forehead.

Hurriedly, small children were manhandled out of the *Chinook* and ushered away. Even before the last child was out, the helicopter was climbing back into the sky.

"Let's go!" One of the soldiers led the children away from the landing site towards a copse of Joshua trees. Unknown and unbidden, Sophie took up the rear. Several of the five-year-olds were falling back, their eyes drawn to the helicopter, rotors beating hard. Invisibly, she urged them forward.

Behind her, the co-pilot was standing in the open doorway, watching the dark mass of children shuffling away, waving gently goodbye.

As the *Chinook* ascended above the hill, the pilot turned the aircraft so that it was facing back the way it had come; a loud 'Whoosh!' sounded followed by the sonic boom of the *F-15* as it flew past. A moment later and the whole world seemed to recoil and a deafening blast erupted from the sky above as the *F-15*'s final payload hit home.

Slowly it seemed, Sophie watched as the helicopter she only moments earlier had flown within, exploded into a fireball and started to rain charred metal, flaming helicopter parts and an unidentified boiling hot liquid down around them.

CHAPTER FORTY-NINE
EMILY

A LAMO IS THE LARGEST town north-west of Las Vegas in the harsh, dry, inhospitable lands of Nevada, and the only settlement close to Area 51 remotely resembling a town, in the traditional sense. With shops, restaurants, schools and hotels, it was everything Rachel was not.

It was the place Ryan had selected as a meeting point for after, when the mission was complete – a stepping stone before their rendezvous with Alby and the *Boeing C-17 Globemaster III*.

It was also where Emily was tasked with procuring transport for 250 children, not exactly an easy ask after one in the morning when everything, including the hotels, were shut, and where the biggest vehicle available to hire at the *Alamo Rent A Car* was a family saloon.

But then, what did she expect from Ryan? The nature of the request wasn't something you could seriously obtain from a high street dealer. She needed coaches – five, perhaps four, minimum. *Greyhound,* the largest provider of bus transportation in North America, seemingly visited every town and hicks-ville in the States, except, it turned out, Alamo.

She might as well have been in Alaska. Isolated was a word that did not come close to describing it; and at one in the morning, it was more desolate than a ghost town. A large tumbleweed blowing lazily across a highway brought a wry smile to Emily's lips.

After a ten minute drive around the empty streets of Alamo, Emily soon established that the town was not going to yield what was needed.

"What about trucks?" suggested the driver of the SUV, steering the vehicle right off North Main Street onto Broadway Street. Emily was sitting next to him. He couldn't see her face beneath the gloom of the car's interior.

"It could work," she said. "Illegals stow in the back of containers from Calais all the time..." Emily was referring to the many immigrants who attempted to access England every day with varying degrees of success.

"Look... up ahead." The driver steered with one hand and pointed towards the end of Broadway Street. On the corner of the junction leading onto Route 93 was a truck stop and what the Americans called a Gas Station. A large green sign with *Sinclair* written in red font accompanied by a green cartoon dinosaur in the form of a *brontosaurus* was erected at the entrance from the highway and, like petrol stations in the UK, had a cover built over it. The *Sinclair* logo appeared on all four sides.

A small pay-in store that doubled-up as a deli was just out of sight, its windows lit, a beacon of hope for many driving Route 93 low on fuel; it was the first petrol station in over 150 miles.

"This looks promising..." Emily was thinking aloud.

The driver of the SUV turned the silver vehicle left and then left again, manoeuvring the car into the petrol station. A short distance beyond the paying booth was the truck stop. Eight trucks were parked up for the night.

"You fill up whilst I take a look..." Emily unbuckled as the SUV came to a halt beside a petrol pump. Through the window of the pay-in store, a woman in her early twenties looked up from behind a counter and studied them for a moment before returning to reading a *Dean Koontz* novel. Emily climbed out of the car. "I'll probably use the restroom whilst I'm here."

"Knock yourself out..." The driver opened his door and moved to one of the petrol pumps. "Just don't be long..."

Emily walked around the SUV, stretched a bit of cramp from her legs and then carried on through the parking lot towards the rear of the pay-in store.

<hr>

Ryan was subdued when he called Emily with an update via his satellite phone. His brief highlighted the success of the mission but was overshadowed by the disturbing news that the three helicopters ferrying the children had been destroyed by an American fighter plane.

Emily was back sitting in the passenger seat of the SUV, a *Styrofoam* cup in one hand, her mobile phone in the other. An inexpensive Bluetooth hands-free headset was slipped around her left ear.

"*So... looks like we won't be needing that transport after all,*" said Ryan sadly.

"Oh..." was all Emily could think to say.

It went silent for a moment, both Ryan and Emily grappling with the information, though Ryan alone agonising over some information.

"*Sophie was on one of those helicopters...*" Ryan blurted.

A dozen images of Sophie flashed into Emily's mind as she tried to grasp what Ryan was saying.

"Is she..." *Dead?*

Ryan sighed. "*We don't know... Dominic is driving out there now, but... it's dark and chances of finding survivors, even if there are some...*" he let the sentence dissipate.

"What are you saying Ryan?"

"*We may need to leave them behind...*"

"No. We can't…"

"*We have little choice. What would you have me do?*" There was pleading in Ryan's voice.

"We find Sophie. We need to know whether she's alive or… well," not accepting the alternative, "alive."

"*And how do you propose we do that?*"

"Back in Washington, Sophie shared a secret with me," Emily spoke priggishly. "She has a GPS tracker surgically implanted inside her skull. It was George's safeguard in the event something untoward happened to her. It was never documented; other than Sophie, only George knew. As the stakes were high, she wanted a way for us to locate her… should things go bad."

"*Like now, d'you mean?*" Ryan didn't wait for a reply. "*D'you think you can track it?*"

"I think so," she said, adding as though it was necessary: "Yes. I just need to find a computer…"

CHAPTER FIFTY
DOMINIC

DOMINIC WAS KNEELING IN the back of the SUV manning the *M61 Vulcan*, firing wildly at the American helicopters that followed at a safe distance. The eight soldiers who'd chosen to remain with Barry made their way to the transporter vehicle Sophie had seized from the perimeter guards at the start of the mission.

"Dom… Barry… there's only one way this is going to turn out if we stay here. Let's get going whilst we've got a margin…" Ryan competed for attention over the unceasing staccato of the rotary gun and the return gunfire.

"I'm on it," said Barry, climbing into the front passenger seat of the SUV. Liam was getting into the driver's seat again.

"And Sophie?" Ryan enquired.

"Sophie? Why, didn't you see her?" Barry chuckled as though his life wasn't in any danger. He was speaking as though Ryan was sitting just there instead of through the communication device pinned to the inside of his shirt. *"She's* fine. She went with the first helicopter."

Liam started the car and waited for the transporter vehicle carrying the remainder of Ryan's task force to pull off so that Dominic could provide a defence at the rear for their withdrawal. Once a sizeable gap had appeared, Liam began the drive back to where Ryan was watching in safety a mile away.

When the first helicopter was blown out of the distant sky by the *F-15*, Barry had been stunned into silence. His mouth fell open. Dominic had ceased firing the *Vulcan*, having watched the American helicopters fall back and seemingly give up on the fight.

"*Are you sure she's okay, Barry?*" Ryan had asked anxiously, just before the Chinook had been turned into a fireball.

Answering for him, the *F-15* fired another air-to-air missile and blew the second *Chinook* our of the sky. The mid-air inferno drifted down to the ground and exploded further on impact.

"There's always hope," answered Barry hesitantly.

And hope began to shine brighter when the *F-15*'s third missile fell short, thwarted by decoy anti-missile flares. The multiple detonation of the flares and the bigger boom of the missile was moderate compared to the exploding helicopters.

"*Hope is just a measure for repressing grief and disappointment,*" said Ryan resolutely. "*I don't put much stock in it.*"

"Nonetheless… you don't know everything…"

Almost as though the pilot of the *F-15* was working in tandem with Ryan so as to cue him the last word, he fired his final missile. The last of the appropriated *Chinook*s lit the whole night sky as it exploded, ending its flight and extinguishing Barry's confidence in the preordained.

"*You're right Barry. I don't know everything. But I know when we're getting our arses caned.*"

Dominic let go of the *M61* rotary gun and turned to sit forward-facing in the back of the car. He watched Barry slump down dejected in the passenger seat in front of him; he laid a hand on the younger man's left shoulder and squeezed it reassuringly.

"Don't for a moment think that it's over. She's stubbornly resourceful. Surviving is in her DNA. There's no one like her." Dominic spoke quietly with almost a hint of compassion.

Against Barry's protests, Dominic took the SUV and went searching for Sophie and any other survivors alone.

"You go ahead. I'll meet up with you in Alamo." Dominic was behind the wheel and leaning out of the shattered window, crystals of glass and a few jagged barbs glistened along the bottom edge like crocodile teeth coated with glycerine. No time had been given to cleaning the former driver's blood from the door or the dash.

Time had sped up and was nearing 3:00 a.m. With dawn fast approaching, chances of escape were beginning to diminish. At night, the wilderness provided sanctuary and aided Ryan's plan for withdrawal. Daylight on the other hand, gave the Americans the advantage. Dominic wasted little time and floored the accelerator, steering the vehicle along the dusty track for ten minutes before taking it off-road to follow a path that appeared to lead directly towards the glowing beacon that was the burning wreckage of the third helicopter on the other side of a rugged hill that offered no palpable route, other than around. Driving up it wasn't an option.

Changing direction, Dominic manoeuvred the SUV across a bumpy stretch that rocked the vehicle and threatened to damage the suspension. Not bothered, he continued forward as fast as able, soon finding a clearer route that seemed to follow the small mountain round.

Peering through the windscreen, Dominic spied a searchlight in the sky. No longer under threat of his *M61 Vulcan*, the Americans had ventured forward with the same purpose as Dominic's.

To search for survivors.

Cursing, Dominic killed the headlights on the SUV and turned a corner blindly, pulling out into a small clearing that was well lit.

The carcass of the third *Chinook* helicopter blown from the sky burned brightly, radiating a fierce heat that Dominic would swear he could feel through the metal of the SUV.

Turning the vehicle and driving it around the burning wreck, Dominic stopped at a safe distance close to where the first of a thicket of Joshua trees started. With the engine idling, Dominic stepped out of the vehicle and unholstered his handgun. Without thinking he released the almost-empty clip and replaced it with another, which he slipped from a pocket. The magazine clicked home and Dominic chambered a round.

"Hello?!" Still limping, Dominic walked around the edge of the clearing, his large steps towards the trees aggravating the gunshot wound in his rear. Ignoring the pain, he took a little comfort from the shadows, relishing the cover the trees gave from the search party hovering high up in the sky. "Can anybody hear me?!" He was shouting to be heard over the conflagration that echoed behind him. The intensity of the burning had caused heavy sweat to form on his face and drip into his eyes. "Hello?!" he repeated a couple more times as he walked gingerly within the trees; light from the fire behind him had receded to a point where nothing but a wall of blackness met him; amazingly, the short distance had lessened the sound of the inferno.

"*Dominic... d'you read me?*" The small earpiece came to life in his left ear, the sudden noise deafening. Dominic raised a hand and touched his ear as though to nurse it.

"I hear you Ryan..."

"*Any sign of her?*"

"Negative," replied Dominic, eyes trying to pierce the darkness ahead. A couple of steps forward and he tripped on something jutting from the dirt. Falling forward he landed with an OOMPH!

"*You okay?*"

"Just dandy." Dominic picked himself up from the floor and carefully continued forward.

"*Listen. We might be able to help you pin Sophie's location.*"

"How so?"

"*She possesses an electronic transmitter. Emily is currently tracking her whereabouts. We should have her coordinates momentarily.*"

"Then what?"

"*Using the GPS signal in your phone together with her transmitted location, we'll coordinate your search. Should be easier than searching in the dark.*" Dominic couldn't fault Ryan's reasoning.

"Okay. How long?"

"*Your luck's in. Emily has just found her…*"

CRACK!

The sharp snapping sound as of a stick underfoot sounded from ahead; loud and close by.

Incognizant to the elevation in his own heart rate, Dominic hesitated forward, his gun hand sweeping from side to side nervously.

"Okay… where?"

"*She's…*"

CRACK!

"*Behind…*" *you.* Dominic didn't hear the end of the sentence, his focus was trained fully on his surroundings. A further snap sounded; this one closer, just behind him.

Dominic whirled round and, without thinking, fired his gun.

BANG!

Within the grove of Joshuas, the shot rang out for seemingly ages; what the cartridge hit, Dominic didn't know. The bullet struck something meaty, its progress halting with a dull 'thud'.

"*Dom? Dom! Didn't you hear me? She's right there,*" Ryan spoke desperately having heard the gunshot. "*Sophie is standing right next to you!*"

CHAPTER FIFTY-ONE
SOPHIE

Slowly, the fiery wreckage of the *Chinook* descended from the night sky, large glowing embers falling down with it. Aviation liquid rained down mist-like in a sheet, soaking the stunned on-lookers who stood under the cover of the Joshua trees.

Sophie watched in horror as the helicopter crashed and exploded, the impact forcing a wave of intense heat to knock her off her feet; she flew backwards through the air, colliding with one of the task force soldiers who, crumpling to the ground beneath her weight, didn't know what had hit him.

Sophie stood up and assessed the situation. The soldier she'd knocked to the ground had picked himself up and was limping towards one of the other two soldiers muttering expletives to himself. The third soldier was trying to communicate with someone in command through his comms-link, but having no success; it was either due to a fault with the communication device or because the distance was too great for the frequency. Sophie guessed the latter.

She would have tried contacting Ryan herself had she not removed her comms-link on the helicopter in favour of the large earphones. Both were lost to her now.

I guess we're on our own, she thought to herself.

"What should we do?" the soldier wearing the bandage conferred with his colleague.

"I think we should wait. Someone will come and find us..." asserted the soldier that had been Sophie's safety mat.

"The Americans, you mean?" the third soldier had joined the conversation. All three men held assault rifles.

"Ryan wouldn't leave us hung out to dry..." asserted the soldier Sophie had floored moments earlier.

"Why wouldn't he?" challenged the third soldier. "We're Kaplan Ratcliff's." On closer scrutiny, Sophie saw that he wore a tattoo of a spider's web on his right cheek.

"Because... I'm here too." Making all three soldiers jump, Sophie stepped into the midst of the bickering.

"What...?"

Knowledge of Sophie and her abilities were on a strictly need-to-know basis. Aside from Barry, Jack Wyatt and Marty, no one on Ryan's task force knew of Sophie. To see her – or *not*, in this case – was above the soldier's pay grades.

"I know... I know... you can't see me; boys, you're not imagining this, believe me, I really AM here. I'm Ryan's secret weapon... I'm also your guarantee. Trust me, he won't be going without us."

"This is crazy messed up," said the third soldier. "How can we trust something we can't see?"

"You might not be able to see... but you can feel, can't you?" Sophie pressed the barrel of her *Glock* against the soldier's forehead, "And hear?" she chambered a round in the gun. "You can TRUST this. I could've put a bullet in all three of you had I wanted."

"Okay, that's settled then," said the soldier who'd tried calling for help. "We wait it out... for now at least."

⚊⚊⚊◆⚊⚊⚊

Under the cover of darkness and deep within the copse of Joshua trees, the three soldiers escorted the children away from the burning remains of the helicopter to somewhere safer, less exposed. Sophie hung back, volunteering as a lookout for anyone in pursuit, her invisibility once again providing an invaluable advantage.

Once relatively shielded, the soldiers drew the gathering to a halt. Despite the distance, the roar of the fire could still be heard – less fierce, but there – a constant reminder of what had just happened.

"I think here will be as good as anywhere. If we go much further we'll come out of the trees. We'd be easily seen again." The soldier who had recommended waiting it out spoke once again, unintentionally assuming leadership of the group.

"I agree," said Sophie, making her presence known.

"How long do we wait? We've probably got three, maybe four, hours of darkness. After that, it won't take long for the Americans to find us."

No one saw it, but Sophie shrugged. There was an inflection in her voice. "Knowing Ryan, he won't want to lose too much time against his schedule. I'd say someone will come within the hour. If not, then we'd best assume we're on our own."

The acoustics of the wooded area amplified a sound in the distance, it could be just heard above the din of the burning helicopter. A car engine, driving fast, entering the clearing.

"D'you hear that?" the soldier with the spiderweb tattoo spoke up. The other two soldiers cocked their heads, turning an ear towards the sound.

"Y-Y-E-E-S-S..." said the first soldier slowly. "Someone should go and check..."

"Not yet..." Spiderweb tattoo stood up anxiously.

"I'll go," volunteered Sophie assertively.

"Be our guest," accepted spiderweb tattoo quickly.

Sophie turned and jogged silently the way back to the clearing. After a hundred feet she stopped; she listened hard and waited.

Leaning against a tree, slowly, ever-so-carefully, she unholstered one of her *Glock*s and held it, right arm bent at the elbow, the barrel pointing skyward.

"Hello?!" A familiar figure was skirting the area clear of the Joshua trees. He was scanning his immediate surroundings, searching for something.

Someone.

Her.

"Can anybody hear me?!"

Sophie resisted the urge to move, wishing to see how the scene played out. She also wanted to see if Dominic was alone. Had Barry come with him? A confusing warmth spread through her as she hoped that he had.

"Hello?!" Dominic called out again, stepping in amongst the Joshua trees. Nobody followed him. He was alone.

Pity. Sophie sighed inwardly. She took a step forward and angled herself so that she was ready to fight if she needed, her stance loose and alert, her weight balanced on the balls of her feet.

She should have felt relief to see Dominic, a member of the team; but she didn't. There was something about him, aside from the fact that he had killed her mother. Something peculiar. Her father used to have a little saying: you could give friendship freely, but trust and respect always had to be earned. Sophie could not trust the man... not now, and doubted she ever would.

"Hello?!" Dominic called out twice more as he walked deeper into the small wood; fifty-feet from where Sophie watched, he stopped, a hand absently reaching up to his ear.

"I hear you Ryan..." He was listening to a voice from the earpiece pushed within his left ear. "Negative," he replied to a question only Dominic could hear. He was staring fixedly into the darkness ahead, his eyes almost trained on Sophie's position. A couple of steps forward and Sophie watched as he tripped on something jutting from the ground. He fell forward hard, winding himself slightly and grunting as he landed on his face.

For a few seconds Dominic just lay there, not moving. Sophie was about to go to him when the man muttered:

"Just dandy." Dominic picked himself up and started forward, not bothering to dust himself down.

"How so?" He answered the voice in his ear again, following it after a long pause with a another question. "Then what?"

Dominic was ten feet away. Another long pause before he said: "Okay. How long?"

Sophie moved away from the tree she was leaning against and sidestepped carefully, manoeuvring herself into a position that enabled her to circle Dominic; her eyes were fixed on him as he closed the gap between them, settling on the gun in his hand.

Why is he pointing his gun? The fact that she had her own gun levelled dangerously did not register as incongruous. She moved a step forward.

CRACK!

The stick beneath her feet snapped, making her jump back. It was surprisingly loud. At first, Sophie thought maybe Dominic hadn't heard it, but soon dismissed that. There was no way the sound could have gone unnoticed.

Under close scrutiny, the way Dominic moved forward, careful and tentative, indicated he knew he wasn't alone. If Sophie had thought the man looked like he was ready to use his gun before, his new trigger-ready stance looked even more menacing.

"Okay… where?" Dominic barely heard what he was saying, his focus completely trained on his surroundings. His eyes were searching the darkness for movement; his ears were straining for the slightest of sounds.

Sophie had moved stealthily around Dominic, avoiding twigs and foliage as she progressed forward, but as she was all but behind the man she stepped on a large bone-dry stick.

CRACK!

Startling herself, Sophie leapt to the side, her weight landing on a piece of branch causing a further snapping sound, one which she knew Dominic could not have failed to have heard.

Dominic whirled round and, without thinking, fired his gun.

BANG!

Sophie anticipated the Intelligence Director's action, diving headlong to the right of him, rolling a couple of times before settling in a half-kneeling crouch, her gun pointing directly at Dominic.

The bullet hit a Joshua tree with a dull, meaty-thud.

Had the moment come to exact her revenge on the man responsible for her mother's death?

Without a shot being fired, Dominic reeled backwards before bending over as though preparing to vomit. He dropped his gun, the weapon now too heavy to carry.

"*Sophie?*" Dominic spoke softly. Slowly, he looked up. Even in the sheer darkness Sophie believed she could read abstract fear upon his face. "*Please... tell me you're not... hurt?*"

Surprising Sophie, Dominic looked remorseful, almost anguished. On his knees, he looked pathetic.

"*I'm so sorry... I didn't know... I didn't know,*" he moaned pitifully.

Stepping forward, Sophie made herself known. "Please, for God's sake, shoot yourself already, will ya?"

"Did I..." he started, "... did I *hit* you?"

Sophie snorted. "Don't flatter yourself. Only one bullet has come close, and yours wasn't it." Her ear was still sore from being grazed at Dulles International Airport, a going away present courtesy of Washington's PD and a reminder of how near she'd come to getting her head blown off. The memory seemed to belong to a distant past rather than just the morning before.

Making an instant recovery, Dominic retrieved his gun and stood up. "Well, that's a relief," adding with hubris, "I much prefer to see the actual face on a person when I kill them."

"That's the truth," Sophie whispered, recalling the look of horror on her mother's face when Dominic had shot her in the stomach.

Turning away, he directed his attention back to the speaker communicating into his left ear. "I've found her... yes, she's fine... others? I don't know." He turned around to where he'd heard Sophie talking. "Are there any other survivors?" She hadn't moved from her position.

"Is that Ryan?"

Dominic nodded.

"Apart from the two pilots on the helicopter who made a sacrifice, all of them," Sophie said in a confident tone.

"All of them? The kids an' all?" Dominic raised an eyebrow and couldn't contain the surprise from his voice. Not needing Sophie to reply, he circled away and relayed the information to Ryan, adding, "I think we're going to need the transporter to pick them up."

<hr>

The transporter vehicle, filled to bursting point with child passengers squashed three and four to a seat, rolled along the tarmac of the small airport twenty-five miles east of Palmdale, a setting familiar to Sophie and her travel companions, having arrived there on the *Bombardier* jet a little less than twenty-four hours earlier. The small jet aircraft was standing to one side, off the runway.

After confirming his sighting of survivors from the last helicopter blown from the sky, Dominic had momentarily left the crash site in search of any survivors from the other felled aircraft. Sadly, the short expedition proved unsuccessful. On his return he had led the three soldiers and the children out from the cover of the Joshua trees to wait by the burning helicopter for pick-up and their rescue. Sophie once again had trailed the group, ensuring no one got left behind.

Less than ten minutes later salvation arrived.

In the early hours of the morning, Dominic drove his SUV into the Alamo service station, Liam following in the transporter close behind. They parked in a dark area out of sight from the road, the drivers disembarking and approaching the other SUV within which Emily, her driver, and Ryan were waiting. Sophie joined them for the short walk, anxious to be reunited with Emily. She hadn't realise how fond she had become of the woman in such a short space of time.

Seeing them approach from the back, Emily spotted Sophie in the rear-view mirror. She climbed out of the car and waited, unable to contain the excitement bubbling from within. She smiled. "Thank God!" she said. "You had me half-scared to death!"

Quietly and unobserved, Sophie embraced Emily and buried her head into the older woman's shoulder. Ryan appeared at their side, coughing loudly to make himself noticed.

"We need to get going. Sunrise's in a couple of hours," he said.

Unseen, Sophie glared up at him in annoyance. Emily made no sign that she had heard him but broke free from Sophie's grasp.

"Be ready in five minutes." Ryan stomped off, joining up with Dominic and Liam who were deep in conversation. Whatever they were discussing came to an abrupt halt. Ryan led Dominic away to speak in private.

"What's that all about?" asked Sophie.

Emily could only guess what Ryan wanted to discuss with Dominic. From where they were standing, Emily and Sophie witnessed the heated exchange between the two men, but not what they said;

Ryan was pointing angrily towards the younger man, whilst Dominic appeared to be shouting something back.

"Probably best not to ask," replied Emily lightly, knowing full well that it stemmed from liberating the children. "Come, let's get out of the cold. You can travel with us… it'll be better than being cooped up in that bus, even if Ryan is travelling with us."

Five-and-a-half hours later, Liam steered the armoured bus into the small airport tailing the SUV driven by Dominic. The vehicles came to a halt a short walk from where the *Boeing Globemaster III* was preparing for take-off, its four turbo-fan engines roaring. The pilot, Alby Goodall, was peering through a window, his head looking small from down where the two vehicles were parked, framed by giant headphones. A short distance away, the other SUV along with one of the 'borrowed' *Jeep Wranglers*, stood unattended having arrived half an hour earlier, their drivers and passengers descending upon a small hut where the airport owner offered refreshments and a bite to eat, his hospitality provided – along with his silence – in exchange for a million dollars wired to his bank account a day before.

Sophie and Emily were sitting by the window and watched Dominic and Liam alight from the two newly arrived vehicles. They were talking with each other as they came together. Barry, Ryan and the remnants of the task force were scattered around the small room, some sitting nursing coffees, eating bagels and having a laugh; others stood in solitude, quietly reflecting on the events of the night before.

Small plates were placed in front of both the women, a bagel and a muffin on each. The caterer made no comment to placing a breakfast in front of an empty seat where Sophie sat, thinking that its occupant had left to go to the bathroom.

Steaming mugs of tea sat to the side of their plates, the liquid looking very milky. Americans weren't renowned for their tea making abilities. Despite feeling famished, Sophie gingerly pushed her muffin around her plate.

Neither woman had taken a bite from their meagre breakfasts, and up until that point, neither had spoken except to say "hi" or "hello".

"Some night, huh?" Emily broke the deadlock. She couldn't imagine what was going through Sophie's head despite Ryan's update on events when he'd joined her at the service station in Alamo.

"Some night… yeah… you could say that…" Sophie spoke in a hushed, solemn tone.

"At least it's over…" said Emily breezily.

"For you, maybe. My father is still out there." Sophie was staring through the window, her attention drawn to a spider spinning a web towards a corner of the pane of glass. Across the asphalt, Dominic had finished talking with Liam and had jogged to the steps leading into the large cargo plane. Liam returned to the armoured bus.

"We'll find your father… WE WILL. We'll put all our efforts into it now that *GYGES* is done. Once we get back…"

Emily knew that Sophie didn't approve, the invisible girl's theatrical sigh more than confirming it.

"I will dedicate my life to helping you," Emily added pointlessly, feeling the need to carry on speaking.

"Do you think us destroying their lab and taking away their toys is going to stop them?" Sophie snorted. She slammed her fists down on the table making the plates rattle and upsetting the tea a little. "THEY STILL HAVE MY FATHER! All we've done is bloodied their nose. How long do you think it will be before they start up again? Now they know what we're capable of, don't you think they'll be more determined and even more careful next time?"

Ryan, hearing the commotion, excused himself from his

conversation with Barry and moved to the vacant chair next to Emily. "Sophie, let's calm down. We should be celebrating… it's over…"

"Don't think for a moment that this is actually over, Ryan."

"I know, Sophie. And I said, once *GYGES* was destroyed, I would help you with finding George…"

"You promised me," Sophie reminded him.

"Right… right. Listen: I know where your father is," he said.

Before Sophie was able to reply, the engines of the *Boeing Globemaster III* began to thunder and the large cargo plane started forward, slow at first but quickly gaining speed as it cannoned up the runway. Just before running out, the aircraft defied the odds and ascended majestically into the sky.

"Where's he going?" It was meant as a thought; Ryan unintentionally said it aloud. Sophie turned to look back out of the window.

The door into the catering hut opened and Liam's large frame squeezed in. Seeing the puzzled look on Ryan's face, Liam spoke as he walked. "Dom thought it best not to hang about. He said he'll see you in London?"

"And the kids?" Ryan raised an eyebrow, faking incredulity and hiding whatever information he knew. It was all part of the plan.

"Them too, I guess." Liam crossed the hut to the serving counter and helped himself to breakfast, moving along to a coffee dispenser where he poured a steaming hot drink. The catering assistant, wearing a white apron that was smeared with grease, was close by frying bacon and eggs for one of the soldiers.

"It wasn't altogether what we planned," Ryan whispered, his mind still with Liam's message.

Momentarily dismissing thoughts of Dominic from her mind, Sophie asked Ryan distractedly: "Did you say you know where my father is? When did you find out?"

The *Boeing* climbed higher into the sky and together, Ryan,

Sophie and Emily, watched it until it turned into a speck before disappearing altogether.

"Yes," replied Ryan, adding hesitantly, "the information was included within the same file recovered from Agent Spencer Roberts."

CHAPTER FIFTY-TWO
MILO

BASE COMMANDERS AT GROOM Lake had been slow in reporting the incident that had counted more than one hundred personnel killed in action and a good many more injured. The loss, though the greatest ever inflicted on US soil by an invading army, was almost insignificant alongside the news that Project *GYGES* had been completely destroyed. All their research, the data, and years of progress had gone up in flames, and all the children were presumed dead.

"Who's responsible?" Milo spoke calmly but felt anything but. Deep inside he was trembling – not through outrage at the tragedy of the situation, though he was angry – it was from fear of the repercussions and the likely fallout.

"Deputy Director, if we knew THAT we wouldn't be having this conversation." General Marcus was speaking via a video conference call, his face grave as he stared through the flat screen TV; he looked extremely tired. "Whoever it was, they were well organised, well equipped and well informed." The General looked away for a second whilst he collected his thoughts. "Our guys on the ground weren't prepared for such an attack; we were outgunned, outsmarted and up against a foe never before seen. In fact, some of our wounded claimed not even to have *seen* their attacker, most rationally putting it down to a highly skilled sniper; but one-or-two insist that the shots came from up close. It was as though their assailant had been... invisible."

Milo's eyes widened. He swivelled in the leather chair, turning his back on the General.

Sophie Jennings.

It was beginning to make sense. She hadn't come to America to find her father, that was too obvious. If she'd been working alone, maybe... but she hadn't. There was that other woman who they'd still been unable to identify, and then there was Dominic Schilling.

Brayden Scott had been right all along. He'd vehemently protested that they were going to be making a move for her father. Like a fool he and the President had dismissed him, allowing the frustration of Brayden's earlier failing in capturing the young woman to cloud their judgement and to ignore his advice.

Damn it!

Why else would Sophie ally herself with the man who'd killed her mother? Utilitarianism! It had been for the greater good, or the bigger picture, however they deemed to see it.

Milo rotated back around in his chair and faced General Marcus once again.

"Thanks General... that'll be all."

"Sir..."

Before the man in his fifties disappeared from the screen, a knock came at the door. Not waiting for invitation, Milo's secretary poked her head through a gap.

"Deputy Director, the President would like a word with you."

Milo swung round to face his secretary. "Tell him I'm in the middle of a video conference and that I'll call him back." It wasn't altogether a lie, but Milo couldn't face President Avery Harrison's wrath just yet. He knew what the outcome would be and wanted to cling to his job... for a little longer at least.

"Sir... he's here in reception. He says it won't wait." The door which she had been blocking was pushed aside, her along with it.

Flustered, she straightened up, smoothed out her clothing and stood aside. Two burly secret service men in black suits and with what looked like *iPod* ear buds in their ears, bustled in. They were followed closely by the President of the United States. The secretary made a hasty retreat, closing the door behind her.

Deputy Director Calland leapt to his feet. "Mr President." Nervously, he offered a hand in greeting; he was unable to hide the tremor he felt. President Harrison looked at it in derision, as though Calland was trying to give his visitor a live grenade with the pin pulled free, or he'd just removed his hand from the back end of a cow and had forgotten to wash it.

"Tell me Milo, are you still sure the girl IS after her father?" he didn't wait for an answer. "Take a seat. I want to hear YOUR take on events… before I blithely accept your resignation…"

CHAPTER FIFTY-THREE
BARRY

SAYING GOODBYE HAD BEEN especially difficult between Sophie and Emily after all that they'd been through those past few days. With the arrival of Sophie's bags from Washington – delivered by a small, mouse-haired guy who looked like a junkie (he kept sniffing and rubbing watery, bloodshot eyes) – she'd been able to inject five vials of serum into her arm using the jet injector, visibility making it more comfortable for everyone around her, though she wore a troubled look. Closely scrutinising her holdall she was overcome with dismay; there appeared to be less vials of the serum than she remembered.

Misinterpreting the pained expression on Sophie's face, Emily had hugged her hard and kept saying 'sorry' for not being able to continue on with the search for her father, almost crying. The truth was, she felt helpless away from a desk and computer and didn't think she'd really offer much. If anything, she believed she'd be a hindrance – exemplified by the incident three days before at Georgetown University Hospital, when she'd narrowly escaped an assassin's bullet.

"It's okay," Sophie reassured the analyst softly. "I'll be fine, you'll see."

"Wow!" exclaimed Barry on seeing Sophie 'in the flesh' for the first time. "Mirrors don't do you any justice," he said.

Sophie's cheeks became hot. "Um… err…" she had no response.

"I'll stay to help you," Barry volunteered too easily, a strange look crossing his face.

She didn't know why, but Sophie found herself blushing even more.

"Be careful here Sophie," Ryan warned. "They will be hunting for you now with greater commitment. Never let your guard down… not for a second…"

"Don't fret. I can handle myself…" Sophie said, peevishly. She hadn't forgiven him for not telling her about her father's whereabouts sooner. When she'd demanded to know whether he'd had the information before the mission to destroy Project *GYGES*, he'd shrugged and sidestepped the question, all but confirming that he had.

"I know… that's what I'm afraid of…" Ryan spoke softly, *grand*-fatherly brushing a strand of blonde hair away from the young woman's eyes. "You look a bit like your mother… Clara, I mean," He smiled tenderly. "Whatever you need… give me a call." Ryan nodded and turned to leave.

Sophie and Barry took a couple of backward steps and watched as Emily and Ryan took the short flight of stairs up into the *Bombardier* jet that had provided transport into the airport from Washington a day earlier. Liam and a couple of the other soldiers were already inside. There wasn't room for them all.

At the top of the steps, Ryan turned back. "Go to Guantanamo, find your father… and get out. We'll give you as much assistance as we can from London. Be home for Christmas; you and your father can come for dinner, there'll be plenty of turkey. I make a fantastic pavlova."

Sophie made no further comment and watched on impassively, her arms folded across her chest.

Without formality, Ryan gave a little wave and stepped into the *Bombardier*, pulling closed the door behind him.

The journey time from the remote airstrip outside of LA to London in the small jet aircraft was twelve hours. By the time Ryan and Emily were back on terra firma, Sophie and Barry were holed up in a cheap hotel a taxi ride from Miami's International Airport; a tawdry-looking building that was famous in the locale for hosting illicit after dark activities and holing up drug users. It was notoriously overlooked by the authorities and not a nice place, but it was ideal for a person (or persons) wishing to avoid notice.

Masquerading as a married couple in the name of Mr and Mrs Mason, the pair had walked into the hotel's foyer in character; arm-in-arm and giggly, as though they had arrived to spend their honeymoon. Behind a squat reception desk, a Puerto Rican in his sixties watched them approach.

Courteously, Barry offered over the passports supporting their deceit, which the Puerto Rican, a small faded label stitched into his lime-green plaid shirt declaring him to be the hotel's manager, accepted begrudgingly. A quick glance and he was easily satisfied. He swiftly passed them back, disinterested.

"How are you going to pay?" The Puerto Rican spoke with a strong South-American accent.

"Credit card," Barry pulled out a *Visa* from his wallet. The name matched his passport.

The Puerto Rican raised an eyebrow but said nothing. Most of his customers paid in cash for anonymity. Credit cards left a trail. He accepted the card and went through the process of checking the 'Masons' in.

Without sleep for more than forty-one hours (not counting the naps taken on the six hour flight from LA on the Red Eye), the pair dumped their bags in a corner of their sparsely furnished room, dropped small items (mobiles, passports and wallets) onto the bedside tables, and crashed on the double bed fully clothed. Sophie on the right side, Barry on the left. They both lay with their backs to each other.

"Don't get any ideas during the night …" Sophie said sleepily. "I don't want to wake up to find that I've broken your neck in my sleep."

"Do you… do that sorta stuff whilst sleeping?" Barry asked nervously.

Sophie yawned. "I don't know… possibly… I've never slept *next* to someone before…"

Barry slowly climbed off the bed and crossed the small room to a grubby-looking armchair. "I think I'll sleep here," he said, not wishing to take a chance. He dumped himself down into the seat and winced from the discomfort immediately felt. The chair had seen better days, not only was the fabric covering it threadbare in places, many springs were broken, one poking up into Barry's right buttock.

Sophie rolled over to her back, smiling. "Don't be silly… come on. I was joking." She patted the place on the bed he'd vacated moments earlier. "I trust you."

Barry went to spurn her request, starting to shake his head, but the look on Sophie's face, and the sharp pain felt in his buttock changed his mind. He crossed back to the bed and gingerly lay down, his body teetering close to the edge.

"Come closer… I don't bite…"

Barry shuffled over to the centre and found Sophie suddenly nestle up against him, her blonde locks falling onto the side of his face; he could smell her hair and feel the rise and fall of her chest close to his arm. Involuntarily, despite fatigue and aching muscles, he felt something stir within him, felt an urge, a hunger, that he'd not felt in a long while.

"I… I don't understand this feeling…" Sophie whispered into Barry's ear. "I feel hot and tingly… and my heart…. it feels like it will explode. Boom-Boom-Boom-Boom-Boom…" Sophie went to grab Barry's hand, not knowing exactly what she was going to do with it.

"Stop," Barry said forcefully. "Sophie… stop!" He pulled away and sat up awkwardly, throwing his legs over the bed, careful to conceal an embarrassing bulge in the front of his jeans. "I knew this might be a bad idea…"

"I'm sorry. I'm so sorry…" Embarrassed, Sophie turned over, looking away. She felt tears spring for some unknown reason, taking her by surprise. "I don't know what came over me… I'm not sure what I am doing…"

Barry looked over his shoulder at the woman who was really just a girl, lying behind him.

"You really don't, do you?"

Sophie shook her head into her pillow. She knew how to kill in a hundred unique ways, but her body, her feelings? She didn't have the faintest clue.

Barry laid back down and turned the overhead light off. "It's not a bad thing. I'm sorry. Try getting some sleep," he comforted drowsily. "We'll have a talk when this is all over."

※

Barry's mobile phone was on vibrate and buzzed on the bedside table alongside him, reverberating against the wooden surface, causing a few coins to rattle and jingle. He stirred slightly but made no moves to answer it.

Sophie nudged Barry in the ribs with her elbow, making him grunt. She was lying on her front, facing away from him – not that he'd be able to see her. Sophie's serum had worn off during the night.

"I'm… on… it…" Barry grumbled, his left hand snaking out to fumble for the offending device, falling upon the mobile by chance, but not until he'd knocked his passport, a few coins and his wallet onto the floor.

Accepting the call, Barry raised the phone to his ear.

"Y'ello," he said languidly, stifling a yawn with his other hand. Next to him, Sophie turned away, trying, without success, to return to sleep. Had she not elbowed him in the side, he could easily have forgotten she was there. A sideward glance fell on the vacant space alongside him, an almost unnerving experience.

"*Barry? Barry?*"

"Hi…"

"*It's Ryan. It IS day time there, isn't it?*"

Barry looked across the room to the window. Sunlight streamed through the cracks to the sides of the curtains. "I guess," he said in a yawn. "I must've needed my sleep."

"*Listen,*" showing no interest for small talk, "*I think something's gone awry.*"

"Awry? Do people still use that word?" Not getting an answer, Barry continued after a few seconds, "how so?" He'd awoken a bit more fully and was pushing himself up out of bed. Unseen, Sophie climbed out of bed and crossed to the bathroom, her image fleetingly appearing in a mirror across the hotel room.

"*I'm not sure at this stage… I mean, it could be nothing,*" Ryan sounded serious. Barry could tell that it wasn't *nothing*. "*Dominic's missing.*"

"Missing?"

"*Well, the full version of it is, our RAF Boeing is missing; Dominic, the kids, Alby – everyone else on that plane; all gone.*" Ryan paused. "*Air traffic control lost contact with the flight somewhere over the Atlantic, one hour outside British airspace. We're using advanced satellite tracking technology, military radar and working with the CAA, but as of yet we don't know where the plane is, or what's happened to it.*"

"What about the aircraft's transponder, surely that will give you something."

"*You'd think… but no. No such luck, which leads me to believe the whole incident has been staged. The signal emitted stopped around the same time the flight disappeared off radar. For all intents and purposes, that Boeing has just vanished.*"

Behind him in the bathroom, the toilet flushed and Sophie reappeared, in the flesh though a little dishevelled. She disposed of five empty serum vials in a small hotel bin and crossed the room, hovering close to where Barry sat. She started brushing her hair.

"What do you think has happened?"

Ryan was slow to respond. "*Honestly… for some reason, I think someone on that plane doesn't want us to find it.*"

"Someone?"

"*Dominic,*" Ryan said. "*I think Dominic has hijacked the plane.*"

CHAPTER FIFTY-FOUR
DOMINIC

ST. KILDA WAS THE last place the Director of Kaplan Ratcliff's Security and Intelligence Division expected – and wanted – to find himself late that October. Substituting the warmth of Nevada and Los Angeles for the cold, dreary setting of a very remote Scottish island, he thought himself a fool. His last memories of the island were of a wet, windy, inhospitable place, the kind of location one would look to offload its enemies on (as the CIA had done to him back in July).

Things had changed very little.

His hair was being whipped back and forth by a strong gale, icy cold fingers clawed at his body through thick, but inadequate clothing; it made him realise that his memories of the place didn't come close to how bleak it really was.

The plane had landed on a small island, forty-one miles east of St. Kilda, the closest, most discrete, airport in the vicinity. Under protest, Alby had taken the *Boeing* cargo plane down, muttering surprise when the air traffic controller confirmed the aircraft was good to land with not a hint of suspicion or inquiry. With a gun levelled towards the back of his head, the pilot did as he was instructed. Once past usefulness, Dominic laid Alby out cold with a hefty thump to the back of the head, the butt of his gun slightly bloodied. Benbecula airport, though small, had a runway just big enough to accept the large military plane. Host to daily flights to Glasgow, Stornoway and

Barra, it provided a crucial link to mainland Britain for its 1,300 habitants. It had also been the place Elspeth Brown had arranged for Dominic to land his plane, and where Elspeth had walked out to meet him once the *Boeing* had taxied to a halt a short distance from the tiny terminal building, and a short journey off the main runway.

Spots of sea mist sprayed against Dominic's cheeks, tiny pinpricks that stung and made his eyes water. Walking away from the jetty, he quietly reflected on the moment he'd set eyes on the plainly-dressed woman again and an earlier conversation with Elspeth, which ultimately led to him returning to the place he now considered living hell.

"I wasn't expect-ing yous back so soo-en?" Elspeth had spoken in her strong Scottish accent.

"I hadn't figured on it. Did you get what we needed?" Dominic had called nine-hours earlier from the plane in Los Angeles shortly before take-off. He'd requested a place to stay, somewhere not likely to draw attention, and big enough for ninety kids. A follow-up call from a 'friend' in a very high place soon after cemented the deal. Arrangements were hastily made.

"Aye," she said. "Your lot wired the money, so t'ings are in place. Are ye goin' ta tell me what 'tis is aboot?"

"In time, yes..." Dominic had said, intriguingly.

"Are ye oka-yee?" Elspeth had walked up behind and startled him back to the present. His memory of earlier that day evaporated inside his mind.

"I'm fine, yes... just tired... jet-lagged."

"Com'on. I'll show ye to ye whum... Might'is well bring t' kids wit' ya..." Dominic guessed she meant the place they were staying. He looked over his shoulder towards the ferry, a much larger vessel than the one which had taken him to the mainland during the summer.

It had to be to accommodate ninety children, Dominic and the three soldiers who Dominic had selected to accompany him from what remained of Ryan's task force; military personnel who were in Kaplan Ratcliff's employ and loyal to the Corporation; part of Jennifer Ratcliff's contribution towards the joint venture. Skip Williams, who he remembered as the captain of the *Stormforce 11* which had carried him to Oban, was helping the children out of the boat one at a time onto the narrow pier. One of Ryan's former task force soldiers was standing nearby providing assistance. The single file line of five-year-old boys walked confidently along the wooden jetty, approaching Dominic who'd been first off the boat, and Elspeth who watched, fascinated. She was curious but did not ask any questions. The children were all identical.

"Can we trust your boat man?" Dominic asked sincerely.

"Skip? Aye… he family. No worries there. Come… 'tis Baltic. Colder still at night…" The dark-ginger-haired woman walked ahead, turning to look over her shoulder after half a dozen strides. "Com'on… what'ya waiting for?!"

<hr>

Behind the row of stone cobbled cottages, a good many restored into habitable condition (though a lot more in complete ruin), stood a hastily constructed, heavily fortified, rectangular-shaped building; built with military precision, it was taking no time to put together. Coming in parts, it was just like putting together a giant 3D jigsaw puzzle.

Dominic was visibly impressed by how swiftly things were taking shape.

As night had descended upon them, a helicopter hovered above what could easily have been a warehouse, a searchlight beaming down, providing enough illumination for workers to continue with their work, adding the finishing touches to the externals of the building.

"I guess this will do." Temporarily, Dominic, the three soldiers, and the ninety small children, had taken refuge within a number of the small cottages that dotted the coastline. Elspeth had provided sleeping bags to each of them for the night. Excepting herself, Dominic and half a dozen others within the travelling party, everyone was going to be sleeping rough on cold, draughty floors for a few nights. "How long until it's ready?" He had to shout to be heard over the noise of the helicopter and the sounds of ongoing construction; metal grinders whirring, hammers clattering and builders calling out instructions to one-an-other.

"Two deeys... three tops," Elspeth replied. She was bunched up inside a *Salomon Icetown* faux fur insulated white jacket. Despite its design for the ski-slopes, Elspeth was still feeling the cold. Her hands were buried deep within the jacket's pockets.

"And you have no qualms about us being here?" Dominic had turned to face the Scottish woman, an earnest look just visible under the dim light.

Elspeth shrugged, smiling nervously. "I would nae say that; but yous seem to have a nice wee face." Elspeth turned to go. "See no evil, hear no evil, speak no evil – that's *me* motto..." she stopped and looked back over her shoulder. "Besides, the pay is pure barry..." meaning, fantastic.

After a long moment studying the construction works, Dominic twirled round and jogged after Elspeth as she disappeared over a hillock towards the back of the first building within the row of cottages.

EPILOGUE
MITCH

W**HEN** S**OPHIE HAD KNOCKED** him out in the warehouse, stole his key card and all but successfully rescued her mother, Mitch Youngs had thought his career in the CIA was over. Removed from fieldwork, he'd been assigned to a back-office function and one which put him in close contact with the Director of CIA, Thawn Montgomery, who held the veteran agent in high regard despite failing to thwart Harriet's rescue attempt, and also directly with President Avery Harrison.

Several years earlier he'd worked on an Anglo-American mission with an English counterpart during the Cold War. Their association had never been documented, but a long distance friendship was developed and from time-to-time their paths crossed. Occasionally they'd discretely contact each other with requests or offers of information. Such communications had taken place in the weeks and days leading up to the events that saw the Director of CIA suggesting his reassignment to fieldwork, a proposal which the President himself encouraged after a failed attempt at capturing a wanted fugitive in the heart of the capital.

It had been the events leading up to his reassignment that had stoked the most interest in his contact in London. Marty Heywood had listened intently as Mitch spilled details of an operation which he'd overheard from the lips of the President, with the intention of capturing the girl, Sophie Jennings, who'd played a part in ending his fieldwork days. Before he knew it, Mitch had all but disclosed the whole plan, the likely ambush points and details of what was intended.

It was this level of honesty and Mitch's reliability that preserved their relationship. He knew that Marty would reciprocate at some point in the future. Information was collateral. His conscience was clear, despite betraying his country. Mitch believed he was doing it for the good of the nation.

When Marty had called again after the CIA's mission had failed, Mitch had already reluctantly accepted his reassignment that saw him once again partnered with Brayden Scott. It was a fortuitous piece of luck, despite his aversion to seeing the man again. The arrangement made Marty's request conceivable.

The fact that he was going to be in the right place, at the right time, almost made what Marty requested a divine thing; some might say it was destined.

Sneaking back into Guantanamo Bay's military hospital undetected had been easy. If anyone had approached him, Mitch would've flashed his ID, ending interest in him. He was a senior CIA operator in joint command with Brayden – he could go wherever he liked, no questions asked.

Most of the 5,000 soldiers ordered in to provide additional protection were in bed, with just a small number of soldiers on heightened alert, patrolling the perimeter of the Navy base, armed to the teeth, panic buttons at the ready.

As the hospital was deep within the prison grounds and deemed 'well-protected', just a handful of guards stood sentry or skirted the building.

Bypassing the lift in favour of a set of stairs, Mitch made his way to the second floor swiftly, gently pushing open the door leading into a wing off-which George Jennings' room was annexed. Only a few fluorescents burned brightly in the ceiling, many turned off to save energy. Deep shadows fell in various places, and Mitch used the advantage to slink into the hospital proper without detection, not that there were anyone around to avoid.

A glance at a clock affixed to the wall indicated the time was 3:20 a.m. Mitch guessed most of the hospital staff were off duty and tucked up in bed. The thought made him yawn involuntarily. He felt tired. Very tired.

It had been a long day.

Creeping along a narrow corridor off which closed doors watched him impassively; Mitch came into a familiar open area, which included a reception desk and nurse's station. The roomy space was empty of people, but overhead lights burned brightly and a computer screen was on – Mitch knew that a nurse or an orderly was on duty somewhere not far away. A steaming mug of cocoa indicated she (or he) was prowling about. He didn't wait around, instead darting across the reception area and entering another corridor. This one, also brightly illuminated, led towards the private ward where he and Brayden had earlier visited George Jennings.

Outside George's room stood a soldier in the blue uniform of the navy. On seeing Mitch, the soldier saluted. As Mitch held no military rank, there had been no need.

"At ease," Mitch said, his voice gravelly. "Go grab yourself a coffee. I'll take it from here…"

"Sir, I've been ordered to stay here… no exceptions."

"Son. I'm working directly for the President. I have your back… go take a break." Mitch spoke with more authority. This time the Navy officer did as bidden.

Now alone, he quietly pushed down on the handle and gently opened the door, entering the private room within which George Jennings lay asleep, lightly snoring. Inside the darkened room – all lights and the television were turned off – Mitch took a few tentative steps towards the man lying in the hospital bed. Light from the hallway behind him gave enough illumination to see that George was comfortable. The cannula attached to the back of George's hand was connected to a saline drip regulated by a small electronic pump device affixed to an IV trolley. The pump made a slight mechanical-groaning sound, undulating and continuous.

Mitch moved to where Brayden had stood a few hours earlier, though didn't sit. He quietly studied the sleeping man. George continued to snore, deep in sleep, oblivious to the spectator at his bedside.

For almost five minutes Mitch watched the sleeping man, counted the seconds between each breath he took, inadvertently synchronising his own breathing so that he inhaled and exhaled in time to George's; it was slow and relaxing. Before he'd entered the room he'd felt tense and nervous. Now, those feelings were gone.

He felt calm and composed. And ready. Ready to carry out what Marty Heywood had asked him to do.

"Good night George," Mitch whispered tenderly. He picked up a stray pillow from beside George's head and slowly positioned it an inch above the man's face. "Think of this as… a *blessing*."

George's eyes sprung wide open just as Mitch slammed the pillow down against his face, pressing it hard over the man's nose and mouth, smothering him.

George attempted to scream but the pillow suppressed the sound, muffled his voice. He tried to kick out, his body bucking, his legs flailing to the side, but Mitch belied his looks and applied much more strength than one would expect. George's arms thrashed about him hysterically, the IV attached to the middle vein in his right hand ripping out; his hands beginning to claw at the sides of the pillow desperately; to no avail, his fingers slipped off the material weakly.

Lack of oxygen, the side-effects of the chemotherapy and the sheer panic that screamed within him, made him defenceless and feeble.

Mitch now climbed on top of the bed and was straddling George, putting all his weight down on the pillow so that George's airway was completely obstructed. George tried to fight some more, his right arm slapping limply at Mitch's face; his left hitting him on the arm. Nothing thwarted the CIA agent from his intention.

Then it was over and Mitch felt no more resistance. George had put up a good fight, but it was done.

George's arms became lifeless and fell to the side, his left dangling over the edge of the bed, his right falling just to the side of him. His legs became completely still.

Mitch kept the pillow pressed down on the man's face for a little longer than necessary before he was satisfied the job was done, only then relaxing the pressure and climbing down, sliding off the bed.

George Jennings was dead. At Mitch's hands, the genius biochemist who'd genetically engineered a girl with enhanced abilities and a talent for turning invisible, had stopped breathing and lay motionless on the hospital bed.

Mitch tossed the pillow back onto the bed next to George's head and, before leaving, tidied his body and the bed up. He placed arms and legs back onto the bed, replaced the bedcovers and straightened the man's pillows beneath his head. Finally, he gently closed George's eyes, giving him a peaceful look.

At the door of the room, Mitch glanced back towards the man. To any one peering in, George just looked sound asleep. He closed the door gently behind him.

"Marty, you owe me one…" Mitch whispered to himself, totally unaware that his friend and MI6 contact lay dead somewhere in Nevada 2,600 miles away having plummeted to the earth whilst parachuting from 13,000 feet.

Walking towards him was the Navy Officer on guard duty, a cup of steaming coffee in one hand and a large bag of peanut *M&Ms* in the other.

"Did you get what you were after?" asked the guard returning to his post, only half-interested. He had placed his coffee on the floor and had made to open his bag of chocolates.

"You could say that, yes," replied Mitch walking away. "But he's now dead tired, bless him." Casually he turned around, "Could you do me a favour and make sure he doesn't get disturbed anymore tonight; he looks like he could sleep for an eternity…"

"You got it," said the Navy Officer.

ACKNOWLEDGEMENTS

G RATITUDE AND THANKS ARE extended to the following people who assisted in some way or another, great and small, with the production of this book.

Once again my editor/agony aunt, Laura Ling, relentlessly helped with finalising the copy of this book. Thanks for putting up with the many rewrites I asked you to check, and for your continued support in bringing Sophie Jennings and her narrative to life.

My wife Beth, for being a sounding board on some of the crazy story lines and angles used, and for keeping the kids entertained whilst I locked myself away to write!

My valuable reading team: Lynne & Paul Cotton, whose early review helped mould the story, and Natasha Darlow, who I hasten to add, read *The Girl in the Mirror* as part of my original beta-reading team, but whom I failed to give proper credit.

Notable others to mention who had no involvement with writing this book, except for being a friend and keeping me sane during the lonely months working: Darren Staff (who did help with some plot points and gave counsel regarding the front cover), Martin Kendray, Kelly Tinsey, Sonia Jennings, Louise Ruse and Steve Ellinor. Now, you've had a mention… go forth and buy my book!

Finally, to those of you who took a chance and bought *The Girl in the Mirror*, thank you for coming back for book two. I hope you stick with me for the third, and final instalment!

ABOUT THE AUTHOR

PHILIP J GOULD was born in Ipswich in 1974, and still lives in Suffolk with his wife Beth, and three children, Rebecca, Sophie and Matthew. At an early age he discovered a vivid imagination and an affection for the written word. Leaving school at sixteen, he went onto work in shipping and insurance, and is also a qualified personal fitness trainer. He quit the day job in 2012 to develop his career as an author and to spend more time with his family. His first book was *The Book of Alternative Records*, first published in 2004 by Metro Publishing Ltd.

Be the first to hear news and read exclusive content on the official website: www.philipjgould.com

 Join the official Facebook page: www.facebook.com/philipjgouldbooks

 Follow Philip on Twitter @philipjgould